NEW STORIES FROM THE SOUTHWEST

NEW

STORIES

FROM THE

SOUTHWEST

Edited by D. Seth Horton

Foreword by Ray Gonzalez

Swallow Press / Ohio University Press

Athens

Publication of this book has been made possible,
in part, through the generous assistance of the
Charles Redd Center for Western Studies.

Swallow Press / Ohio University Press, Athens, Ohio 45701
www.ohioswallow.com

Swallow Press / Ohio University Press books are printed on acid-free
paper ⊗ ™

15 14 13 12 11 10 09 08   5 4 3 2 1

Library of Congress Cataloging-in-Publication Data
New stories from the Southwest / edited by D. Seth Horton ; foreword
by Ray Gonzalez.
   p. cm.
 ISBN-13: 978-0-8040-1106-8 (acid-free paper)
 ISBN-10: 0-8040-1106-0 (acid-free paper)
 ISBN-13: 978-0-8040-1107-5 (pbk : acid-free paper)
 ISBN-10: 0-8040-1107-9 (pbk : acid-free paper)
 1. Short stories, American—Southwestern States. 2. Southwestern
States—Social life and customs—Fiction. 3. American fiction—21st
century. I. Horton, D. Seth, 1976–
 PS566.N49 2008
 813'.0108978—dc22
                                          2007043471

CONTENTS

Tas A:ga (Ode to the Sun)

Bapt t-ma:k g tas tonlig matt 'o hekaj ha'icu ñeidat
Nopi g m-tonlig 'am tonod t-mo'o da:m
Nopi g m-tonlig 'am 'e-ma'ikos su:dagi da:m
Nopi g m-tonlig 'am 'i ha-we:mt g ha'icu t-e'es
Nopi g m-tonlig t-hu:kajid hab masma mo s-hu:k
    cukuladi
Gm 'ap 'i-ñu'ikwup g s-cuhugam hab masma mo
    hemajkam 'am'e-ñu'icsulig
Am 'añ hugkam m-ñeid mat 'ab 'o 'i-ces g masad.

Because you give us sunlight to see
Because your bright light shines on our hair
Because your reflection shines on water.
Because you help our plants grow.
Because your brightness keeps us warm like hot
    chocolate does.
Because you push the darkness away like people push each
    other away.
I always see you until the moon comes.

This poem by Clarinda Valenzuela, a ninth grader at Ha:San Preparatory High School, was translated from the Tohono O'odham by Janice Ramón and Danny Lopez and published in the journal *Dancing with the Wind*.

FOREWORD

The Southwest region of the United States is a land of storytellers. Its vast landscapes, along with its volatile border and cultural history, have been the sources of stories for centuries. From Hopi and Pueblo myths to the early-sixteenth-century journals of Cabeza de Vaca and the birth of Mexican American identity in the modern novel *Bless Me, Ultima* by Rudolfo Anaya, the Southwest storyteller has been at the forefront of documenting, reimagining, and celebrating a region that is unique in the United States. To write a story set in the deserts of New Mexico or in the canyons of Arizona means the storyteller is immersed in environments where fiction redefines human interaction with the natural world. When a short story that takes place in the streets of El Paso or Phoenix brings the reader closer to experiencing the vast growth of southwestern cities, it is not fiction that could be set in any large urban area. Southwest fiction recreates life in a unique region whose history, culture, and environment have played themselves out for hundreds of years and influenced the character of the entire country. The writer who brings fictional characters to life on the freeways of Los Angeles, or the back roads of West Texas, knows that a modern storyteller of the Southwest must be aware of its great literary traditions while attempting to show how language reflects vast change and creates new stories.

Southwest fiction is more than writing about place, a term often used in too general a manner when it comes to identifying writers from specific areas of the country and the topics they write about. After several centuries of a rich literary tradition, and ongoing transformations in the region's established canon, writing from states like Arizona, Texas, New Mexico, and southern Colorado (the traditional Southwest), a "sense of place" has been redefined many times. "Home" with its environments and characteristics has always meant one thing to a Native American writer, while a Mexican American author has approached the concept from a different perspective. Writers new to the area or writing about it from afar may never know the native impulse, yet their stories and characters deal with place as a complex metaphor for a magnetic area that, like it or not, keeps attracting more people and calling for more stories. Today, the Southwest as a fictional center of triumphs and tragedies is a construct whose geographical boundaries expand beyond worn-out ideas about the frontier or *la frontera*. In other words, place as a literary concept in the stories collected here functions as a world where anything can happen, usually does, and the fascinating characters experience their human conflicts on a universal stage.

The fine stories in this book prove their authors recognize that literary and real territories no longer have to be inherited or conquered. Desert and mountain vistas shimmering in the distance and small towns getting closer on the passing two-lane highway await a new day of discovery and a different kind of reading experience from familiar territory. To approach these places as lovers of good stories is to recognize the storyteller and, in finding these writers, be immersed in a Southwest that offers a wide range of identities.

RAY GONZALEZ

PREFACE

When one is writing about the Southwest, it has become common to quote the famous D. W. Meinig quip, "The Southwest is a distinctive place to the American mind but a somewhat blurred place on American maps, which is to say that everyone knows that there is a Southwest but there is little agreement as to just where it is."[1] It is only a slight exaggeration to say that there are almost as many definitions of the region as there are people attempting to define it. One of the most important decisions made in the early stages of this project concerned what to include under this regional rubric. My previous travels throughout the region, extensive though they were, didn't provide a sufficient answer to this problem. I therefore spent several months poring through books and articles, obsessively consulting maps, and, most importantly, talking the matter through with a number of writers from the area. I slowly came to believe that essentialist definitions excluding the region's border zones were inadequate. For example, the Navajo Reservation stretches into Utah, but does that result in part of the area being excluded from the Southwest? Similarly, California's desert towns and cities, places such as El Centro and Barstow, strike one as more southwestern than Californian. Regions obviously blend into one another, so the question is, where does one draw the line? In the end, I decided it was better to err on the side of inclusiveness, and I thus considered those stories that take place in Arizona, New Mexico, the southern parts of Utah and Colorado, Texas southeast of Austin, Nevada south of Reno, and California south of Los Angeles.

---

[1] D. W. Meinig, *Southwest: Three Peoples in Geographical Change: 1600–1970* (New York: Oxford University Press, 1971), 3.

However one finally defines the Southwest, the region continues to play a unique role in the imaginations of many North Americans, in part because we, as a nation, tend to romanticize the area. Such a disposition might at first appear benevolent, but a visit to the New Age Centers of Sedona, the supposed vortex capital of the world, will quickly highlight the artificiality that often results from this dynamic. Likewise, there is a degree of historical resonance to be found in colonial Williamsburg, but the same cannot be said of the staged shootouts held outside Tombstone's OK Corral, which feel kitschy, overly theatrical, and commercialized. The point is that authenticity is an ongoing problem in our region, and one that is often keenly felt by our artists and intellectuals, a fact I was recently reminded of when I asked a group of students at a Tucson art college to write an essay about southwestern aesthetics. Many of them argued that such a concept was mostly, though not entirely, market-driven, touristy, and irrelevant to their creative work. This doesn't necessarily invalidate southwestern aesthetics as a useful hermeneutical tool; rather, it illustrates the challenges of writing and thinking about our region authentically.

Misinterpretations of the Southwest are rooted in the history, geography, and cultures of the area. While this brief preface is not the place to delve into such topics with any degree of depth, it is important to note that standard histories of American literature usually begin with the Puritans and either overlook or underemphasize both the Native American oral traditions and the numerous Spanish texts written in what is now the Southwest. The first European to explore our region was Alvar Núñez Cabeza de Vaca, who published *La Relación* in 1542, sixty-five years before Jamestown was founded. This book, which details his adventures throughout the South and Southwest, could be seen as the beginning of Chicano literature. Such an interpretation resists the historically inaccurate notion that English is *the* literary language of America and, by extension, the Southwest, a move that would entail, amongst other things, classifying *Relación* as an American classic. This canonical repositioning allows for the emergence of a dynamic regional literature that avoids both mimicry and provincialism by accurately reflecting life here in the hybridized Southwest.

Masters such as Momaday and Abbey, Silko and Anaya, to name just a few, are proof that contemporary southwestern literature continues to thrive. Their work has justifiably been anthologized in a number of collections, chief amongst them being *Writing the Southwest,* edited by David Dunaway. *New Stories from the Southwest* takes a different approach, primarily focusing instead on the emerging voices who write about the region. In order to be considered for inclusion in this volume, a story had to meet two criteria: it had to have been published in a nationally distributed North American periodical between January and December 2006, and it had to illuminate some aspect of life in the Southwest as defined above. Almost two hundred journals were consulted, the names of which appear in the appendix. Nineteen stories were finally chosen for this anthology. It is hoped that by reading them together, in a single volume, the reader will experience the diversity of southwestern fiction and the nuanced aesthetic delights it provides.

Anthologies are collaborations, and this book is no exception. Without the assistance and support of a number of people, this volume would never have been published. I'd like to thank David Sanders at Ohio University Press for helpful suggestions; C. E. Poverman, Bob Houston, and Aurelie Sheehan for support and advice in the early stages of this project; Justin St. Germain for his willingness to listen; Robert and Victoria Schnettler and, especially, Jeremiah Fletcher for their help in creating the Web site, www.southweststories.com; and the staff at the University of Arizona's Poetry Center for their research assistance. I owe a special debt of gratitude to the many editors working at our nation's literary journals, many of whom were kind enough to provide me with complimentary subscriptions. The work they do is as underappreciated as it is essential to the ongoing development of North American literature. This volume obviously wouldn't be possible were it not for the twenty contributors. I thank each of them for their participation, especially Ray Gonzalez, who kindly agreed to write an introduction for this first-time editor. Most importantly, I'd like to thank my wife, Catherine Chen, for her love and generous spirit. Too many times this past year she's had to sleep alone while I've read stories long into the night.

MOONRISE, HERNANDEZ, NEW MEXICO, 1941

Alan Cheuse

IN THE FIRST HOUR NORTH out of Ghost Ranch in the station wagon packed to the roof—and him on the verge of grief—they had stopped along the river, and he helped Michael with the viewfinder of the small box camera, while Cedric, his tall, jaunty-nosed former best man, wandered off along the pebbled bank in search of his own visions.

"We'll sit awhile," AA said to his son.

As if on the mark of some invisible choreographer, together they sank onto their buttocks on the hard surface, feet pointing toward the sparkling rushing water. For a short while, they watched their breath curl up in the cool air. The morning light had given him such hope—fierce cool luminescence that seemed to emanate in perfect harmony from every cliff face, rock formation, and stand of pines. So far, nothing had come of it.

"See that cliff?" he said, breaking the silence.

"Yes, Daddy," Michael said. He was a thin child, built like AA himself, with soft touches that certainly came from his mother's side. How odd that in nature you could not make out such easily divisible mathematical properties; but in your own family, in your children, you could do the math easily. Head, mine. Eyes, hers. Nose, mine. Lips? Well, he couldn't really make a decision about

From *New Letters*.

the lips. But chin? Yes, his chin. For his daughter, at home with her mother—this was an excursion for men and boys—he could do the same.

Insects floated past. Buzzed, buzzed.

The river sparkled.

"Do you recognize it?" AA said, pointing to the cliff face to their north.

"I don't know."

"Miss O'Keeffe made it."

"She made the cliff, Pop?"

"She made a painting of the cliff."

"Did I see it?"

"It's in a museum in . . . somewhere. Did you like the stew she made last night? The chicken fell away from the bone."

"The peppers made me sneeze."

"Your taste leans toward your mother's side," AA said. "Your mother doesn't like things spicy."

A light came into the boy's eye.

"Do you miss her, Daddy?" Michael said.

"I do," AA said.

"She says you're happy to get away from her," Michael said.

"She shouldn't say those things." He quieted himself down and touched his son's shoulder. "Look at that."

A hawk paused high above the river, as though pinned against an azul cloth backdrop.

"Daddy, are you and Mom going to get a divorce?"

AA shook his head at the thought, at the air.

"Did she say that, too?"

"She asked me not to say what she says."

"But you just told me."

"No, I was just asking."

"She writes me another letter like the kind I got last night—"

He fritzed air across his lips, trying to stop himself from further speech. Oh, speech! What good did it do? Always getting him into trouble. And her. Writing that letter.

"What did she write, Daddy?"

Foolish naïve fellow that he was, he was about to explain when Cedric came wandering back.

"Sun's nice," he said, removing his eyeglasses and wiping the back of his hand across his brow.

"Any luck?" AA said.

Cedric shook his head. Flecks of gray in his hair caught the early sun.

"I'm not like you, Ansel. I don't know what to look for. I didn't see anything."

"Oh, no, no. Everyone has an eye. It's like fishing. Some days they just aren't biting. Let's try somewhere else."

They got up and returned to the station wagon.

"What's not biting, Daddy?" Michael spoke up from the back seat.

"Things," he said.

"What kind of things?"

"The way things look," he said.

"Pictures?"

AA glanced into the rearview mirror, seeing just the top of his young son's head.

"*Photo*graphs, *photo*graphs."

"Votographs," the boy said, catching the rhythm of the game they had played on and off in the car all the way from Yosemite.

"Smotographs," Cedric said.

"Hopigraphs," AA said.

"Navajographs," Cedric said.

"Uh-uh," AA said.

"Ok, then, Smokographs."

"Good."

"Daddy?"

"Yes?"

"Eggographs."

"What?"

"I mean, yolkographs."

"The yoke's on you, son."

"Ansel," Cedric said. "Now I know why you take photographs."

"Why?"

"Because you're not much good at anything else."

With a nod, AA acknowledged his friend's joking remark and then kept silent awhile. Cliffs made a blur of clayey orange and soft browns. The river, which they were following, curved into a small canyon and dipped out of sight.

"Daddy?"

"Yes, Michael?"

"What is it?"

"What's what?"

"What's divorce?"

Cedric frowned at his friend.

"What have you fellows been talking about?"

AA shook his head.

"Nothing. Virginia talks to the kids, tries to turn them against me."

"She says you want a divorce?"

AA shook his head again, staring at his son in the rearview mirror.

"Let's not talk about it now."

They rode in silence. Light danced along the tree line. Miles and miles up the Chama Valley they stopped for lunch, a lovely repast, as it turned out, that Miss O'Keeffe herself prepared for them early that morning before she set out on her daily work.

Slices of roasted turkey.

Freshly baked tortillas.

(He had awakened to the sound of Miss O'Keeffe's housekeeper slapping the masa between her hands before setting it in the oven to bake. Patta-pat, patta-patta-pat.)

Sweet peppers.

Almond paste sweets.

Lemonade from a tall jug, which he poured into the cups she had packed along with everything else.

Now the sun poised at full mast. Nothing but approving mouth noises as the three of them ate.

Then Michael went down a few yards toward the river—it had reappeared again at the turn of the road where they had stopped to eat—to pee.

Which gave Cedric the opportunity to speak about what—given the look in his eyes—seemed to have been troubling him.

"This makes me sad, Ansel," he said.

"What does?"

"What does? This talk about ending it."

"Me, too," AA said.

"But you're just the husband," Cedric said. "Think of how it makes the best man feel."

They both laughed just as Michael worked his way back up the slope, arms swinging for ballast.

"What's so funny?" he said.

Children had it both ways. They could disengage easily from the talk of adults. Then, on occasion—right now—they fiercely demanded their rights to be included.

"Nothing."

"It's not nothing. Tell me what."

Cedric spoke up.

"Your father and I were recalling something funny that once happened to us."

"What?" Michael said in a rather ferocious manner that was unusual for him.

"I . . ." AA talked now. "I was taking a picture but forgot to take the lens cap off. One of the oldest and dumbest mistakes known to man."

"Whose picture?" Michael said.

"I don't remember that."

"You remember the joke," Michael said.

"Sometimes that's all we remember," AA said. "A joke is like a ghost of something funny that's happened. Hey, see those trees?" He pointed up the slope. "Who's for a little nap in the shade?"

"I thought we were going to take pictures," Michael said.

"You can't just take a picture for the sake of taking one," AA said. "You have to find the right opportunity."

"All you make is trees and rocks and sky," Michael said.

AA shook his head.

"Did you just think of that?"

"Why?"

"Nothing."

The boy's eyes flashed.

"Mom said it. I agree." The boy folded his arms across his chest. AA felt an icy heaviness slant along his own sternum as he walked the few yards to the spot that a few moments before had seemed ideal for napping.

Now he couldn't rest, his mind roaring with all this turmoil, Virginia's arguments against him, poisoning the children, dissenting from his art. Once she had understood him so clearly; now it seemed—now, now, the miserable now of now—that she was turning against him and, worse, turning the children against him.

The brushing of the wind in the leaves, sounding like a river running in air—the shift back and forth between light and shadow as clouds played across the face of the sun—Cedric's labored breathing as his friend sank into slumber—all this kept him awake—and then he was out

—awakened by Michael's shout.

"Look! Look!"

The boy pointed up at the blue scrim of sky where a hawk rose high above them, a wriggling vine—rope?—snake!—in its talons.

Cedric sat up.

"What is it?"

His eyes followed Michael's pointing finger.

"Oh," he said, "the flag of Mexico."

Why was he doing this? Driving along, wrestling with life, with time, damned drag on all, himself, the children, not to mention HER, time and light, f-stop of things, flash and ripple sunlit river, glint of hawk's eye, eagle claw, driving down this road look at cactus sky mountains horizon, what? Michael asks me something what? Sorry I was daydreaming, go back to sleep . . . Ice-chill in my chest thinking of her words can't even remember specific but she makes a mood even at this remove using the children I would write you my love in a myriad shining lines shine on Republic roll on Jeffers' lines there's a poet I would be the ocean. The deep dark-shining Pacific leans on

ALAN CHEUSE

the land feeling his cold strength to the outermost margins let me see do I remember? Yes, I remember. The extraordinary patience of things! This beautiful place defaced with a crop of suburban houses— How beautiful when we first beheld it, Unbroken field of poppy and lupin walled with clean cliffs; No intrusion but two or three horses pasturing, Or a few milch cows rubbing their flanks on the outcrop rock heads—Now the spoiler has come: does it care? Not faintly. It has it has . . . all time. It knows the people are a tide that swells and in time will ebb, and all Their works dissolve. Meanwhile the image of the pristine beauty Lives in the very grain of the granite, Safe as the endless ocean that climbs our cliff.—As for us: We must uncenter our minds from ourselves; We must unhumanize our views a little, and become confident As the rock and ocean that we were made from. And if I could make something as beautiful as that what would I be?

From the backseat: "Daddy?"

"Yes, Michael?"

"I'm thirsty."

"Cedric? Oh, he's asleep. Wait, Michael."

"Daddy?"

"I know you must be tired. It was an empty day. We didn't catch any fish. We're going home," he said.

"We weren't fishing, Daddy."

"That was a metaphor, son. Comes from poetry. You have to listen to some poetry. Want me to say a poem for you?"

"I'm tired," Michael said.

"All right. Now just dig into the pack, and you'll find the water bottles. Just behind you."

"So much stuff here, Daddy."

"I know, I know. Who knows where anything is? Can you wait a little while? We'll be back in Taos before too long. You can get a long cool drink at Mrs. Luhan's. And we'll eat a good dinner. They'll roast something. They're always roasting something. Can you wait?"

"I think so."

"Good. You're a good boy, Michael."

They traveled a few more miles on this rocky road.

Then he spoke out.

"What's that, Daddy?" Michael said.

"More poetry, son. I'm saying a poem. 'The extraordinary patience of things! / This beautiful place defaced with a crop of suburban houses— / How beautiful when we first beheld it . . . ,"

The voice—his own—fell silent, and he saw it happening in front of him.

As they approached the village of Hernandez, a moon the size of a small coin was rising in the east over distant clouds and snow-peaks; and in the west, the late afternoon sun gained the crest of a south-flowing cloud bank and splashed its final brilliance upon the crosses in the cemetery of the church rough-tough O'Keeffe had painted some years before.

He steered the station wagon into the deep shoulder at the side of the road, and stopped and jumped out, running to the rear of the vehicle and wrenching open the gate.

"Cedric. Michael. We don't have much time."

View camera, lens!

He was breathing heavily, heavily but steadily.

Assembled!

Still in control of his breath.

Image, composed and focused.

"Ansel?" Cedric called out.

"The light meter, where is it?"

He heard his voice rise, nearly as high as the rising moon.

"Daddy?"

"Help Cedric find the light meter, son. Hurry, hurry."

Behind him the sun was about to disappear again behind the clouds. He was desperate, holding his breath. Here was the dream part, the rest all real. Doing the math for a celestial body as easily as he might have for someone in his own family posed there before him—it came to him that the luminance of the moon was two hundred and fifty candles per square foot. He placed this value on zone VII of the exposure scale—with the Wratten G (no. 15) deep yellow filter, the exposure was one second at f/32. He had no accurate

ALAN CHEUSE

reading of the shadow foreground values. He released the shutter and breathed deeply at last. After the first exposure, he quickly reversed the 8-by-10 film holder to make a duplicate negative, for he knew in his nerves he had visualized one of those important images that seem prone to accident or physical defect. As he pulled out the slide, the sunlight left the crosses.

"Daddy?"

"Yes, Michael?"

He was drenched in sweat, as though he had waded into a pond up to his shoulders.

"I found the light meter."

"You did? Good lad. I'm amazed we can find anything in this car."

"Here," Michael said.

"Too late," AA said, taking the instrument from his son. "But thank you. I think we did all right."

Cedric, taking off his eyeglasses, rubbed his face with his knuckles.

"What did you get? Were they biting?"

"Maybe a big one," AA said.

"I don't see what you were looking at," Cedric said.

"Put your glasses back on."

Cedric complied. The sky had darkened in the east, and now all the horizon had melted into a dense muddy line broken here and there only by larger trails of dust and smoke.

"I still don't see."

AA took another deep breath and nodded at his dear friend, best pal, member of the wedding a long time ago. And the boy standing next to him, this child he loved so much. What would happen to him? And to his daughter? To all of them?

"You will see," he said, feeling his grieving heart turn into a bright cold moon the size of a coin. "I hope. I do hope."

THE SECRET HEART OF CHRIST

Matt Clark

THIS IS NOT A STORY: I am thirty years old. I teach college in Louisiana. At the moment I am in Taos, New Mexico, where I'm living on a summer college campus, writing, acting like I'm the resident assistant, the person who makes sure the students don't kill each other or themselves during their sojourn in the Southwest. I'm here for two months and two weeks, and I miss my boyfriend more than I imagined I would. I struggle not to call him so often that my phone bill overwhelms me—with this in mind, I spend very little time mocking the students who pine so for their lovers at home in Dallas; they sometimes look like zombies, sunken eyes and pale skin, anomalies here in the heart of sun country. Mainly I try to keep out of the students' way, let them have their fun—as long as it stays sane, I stay on the periphery. This is safest . . . on any number of levels.

This is a story: I am thirty years old. I teach college in Louisiana. At the moment I am in Taos, New Mexico, where I'm living on a summer college campus, writing, acting like I'm the resident assistant, the person who makes sure the students don't kill each other or themselves during their sojourn in the Southwest. I'm here for two months and two weeks, and . . . you get the idea, right? You

From *American Short Fiction*.

can follow this without any problems, can't you? You can trust me, can't you? Why wouldn't you?

This is where the story really starts: at the church seven miles away in the tiny community of Ranchos de Taos. You've seen it in the work of Ansel Adams, Georgia O'Keeffe, anyone with a camera who's ever driven up 68 from Santa Fe. Its adobe walls and vaguely sexual buttresses capture the sun spectacularly, creating shadows so rich in color and implied texture one can't help but feel his or her own Kodak snapshot of the place will rival the ones nearby gift shops sell framed and matted for hundreds of dollars. Good luck. Art is harder than it looks. It may in fact be more closely related to miracles than to hard work.

Everything that preceded this: Exposition.

This is not a story: This is a story.

This is where the story really starts: The St. Francis church is re-mudded by the community every year in the late spring/early summer. Several students and I volunteered to help. For me it was more about nostalgia for Play-Doh than a good, Christian heart. Put simply, I wanted to play in the mud. So early on a Tuesday morning we drove—in a number of cars, as nobody wants to be at the mercy of a driver whose plans don't dovetail perfectly with their own—to Ranchos and presented ourselves to Rudy, the foreman of the *enjada:* all of us smiling, putting on our best faces, excited, yes, but maybe faking it just a little.

There are stories behind stories: Some of the student volunteers were enrolled in a class on Native American Mythology. Their professor thought it would be a good idea for them to participate in the *enjada.* (So add him to the list of people present.) It was forced volunteerism. Gently forced. Their being there reflected upon them not as people but as students, men and women who navigated life with a compass sometimes vaguely affected by the concept of grades.

There are stories behind stories: I write. I'm out here for two months and two weeks to work on a novel that needs revising. Last year I came out to do the same thing and never touched the novel that needed revising. I wrote a whole new novel, one with which I am much happier than I could ever be with a revision of the older novel. This year I came out once again to revise that first novel. I hate the first novel, hate the way it expects me to help it. I have decided to write something all new this summer, just like last summer. Maybe not a novel, maybe a series of short stories set in New Mexico. This is my plan.

This is not a story: The students here are mostly enrolled at Southern Methodist University in Dallas. This is where I went to school, too, which partially explains how I got this very comfy gig. SMU is known more than anything else for its high tuition and a student body composed largely of young men and women with wealthy parents and all the accompanying affectations. Almost half the student population of SMU belongs to a fraternity or sorority. The hierarchy of importance attached to these houses is based on wealth, looks, political outlook, etc. You get the picture, don't you? It is handsome but not especially pretty.

This is a story. This is not a story. This is not how a story works.

This is how a story works: You are a witness. Even removed somewhat from the action, you are a witness and therefore a participant. You are a volunteer in a project you trust has been well planned—but not so much that there remains no room for the unexpected. Surprises are good, but they shouldn't strain logic. The careful planning and hoped-for but unexpected surprises should play off one another in such a way that the ending provides not necessarily a lesson, but a sense of completeness, satisfaction.

Boil that down: Witness, action, trust, unexpected, logic, satisfaction. Is this a formula for writing stories? I don't think so. It is not something I teach. It's something that just came to me. It may be nothing more than bullshit, a list of words that equals bullshit.

This is how a story works: Bullshit.

The beginning of a scene, nothing more, only its promise: Rudy asked us what we wanted to do. He gave choices, recited a list of opportunities. Hauling, mudding, digging, painting, mixing, working in the flowerbeds. We looked around us, seeing people on high ladders, scaffolding, balanced on platforms suspended from cranes. A very old woman in a long dress and bonnet—a bonnet, no lie—was poking around in the flowerbeds lining the low adobe wall of the church courtyard. She smiled at us, a toothless, gaping grin. The shadow of a sunflower fell across her shoulder. Hauling, mudding, digging, painting, mixing, working in the flowerbeds. We looked around us and we chose painting, all of us, assuming it would involve slapping some brown dye on the adobe walls. We thought the adobe got painted its delicious chocolate color. We were wrong.

Setting: The interior of St. Francis is one of the most beautiful in the U.S. White adobe walls (painted) reach high up to a roof of ancient pine vigas and *latillas*. The *retablos* behind the altar and to the altar's right are some marvelous examples of religious folk art. Picture-taking is not allowed inside the church; this is a sacred space. Postcards may be bought in the gift shop.

Character: Rudy is thin. (Later we hear a fat man say that is because Rudy never stops moving.) He has long hair and a beard. He smiles broadly and seemingly without cease. His sentences all sound like questions, the inflections rising and rising. He has until Sunday to finish the church; it has to be ready for Sunday mass. Usually they just re-mud the outside, but this year they are also repainting the interior. The good Lord has sent us to him. The good Lord provides. Rudy tells us this, and I don't doubt that he believes it.

A more detailed picture: There is one set of scaffolding erected between wooden pews at the back of the church. Men stand on it, painting high up, close to the vigas supporting the roof. Women work along the bottoms of the walls, slowly, careful not to get the new white enamel (enamel: a first-time application, easy to clean, sure to shine) on the pews. Everyone is speaking Spanish. The students who have just entered the church are Anglos. Nobody else here is.

Character: Rudy's wife Sylvia is unofficially in charge of the church's interior makeover. She is short, plump, wears glasses. She means business. She doesn't appear especially glad that the students are here, but help is help. Just so they be careful. Don't tear anything up. This is not a game.

This is not a story: The students are out of their element. They do better in bars. They can talk to just about anybody in a bar, provided the anybody looks like them, dresses like them, drinks like them. These people are not like the people they talk to in bars. These people work for their parents. These people speak a different language sometimes. These people are telling them there will be a break at ten, another at noon for lunch (frito pies, being made by the ladies behind the parish office), then all work ceases at four and things get cleaned up by four-thirty. The students have little intention of staying that long. They have little intention, most of them, of staying until lunch. Indeed, when Professor Hendel leaves earlier than expected, some students wait a few minutes and clear out themselves. Why keep working if the person who's supposed to be watching you is gone?

"OK," Rudy says, "so you guys go get another set of scaffolding out of the garage over there and set it up at the front of the church. And that extension ladder there, a couple of you—who's not afraid of heights?—can set that up by the confessionals and start painting right away. There are brushes and rollers and extensions back here. OK. I'm going to go check on my outside crew. Let's all be safe and work hard." The group stands there. There is no leader. The man who would normally be taking orders from their father or one of their father's underlings has left. He was leader by default, and now he's gone. Now what?

Cultural studies: The girls have been directed to help the women. I should say the women have been directed to help the women. This is of some concern to the students, who are aware of the sexism but unsure how to deal with it. This is not their culture. These are not their people. At the same time, the scaffolding looks shaky, and the ladder, well, never mind that. Screw that. OK, the girls seem to say as they begin to help the women. OK, the women say without saying.

A short jump in time: The women are making some headway. They've put extensions on the roller handles and are hitting the walls almost halfway up along the sides of the church. You can see the new white against the old; you can watch the transformation. The men, myself included, are just standing at the front, close to the altar. We're looking at the scaffolding we're supposed to be putting up. It seems to be missing parts. Instead of doing something about it, we're just looking at it. The ladder is behind us, next to the confessionals. We're not touching it. There are worse places to die than in church. But church is bad enough. We're waiting, but we don't know what on.

The story behind the story. Of the fraternities at SMU, the one that bothers me the most is Kappa Alpha. These are what I've heard called "Executive Rednecks." They grew up in affluent suburbs, but they drive four-wheel-drive vehicles with Confederate symbols on the license plates. Indeed, they are "gentlemen of the Old South," and they have the world's largest Stars & Bars flag to prove it. Yearly, they organize the "Old South Ball," to which a great many of them wear Rebel uniforms. Some of their dates wear hoopskirts. Let me jump to my point: they are racist, sexist, homophobic, spoiled-rotten white boys who think they have a claim to greatness because they are pale.

Characters: There are four Kappa Alpha members at SMU-in-Taos this summer. They aren't such bad guys. Oh, sure, they keep pretty much to themselves and they drink too much (though not so much more than the other students) and they observe everything with an air of superiority. (You should see them tolerate/buddy up to members of lesser fraternities. They're equal-opportunity dickheads.) Three of the four are students. The fourth is a teaching assistant for the physical education class. His principal job is to undertake most of the "Wellness" activities with the class (excepting yoga, for obvious masculine reasons—wouldn't want to turn fruit halfway through a lotus position) and to rake the sand volleyball court before tournament matches. The latter activity he does shirtless. This is no great thrill. He is what might be called a biscuit-neck: he's worked out enough to get that thick, brontosaurus look about his upper torso, but sadly he's got a gut. One more detail, a fair one I think: he maintains a blond Nazi-short haircut.

Unreliable narration: Can you trust me? What's my agenda? Is it too clear who the bad guys are?

First person: I'm having a hard time organizing this; it's impossible to deliver the truth all at once. The truth is so much more than the story, but it makes itself clearest in a narrative, I think. A great many religions agree with me on this. You can cover a lot of philosophic ground with a good narrative.

The narrative: Good luck. To me and you.

Confession and clarification: I'm gay. Nobody out here knows this. The administration would be very unhappy to learn of my aberrant lifestyle. The students would be apoplectic. Their parents are Republican, paying a lot of money for this summer camp stuff. No deviants need apply. After all, a gay man might jump one of the students about whose safety he should be concerned, right? A straight man would never touch one of the female students, surely, even though that's happened before out here. (Some truths exist in modified form.)

The story behind the story that is not a story: I was not gay when I was at SMU. Of course, I was—I just didn't do anything about it. If anything, being in the conservative stronghold should have warped me out of my natural/unnatural tendencies. In truth, it wasn't until my third year of grad school in Louisiana that I did anything about what I'd known all my life. While at SMU I ignored the urge to even look at the handsome youths around me, my peers. Instead I developed a smallish drinking problem and dated girls willy-nilly, trying to prove something—to myself more than anyone else.

Ancient history: When I was little I had crushes on boys. These were not instances of hero worship; these were crushes. Even my sisters identified my idolatry of a dark-haired, James Deanish neighbor as a crush, and my sisters were ten years older than me—they knew crushes. They were experts on crushes.

Repetition for the sake of emphasis—you've read this before, I know: I miss my boyfriend.

I am sick of waiting on these students to get the scaffolding up. And I'm really sick of watching the KAs watch the other students with disdain. They are more helpless than the men they scorn (you should see them with a hammer), but that doesn't stop them from nurturing their clan-prescribed superiority complexes. The fact close at hand, that they are helpless in the ways of construction, labor, usefulness: that fact is easily ignored, set aside. Why do something menial when your parents can pay people with skin the color of Rudy's or darker to take care of life's trivialities for you?

Whoa, this is pretty bitter stuff. Is it fair? Probably not, but I doubt anybody else will jump in here to balance things out.

Valid question, not worded particularly well: An essay is not a story, but is a story not an essay?

A qualification: One of the KAs appears to be an OK fellow. He's trying a little harder than the others. I will not give his name. Each of the KAs may now believe he is the good guy.

The truth: Only two of the KAs are present. The Führer, of course, is not here. Keep in mind, he is not in the class that "volunteered" to do this. The Führer is home asleep. The Führer is belly down on a beer gut growing larger even as you read this.

The story, true: So I get the ladder and I extend it and I set it against the wall to the right of the altar. Somebody's already painted to the level an arm holding an extended roller might reach. On the ladder, I can get within two or three feet of the ceiling, leaving that high and dangerous space to the scaffolding painters. Before I can begin, though, I have to cover a saint with plastic. She's in a glass-fronted case on a shelf about ten feet off the ground. The case is framed by punched-tin scallops. The saint—it may be Mary, I'm not sure—is a wooden doll with an elaborate white dress. I don't look at her very long. I'm on a shaky ladder, and no one is helping me, steadying the ladder. I cover the case with plastic, secure it with a couple pieces of masking tape, and climb down. Step one.

Character history, first person: I was raised Catholic but stopped going to mass in ninth grade when I got in an argument (about an ice-skating field trip to Fort Worth) with my parish priest. This was a new priest. The old one, who had been with the parish forever, was replaced after being accused of what—fondling, touching, propositioning one of my fellow altar boys? Did he do it? I don't think so. Listen, I may not have acted upon any sexual yearnings until I was twenty-five, but I've had gaydar since before I can remember.

Not a flashback, exactly: My grandmother died not long before I came to Taos last summer. She'd wanted a Catholic funeral, but my wickedly unscrupulous aunt denied her this. On one break from campus I went to Chimayo, a beautiful chapel about forty minutes away, famous for its "healing dirt." It was a feast day, and there was a mass starting not long after I got there, so I stuck around, thinking I'd do some thinking about my grandmother, sort of substituting this for the funeral ritual she'd desired. I was surprised how easily I remembered the creeds and responses, how the words came out like the poems memorized in grade school. I was not surprised that the sermon was about how the world was evil and dangerous and *look out*. The priest's near-frantic assurances and admonitions reminded me why I didn't go to mass anymore—I mean besides the fact that the Catholic church is inherently hypocritical and mean-spirited and I'm not exactly their idea of a good boy—but I lit a candle on the way out anyway, in memory of my grandmother. There was a dollar charge.

A change is necessary in order for a character to grow: I'm getting used to the ladder. I don't mind the height so much. I put the distance between me and the floor out of my thoughts. I wield the roller carefully, trying not to drip. I hang on with one hand and stretch as high as I can. Every time I climb down to replenish the paint, I look to see how the scaffolding is coming along. They're getting it put up, but I can't help but feel a little ahead of them, as though this were a competition.

Facts taken from a book,[1] presented here out of the line of narrative, meant to be useful to a reader interested in history: The San Francisco de Asis Church was constructed in 1850. Its cruciform shape is unusual, one reason the shadowplay on the adobe is so dramatic and attractive to artists and photographers. Visitors to the church may wish to view *The Shadow of the Cross,* a painting by Henri Ault that's on display in the parish hall. Painted a decade before the discovery of radium, the painting nevertheless glows when viewed in darkness, revealing shapes within the portrait that are not detectable otherwise. The mystery of the painting deepens when one considers that no luminous paint has yet been developed that doesn't darken and oxidize within a short time. There is no charge to see the painting.

Useless poetic image #1: From where I sit I can see three magpies pacing the sand volleyball court, stalking bright grains, jewels in the sun.

---

[1] Adapted from *New Mexico Off the Beaten Path: A Guide to Unique Places,* by Todd R. Staats, 2nd ed. (Old Saybrook, CT: Globe Pequot Press, 1994).

On tense: Some of this is in present tense, when obviously it could not have been written at the time. How could I write about holding onto a ladder with one hand and painting with the other while typing? I couldn't. The use of present tense is to create the illusion of spontaneity, to heighten intensity, immediacy. It's mainly a cheap trick, but it works now and then.

Ten o'clock break: A long line behind the parish hall. Patient. Slow-moving. Watermelon, sliced. Oranges, cut. Cookies. Pepsi. Lemonade. Coffee. I take a piece of melon and orange, some lemonade. I sit against an adobe wall, talk to some students. One is particularly outgoing and funny. She's a theater major. She uses the word "amazing" a lot. Nine out of ten times she means it.

Rudy comes in to tell us we're doing a fine job. *Bueno, bueno.* I move to a different wall, one that isn't next to the altar, but faces it in part. I've mentioned the church's cruciform shape, and now I'm working on a wall that's the bottom of one of the cross's arms. It occurs to me that whereas everyone in the church will see the wall I was just working on, few will look at the wall I'm painting now. Does that matter? Can I get sloppy, or would it be better karma to paint this side with even more deliberate care?

Only a few of the students remain.
The others, they'd done enough.
They helped.
They grew bored.
They left.

I've moved my ladder to the rear of the church, where I'm painting the adobe immediately below the choir loft. After that I need to paint in the corners. Then below the vigas holding up the choir loft, then above the beams over the doorway, then the uppermost parts of the doors. I've got a lot to do, and I'm a bit frustrated. Sylvia keeps piling on the work. The person with the ladder is the only one who can do these things, it seems. Right now I'd rather be outside helping put adobe on the walls, getting muddy, getting some sun. I resent that I'm expected to keep working at this tedious task. It takes many minutes to arrange the ladder, to make sure it doesn't damage the wood or the adobe, to make sure it's balanced properly. I'm tired. My arms are sore. I'm taking a break. It's almost lunch, but I'm taking a break.

I go to the front to see how the scaffolding painters are doing. They need help. They're looking up at Christ on the Cross. "Should we move him or cover him?" Brian asks. (On the campus roster Brian's name is typed "Brain." The irony is grand.)

Covering him would be a real pain and seems like it might damage him somehow. We should take him down. "Sylvia, should we take him down?" we call. She comes back, and together, we barely lift the crucifix to examine the chain upon which it's hung. "Take him down or cover him up?"

"Take him down," she says, turning back to her work. "Carefully," she adds.

We fetch and lean the ladder close to the crucifix. "I'm not going up to get him," Brian says.

The faculty member's son, Steven, says, "He's taller than I am. I don't know if I could wrangle him."

"I'll go," I say. "I'll get him."

And so I ascend the ladder again. It's not fully extended, shouldn't be as scary. But it is. How heavy is he? How to balance him as I descend? What are the cosmic penalties of dropping Jesus? I take a good grip below his outstretched arms and slowly lift the hook on the back of the cross off and out of the chain-link from which it depends. Unwieldy, dusty crown of thorns. Help me. Help me get him down. Help me land him safely. Help me find a place to rest him out of the renovation. There. Thank you. Thank you, let's put him here, behind the altar. He's dusty, long, more intense-looking on the ground, sprawling, unsteady on the fulcrum of the hook. There. There. Back to work. No, to lunch. It's lunchtime. Leave him. OK. To lunch.

Behind the parish hall again, another line. Put Fritos in a Styrofoam bowl, let one of the ladies ladle on chili—spicy or not-so-hot? Cover with cheese. Take a tortilla. What else? Tomato? Cookies? Pepsi? Lemonade. Napkin. Smile, thank them. They thank you back. They're glad you're here, you imagine. You insert thoughts into their heads, gratitude. You take pride in what you're doing, even as you suspect it is in opposition to the "reason" you're here.

So, I'm writing, right? I'm out here to write. Stories. So, what am I writing? Is it any good? Not yet. Is it finished? Not yet. This is what it looks like so far:

THE INEXPLICABLE AND UNEXPLAINED SHOW

People, they blame me, like it's my fault. "Your Rigo stopped me. Tuesday," someone will say after mass, and the others around us, flowing out the door toward Father John's soft handshake, the others will cluck, shake their heads sadly, sometimes adding, "Me too. Thursday."

They say this not long after we've all shared peace, after we've all celebrated the mysteries of the faith, like there's something I can or should do.

"Were you speeding?" I ask.

Maybe occasionally they'll blush. "Yes, but not so much. It's me," they say. "I live here."

What they mean is that mainly the tourists coming over the mountains are the ones who get caught. They're so close to Taos they can almost smell it. So why brake to thirty-five going through Talpa? No stop signs. No blinking yellow lights. No nothing. Even the tavern is closed, abandoned; no blue neon-beer signs flash there. Why slow down?

"The rules apply to everyone," I say, crossing myself with holy water and exiting into the bright courtyard. The flowers I planted there are blooming, but nobody wants to talk about those, nobody gives me credit for the poppies being prettier than Georgia O'Keeffe's, redder. They just want to complain about Rigo doing his job. The rules apply to everyone. "Everyone. Even me," I say. Even me.

When I ask Rigo about this he says, "Don't be stupid. Besides, you don't speed."

"You're calling your mother stupid? Standing in a house of God you call your mother stupid?"

Rigo rolls his eyes. "Number one, I didn't call you that. I said 'Don't be' that, like a warning. An admonition."

"I fail to see the difference."

"Well, there is one. Number two, this isn't a house of God. That's across the way. This is a tourist trap, Mama."

"Shut up! You are a tourist trap. You'd give your own mother a ticket."

"Mother," Rigo whines. "Mother, please. If you really think—"

"No, I don't want to talk anymore to you. Here's your lunch." I hand him his bag. "Now go. Get out of here and do your job, go hunt down the speeders. Go."

And he does, whistling the *Andy Griffith* theme, badly.

As he leaves, a young couple comes in, sheepish-looking, arms and hands awash in just-bought turquoise. "Hello," I say. "There will be another showing of the Mystery Painting in just a few minutes, after the last group lets out." They nod at me and then stand there, eyeing the sign that asks for donations. We are a church. We do not charge admission, but if people feel like giving as they go in or come out—and they should—then there's a box into which they may slip a dollar or two. "There's a gift shop next door," I tell them. "If you'd like, you can look around in there. Work by local artists. Art. And postcards." I smile at them until they leave. They haven't said a word, as though they are afraid there is a vow of silence associated with being here, as though this is a library and they are in danger of being shushed. They leave, headed in the direction of the gift shop, and I go back to my desk.

On days like today when it's slow, I sit and read. Not always the Bible. Rarely the Bible, actually. I like detective novels, not the gory ones. People who do come in, and see me reading a novel, sometimes give me a funny look, like they expect I should be reading the Bible, but to be honest, despite all its wonders the Bible is no good for passing time. Some days, if I'm sick of reading, I may go in and look at the painting myself, first with the lights on, then with them off. When the lights are off, I get very close, I step over the velvet security rope and put my eye right up next to the painting, until I can see some of the little cracks beginning to form. The glow is still there, but that close it doesn't look like a glow. It looks like a color, a bright color in dim light. I look at it until my eyes water sometimes, then I go back to my novel, or maybe I clean the bathroom, make sure the paper-towel holder is full.

When the door to the left of my desk opens and the group lets out, a man in a yellow Hawaiian shirt says to his wife, "It's some kind of radiation, radium or something in the paint," even though the video explained quite clearly how the paint was tested for just that, how radium hadn't even been discovered when the painting was created, how the artist, Henri Ault, thought he was mad the first time he went into his studio at night and found the painting aglow.

"So it's an atomic Jesus," the wife says, and they both laugh. They must know I'm sitting right there, but they don't look at me as they leave. They don't say good-bye or thank you, nothing. They are just gone into the heat and I'm glad, I don't want to debate with them. You can't reason with white men in Hawaiian shirts — more than likely they're from Dallas. Other people are coming out now, blinking against the light, and they nod at me and mouth silent thank-yous and wows. When the last person has left, I go into the viewing room and turn on the overheads to make sure nobody left anything behind. Sometimes they leave cameras, a backpack, a half-full bottle of fancy drinking water, water that costs a dollar-plus for not much more than a couple of gulps. There's always something left behind, it seems like. But a quick glance reveals no new item for the lost and found, so I rewind the video for the next group, wondering if that young couple I sent to the gift shop before will come back. Maybe they wandered down to Teo's for some iced tea or into one of the galleries around the Plaza. Maybe they left, though. Maybe they're headed away in a nice Ford Explorer or one of those Range Rovers that used to be rare but now are everywhere around here. I say a tiny prayer for the couple, one that is more like a focused thought sent their way. *Drive slow going through Talpa.* Not because I was fond of them and would hate for them to get a ticket, but because it would be nice for Rigo to be able to eat his lunch without interruption. He eats alone in his car. He could go into town to a café, but he prefers to save money and doesn't like sitting in the break room at the station, where apparently people are not shy about impounding my white-chocolate-chip cookies. So like I said, he sits in his car, alone, eating a lunch I made this morning. Sometimes he eats at one of the turnoffs out on 518, maybe next to Pot Creek, sometimes behind the new post office in the shade of the loading dock. Sometimes he picks up his lunch and eats right out front in the parking lot, in his car with the windows rolled down and the dispatcher breaking the silence every now and again just to say something, just to hear the silence broken. Maybe he'll wave to me, maybe he won't. Every so often a tourist will see Rigo in his car and say to me, "What happened? Is everything all right?" as though there's been a crime Rigo's come to investigate. "My son," I tell them, nodding at him chewing on a sandwich, very handsome in his uniform. "Eating his lunch. My son, my boy."

The young couple from before never comes back. Instead a busload of Germans arrives. I watch them out the window, taking their pictures of the church from every angle, see them gather in a sturdy, blond group and almost march toward me in the parish hall. Most of them have guidebooks as well as cameras, so I figure they'll know what they're about to see. Even so, the video is English only, so I hand each of them a Xeroxed sheet that says in German all the kinds of things they might miss in their guidebooks. Though I doubt anyone understands me, I stand in front of them in the viewing room and explain about how flash photography is forbidden and how it's important that we maintain respect for the sacred. They sit quietly, listen carefully, politely, and then I push PLAY on the VCR and leave them, turning out the overheads as I close the door.

Twenty minutes pass. I go in and turn the TV off as the credits are rolling upwards, catching my name on there, *Thanks to Irene Luhan,* it says. I invite them to stand closer to the painting, motioning them out of their seats. I point out the rope and make it clear that they are not to cross it or lean so far over it they lose their balance. They nod, smiling. In order to keep their eyes adjusted to the dark, I did not turn the overheads on when I went back in, so everybody is shadowy-looking, some grins appearing dangerously sharp. "OK," I tell them, "I'm going to shut the door, and then you'll see it. Give it some time," I tell them. And then I go back to my novel, which is starting to get a little gory, so maybe I won't finish it. After a few seconds I hear them in there, the Germans, trying to say what they see. At least that's what I guess their words mean. That's what the English-speakers do, the Spanish-speakers, too, try to second-guess the glow before it's probably fully ready to be understood. Some people's eyes work faster, sure, but I know it takes a few minutes at the minimum, I know even in German that the people talking are trying to point out the cross before they really see it, that they're jumping the gun, relying on what the guidebooks and the sheet I handed gave away. If I listen carefully I might recognize some of the words off that sheet, the grunting sounds of *ship,* and *cross,* and *miracle.*

Minutes later, as they leave, the Germans nod at me, some trying out their thank-yous and *gracias*'s. Most drop a dollar or two into the donation box, and I smile, wish them a safe journey. I like them, the Germans. I like foreign tourists the best because even if they are saying snide things about the painting, I can't tell. And in general, from the way their voices sound, softer inside the viewing room than American voices, I believe they are saying nice things. Even if they think the painting is hooey (my late husband's word), they know enough to keep that to themselves until they regain the privacy of their big, black bus.

I don't like hearing the words *hooey,* or *fake,* or *gyp,* or any words like those. Here's one reason why: *Hooey* is the last word I heard my Rudy say before he disappeared. I had just taken this job—this was twelve years ago and he didn't like it. It didn't, and doesn't, pay much, and Rudy thought the Mystery Painting was not a good thing for the parish.

"And what's it doing here? It was painted where? Italy, somewhere like that. This is New Mexico. Why do we need it here?"

"It's been all over the world," I told him. "We're lucky to get it. It's a treasure, and we are its caretakers. We are blessed by its being here."

"Baloney," Rudy said. "Hooey. Makes us look like simpletons, diminishes the beauty of the church, the true mysteries of the Sacraments."

"You're exaggerating," I told him. "You're overreacting."

It was a Saturday. He had the day off and was taking Rigo fishing at the Gorge. The car was packed with their tackle, all that stuff, and the lunches I'd made them. "Hooey," Rudy said, and he steered Rigo out the door by the back of his head. I can still picture Rudy's hand that way, his palm almost as big across as all of Rigo's head.

"Good-bye," I said, not mad, wanting this not to be something between us. It was my first job since high school, and I was pleased. I'd waited until Rigo was old enough to be alone after school, and I'd applied for the job, beating out a couple women from the parish who still won't speak to me beyond a gruff hello. I was excited about it. "Good-bye," I said to his "hooey," the last word I ever heard Rudy say. "Good-bye," I said, waving to his back.

There is a program on a station out of Los Alamos that only broadcasts on the first Friday of the month. By the time the announcer has closed out his hour, you are glad it doesn't air more often. All he does is read stories about mysterious happenings from around the world, mainly UFO sightings in South America and Bigfoot incidents in Washington state. Sometimes there is a report of some oddity in New Mexico, and on these occasions the announcer gets a little antsy, his voice rising to squeaky heights. He invites people to call in, particularly "witnesses" to these phenomena; he promises to believe them and ensures anonymity. I listen every month, and nobody ever takes the poor guy up on his offer. He says he understands that people are afraid to tell the truth, he says his knowledge and beliefs affect his daily life, the way people treat him, so of course he can see how people would be shy, unwilling to sacrifice the security of a good job, the love of friends and family. It's a sad show, tragic and compelling, impossible to turn off once you've tuned in. And it's not the kind of thing you want people to catch you listening to, so when one of the vacationing Germans comes chugging back in, looking upset, I turn the volume down low, though I know from the way the poor fellow is struggling to think of the words to say to me he couldn't possibly understand the announcer's pleas for people who saw a flying saucer over El Prado to call in and testify. The German is holding his wallet and gesturing at me and searching his English vocabulary. I can see him rolling through the list of words he knows, grimacing as he does so, squinting. "I," he says. "I . . . forgot."

"You forgot something? Hang on." I go back into the viewing room, thinking maybe I'd missed something. Credit card? Ring? Passport? I bend to look under the rows of folding chairs. Nothing. *Nada.* Maybe it fell under the velvet rope and rolled into the darkness below the Mystery Painting.

"Mom?" I hear Rigo say from the foyer where I left the German.

"What?" I'm stooping to see if maybe there's a ring in the shadows around the bottom of the Painting's frame. It's dusty here, needs a good sweep. "What is it, Rigo?" I call. Did I forget to pack his orange? His Coca-Cola?

"Come out here," Rigo says.

"Hang on," I say, giving the room a last scan. Nothing.

I find the German in tears, hands above his head as though he's being mugged, pulled off the stagecoach and robbed. "Calm down," Rigo's telling him. "It's OK," he says, then to me: "Who is this guy?"

"A German," I say. "He thinks he forgot something."

"I forgot," the German says once again. He's perfected those two words in his head and uses them meekly, nearly sobbing. "I forgot." He uses his empty upraised hand to tap the one holding the wallet. "I forgot."

Aha. He'd come back to put some money in the donation box, and then Rigo had shown up in his patrol car, in his good-looking uniform, and the poor German assumed I'd called the cops on him. "No problem," I tell the German. "You're not in trouble." I walk to Rigo and put my hand up on his shoulder, patting it. "My son," I say. "He's my son. You're not in trouble." I tell Rigo what I've deduced, and he laughs.

"No problem here," Rigo tells the German. He steps forward and gently pulls the man's arms down, like he's posing him for a photo shoot. "You're fine," he tells him, "fine and dandy."

The German looks at us a moment, more confused than ever. Sniffling, he fishes a five-dollar bill out of his wallet and shows it to us, demonstrating its strength and genuineness by tugging on its ends, popping it. He folds it and slides it into the box, then, wiping his eyes, flees into the afternoon glare.

"Highway robbery," Rigo says to me, shaking his head.

"You should know."

"Which is why I'm here," Rigo says. "I just gave a ticket to Nadine. Sixty-five in a thirty-five. Figure you'll be hearing about that."

I sigh. "Yes, I will."

"Wanted to give you a chance to prepare yourself."

"Honey," I tell my boy, "it is not possible to prepare for such an onslaught. One does not prepare. One survives. If one is lucky."

Rigo smiles, then stops. "What's that noise? I hear a voice."

The radio. I don't want him to hear the program, so I push him toward the door. My hand on his starched shirt. My tiny hand. His broad, strong back. "Nothing. Now go back to work. Go ticket the rest of my neighbors, make them all hate me. Go on."

"OK, OK," he says, strutting to his patrol car. He knows what I was listening to, the silly UFO report, and I am ashamed. "See you later," he says before he ducks into the car, tossing his hat in before him.

"Later, gator."

As soon as he has backed out and driven away, Nadine pulls up in his spot. She gets out and sees me in the doorway. "Was that him?" she snaps, knowing perfectly well it was.

"Yes, it was. That was Rigo. My son. Who works for the State Department of Public Safety. Why do you ask?"

"He told you?"

"Yes, he did. Sixty-five in a thirty-five."

Nadine huffs. "His thingy is off," she says. "Way, way off."

When they called to tell me that they had Rigo twelve years ago, I asked what did they mean. Where was his father, I asked. Nadine was in the kitchen and already had her hand to her mouth, covering the look there. She knew it was bad.

"Ma'am," the man on the phone said. If he were to call me right now, I would remember his voice. I can hear it in my head the way I can remember Bing Crosby's voice singing "White Christmas." "Ma'am," the man said. "That's what we need to come talk to you about—"

And so they did. They brought Rigo home and told me he'd been found sitting in the truck alone. He'd hiked up out of the Gorge, thinking maybe his father had come up without telling him, even though all their fishing gear was right where it had been when Rigo went downriver a little to play. They'd found Rigo sitting in the truck, crying.

"So where is he? Where is Rudy?"

"We fear he may have fallen in. He may be drowned, ma'am. Or he may have just wandered off."

"Maybe he broke his leg," I said. It made sense to me, and saying it was the only way I could keep my lungs from curling in on themselves and dying. I had to talk. "Maybe he went to use the bathroom and broke his leg. He's still down there, I bet." Nadine saw that I was getting a little hysterical, and she took Rigo into the yard. "Did you look? Are you looking for him? He may need help, that's all."

"Ma'am," a man said. This was not the same man from the phone. I'd heard the voices of all the men who came to my house—there were four of them, four of them brought my Rigo home—and none was the man from the phone, not one had a voice like his. I only heard that voice once. I never heard it again, but it's the voice I'll always remember from that night, coming from someplace I couldn't fathom, from a mouth I would never see, never. "We've been looking," the man said. "And will continue to do so. You're absolutely right. He may have just gotten a little lost. For all we know, he wandered up out of the Gorge on a different trail. For all we know, he's fine."

And I looked at the man, him in a uniform my Rigo would grow up to wear someday, him holding his Stetson hat in his lap, I looked at him and I thought, *Hooey,* knowing the man was thinking the same thing about the line he was feeding me. *Hooey.* Rudy was gone. Why waste time beyond that? Why waste my heart when it was perfectly clear Rudy was not coming back? *Hooey,* I thought, and I rocked forward on my legs and off the couch and I went out to Rigo in the yard, on his swing, not swinging but sitting and looking at the ground beneath him, the worn spots where Rudy would stand to push him toward the sky. "Rigo," I said. "Baby—"

Rigo later said he had waited for him, then called for him, then looked for him, then cried for him and for himself, alone at the bottom of the Gorge. He kept expecting Rudy to find him crying and make fun of him, which made him cry harder, and when Rudy didn't come, didn't find his boy crying, that made Rigo cry harder still. But then he thought maybe his father had hiked out alone, maybe he was looking for Rigo up top by the truck, or maybe he'd gotten a stomachache and gone up to rest across the truck's long seat. So Rigo left everything where it was but the canteen he'd been given on his last birthday, and he carried the water and himself up the trail past Little Arsenic Springs and up and up to the lip of the Gorge, from which he could see the truck but not Rudy. Maybe Rudy was spread out across the truck's seat, like Rigo had thought way down there at the bottom of the Gorge, and Rigo, breathless from the climb, ran as fast as he could to the truck, afraid to call out for his father, afraid to show that he was afraid. But the truck was empty, with no sign his father had been there at all. Crying more, he made his way back to the river, looking all the way down for a glimpse of Rudy's red ball cap but not seeing it. The fishing equipment was just the way he'd left it still, and that was bad. It was bad, all this was bad, Rigo knew. The sun was shining in such a way that the Gorge was only lit on its east side. The west side was getting darker and darker as the sky above it turned orange, and if he watched carefully Rigo could see how the east side's light was creeping upwards, disappearing, and it would be bad to be in the Gorge past dark. His father knew that, and his father would want him to do the right thing, to climb up and wait for him at the truck, to wait for him to come back from wherever it was he'd had to go. Rigo would leave the equipment, but he couldn't find anything with which to compose a note for his father, no pen, no paper. So he just turned his back on all of it and hiked up out of the Gorge feeling cold, sensing the night coming, the temperature dropping. He found the truck empty again. Still. But there was an old blanket behind the seat, one that smelled like sage and dust from the ground where they'd spread it to watch fireworks on the Fourth, and Rigo covered up with it and sat in the truck watching the lip of the Gorge, afraid that his father was not going to come up over that lip, worried that all this bad stuff that was happening might get worse, worried that this was all his fault somehow, though he couldn't imagine exactly why that might be. He sat watching the trailhead, watching it like a hawk, not sleepy at all, and when a Forest Service ranger came to change out trash bags by the trailhead, he told him he was waiting for his father, crying so hard as he did so that the ranger knew the father was probably not going to come up that trail. "It's going to be OK, your daddy's fine," the ranger told Rigo.

"He lied to me," Rigo sobbed later that night, sitting in his swing with Nadine crouched on the end of the little slide attached to it, me standing there in front of Rigo. "He lied to me," Rigo said. "Lied."

I didn't yet know about the whole of Rigo's experience. I didn't yet know about the ranger. I didn't know who my son meant, who had lied to him, but I told him this anyway: "He didn't mean to," I told Rigo.

"He lied."

"But he didn't mean to," I said.

There. That's all there is so far. I know what's going to happen, I know pretty much what's left to write. But it's not coming. Is that because it's the wrong thing, the things I think should happen are not the right things? How do you move in a maze you can't see, a maze you're creating with every step, one you know you must move

MATT CLARK

out of eventually with some grace, leaving it knowing that the maze itself was a lesson, an experience valuable not just for yourself but the others who follow in the footsteps you leave as markers? How do you do that without running smack into a wall you made?

Back at the church, behind the parish hall, having lunch with students: quickly sounding each other out about campus. Yes, the frat boys are asinine. We can agree on this, even though one student in this conversation belongs to a top sorority, one of the most elite of the elite. "You get out here and none of that stuff should matter, but it does," she says. "It's sad, but it does."

The Story of Mud: Going back to the church, you stop and finally get your hands muddy. There are buckets of mud and water mixed with hay, and there are sheepskins torn and stuck into the muck. You take the sheepskin, which looks nothing like a sheepskin anymore, and you get it good and mucky. Then you slap it lightly against the adobe wall and begin to wipe it around in a circle, watching where you leave the mud and water. Around. Around. Around. Re-mud. Around. Around. The dirty water begins to run down the sheepskin onto your wrists, down to your elbow. It's cold in the hot sun and feels good, but also more than a little discomforting. Can something be those two things at once, good and discomforting? After only a few minutes your arm tires, and you become glad you've been painting in the church where it's cool and the paintbrush has a handle, is clean, where the work is just as tedious as it is out here but differently so. You hose off your arms, rubbing away the mud that has already begun to dry on your pants. You go back inside.

The Curator of Objects is inside. She sees we've taken down the Jesus on the Cross, she's been told this by somebody, and she's come to look after it. She's dusting it lightly with tiny brushes, blowing away the years of accumulation with a can of compressed air. She introduces herself as the Curator of Objects. She is in charge of the *santos* and *retablos* and this crucifix. She doesn't strike one as somebody who attended a school in curatorship, but she likes the word "curator" and introduces herself in connection with the word and uses it to describe what she's doing. It's easy to tell she wished we'd asked her and not Sylvia about taking down the crucifix. At the very least she should have been there, been a part of its descent from the wall where it's rested since the last time the church was painted. With help, she raises the crucifix and says, "Let me show you this."

Suspense: What is it the curator will show? Why is she standing the crucifix up? Why is she whispering? Why are you whispering back?

Lust and villainy: OK, so I'm gay and it would be a bad idea to tell anybody this because of the obvious paranoia felt by people (men) about homosexuality. Never mind the psychology of fear and desire, all that stuff; the simple fact is, it's best kept under my hat. And though there's no way in hell I'd ever hit on a student anyway, even if he was hitting on me (fat chance, remember my experience at SMU, in which true identity was buried deep out of the sight of my fellow students and myself—isn't that probably still the case for students following in my footsteps?), even though I'd never do anything to jeopardize my job or a set of ethics I feel comfortable with, even so, let me point this out: There are no cute boys at camp. The closest we get this year is one of the KAs, a dark-haired guy with a too-bright smile and in-shape physique. He seems nice enough, but he is not at the church on the day of *enjada*. He's no volunteer. He plays volleyball well, though, and looks good in shorts. He wears aviator sunglasses and resembles Tom Cruise. He's picking up a nice tan out here.

Tease: "What every story needs to succeed: A little religion . . . a little aristocracy . . . a little sex . . . a little mystery, as summed up by this sentence: 'My God,' cried the Duchess, 'I've been @#$%! But by whom?'"   —*Source unknown*

Suspense: Is it building? Was it incorrectly set up? Again: The Curator of Objects is whispering. She hisses, "Let me show you something" as she stands the crucifix up and begins to turn it slowly around so that you are looking at the back, into the hollow torso of the Messiah. "Look at this," she says, balancing the cross with one pudgy hand, pointing with the other.

The students have all left now. I am back atop my ladder, painting corners white. The shadows and crossbeams make it difficult to tell what has been painted already by the women with their rollers and what needs my hand. I skipped one troublesome corner earlier, but now, feeling guilty, I go back and hit it good, make it shine. The men on the scaffolding continue to work just as hard as I am, but they have one another to talk to—and the women below me are washing the floor, mopping up spilled dots of paint with mineral spirits, talking quietly in Spanish, gossiping, I imagine. So, above the women, below the choir loft, with a tiny brush in my hand, one that needs constant refilling (is that the right word?), I am alone, it feels. My back really does ache, and every complicated ladder move involves pulling in the rungs, scooting the heavy aluminum steps sideways a few feet, re-extending the ladder, picking up the brush again, ascending. I repeat this move I can't count how many times. Lunch was hours ago. It's getting close to four. And I'm going to finish soon. I've lost the feeling of urgency, the hurry. I'm going back over spots I thought I'd covered that now look slightly yellowish in the altered, late-afternoon light. When several students eventually return, including the theater major, they're surprised to see me still at work. "We did a lot today," they say, looking around at the church. The men from the scaffolding are beginning to climb down; almost but not quite done, they have to tidy things up for the mass that will take place in the unfinished church in the morning. "We did a lot today," the students say. "Didn't we?"

Outside, the cleanup is efficient though slightly chaotic. Scaffolding must be dismantled and stored; cranes must lower platforms upon which sit men who've been applying adobe to the highest sections of the church. Water must be dumped, tools sprayed clean. Everyone helps carry things to the garage by the parish hall. The women are setting up a table in front of the rectory, a banquette they're crowding with cookies and juice and soft drinks. Men try to take a break to grab a soda, but Rudy stops them. "Not until we've put everything away," he says. He's not smiling. He wants this done right. The old woman who was working in the flowerbeds this morning now shoos people into working harder, badgering them in Spanish. During the day I've seen her digging, mudding the wall, helping put out food. She is not pampered or treated as a fragile item. She's tough, as she's no doubt proven at dozens of *enjadas* before this one.

The theater major, Leslie, tells me that the old woman came up to watch her mud and said something in Spanish that she didn't understand. A woman nearby translated: "You don't have any mud in your bucket. You're just getting the wall wet, that's all. All you've got there in that bucket is brown water."

Leslie blushed, but the old woman smiled and patted her on the back, comforted her in Spanish. Though the language was foreign, the meaning was clear.

Leslie and I lug scaffolding, boards, and crossbars from the church to the garage. The men are surprised that she's doing man's work, but nobody says anything. There is still one high scaffold to take down. The young men atop it have only just stopped mudding, and they hand their tools and buckets down. Like circus acrobats they begin to deconstruct the very platforms on which they stand. Their friends call up to them, and they smile back. Dazzling. Their arms are brown, strong, beautiful. I have to stop myself from staring. They are gorgeous, brave. Don't stare. Don't get your ass kicked out here. Rein it in, bucko.

The priest is in front of his home, talking to the women. I saw him earlier in the day. He came into the church to inspect the progress. Young, much younger than I expected for a church of this antiquity and historical importance. Hispanic, with a soft voice and owlish glasses, wearing jeans and a sky-blue polo shirt, handsome and soft-looking. I wanted him to notice me, to introduce himself. He was speaking to everybody in the church, complimenting everyone's work, but he passed me by. I may as well not have been there. But why was it I wanted to meet him? To gain his praise? Or to look him in the eye? His voice, his dress, the way he carried himself—he was familiar in many ways. Why was it so important for me that I meet him? And why was it he saw me but did not stop to speak? What about me made me invisible, that he didn't know me—or knew me too well?

Now the priest is talking to the women as they set up the refreshments and the men finish putting things away, meandering from their duties, dusty, tired, smiling. Rudy is smiling again now, slapping people's backs, shaking hands. "Good work today," he tells me, clutching my hand tightly in something that's a cross between a traditional grip and a jivey ballet. He rubs Leslie's shoulder and tells her the same thing he told me.

"We should get dinner in town tonight, do you want to do that?" Leslie asks me, and I say yes, thinking tonight is pork chop night. Almost immediately after I've said yes I realize that tonight is not pork chop night—and worse, what she may have just asked me was to go on a date. And I said yes.

A date: would be wrong on how many levels?

I give her a ride back to campus, a little uneasy. Is it just me, or has she begun to act differently, a trifle girlish? Is she touching her hair more? (Or is that only in my memory? This happened a week ago: has my mind filled in the blanks with clichés? John Irving in his essay "Trying to Save Piggy Sneed" writes, "A fiction writer's memory is an especially imperfect provider of detail. We can always remember, or think we remember, a different, better detail than that which actually happened." Now in my memory that's what Irving wrote, but I don't have the book here in front of me, so am I sure? Yes for the first sentence, no for the second.) When we get back to camp, Leslie says, "So I'll meet you here when?"

"I don't know," I say.

"I don't take a lot of time to get ready." As opposed to other girls? Is she setting herself in opposition to them, making it clear she's different, better?

"How about forty-five minutes then?"

"Great."

I'm filthy. Covered in paint. Need a shower. And what to wear? Am I really spending more time getting ready than I usually do? Why? Am I putting on the shirt I brought for special occasions? Why? Am I dabbing on cologne? Why? Isn't it cruel in some way? Isn't it mean-spirited? Am I enjoying the idea that Leslie may have a slight crush on me?

Desire: is nothing more than vanity all curled up, biting its own ragged tail.

We get sushi. It's early for dinner; we're the first in the restaurant. Leslie has dressed up, I think, though it may be more about being away from campus than about being in my company. Nevertheless, she looks me square in the eye for periods that last two heartbeats too long. We talk about camp. We talk about plays, specifically musicals. I talk about my recent trip to New York with "a good friend." Isn't this Chad? Isn't this the boyfriend I miss so much? We talk about museums. Am I making it clear enough that I'm gay? I'm reveling in the stereotypes. Are they a defense now, an out, so to speak? "Are you married?" Leslie asks. No, I say. But I don't take it further than that, and I'm ashamed. Clearly Leslie suspects, and she wants me to say it. Tell me, tell me, is the subtext of the conversation now. Let's talk secrets. Let's give stuff away.

No.

Absurdism made easy: Sushi in Taos. Raw salmon in the high desert. Octopus within miles of a pueblo without electricity or plumbing. Tuna. Quail eggs. Squid. Kachinas. Kokopelli. Blowfish cut not to kill.

How did she say it? How did it come up? What prompted this revelation, this: One of the KAs has a gun. In his casita. Leslie was present for the gun's appearance, its debut, its coming-out party. The boys were questioning the sexual orientation of one of their bunk-mates. Seems he'd had the gall to reach in and get his shaving kit out of the shower while one of the KAs was bathing. Sure, it's a big bathroom, and the showers are equipped with multiple heads to accommodate more than one person at a time, but that wouldn't do, group showering. Shades of homosexuality and communism. So he must be gay, right? Right? Isn't that what gay men do, sneak glances at beer guts and shriveled dicks while a Nazi is blinded by his own emerald Prell?

My gaydar: Pretty polished. Rarely off. This guy, this suspected person: he lacks social skills, he's awkward, not good at volleyball, dresses like a dork. He is not gay. He is not of my tribe. He is a geek, that's all. Frankly, I'm insulted.

An aside, useless: It's Gay Pride week; in magazines those clever Absolut admen have filled their bottles with rainbows. When I smile at this I only do so for a second, fearful somebody might see, might peek through my blinds and witness me admiring an ad. An ad, for God's sake.

Manly soliloquy: Motherfucker touches me—any of us—I'll blow his motherfucking head off.

Ethical dilemma: Is this being told to me in confidence, this gun business? How am I to respond? Clearly this requires my attention. A firearm on campus is a violation of the student code.
    Shit. I'm going to have to do my job.

Leslie may still be thinking about the possibility of *what* between us—romance? I'm thinking about a gun. I'm thinking about a guy with a gun in his casita who might shoot a guy because he doesn't know better than to let these manly (but not studly) men shower in absolute privacy. I'm eating raw fish and rice and soy mixed with wasabi and I'm hearing this girl across from me, who looks a little like a girl I dated some years ago, I'm hearing her talk about the plays she's been in and I'm thinking: gun. I'm thinking, you jerks, now I've got to do something aggressive. Now the real fag in your midst has to bust you. Leslie played the Audrey Hepburn role in *Wait until Dark* last year, and I'm obliged to play sheriff now, later tonight, against Nazis with guns.

I convince myself it's the one who looks like a Nazi, biscuit-neck recruit for a new army, one above skinheads, below Republican congressmen. He's the Wellness assistant, is being paid by the same university that's paying me, and he's got to go. He's got to go home and tell people how he fucked up, and he's got to forfeit part of his paycheck and reorganize his summer plans and get over himself and his politics and his baseless homophobia. So long, farewell, *auf Wiedersehen,* good-bye.

I'm using the wrong ends of the chopsticks, the thicker ends, but it's too late now and there's a girl with a crush on me across the table and I shouldn't be here, I shouldn't have heard this thing about the gun, if I hadn't heard it I would not have to do this, I could avoid the confrontation. I'm eating raw fish and I'm miserable and I'd like another beer, please, but I don't order it. I'm clear-headed, my sinuses burn from too much wasabi and I'm in New Mexico and I miss my boyfriend and I'm responsible. I'm going to have to act. Shit.

Shit.

Linear storytelling and the possibility of the truth: Fuck it. This morning I was telling one of the painting instructors about my trip to Chimayo last year. But I changed the way the story worked. It was more cynical. I left out the part about my grandmother. I turned up the volume on the kitschy miracle dirt, the dust that heals; in this new version I got trapped in mass, said I was leaving the church with the miracle dirt in its dark, miraculous hole, the thousand abandoned crosses, said as I was coming up the aisle the priest and his altar boys were coming down, and I had to duck into a pew and there sat out the mass like one waits out a storm, a thundershower. It was a better story this way, I think, a better breakfast-table tale.

Wait. I didn't tell that story this morning. I did tell the story that way, but it wasn't this morning or yesterday morning. It was two mornings ago, and I fully intended to get to this point in writing this "thing" two days ago, fully intended to use the story of that storytelling then, two days ago, sitting here where I'm sitting now, in front of my keyboard with sore shoulders. Except I didn't.

So the past is gaining distance, fleeing. And I'm trying to come back to it, but I'm not bound to tell the whole truth because I don't know if this is a story or an essay, and even if I did I'm not sure I'd be doing a better or different job.

Determination: I plow ahead.

Time: doesn't matter, does it? Are you really concerned about when all this happened? Doesn't my putting it down on paper, this sequence of events, my interpretation/version/impression of those events, doesn't the act render the concept of time a lie? You're going to read this perhaps months or years after it is written. Does it matter that I can predict my future in small ways? Saturday night we'll have hamburgers in the dining hall. Tomorrow the fourth *Batman* movie starts at theaters around the country—including here. Next Thursday, a week from today, for breakfast we'll have blueberry pancakes. By the time I finish this "thing" those pancakes will have been eaten, digested, expelled. Will I need to go back and update this paragraph? Should I make new predictions or merely confirm my accuracy? Does any of that matter to you? Or are you unimportant? Am I really asking these questions of myself, stupidly and somewhat selfishly involving you to justify my not simply moving on with the narrative? Should I just get on with it? Home, James.

How a date that is not a date ends: awkwardly.

Useless poetic image #2: Walking through the high grass, she takes care to avoid pinecones knocked free by the breeze of a coming storm. They fall around her, into the places she might have stepped, into the steps she leaves behind.

Reaction, non-action: I didn't confront the KA about his gun when I got back from sushi. It was only an hour until yoga, and I didn't want to ruin my mood. That's what I told myself. Keep in mind my mood was already ruined.

Yoga: is not really yoga. It's more stretching and breathing, Lynn informs us. She is the Wellness instructor and leads the yoga class. It's more breathing and stretching, stretching and breathing. It's not yoga, but it's enough like yoga that we are calling it yoga. There is no name for this near-yoga experience. We rely on imprecision for communication, but know for a fact that the word would have sufficed had Lynn not told us that actually we are not doing that at all. "Are you going to yoga?" we ask each other, hiding our distrust of the word, hiding the truth from anyone who may overhear, who may not realize that we are essentially speaking in code, that more or less we're liars.

Reaction, non-reaction: I didn't confront the KA about his gun the next morning because they and practically everybody else were leaving on a long hike at Ghost Ranch, the place where Georgia O'Keeffe found such inspiration. I didn't see the need to ruin everybody's day, make the vans run late, etc. That's what I told myself. Be the good guy here, I thought. Use some judgment. I watched the vans pull out, full of students ready to nap on the ride, though they only woke up a few minutes before. Using some judgment, I waved good-bye.

Coward: Am I one? Is my cowardice—if that's what it is—about guns, about Nazis with guns? Or about the reason that gun made its entrance to begin with: "fucking faggots . . ."

Procrastination, perspiration: I was not going to confront the KA about his gun the next day because everyone left early for a hike at the Great Sand Dunes in southern Colorado—again, why ruin everybody's beautiful day? But, riddled with guilt about slacking on what was surely an important duty, I was pacing the roads around the fort when Ed, SMU grad student and head of Food Services here, stopped me. He was in his Volvo, leaning out his window, and I blurted out that these morons had a gun in their casita. I added that I was pretty sure it belonged to the teaching assistant. I said I was going to do some confrontation as soon as everybody got back. I did everything but hitch my thumbs through my belt loops and spit Skoal. Howdy, Pilgrim.

"*That's* not your problem, their absence," Ed said. "They're not *all* gone. The teaching assistant's in his casita now—didn't go on the hike because his mother's flying in to visit this afternoon late. You want to wait and go in *after* he leaves to pick her up at the airport, before the other guys get back? You want to search the place and get the gun, avoid them lying to you about it, hiding it, pulling it on you, whatever? What's our first move?"

Ever want to make your characters quit their philosophizing, their whining, and get on with the story? Make them involve another character. Then they've got to make decisions. Then they've got to get down to business. Then the royal "we" they've been using suddenly splits into a real "we," a live-action "we."

Ed volunteered to meet me at my place after he went back to his room to check his messages—he was expecting friends to call him for lunch. I started walking back down the nature trail, getting caught up in conversation with the photography prof about whether it would be OK to have a fire and marshmallow roast, if there were regulations against that. Halfway through the conversation I thought about Ed beating me back to my trailer, going inside, seeing the novel I wrote last year sitting on my table, topped by a letter to an editor who was going to look at it. The letter included a shitty little synopsis which made quite clear that the novel was about a gay man who teaches at a university in Louisiana. Oops. Shit. Damn. I finished up my answers to the prof's questions pronto and began to trot back to my place posthaste, feeling the burn in my lungs as I chugged up hills. Surely Ed wouldn't just go in and start poking around on my table. Surely he wouldn't, though that is precisely what I would do in his position.

Coming over the last rise, I could see Ed. Was he coming back from knocking on my door, or closing it behind him? Was he already looking at me funny? "Hey," I said, breathing hard. Speak first; everything's normal.

Everything.

Breathe.

Is.

Breathe.

Normal.

"Hey," Ed said. "My friends are in town. I'm going to meet them for lunch. We'll check out the casita later?"

Paranoia sets in. He read it. He's in possession of my secret. He's unsure how to act. He's ready to get away from me right now, before I jump him, before I pull him into my lascivious lair. Don't get too close; don't get trapped in a confined space; never turn your back on a pervert, a freak of nature, an abomination. Is that what he's thinking?

"We'll search the casita later," Ed says.

How to remedy this? How to make the Universe like me again, forgive my carelessness?

Bravery. Action. I'm gasping a bit. I haven't had an asthma attack in a decade, but here comes one. "I'm just going to go ask him about it," I tell Ed. "Right now. If he's in there, I'm just going to ask for it. Fuck it, why put it off?"

Indeed.

Footnote: In truth, this straight-on approach was my boyfriend's idea. I asked his advice over the phone, and he said just to do it, don't investigate, don't search, just ask for it and if they screw around, tell them to start packing, all of them.

So much for the stereotype of the gay man as sissy.

I'm still a little short of breath when I get to the casita. I go in, and he (let's give him a name, how about Adolf) is near the front door, possibly on his way out, possibly escaping. "Hey," I say, "I've got a problem I want you to help me solve. There's a gun in this casita, and that's a big no-no. Let's avoid all the bullshit and you just get it for me, OK?"

Listen to my machismo, my *High Noon* no-nonsense nuances. Keep a straight face. You and me both.

Watch his eyes. The panic.

He sputters a second. "I don't know where it is," he says, adding, "It's not mine."

So *it* exists. *It* has been seen. It is an *it* without gender, an androgynous death-god with a story behind it, too, just like people.

It lives.

"I think it's in one of the guys' cars," Adolf says. "I think it's off-campus, I mean, I think the car is gone, not here."

"OK," I say. I'm pretty sure he's lying. I'm pretty sure he's shitting bricks. His mom is due in town soon. He does not need any misery coming down on his fresh-barbered head. He does not want to leave his mom waiting at the gate, looking for him to show up, getting good and steamed with her little golden Nazi. "Listen," I say, and I sound weary, tired, ready to use a gun myself perhaps, just to end this malarkey, "listen, I need the gun as soon as possible, so the minute your amigos get in, whoever owns said gun needs to give it to me immediately. Let's keep this from getting ugly and stupid, OK. Let's make this simple, stress-free."

I'm expecting he'll figure out the best thing to do is just get the gun now and hand it over. Now. But he holds his ground, and I have to be satisfied just in seeing that he's a little shaky. Trembling.

Power is an aphrodisiac, sure. And I wielded a little, but I'm by no means made horny by this encounter. I am not getting off on facing Adolf down. I miss my boyfriend, I'm lonely for companionship, but setting this fellow on edge doesn't get my motor running. Instead, walking back to my place I feel empty, like I want more, like I need a resolution, which surprises me because by and large resolutions bore me. (Is that bad? Does that worry you, you're fifty manuscript pages into something and the writer confesses he's not crazy about resolutions, does that create some concern in your mind?) Would I feel this empty if the gun had been surrendered? Would I feel less empty if I were walking back to my place with a pearl-handled pistol in my paw?

But what about suspense? The lady at the church, the Curator of Objects: she was holding up the almost-life-sized crucifix, spinning it on its base, readying to show you something. What was it she pointed to? The altar was brightly lit, but it was hard to see. Where were all these shadows coming from? From the lights, yes, from our bodies blocking the lights. We bent closer, wondering, What is she pointing to? What are we supposed to see?

Suspense, you want suspense? Wait a bit, I'll give you suspense. What? You insist on seeing ahead, predicting the forthcoming suspense has something to do with a certain gun? It might. It just might.

Then again, it might not.

Maybe this suspense has something to do with the gun in whichever part of this you're reading that is "story," or maybe this suspense is central to whatever part of this that might be called "the truth."

Confused? Wait. You'll have to wait.

That's suspense.

In the dining hall, one of the KAs, the nice one, comes up to me. He says, "Andrew (not his real name) says you were asking about the gun."

"That is correct."

"It's Brad's (not his real name). He went home for the weekend and took it with him. So it's gone. He took it with him."

Could be complete bullshit, but this guy is not the type to lay it on thick. "Very good, then," I say. "When he gets back, would you have him come see me, *por favor?*"

"Sure thing," Derek says. Derek is the good guy.

I sit at a table with some other faculty; they're talking about Brad, having no knowledge of the gun. They're concerned because he's missed a lot of class because of some family problem that keeps dragging him home. They suspect his ill-relative story may be a fake. They think the family problem has something to do with a girlfriend back in Texas. The mind leaps straight to scandal, pregnancy. Lynn, the Wellness instructor, has asked her assistant the Nazi what he knows. Can't say, she says he says. But it definitely has something to do with the girlfriend. If I could tell you I would, but I can't, she says he says.

So the girlfriend's pregnant, and he's waving a gun around to ward off fags who aren't even fags. He wears mirrored aviator sunglasses and cuts his hair too short. He has nice legs, but probably is perfectly aware of this; these nice legs no doubt helped land him in the trouble he's currently in with the señorita back in Big D. Is this guy the real bad guy? Is the Nazi off the hook? It appears the answer to both questions is yes. The Nazi is still a Nazi, however, guilty of trying to cover for another Nazi, the newly discovered Nazi, the handsome Nazi, the Nazi with big puppy-dog eyes and too-white grin, the PR Nazi, the spokesmodel Nazi. I was wrong about the first Nazi, but I owe no apologies to the first Nazi. They're all Nazis, excepting perhaps Derek, who has developed a serious headache, I hear. Stress. All this stress.

Later that night I'm in bed, reading. Lynn knocks on my door. She says Derek just went to the emergency room. This is not good. His headache is a migraine; he's blind in one eye, nauseous, dizzy. Here's the ghastly spin on what's already pretty scary: his younger brother has survived two brain tumors. OK. Maybe we're overreacting. Maybe this kid, Derek, who's a nice guy, sure, but a KA after all and therefore prone to bouts of drunken rowdiness, maybe he's a little hungover, don't these crazy kids go out every night and come home blotto? Sure, that's it, this fellow's headache ain't no tumor, it's a bad second day, one that's lasted all evening and now it's eleven and it'll be gone tomorrow, hell, I've had worse. Except, Lynn points out, he's a recovering alcoholic. He doesn't drink. And he's sitting in the emergency room in Taos right now with his sweet, devoted girlfriend—seriously, no irony here—and it's all going to be OK, for sure . . . but it's good for me to know what's going on, right, important, right, important for me to know, true? Isn't it part of my job, keeping tabs on the students' well-being? This is something I should be told, right? And I say yes, and thanks for filling me in, and then I'm getting fully dressed, pulling pants over my shorts because it's cold out on my way to my car and then to town, praying for this kid a simple prayer, thinking, Shit, nobody deserves a brain tumor, not this kid certainly—a Nazi, maybe, maybe a little brain tumor, a tiny, operable one, but fuck, not this guy, not Derek. Derek doesn't deserve this. He's *not* cute, don't mistake my compassion for imagined passion, he's just an honest, laid-back student, a likable lug, and I want him to be OK, I want this to be a simple migraine, one that's fixable, one you take a pill for and wham-o, it's over. It's over.

FROM MY JOURNAL, 6/16:

Notice the slightly affected tone—who was I expecting to read this, for whom was this written?

> *Set aside an ad from the NYT magazine yesterday. Polo underwear, knit boxers, modeled by four perfect bodies on a windy beach. I'm uncomfortable having anything resembling pornography (even* Men's Fitness*) in my trailer, so a surprise Calvin Klein or Ralph Lauren spread tends to excite beyond its intentions, I'm sure. I wasn't especially horny this morning, but I thought I'd give it a go anyway, out of what? Boredom mainly, I guess. It was an uneventful orgasm—followed almost immediately by a quiet knock on my door. Shit. I open up to find Phillip Eidson, the camp geek. I've felt sorry for him the past two weeks. He has zero social skills, no friends to hang out with. Add the fact that he's careless, and you get a sense of just how sad this lad is. He just stands outside my trailer looking at me. "Can I help you?" I say.*
>
> *"My toe hurts," he says. "Somebody says you drive us to the doctor or whatever."*
>
> *"Your toe?"*

"Yeah."

"Is it broken?"

"No. I think it's ingrown."

An ingrown toenail. Ye gods. "Come on in. I'll call town and get an appointment." *And so I do.*

As we drive to Taos, Phillip asks a million dopey questions about SMU, all the while grunting about the pain in his foot. He's going to be a frosh in the fall, which partially explains his utter interpersonal incompetence. "So is the cable good? What's the party dorm? How much is a single room? What if you hate your roommate? Is it a problem if I bring a sword to school? Would I have to register that with the Department of Public Safety?" *Etc.*

"What's your father do in Miami, Phillip?" *This kid's from Miami—shouldn't he be fabulous, tanned, fashion-conscious?*

"Lawyer. Personal injury."

Sigh.

He has no idea how to fill out the forms the nurse hands him at the check-in desk. Indeed, he was unable to announce his presence to her, requiring that I do that for him. "Do they want my social security number or my mom's?" *he asks me, dragging out the process of writing down things like* NAME, ADDRESS, AGE. *Each blank flummoxes him like a trick question on a test. Finally he finishes and sits anxiously, starting each time a new patient's name is called. When a nurse finally summons him, he walks toward her, but when she turns to show him the way, he spins and heads back for his chair in the waiting area.* "What are you doing?" *I ask.*

"She took off," *he says*

"Follow," *I suggest.*

The nurse has returned and says his name again, gives him a funny look.

"OK," *Phillip says.* "OK."

So I'm left in the waiting room, where there are tons of magazines, and I'm thinking, Come on, Calvin, produce the goods. *Surely there will be one* GQ *or* Esquire, *something of that nature. I've come to rely upon the occasional thrill found in* Vanity Fair. *But of course there are none of those magazines about. This is Taos, New Mexico. And the underwear ads in* Modern Maturity *fail to excite in the least.*

When Phillip emerges, limping madly, near tears, the payout procedure is as exasperating as check-in. (Should he sign his mom's name? It's her MasterCard.) He hobbles to the car, announcing once we're back on the road that he needs a prescription filled. We've passed two pharmacies already, so I circle back to a grocery store, a place I can shop while Phillip waits and groans for the antibiotic and Tylenol 3 with codeine (if students were to discover him in possession of the latter, his popularity might rise). My first stop at the grocery: the magazine aisle. (What's my problem? How much is enough?) It offers the usual ridiculous fitness and muscle magazines, but I've seen them all before and the models are beefy in the extreme, more frightening than flirtatious. Plus, I'm not exactly in the mood again so soon after this morning's Polo match. I leave the magazines and pick up chips and salsa, postcard stamps, head back to pick up Phillip at the spit-polished pharmacy counter.

He dry-swallows the pills in the car, complaining about the pain and the taste (the taste?) of the pills. He needs a haircut. He needs new glasses. He (desperately) needs new clothes. He needs to find a nice large state u. into which he can disappear. SMU is going to eat him alive. His mother's credit card is a good start, but is it enough to effect a complete transformation?

Does this sound merciless? I'm sorry. I can't turn back now. Besides, Phillip and I are almost home.

An hour or so later I trek up to Doble South casita for a shower. As I'm getting out, I can hear someone in Doble North's next-door bathroom, retching. It's Phillip, I know it. The medicine has made him sick. Shit. I take my time shaving and cleaning up, then wander to Doble North. Phillip is in the bathroom. I knock, but he doesn't bid me enter. I do anyway and find him just exiting a stall, looking pale and sad. "You doing all right?"

He smiles at me. "I'm wide awake," he says, meaning what, I don't know. "Everything's fine."

End of entry.

When I get to the emergency room, Derek and Whitney, still waiting to be seen, are crouched forward in stiff, uncomfortable chairs. He's miserable and surprisingly not surprised to see me. I say, "What's up?" and he lets loose, telling me the facts, telling me words for the pain that make me cringe. He lets it all out, and he's scared. He's a big guy, a senior, and he's sitting next to his adorable girlfriend and he's scared shitless. His hands tremble I know what he's thinking. He doesn't know that Lynn told me about his brother, so he can't tell that I can see it in his eyes, the fear. I've got it, he's thinking as he tells me about his eye acting crazy, sight going black, I've got it, he's thinking. I'm finished.

Personal crisis: I don't want to address this for very long because I'll get all worked up, but I have a similar thing happen to me occasionally. Not migraines, but fear. I have these crises in which I become convinced I'm HIV-positive. Like I said, I really don't want to go into it, because I can feel my shoulders tightening up right now, but I know fear. I can understand this kid's eyes, the way they're seeing (or not seeing) the world right now.

Suspense: Not knowing if you're going to die, if the end is the day after tomorrow. There's a gun in one of the casitas, though it is rumored to have been removed, gone back to Dallas with its troubled master. One of the good guys may have a brain tumor. I may not be as well as I would like to think. Enough. What else? What more? Isn't this enough?

"There's not much need in you staying," Whitney tells me as she emerges from two swinging doors with wire-hatched glass windows.

She went in with Derek, holding his hand; I stayed in the lobby, watched the MTV Movie Awards with three girls working for Ameri-Corps. I don't know why they're here, who they brought in. I can't understand why they cheer the exact people on the Awards whom I'd like to see disappear. "They're going to run a bunch of tests. We're going to be here all night." The AmeriCorps girls damn near swoon over Will Smith. I stand and give Whitney a card with my number on it, leave the emergency room, walk around a sprinkler that has suddenly erupted on the hospital's wastefully verdant lawn. I drive home, radio on loud. With one hand I feel around in the passenger seat for a tape I want, some music I want to hear, something I choose, not a disc jockey. Where is it? I know it's here.

Escape: *Batman and Robin,* the fourth movie in the series, is precisely as rotten as I expect, though it does take me away from worrying about all the things that could be going wrong out here. The only vaguely interesting bits in the film: 1) Uma Thurman's over-the-top performance as Poison Ivy, diva/femme fatale—her character will be copied ten times over at Lazarus, the five-thousand-plus-attended Halloween party/AIDS benefit in New Orleans; 2) the relationship between Batman and Robin, both with their adorable Caesar haircuts and tight rubber suits, living in that fabulous mansion, inexhaustible supplies of cash spent on toys, bickering almost constantly but clearly in love—at one point Bruce Wayne says to his supermodel (gay icon) girlfriend, "I'm not the marrying kind; there's a lot of stuff about me you wouldn't understand." Hello? I'm sitting in a matinee in Taos, New Mexico, and I'm laughing at things nobody else is laughing at. This film, for all its dreadfulness, is the kind of thing I'll be able to work perfectly into my second-semester freshman composition class. We look at urban legends for a few weeks, and one of the most popular revolves around "Batman in the Closet," in which a freshman at Columbia gets picked up by a gorgeous woman, taken home, handcuffed to a bed, then raped by a big, black male in a Batman mask who leaps out of a closet. Students are repulsed and fascinated by the story, and its emblematic meanings are so obvious they feel some measure of success in taking it apart and looking at the WHY of the whole thing: Why a bat, why Batman? Why a black man? Why a freshman at Columbia?

Now for the true-life coincidence wrinkle—a few nights ago the only two African American women on campus here asked me to help them get into the computer room. To reach that space you have to move across an anteroom with doors that open, like all doors in the Fort, to the outside. This anteroom is prone to having bats fly in, tiny, harmless things. Despite posted signs, students can't seem to perform the simple task of closing the doors, and some nights you find one or two of the little critters bouncing around, hitting the low ceiling, more scared and lost than lurking. "It's full of bats, and we can't go through it," the two women wailed to me. "And we have an assignment due tomorrow that we have to get done."

"I'll go down with you," I said, having no idea what my presence might do to make the situation less scary for them. I drove the three of us the half mile or so to the Fort; they sat in the car while I checked out the situation: the room, with both doors wide open, was dark, and I entered cautiously, a little wary myself, despite thoughts of how silly the girls were. I listened for the flurry of wings, heard none, saw none in my flashlight's beam, and turned on the overhead lights. Empty—there were no bats here, though that didn't mean there hadn't been fifteen minutes ago.

I fetched the girls from the car and escorted them quickly through the bat-room to the computer lab. "Thank you," they said, laughing, feeling a little goofy, I could see that now.

When I went to check on Derek the next day, he was laid out in considerable pain. The doctors, after tests, including a CAT scan, had determined it was a migraine. They prescribed painkillers; what else could they do? A headache, nothing more, doctors had assured Derek and Whitney. Good. We were in the clear. Sure we were. Life is good. Life goes on. Life is but a dream. Etc.

Suspense: There's still the gun to deal with. When does this kid get back from Dallas and—what? His girlfriend's abortion, a hasty wedding? Is it best to confront a man with a firearm after such intensity? Is it wise to give a ticket to a speeding wasp?

Scary movie: The moon is full, it's the summer solstice, the longest day of the year has just ended, and the students are a bit weirded out, not by the silver moonlight washing the campus like a floodlight but by radio reports that a serial killer on the run from the Northeast has been spotted in Taos. The FBI is searching the area. We've seen no killers here on campus, and the fugitive, known to be gay and so far restricting himself to killing affluent gay men with whom he has had dates, offers little threat to the students. (But what about me!?) Nevertheless, the camp has grown quieter than normal, as though a dread has found the vocal cords of these children. They are not going camping tonight, not away from the rules of the Fort to smoke pot and wrestle with their lust in the wilderness. They are not convoying into town to their trendy bars; the FBI has pointed out that the killer leads a somewhat flashy social life, and pictures reveal him to be an attractive fellow; why, he could have been standing next to the students last night at the Alley Cantina—excepting, of course, that he wouldn't be caught dead in that breeder meat market. No, my dear ones, only one soul on campus tonight qualifies somewhat for the grisly attentions of the murderer. And though you are certain any killer worth his salt would have researched the area and sought out this verdant summer campus, fecund with toned bodies and raging hormones, I don't think there's all that much worrying to be done here. I'll sleep with my door unlocked, the moon beaming in through the skylight over my bed like an alien transporter beam: old and rotten bumper sticker joke—beam me up, there's no intelligent life down here.

Desire decelerating: Leslie, the theater major—her crush on me is dissipating, I believe. I haven't paid her enough attention at the dining hall, haven't found time to stop by her casita and visit. In addition to being made uncomfortable by the idea of her attraction to me, the sordid undercurrent of misconception thereabout, I feel a bit like a traitor regarding the gun thing. I'm concerned that her telling me about it at dinner was meant to be a secret given as a gift, one the giver intends the recipient to keep, not distribute among acquaintances, colleagues, superiors. Then, too, there's the problem of confidence. What if this Brad character, the gun-wielding, super-potent KA president—did I mention he's head of that organization, King KKK?—what if he decides to take out his anger on her, on Leslie? How does one keep those around him safe? What if the creation of safety inspires other forms of danger, threatens a new group? This is like playing pick-up-sticks . . . but with bullets.

Setting: Walking from where I live to the dining hall, I can catch a glimpse of Taos Mountain ten miles or so away. It's almost July, and there's still snow up there; the students on hikes to Wheeler Peak have played in it, slid down it, cursed it for sogging their boots, freezing their toes. I haven't seen the snow up close yet. I'm waiting for my boyfriend to come so we can hike together to see what is never seen at home in Louisiana. From the peak of Taos Mountain a thin line of it runs jaggedly down the south side like a bolt of lightning headed this way in slow motion, pointing, blaming, moving toward where I stand looking.

Zap.

Foreshadowing: Was that too much? That whole lightning bit? Or was it anything at all? A red herring? Is that snow even really there? Am I making it up? Or am I making something real fit into something unreal, adding to the story with building blocks stolen from life? Faulkner said a good writer knows that if he has to, he should steal from his own mother. "'Ode on a Grecian Urn' is worth any number of old ladies," he wrote.

Responsibility: Anticipating that Ed may have told our boss John about the gun, I mention it to him over dinner, downplaying it, assuring him in a few words that it will be taken care of as soon as the offending student comes back to campus. I also mention Derek's headache and downplay it a little, too, though I saw him again just before dinner and he was still in immense pain. But that's normal, right, normal for migraines? What are the chances of two brothers having brain tumors? They're not genetic, surely.

Furthermore, what are the odds the older brother would first show signs of the same defect (slowly eating away at the thoughts and serenity of a new model of himself) out here, at camp for Christ's sake? It's all circumstantial, not coincidental or fateful. It's hooey, this brain-tumor terror. What about heat exhaustion, sun poisoning, altitude sickness? What about headaches, huh, what about them? They happen. They do. Mr. Tylenol has made his fortune betting on just this fact.

More foreshadowing, more poking and winking: *Why a bat?* It lives where we cannot see it, comes out of the dark, moves in ways we cannot. Small, potent, it wants to bite us, to suck our life away, to feed us to the underworld. OK, all that's true, though worded in terms too purple by half, loaded like a sloppy slingshot. What's all this bat stuff doing in here anyway? John Gardner writes in his *Art of Fiction* that "What Fancy sends, the writer must order by Judgment." What is the writer doing about that, huh? Where do all these bats fit into this train wreck?

Stop. Wait. Back up. The church. We started there, didn't we, and there was some intimation in the way I treated it, the way I described briefly my connection to other churches, to Catholicism, that the church would figure into this narrative more prominently. So did I go back to the church in Ranchos de Taos? Will I work it in again? Is there any chance of a smooth transition, a gentle segue that will not trip up you dancers? This story—if that's what it is—resembles a parking lot so full of speedbumps, well, so full you can't traverse it without making yourself sick. You need great shocks to survive this long, slow drive. To top it all off, it's midnight, there are no security lights, and your headlamps are on the fritz. Who's driving this thing, anyway?

"Stories, like conjuring tricks, are invented because history is inadequate to our dreams."   — *Steven Millhauser*

The church was completed in 1850. Any number of guidebooks will tell you just that, using almost without exception that exact sentence. It's not plagiarism, it's just the easiest way of putting it. What none of the guidebooks manages to point out, however, is when work on the church was begun. It might have been in the mid-1700s or the early 1800s. Parish records aren't that helpful; crumbling letters from Rome are ambiguous at best. The question is apparently impossible to answer—for a number of reasons. I mean, what exactly do I mean by "begun"? The first adobe being laid—or the mud for that adobe being dug, mixed with straw and water? Or was it when the first sagebrush was cleared? The first meeting to determine definite plans? The first time a Franciscan dreamt of the church towering here on the plain? Was that dream preceded perhaps by a dream in childhood, one only to be remembered after construction is completed, recalled suddenly by the oldest woman in the village, a woman who doesn't even try to make this premonition or its slow fulfillment known to the people standing around her, her family, her neighbors, her priest and confessor? What is a beginning? How to track down the conception of any project? Who can pinpoint the germination of human creativity, of a masterpiece, of a miracle, of art?

What sounds like a good story but is in fact true: The night before Father's Day I dreamt of my father's infidelities, the mysterious phone calls to our home when I was eleven, the hang-ups and breathy-voiced women asking to speak to Dan, his acting like what was being said on the other end of the line had something to do with work. When I woke up, I knew I had to call him myself. It was Father's Day, and though the dream had left me sad and a little angry, I was obligated. If he didn't receive calls from all his children on this day, on his birthday, etc., there would be hell to pay—this despite the fact that when I was in junior high and suffering through football for his sake, he rarely attended a game and tried to skip out on the father/son sports banquet, preferring to ride around town drinking beer with my alcoholic brother-in-law. I'll call later. I'll call after church.

I hadn't been to a mass since the one in Chimayo a year ago. Even though that experience had been in equal parts freeing (in relation to my grandmother) and maddening (in regard to the priest's ugly ranting), I was determined to go to the church in Ranchos, the one the students and I had been working on earlier in the week. I wanted to be there to see how people responded to the new white walls, the brightening renovation. Spanish mass was said at seven, and the first of two in English was at nine, so after breakfast I cleaned up and drove into town a little excited, a little afraid for some reason, liking the intoxication of those two feelings mixed.

The church was packed at nine o'clock on the dot, and I squeezed into the very last row, between a man in black jeans and a T-shirt and an older woman parked on the kneeler, praying fervently. I had to pass Rudy getting in, him in a pressed turquoise shirt and bolo tie, but he didn't recognize me, which disappointed in some small measure. Not long after I'd taken my seat and found a missal with which to refresh my memory, the priest came in, preceded by two altar girls. Not altar boys. Girls. In the front of the church a woman strummed a guitar sweetly while the crowd stood to sing a song that sounded vaguely like "Frere Jacques" in Spanish. This was going to be a different experience from Chimayo, less dark and mysterious, more giddy.

Indeed, the air was light, full of sunbeams reflecting off the brilliant walls, and the tone of the mass was quick, celebratory. The *enjada* had been completed successfully. The young priest fairly cheered for the rejuvenation around us before moving swiftly toward a sermon that had to do with, of course, fatherhood. He related how he and his father hadn't gotten along growing up, how there was drinking, abuse, and intolerance. It was surprising to hear a priest be so open and honest, confessing almost, strange in a church steeped deeply in tradition and a truly tangible sense of history. But the people didn't seem shocked. They listened intently, and more than a few heads nodded in agreement when he began to talk about how he'd just gotten around to getting to know his father better, after his maturation, after he had a choice of whether to turn bitter, turn away—or go back and try to see a different side

MATT CLARK

of the man who'd raised him. The Father's father was forgiven, obviously, but more important he had become the fulcrum of a deeper personal project concerned with salvaging some sliver of tradition connecting them to the generations that had gone before.

I shook myself free from the eerie sensation that this sermon had been prepared for me especially. It was for everyone, doubtlessly, was about all parents and children and mistakes made and the opportunity of finding inroads to a better life. It was directed at me, but it was just as much directed to the man in the T-shirt to my right, the woman to my left. This was no cosmic conspiracy, no Pynchonesque practical joke. But it was not coincidence either. Was it? Determined not to cry, I focused on the wall to the side of the altar, the wall I'd painted. Was there anything about it that seemed to mark my having been there? Was its new whiteness especially noticeable? Honestly, no there wasn't, no it wasn't. The walls were equally white, all of them. The whiteness was solid, oceanic, without character or individuality. I was not to be found there by the altar, I was but one of many who'd worked here.

Because of the side of the church I'd chosen to sit on, I couldn't see the altar wall, where the Jesus must have again been hanging. I assumed it was there, of course it was—and just as I made this assumption, the priest began to wrap up his sermon, throwing in a bit from Paul, something about how "We walk not by sight, but by faith." I was struck again by how the words seemed to come directly toward me, how they spoke to something I was just then considering. Of course the crucifix hung where it should. And with it hung what the Curator of Objects had taken the time to show me the day we took the icon from the wall and placed it gently behind the altar. "Look," she'd said, turning the crucifix so I could see between the hollowed-out side of Jesus's chest and the backbone of the cross itself; dangling there was a heart, a carved wooden heart suspended from the throat of Christ by a tiny chain, a chain that dropped the heart, oddly anatomical, into the chest cavity, where it swayed and thumped just barely against the ribs of the dying messiah. It couldn't have been seen from any angle but the one we now had; it was not placed there to be seen by those who came to worship, was not part of the visible atmosphere of mystery, pain, faith. Few knew about it; he hadn't been taken down in at least a decade, but now that we had lifted him from his perch, we were blessed with the knowledge that it was there, the secret heart of Christ. Whether we wanted that knowledge or not, it had been given. How many people now in this church with me, this Sunday morning crowd, packed in for Father's Day, how many of them knew about it? I was sitting in the back row of the San Francisco de Asis Church in Ranchos de Taos, New Mexico, and though my point of view did not currently offer me a glimpse of that Christ, I knew it was there—and I knew more than most of the people who weekly took communion here; I knew that this Christ, like the Tin Man of Oz had had all along, this Christ was not without a heart in that still, manufactured chest.

"Whenever the plot flags, bring in a man with a gun." *—Raymond Chandler*

The bad guy knocked before he came in, saying he'd heard I was needing to see him. He said he knew it was about the gun, that in fact the gun was gone, had traveled back to Dallas with him, had been packed away and carried on a flight from Albuquerque to Love Field. He said there was no problem here. He said he was sorry for having caused any trouble, if there had been any trouble at all. He smiled a smile that had gotten his well-toned, tennis-playing ass out of many a scrape. He was too handsome to be naughty, the smile said, truly naughty at least. "OK," I said, "good deal. A relief. Do me a favor and be sure you tell John at dinner tonight. As director of this whole shebang, he's aware of the gun and concerned. He'll be happy to hear that it's gone. So you tell him at dinner, OK? That it's gone?"

The smile faltered for a second only. It had been constructed so expensively, put together by orthodontists and dentists, polished, practiced. It disappeared between the lips for a single tick-tock, then it came back, glistening.

MATT CLARK

"Sure thing, no big deal."

Whitney comes by to tell me Derek's headache is not better. He's in pain. He's emotionally distraught. We agree to take him back to the emergency room. We agree that this time it would be best to inform the doctors about Derek's brother's brain tumors. We agree without saying so that we're going to manage our mounting fear successfully. We're going to be calm when we ask the doctors to look again at Derek's CAT scan, to search more thoroughly for anything that might show up when it shouldn't, for something there that should in fact not be there. "Was that Brad I saw leaving your trailer a few seconds before I came over?" Whitney says. We're changing the subject. We move on. We forge onward.

Yes, it was.

"Did he just get back from Dallas? Everything straightened out with his girlfriend?"

Question one: The answer is yes. Question two: The answer is I don't know.

"What a crazy mess," she says, laughing.

This is something to laugh about?

"Well, no. Not really. It's just, this place is such a soap opera. I feel sorry for the guy, really. He got tricked into sleeping with this girl out here, and then he tells his girlfriend out of guilt and she of course wigs, and his parents, who the girlfriend tells in a teary late-night visit, his parents make him come home and deal with things."

That's it? There're no tough decisions, no aborted fetus, no shotgun-wedding bells pealing six hundred miles away in the shimmering Texas heat?

Where do we come up with this stuff?

"OK. So we'll take Derek in to the hospital. Hoping to avoid the serial killer, of course."

The serial killer.

Scary movie, take two: Moving across the bridge near Casita Ultima, my flashlight aiming for possible rattlesnakes, the ones that enjoy the warm wood slats, I hear loud squealing near the dining hall. Students in line for the payphone are straining their necks for a glimpse at what might be making such a racket. Sounds like bats to me, but the volume is much too loud; they'd have to be monster-size bats, bats with opera-singer lungs. As the din rises still further—is something being tortured, made to suffer not just death but anguish?—all the students but one move toward the safety of their casitas. One boy backs away, whispering to me, "What is that?"

"I don't know," I say. I look at the remaining student, she who must use the phone even if a wild-animal attack is imminent. She is dialing quickly, trying to ignore sounds that whoever she calls is bound to hear and ask about. (Hi, Dad, I'm calling from the slaughterhouse.)

I duck under the clothesline and move across the little employee's parking lot closer to the thick woods from which the yelps are coming. Something is in anguish. Something is torturing something else. What is it? A coyote, probably, I tell myself, though I can't imagine a coyote dragging out the death of a—rabbit?—quite so long, enjoying its screams. What my flashlight's beam reveals: nothing but piñon and juniper and ragweed. There's a creek running high back in there, but I can't hear its gurgle for the whining hell of what is surely a rabbit. Maybe a cat. That is not a person's voice, no, that's an animal, and this is the wild, and it's best just to stay the hell out of the way. Still, what is it?

When the squealing stops, cut short like a radio being turned off, the creek's mumble leaps into the new quiet.

And then, like a scene from a miniseries based on a Stephen King novel, something is moving, something heavy and plodding is moving through the underbrush toward me, toward where I'm standing. What do all the little articles on the camp bulletin board say about bears? Make noise or not? What do I say to this thing moving toward me? "Stop"? I turn and move. Feeling the gravel shift under my sandals, knowing I can't run in this, I spin and head back to where the student is getting off the phone. "Nobody's home," she says, smiling at me.

"Let's go back toward the casitas," I say. I have the urge to take her by the elbow to aid her speed, but I don't.

"So what was that noise?" she asks.

"A coyote killing a rabbit," I say, not knowing for sure whether I'm right but hoping this simple explanation won't scare her. It might be that, after all, and we know coyotes are cowards, right? They don't attack people. They're cowards, afraid. They're Acme-loving losers; they suck.

"Yuck," the girl says.

"Yuck," I concur.

This is a story called: THE SERIAL KILLER.

This is not a story. Do you believe me?

The serial killer shows up. He's handsome. He's debonair. He's fabulous. I miss my boyfriend. I don't recognize the serial killer as the serial killer. The serial killer introduces himself as a grad student from Arizona State. He eats dinner with us in the dining hall. Using his profoundly sharp gaydar, he pinpoints me and sits at my table. He is dashing. He is Harrison Ford as Indiana Jones. He comes back to my place, walking with just a hint of swagger, pleased with the success of his charade. He is poised to kill me. He is seductive, deadly. He doesn't know that I, just a little while before his arrival, went to the manly Land Cruiser of Brad the white-toothed bad guy/philanderer and removed from the Land Cruiser's glove compartment a gun not unlike the one my father gave me a couple of years ago for protection in my not especially safe neighborhood in Baton Rouge. The serial killer can't know these things because he is a character in a story I am writing. I am the hero in this story. I am the hero because I say I am. He leans to kiss me, the serial killer, and his breath is like honey but as potent as the lips of Poison Ivy in *Batman and Robin,* the very bad movie playing several miles away at the faux-adobe Storyteller cinema. The serial killer leans to kiss me, thinking about Uma Thurman, thinking maybe that'll be his drag for the Lazarus party in New Orleans in late October; he leans toward me for a kiss, and I shoot him—not in the heart, as you might expect, but in the leg, because it's important that characters like this be taken alive and studied further. The serial killer is shocked by all this and more than a little perturbed when the police show up to take him away and I am idolized for having stopped his reign of terror and having saved the students from such awful fates as surely awaited them and having been smart enough to confiscate a gun that was on SMU property illegally. I am a good guy. My actions demonstrate this quite clearly. We leave out all the gay stuff, and I am a hero; my actions demonstrate this to be the truth.

Now: A bat flies into the screen on the window beside which I sit typing. It sticks there like a little gray rag pinned by the wind. Tiny, furry, with a mouth that gasps as though for breath, like it's just come up for air, the interior of that mouth not vampirish blood-red but cotton-candy pink. It is how far from me? Two feet? Can it see me? Blind, does it sense what is beyond the screen to which it clings? Can it imagine that I am seeing it, turning my eyes from my keyboard to its paper-thin wings, then back again, typing its name: bat. How long will it stay there? What does it want? How much longer will I pay attention to it, how long until its novelty, my fear of its teeth, will fade and I go back to something else? What else is there?

Exit: Is this the way out?

How long after Rudy's disappearance did the kids in Rigo's class start telling him his father had been abducted by aliens? I don't know, because it was something Rigo didn't tell me about until I one time rented the movie E.T. and he refused to watch it. "Why not?" I asked. "It's good. Nadine saw it and said she cried it was so good."

And then he told me, told me all of it. Years removed from the moment when the first boy said it to him on the playground, Rigo let it all come out, how everybody said his father's mysterious disappearance was easily explained by aliens. Don't we have Roswell to the south of us? Aren't UFOs seen in these parts sometimes, by tourists and Indians and scientists? Didn't their own teacher tell them she'd seen one once while camping near Serpent Lake? And what about down around Chimayo, all those cattle mutilations? Those were seen on the news. Those made the papers lots. So what else was there to believe? The aliens had captured Rigo's father while Rigo was off skipping stones—and that was a good thing, Rigo skipping stones, or they'd have got him too. Maybe his father was like those cattle, mutilated aboard the spaceship. Or maybe he was still up there, being experimented on, and one day would come back when Rigo was an old man, and his father wouldn't have aged a bit in outer space. His own father wouldn't recognize Rigo, probably, because Rigo would have wrinkles and a beard and grandchildren. "He wasn't drowned," Rigo told me. "They said he'd been taken by monsters, not drowned. And I didn't know whether it was worse this way or not. Maybe he was still alive on a spaceship or another planet. Maybe he wasn't dead and he was watching me on a special alien viewing screen. That's some of what they said."

I couldn't believe it. "Why didn't you tell me about this?" I asked.

He was seventeen. He had just stopped being an altar boy. He played football and basketball and was in the National Honor Society. He thought he'd go to UNM and major in prelaw, maybe history. He was taller than me and once told me he'd tried marijuana but didn't like it so I could stop worrying about him in that way. What else? Did he like girls? I don't know. We'd never talked about it, and I figured if there was something I needed to know he'd say so. What else? He was a good boy. He'd gone to some therapy about his dad, and we spent every Father's Day together at the Storyteller Cinema, watching all four movies on all four screens, no matter what they were. What else? He loved his mother, told me this on more occasions that I can count—and I feel blessed.

"Why didn't you tell me about this?" I asked.

He shrugged and pushed the videocassette still farther from him, pushed it until it was about to fall off the kitchen table. "I didn't know what to do. Was it good, was it bad, did it matter— he was gone no matter what."

"Rigo," I said because I didn't know what else to say. "Rigo."

"Mama, it's OK. I'm fine. I don't like alien movies. This is not such a bad thing, I think. I think coming through all this with just that scar is not so terrible."

"Do you have nightmares?" I asked him. Why hadn't any of this come out in therapy? Or did it, and I just never knew?

"Mama, it's OK. I told you. It's OK. I'm OK. We're OK."

I tried to picture the kinds of nightmares Rigo might have, populated by his father and aliens and visions of himself as an old man. Did you wake up screaming? Wouldn't I have heard? Or was I too lost in my own sleep?

"Mama," Rigo said, and I could see then that it was him now comforting me. "We all have nightmares. If we're lucky we don't remember them. But we all have them. And they're better, aren't they, than the real thing?"

When he took my hands in his the salt shaker fell, hitting the videotape, knocking it to the floor. Neither of us moved to pick it up. "Yes," Rigo answered his own question while he held my hands. Did I think of his father then, of Rudy's hands, the way they looked on my own, the way they looked holding Rigo over his cradle? Yes.

"Yes," Rigo said again. "Of course," he told me. "Of course nightmares are preferable to the real thing. Now I'm going to the library to study. I have a paper due. You watch the movie. I've heard it's very good, too."

The rest of the day after the Germans is slow. The young couple from early in the day, the ones drenched in turquoise, the ones I sent to the gift shop, never do come back. On the radio, *The Unexplainable and Inexplicable Show* gets lost in a series of reports on the chupacabra, the goat-sucker monster terrorizing Mexico, now assumed to be moving this way in search of fresh game. After the announcer signs off I sit down and finish my detective novel—even though it gets too gory and I find myself skipping paragraphs to keep my eyes and mind off the ripped flesh and obscene violations. Maybe ten more people come through. At four-thirty I put the closed sign out, go to my car, and drive home to find Nadine sitting on my front porch holding a folded newspaper, fanning herself.

"Nadine," I say. "I don't want to have this conversation. Rigo was doing his job. Of course he loves you, but how could he not give you a ticket? Sixty-five in a thirty-five? Really, that's over the top even for you."

"Forget that," Nadine says. She stops fanning herself with the paper and holds it out to me. "Read this."

I hoist my purse a little higher and take the paper. Couldn't this wait until I got inside? "What? Which story?"

"Bottom left," Nadine says. She stands and moves toward me, behind me, reading over my shoulder. "That one, yes," Nadine says, though how she can know what I'm looking at is beyond me.

"It's about a skull," I say, because it is. It's about a skull being found south of Embudo. Rafters found it while eating lunch and thought maybe it was of some archaeological importance. They took the skull to an anthropologist at UNM, and he determined the skull was not ancient but modern, was the skull of a thirty-year-old man who died ten to fifteen years ago. The skull was turned over to police and was now the subject of a full-blown investigation.

"Nadine," I say. The world changes around me. The sky is not the right color, and the air tastes sharp in my nose. Where is that noise coming from? What is that, crickets? They sound like tiny trumpets. "Nadine," I say. My purse has fallen onto my elbow, and I let it fall farther down my arm, let it slide all the way past my wrist, feel it graze my fingers as it tumbles, spilling its contents onto the ground. I'm moving toward my door, can see it getting closer but can't feel my feet working, my legs doing their job. Nadine is behind me, and she has her set of keys out, and she is opening the door and I float inside. I float to the kitchen, to the picture of Rudy on the refrigerator, the one I never took down, the one I never take down. Is that him? He looks so young. Is that his skull, beneath his skin, his hair, behind his beautiful eyes, is that Rudy? What shirt is he wearing? "Nadine," I say. "Nadine. Look. Is that Rudy there?"

I am in bed when they come, the lights. I sense them before I see them, a full minute before. Then just the hint of them is there, red and blue, swirling; they are coming, they are close and getting closer, and they are going fast, coming fast. Red and blue. It's so quiet. Surprising how quiet. I can hear the fan, nothing more. Now. They are here, they are outside my window. The lights come in, and they are wild against the ceiling, playing in the shadows of the vigas, bouncing off the walls, sliding across the face of Mary, springing off the glass over her, her immaculate heart. I am not afraid of them. They are here, and they know I am here, and they want me, but I am not afraid. I hear the door open, I hear Nadine's voice, Nadine telling them they will find me in the bedroom, asleep. "I am not asleep," I tell my closed door, the lights spinning there, sparkling on the glass knob, running through the glass, coming out the other side. "I'm in here," I tell them. "Not asleep," I tell them.

But then there is no them. There is only one, and he is tall when the door opens. He is tall and strong, solid, not like E.T., not like any of the aliens in the movies. He is like Rigo, and he has Rigo's voice. He is Rigo, saying, "Mama, I'm here." I'm thinking suddenly of the book I finished this afternoon, how I hated the ending, how it was so easy to see coming and how disappointed that made me. I could feel the book growing thinner in my hands as I turned the pages, and I could see the ending before it was there in ink. Rigo is not them, he is only himself. All around us the room is glowing with the lights from the window, and my son brought those lights.

My boy.

I don't want this. I don't want the mystery solved. I don't want to remember the nightmares that have been there all the time. I want my boy, that's all, and he is here with me, kneeling beside my bed. And I want to believe in miracles. Even if there are answers to every question, I don't want to understand them, I want them spoken only in a language that is not my own. If I choose to have them translated, that's my choice: I don't. I choose not to know. Tonight I want to believe in miracles. There is one holding my hand now. "Mama," he says, kneeling there. "Mama, wake up."

I am sitting now. The lights are splashing across my face, red and blue, official, American, and I shut my eyes against them.

"Rigo," I say. "No." His head is on my mattress, and I put my hand on top of his hair. I bless him and move to kiss him there, and I lie to him, to my son I lie. "I can't," I tell him. "I will not," I lie.

It's flawed. I know. It's a mess, and maybe I'm not a writer. Maybe that's what this essay is about. Maybe the mystery of how to make a story work is beyond me. Maybe I am destined to fail. Maybe everything that precedes this is evidence of that fact. So why am I still writing?

This is not a story: When Brad lies to John about the gun being gone, being left in Dallas, John sends Brad home; he's flunking his classes anyway. Sending him home is doing everyone a favor—except his volleyball team. Even Brad seems cool with John's decision; he can avoid the tanning-booth charms of the girl with whom he slept out here, and he can patch things up with his girlfriend back in Big D. He's like that; he's not without a heart, some emotions. The Nazi has chigger bites that he is afraid may be something worse; they're red, and they itch and swell, and maybe they're something like a deadly spider invitation to rotting skin and paralysis—but when he asks John, who teaches biology and has seen every bite there is out here, John just laughs and says, "Chiggers," and the Nazi is visibly relieved, but continues to examine his legs with suspicion even so. Meanwhile, the serial killer is still at large. A full moon, a big crying baby's head, will rise over the mountains soon, and the students look forward to a night of fear undercut by the knowledge that they are young and therefore immortal, and they will stay awake and together until morning to prove just this fact. Derek and Whitney and I have gone to the hospital, and we've been reassured by the doctors there this is no brain tumor, the CAT scan doesn't lie. It knows the brain's great hidden moments, its wild successes and rare, unearned flaws. This is not a brain tumor, not an aneurysm. This is a headache, is a migraine. It's really bad. It's miserable. But it will pass. This too shall pass, and I'll see my boyfriend in less than a week. He'll ask how my writing has been going, and I'll tell him what Elmer Kelton, a writer of westerns, said, that "Fiction writers are liars and thieves," and then I'll show him all these words, and hope he likes them, hope he finds in them reasons maybe to love me in even greater quantities than he already does, which is so much more than any man deserves, even if he is a character in a love story, even if he is only a hero because he says so, because it's his story, and that's his right.

COWBOYS AND INDIANS

Lorien Crow

JACK WHEAT IS THE PREACHER at my Grandma Ellen's funeral. The February day feels like May, and the sand cliffs that rise in the distance radiate sunlight. This was the backdrop of my grandmother's life: juniper and piñon, red rock and mesa, sand in so many colors there aren't enough crayons. Jack Wheat talks of original sin and is dressed like a Quaker.

I keep my eyes occupied with one of the gravediggers, who stands off to the side, his head bowed. He is brown-skinned and fierce, definitely Navajo. I feel guilty for meeting his curious gaze while Jack Wheat croaks out a rusty version of "The Old Rugged Cross."

On our way to the cemetery this morning, the cars traveling in the opposite direction moved aside to let us pass. Men and boys on the sidewalk removed baseball and cowboy hats to stand with heads bowed as we inched by. There seems to be an innate respect for death out here, one I've never experienced back East.

Days like this you wouldn't mind if it rained. Gray would fit the mood better. Out here, you can't hide from the sun. It creeps into the cracks of dark rooms, garish, invasive. On a cloudy day you could blend in better, slink away to grieve unnoticed.

My aunts and I remove roses from the casket's flower displays. We return to the house to serve coffee and store-bought pastry to

From *CT Review*.

a procession of black-clad mourners who linger like hungry crows, picking at remains, not wanting to be first or last to leave. I'm old enough that I'm expected to replace plastic utensils and thank people for attending, but I still feel like a teenager who needs to escape. I call my cousin David, who arrives in the late afternoon to rescue me.

David is six-foot-six, owns four motorcycles, and works for one of the big oil companies: offshore drilling, somewhere in the seas that border South Africa, one month on, one month off. He lives in a trailer up in Chama, a tiny mountain town further north—more Colorado than New Mexico, and right on the border. David screams rebellion, always has. As a kid, he embodied to me all that was wild in the world.

Today he has the Ducati. It's still too cold to go up to Navajo Lake, our usual getaway spot. David asks me what I'd like to do, with that Native American twinge that sounds Canadian to my pale, untrained ear.

"Margaritas," I say. We take off.

The air is dry and I'm breathing easier. There is something suffocating about my grandmother's house: the green shag carpet, my grandfather's corduroy chair. The relics of fifty-two years of life with another person, flanked by black-and-white photos of kids and grandkids who've joined the army. My dad was one of those kids. So was David. He was one of the few soldiers to see ground combat during the Gulf War. I remember writing to him then, telling him about my fourteen-year-old life in Connecticut. He says this is why I'm his favorite cousin, because I never felt bad for him.

"How about Applebee's?" David asks me. We have stopped at our first red light along the main strip, where teenagers still have drag races at twilight on Saturday nights.

"Cousin," I say, "can't we go to a real bar?"

"Cousin," says David, "you know what kinda people go to bars at 3:30 in the afternoon out here?"

Not sure if it's a joke, I wait expectantly. The light turns green.

When I was little, my Uncle Dwayne took all of us cousins camping in the mountains of southern Colorado. He wanted us to bond,

LORIEN CROW

being that we hailed from so many different parts of the country, and so barely knew one another. The first night, David told my younger cousin Edie and I a story about a crazed Indian trapped in the body of a bear. The bear ate only little girls, and could transform back and forth between bear and human at will.

I believed that story with my whole heart because David was adopted. He was wild and foreign, and I knew that if such a child-eating Indian bear existed, David would know him.

At the next red light, David says "Shit, cousin, even I don't much go to the 'real' bars out here. I don't wanna have to kick some ass the day of my Grandma's funeral. You know it's still cowboys and Indians out here, right?"

He cranes his neck around. I stare at him resolutely. He grins and runs the red light.

On the northwest outskirts of town the gaping silhouette of Shiprock becomes visible, ominous and prehistoric. David steers the motorcycle through the back streets, quaint suburban houses giving way to ramshackle trailer parks where laundry sways against red rocks in the distance. We pass the Apache Queen Laundry with its fading façade of spearmint and seashell pink. Powerful modern structures occasionally jut upward, dwarfing the crumbling adobe ones next to them. People used to run successful businesses out of trailers with hand-painted signs out front. Now the monsters of progression permanently divide the oil field town from its vanishing past.

The rich new settlers have built upward as well, claiming the high walls of the canyon to the east. The outsides of the mansions look like adobe, but are actually made from more durable materials. Natural-looking porches with built-in electric fireplaces gaze out past the trailer parks, where the desert recedes onto the Navajo Rez.

Don't get stuck out on the Rez at night, my uncles tell me. They make their own laws out there.

Scientists think that millions of years ago this land was at the bottom of an ocean. It's easy to picture that now, gliding through jagged rock formations, buttes and mesas looming on the horizon. The landscape is strange and barren compared to New England. I know why cowboys felt like cowboys out here.

Still the sun penetrates everything. The native cultures that thrived here worshipped the sun's relentless omnipresence. It makes even the fiercest rocks look warm and inviting, like they will always retain warmth, even in winter; it tricks the eye, transforming sharp points into curving shoulders.

We pull off the road in front of Dean's Shiprock Tavern. A faded sign swings in the arid breeze. The brown paint is peeling. Three out of the four cars in the parking lot are pickup trucks. At any moment I expect outlaws on horseback to ride up, tie their horses out front, and draw guns. David always says he has outlaw blood running in him; that's why he was given away as a baby. Part outlaw, part Indian, he jokes; never had a chance.

Now he's trying not to smile, wondering if I will ask him to take us somewhere else. He's daring me to back out, but knows I won't. We are the black sheep of the family, and we understand this about each other. Our grandfather, the patriarch of the family, despised us both. Our grandmother tried failingly to make up for it. Now they're both dead, and we're not really sure where that leaves us.

The bar is dark and smoky, most of its windows boarded up. I'm the only female in the place. Any eyes momentarily raised are quickly lowered when they encounter David. He makes an imposing impression on people.

We step up to the bar. David wears a shit-eating grin on his face. Just loud enough for the whole bar to hear, he says "So, coz, still craving on a margarita?"

This is supposed to make me look frilly, dare me to be tougher. Bars like this don't serve dainty pitchers of frothy drinks. The bartender smirks.

"Not if you're buyin'," I say. "Two shots of Patron Silver."

The bartender is not as impressed as I hoped he'd be, but he stops smirking and pours. David raises his eyebrows. "I taught you well," he says.

The bartender hands us our liquor with limes and salt, which I accept and David does not. "To Grandma," we toast.

After two more shots and a beer, I don't care that David drives too fast. We decide to do the sunset up on the bluffs. The sunset here is an event, a time of day to which plans are assigned. If you have the afternoon free, you drive to as remote a place as your vehicle can take you to and watch the sun go down. The bluffs are to the north, toward Colorado and Highway 666.

Highway 666 has a bad reputation. Curvy narrow roads wind through craggy outcroppings of rock, steep inclines alternating with flat desert.

That highway is the badlands personified, my Uncle Troy once told me.

Two years ago a Navajo woman was murdered out there. She was split open from throat to sternum with a machete. Local legends hold that her ghost haunts the road, luring truckers over the cliffs like some wicked desert mermaid.

We stake out our spot on a southernmost bluff. The rocks feel sturdy and hot beneath my fingernails as we scale the sides. The day is still warm.

David lights a joint and we sink down onto the blazing rock. I should be worrying about rattlesnakes, but when I'm with David I forget about worldly dangers.

"I didn't see her enough," David says. "You live across the country and you saw her more than I did. Grandpa's been dead for *twelve years*. I should have gone to see her more."

I realize I am supposed to offer some sort of comfort, but I can't. He's right. He should have gone to see her more. I exhale.

"It's different for me though," I say. "I'm a woman. It's a different level of respect, especially now that I'm older . . ."

As I'm saying it, I know he's already tuned me out. I say it anyway. It needs to be said. I want to go on, but the divide is too great. I can't express to him how full Grandma's life seemed to me. She bore seven kids and raised the five that lived. For half of her life she cooked and cleaned without electricity. She sewed quilts, spit-shined shoes, stroked her children's hair, cleaned rich people's houses when she needed money, made perfect biscuits and apricot jam, wrote me birthday cards every year, and died with her cross in her hands. I am frustrated with my inability to express the importance of these things to David. He would never think of them as accomplishments;

he would never be expected to perform any of them, or even to try. It's expectation that's so crushing sometimes, I think.

I say this out loud as the sun begins to sink more than shine. We are bathed in sherbet colors.

David stares at me for a long time after I speak. I stretch out flat on my back, trying to melt into the rock like ice cream, trying to mold myself into something that retains warmth. I study my hands, which seem too soft, not callused enough. No needle pricks or cast-iron burns, just ink spots and some fading nail polish.

David finally kicks back, stretching out beside me. He is all muscle and brawn and gruffness.

"I've seen the world," he starts, "but I just can't seem to get the fuck out of here."

Then we both just start laughing, laughing so loud it's not even sound anymore. Maybe we couldn't quite feel the sadness deep enough, but the laughter is resonant. It comes from the right place.

The last maroons and purples are lingering over the valley. Only the highest cliffs still hold the tint of sunlight. The tiny town below us, Farmington, is all dusk, the lights slowly blinking on. In the dark it will look like a neon sea.

We're both starving. We decide on green chicken chili and sopapillas from a little takeout stand just off of the highway. The wind has picked up and it's chilly on the bike now. I hunker down behind David as we speed back toward civilization, the excitement of the town's small rush hour becoming palpable.

We are the only customers. Dust floats up from the bike as we saunter over to the dingy window and place our order. Despite the impending darkness and the chill in the air, two *abuelitas* are sitting in fraying lawn chairs next to the stand, wrapped in Apache blankets. They study us expectantly, smiles not on their mouths, but in the beautiful wrinkles at the corners of their eyes.

"Wind's pickin' up," David says to them.

One of them shakes a chubby brown finger at us. "The Navajo women say this wind, it brings devil spirits with it." Her eyes twinkle. "This wind, it came with you! You devil spirits? Huh?"

The other *abuelita* giggles with delight.

David shifts uncomfortably. I try to smile with my eyes as I say, "No Ma'am," but it's a trick I haven't mastered yet, and the question hangs there, and I don't think she believes me.

We lean against the peeling red picnic table only long enough to spoon down the chili, balancing the piquant spice with pillowy soft sopapillas drizzled with honey. We share a Coke, but our cheeks are flushed and our mouths still burn as we get back on the bike, pulling our helmets on.

"Don't let those devil spirits catch you!" waves the grandmother, as her silent friend dissolves into hysterics. David guns the engine and peels out of the parking lot.

"See what I mean?" He asks.

I don't reply. I can't figure out why he is so spooked—they were just having fun with us. Then I consider what the words might have meant if I'd been considered an outlaw my whole life.

"Cowboys and Indians, coz, I told you." David says. "Just the way it is out here."

It's dark when we get back to Grandma's. Cars are still parked outside. David, as usual, says he can't deal with coming inside. I kiss him on the cheek and say I understand—what else is there to say? He winks, morphing back into Wild Charming Boy, and I back into Wise Ass East Coast Girl.

"Hope you make it back out this summer, coz, we can take the boat up to Navajo."

I nod and tell him to get the hell gone before the relatives stumble out like zombies to claim him.

I turn from the Ducati's dust to the well-lit house. Why is it that I can do this, switch gears, when David cannot? I will recount memories of my grandmother to drunken mourners, throw out paper plates, make polite conversation, and clean coffee cups while David rides through the desert with devil spirits at his boot heels.

Walking to the front door, all I can think is:

It's not just here. It's like this everywhere. Cowboys and Indians; that's how it is.

TOGETHER WE ARE LOST

Kathleen de Azevedo

MY FINAL DIVORCE PAPERS were the great paper airplane that would fly out of my Nevada window and set me free. I rarely saw Conrad. He was always on the road in his eighteen-wheeler, his mind too crazy for anyone to help, too wild for me. My husband used to complain that a dozen black ravens flapped inside his head, beating their wings against his skull. He once told me that his eighteen-wheeler had no more brakes, and that at certain points in the Nevada desert, he would bang bunnies crossing the road, killing them by the thousands, the thump and splat unbearable, tearing his sanity into bits. He told me that the sand glittered with thousands of watchful glass eyes and had put curses on him. There is no getting around it; untangling myself and my son Eric from that madness was no simple task. Still, Conrad and I clawed at each other whenever he went off the deep end, tumbling through his cloud of desert dust and raven feathers. Finally, I had to tell him *no más*. No custody, no visits with Eric, *no nada*. In his condition, Conrad shouldn't even have been walking around.

He blamed the Mexican part of me, the one who knew of la Llorona, the mad ghost woman of the arroyos, crying for the children she killed, and who consorted with people who lit candles for saints and against evil eyes. Yeah, he grabbed at any excuse. Ghosts. Raven feathers. My supposed hex on him.

From *TriQuarterly*.

Once my divorce was final, I made the mistake of telling my mother that I'd had it with men, so she of course invited me over to her house for one of her ladies' parties, the ones that celebrated love. "Forget it, Ma," I said, "I'm through!" How ironic when I found myself repeating this above the din of her cadre of friends who filled her living room and kitchen, their voices more animated than the high-pitched chuckle of the mariachis on the record player (no CDs for Ma!).

At her party, Ma wore a pale lavender tulle dress that swept over a purple satin slip underneath. Her hair was all poofed, with a flat lavender bow in back like a prom queen. "For godsakes Ma," I complained, "you look like a bridesmaid."

She grabbed my arm and led me off to the side. "Aye, Celia, you look terrible like you drank the water from Pyramid Lake." I shrugged. I wasn't about to tell her of my surprising broken heart, the one I wasn't supposed to have because good riddance was supposed to have crushed out the flame.

"Where's Eric?" she continued, asking about my son. "Why don't you ever bring Eric to see me?"

"I told you, Ma, he doesn't like old ladies' parties."

"But honey, I'm celebrating love. LOVE. *Amor. Tu sabes?*"

The women around us danced, some with men, but mostly with each other because they were divorced or because their men were in Mexico, or were working, or were sitting in front of the TV at home. Some women wore button earrings and necklaces with big fat black shiny beads. A couple of women wore tunics splashed with two orchids in the back, and four orchids in the front, so their breasts gave the flowers little snout-like bumps. Another wore a turquoise jumpsuit and a Navajo necklace. The women with nice hips wore rayon dresses which rose up on their behinds as they walked in high heels. They danced salsa, moving together in such coordination they seemed like four-legged creatures. And they chuckled to the tune of El Amor, because El Amor was the real purpose of the party: to introduce my mother's new boyfriend to her friends. It was like a *quinceañera* for an old man.

My mom got herself an older Mexican man, sharp nose and elbows, like a three-pronged hood ornament. He wore an all-white suit like a hidalgo, his skin was as brown as a nut, and his long white hair shot back as if he had been riding on a motorcycle with his face against the wind. A small tuft of his white hair was in a ponytail that looked like a rabbit's foot. He was eyeing the ladies and holding his hat in front of him, fingering the brim. He was just another old fox she chased after. Just the other day, Ma had spoken to me of Jimmy Jered—the Elvis impersonator she had been dating, the guy who performs in the Leprechaun Room at the Babaloo Casino, the one she visited every Saturday with her rambunctious old-lady friends to sip Manhattans and flirt—"I've had it with gringos! I'm going down to my roots!"

"What roots, Ma! You're a gringo yourself."

To greet me, the Hidalgo lifted his eyebrows in a *buenas noches señora,* looking a little comical like the Mexican movie king Cantin-flas. The guy was probably a busboy, just like a lot of the women here were hotel maids like my mother, who on the weekends swilled visions of romantic moonlight at the Babaloo Casino. Still, it was too much, his cooing, his lovey-dovey, the way he touched my mother's arm when she swam around with a plate of taquitos, the way the women sized him up and down, a couple of women making jokes about the size of his feet (How large!) meaning his "member" was (How large!). And all the while, the music slid around the women, patted their butts and traced its tongue on their feet swelling from their too-tight shoes.

I couldn't stand the chatter. It made me dizzy. I made my way out to my mom's backyard to the stubbly patches of grass, the deflated doughboy swimming pool, where I could see the horizon beyond the fence, a long mountain with a far-off subdivision wrapped around its base. I recalled Conrad screaming and plowing forward against the wind in one of our arguments, the ones so strong we had to go outside, the ones that needed all the Nevada desert to contain. He'd tear his hair and accuse me of lifting off the top of his head like he was a cookie jar and stuffing black ravens inside that fluttered all day, trapped. At times I didn't know if he was really crazy, or exaggerating a headache to get back at me. Because he was gone most of the time, his insanity seemed a normal part of futile love.

KATHLEEN DE AZEVEDO

The old Hidalgo stepped outside and slipped out a pack of Tiparillos from his jacket pocket. He held the little cigars slick and smart from his fingers. "So," he said to me, "you are Silvia's daughter."

I nodded. His skinny neck was wooden with the burl of his Adam's apple. He sniffed the air and looked a little arrogant. "I know you read cards," he said, "and you always read cards of your mother's new boyfriends. And you always predict disaster. So I won't ask you. If my romance with your mother is going to be a disaster, I'd rather not know."

I walked over to the fence and leaned my arms on the crossbeams. "It's no biggie," I said. "Ma can take care of herself."

"Hmmm." He sucked his Tiparillo with little pops. Obviously he couldn't smoke in the house. If I said something, he'd say something back. He hummed the words of "El Amor Lindo." *My beautiful love.* (Puff, puff.) *A small step is all I'll take. But if I can steal a kiss, señorita, sería un regalito de los angeles. Mi Amor, when I gaze at you, I think this is madrugada and I've woken up in your arms.*

When he was done, he grinned. "I hope I didn't disturb your sleep with that song."

"It doesn't matter," I grunted, "I never sleep." The smell of his smoking swirled with the odor of his cologne. I imagined him getting out of the shower, fastidiously patting himself dry and splashing lotion on his face and talcum on his body. I imagined his feminine bathroom shelves to be full of lotion and Avon.

"Would you dance with me?" he said bluntly. "I've already gotten Silvia's permission. She wants to cheer you up."

"Forget it. I don't dance."

The Hidalgo didn't say anything for awhile. He threw the nub of his Tiparillo on the ground and stepped on it with one swirl. Then he pulled out a pocket watch, checked the time, and clicked it shut. He was an antique, all right. He came forward, his shiny shoes clicking, the shininess defying the dust. "Celia," he said, "be in love with someone. Even if a man is old and ugly. It's worth it. Very very *vale la pena.*" He laughed, lusciously, seductively, from his belly to his heart.

It was so sudden. Only a couple of weeks after Conrad and I signed the divorce papers, my thirteen-year-old son became a vegetarian and a Buddhist. Eric went from being a fierce little punker who wore bandanas as wristbands and black T-shirts and ate steaks like no tomorrow to being almost agreeable, almost a little too soft, and not eating anything that could possibly peep or yowl, no carne asada, no ropa vieja stew. His normally slitty-eyes-with-attitude had relaxed, and I saw that they were soulful, rich and brown, the eyes that I had given him. What mother wouldn't treasure the change, yet we are made of the same clay as our fathers and mothers, and I had the urge to reach inside his head and pull out his thoughts and read them like cards. Eric sat on his bed cross-legged with his textbook on his lap and a few paperbacks to the side. All his posters of rock band fiends and thuggy-looking Peterbilts had been torn down; the wall was bare except for one poster of Buddha, skin bluish-white with a Saturn-like halo of ice chips around the head. Buddha sat on a lotus pad with skin-like petals that pouted at the edges. The words on the poster read: *Be a Bodhisattva: Buddhism at its Best.*

Eric had changed. Oh, yes. Or should I say "que pasa mi hijo?" Did you go to India to look for the truth? Are you a Hare Krishna now? He told me he wanted me to discover him like a temple that had always been buried in the desert. But I was suspicious. I could not see the temple inside his head, the one I feared would be crumbling in pieces, the ones I'd have to mourn for because I couldn't put them back together. But instead, I did the motherly thing. "What are you reading," I said, "Tell your ma." I had to start new, new conversations, new struggle, everything.

"My history book, for one," Eric said. "And this pocket book here is about Zen and this one is about meditating. My counselor got me into this meditating class."

"What do you meditate about?" I asked rather clumsily, as I thought meditating was done by very thin people who ate strange things. "Do you think about me when you meditate?"

Eric rolled his eyes. "It's personal."

Oh. A little annoyed yes. Everyone with their secrets. All busybody. My mother would say, "Celia, at least now he's not taking *drogas* and smoking *mota*." "Yeah," my thoughts yelled over Ma's advice. "Sometimes you don't need those things to invite the devil into your house." I turned to go.

"Wait," Eric said. He turned serious and, just like that, began talking about his father, the last time they were together, the time they ran off for a couple of days without telling me and I called the cops, thinking my son had been kidnapped. Those were the days when I swam in a pool of my la Llorona tears until my body went numb. But Eric, not able to see the insanity of this memory, told me of how his father took him to a place in the desert, not far from here, he said, oh, twenty, thirty miles or so. Eric said he wanted to go there again. "It's a real and spiritual place."

"You want to go there again? Do you have any idea—" I hissed, trying to tell him of the grief I had when I found his bed empty. But couldn't continue on as my anger cut my words off at the bud. Finally, I just said, "No way. Your father is dead to me."

Eric turned away from me deliberately, faced the wall, and he groaned as he unpretzelized his gangly westernized legs. "Fine," he said. "I'll go myself, even if I have to walk."

I boiled out of the room, roiled in the kitchen, got out my pack of cards, the ones I tell fortunes with. I sat at the table and shuffled and snapped the deck. What could I have done? Could I have spotted that crazy eye in the middle of Conrad's massive flesh? Conrad probably told Eric all the worst, that I drove him loco, that I drove him to see ghost women on the road and CIA henchmen riding motorcycles outside of Ely. "Your mother," he would say in Spanish, "is a *bruja*," practically the only word of my language he knew. "She is a witch, you see that, my boy? She makes me see visions with those cards of hers."

Counselors told me Eric was in this kind of fragile state like a fish; you catch him now or let him go forever. So the next day, I got Eric out of school and we drove out to his "place," drove east of Sparks where the pale blue mountains and the more obstinate blonde ones rose from a rocky valley with trails of dried arroyos and sagebrush along what used to be rushing creeks. Eric sat slouching next to me, his large foot resting on the dashboard, his pointy elbow resting on the car door. Thoughts of Conrad filled the car, slid and curled around our heads. My tongue was sluggish and tasted like steel. Eric was maddeningly secretive. His delicate fingers drummed the windowsill. Drumming, he was always drumming, all five fingers, drumming. Then he jabbed at the horizon. "Turn there, see that sign in the distance?"

"We better not have to drive down some dirt road. Better not be in someone's property where they get boards with nails and hide them under the dirt. We get a flat tire here and we are in big trouble."

The sign got closer, just a green square that said Road 14 and was riddled with buckshot, twisted a little to the side, as if to say *Why Go Here, Locos, Eh?* The dirt road went between two properties sectioned off with barbed wire. The road was dry, and the chewy winter mud had molded it into prominent ruts, not worn down by many cars, so the surface was still uneven with rocks and lobes of old clay. "I don't like this, Eric," I said. "Only a mile, then back we go." But Eric leaned over and tapped the front windshield with his knuckle. "That group of rocks there. We'll need to walk out just a bit."

I stopped the car near a group of boulders that were gnashed together like giant molars. Eric jumped out, leapt over the boulders, and disappeared around a bend. I followed, scrambled between the rocks, and called out, "Watch for rattlesnakes, you hear?" Eric climbed further up the boulders and crouched.

We stood overlooking the valley. My son's body looked elegant, like when boys first become men: slender legs and prominent muscle that roped down his calves; the way his torso leaned out almost ready to pounce as if he wanted to hawk-dive over the land that dipped into streaks of blue-green sage and patches of glistening white sand-salt. A small wash of black volcanic ash trickled from shelves of rock. The wind smacked my ear with a sudden blast.

"Look there! Amazing!" Eric cried, "Amazing."

In the distance was a flock of bighorn sheep, not moving, just standing in a group like a spill of white buttons.

KATHLEEN DE AZEVEDO

"Yes," I said, "they are rare." Along the edges, some sheep wandered off, making the group a little ragged.

I wondered how Conrad had found this place. I wondered: Had he seen these sheep? The old veins of waterways? Did he see what I saw, a peaceful desert too raw to have secrets? Did our pupils match, eye to eye? Or did the wind rattle him like cards, shattering his thoughts so that a wave of black pitch rolled over past-present-future, pouring the birds into his brain? I wished I could have done the *bruja* thing: hold Conrad's pounding head in my hands and squeeze out his bat-winged demons so that they popped out of his ears and skittered away. Then I could have held what remained: his crystal-clear mind, one that had my reflection.

Eric came and stood next to me, his arms crossed.

"Is this," I broke the silence, forcing my voice to be steady, "what you wanted?"

Eric shook his head. I could tell he was sad, but he wouldn't let on. "It looks different than before," he said. "I can barely recognize it."

About a week after Eric and I saw the sheep I was told that Conrad had killed himself at that very same place. Perhaps Conrad *had* seen the sheep, who knows? First I heard officially, but then, several people had their version of what they heard, and again, it seemed as complicated as Conrad's head. I felt like I was sewing together strips of old cloth trying to make a long shroud which Conrad could wear for his own funeral. I imagined the last days of his life he must have gone even crazier: the bunnies smacking against the bumper of his eighteen-wheeler sounding like grenades; the glass eyes in the sand bursting out blood; la Llorona, the crying ghost woman, tapping at the windows of his truck.

I created in my mind, Conrad's last moments. I imagined he saw morning beginning to lift, old eyebrows of gray separating the clouds. He probably drove with the window open so he could sense the bulk of whatever he carried, the furniture sliding and hitting against old blankets, or food crouched in cold storage, or cattle shuffling in their own manure. His truck moved along the asphalt zipper that opened the mountains, which, as he used to say, were like two big breasts, and sparkled with the glare of TVs and cellular-phone towers. Behind him, the zipper closed. Gradually, a small rim of orange cracked the horizon at dawn. Conrad remembered the way it used to be at this time of the day when mule deer strolled casually, rubbing their hides against the creosote. At least this is how I wanted to imagine his last day alive.

So Conrad had turned up the Road 14, past the sign riddled with buckshot. He kept going until the line of boulders crunched against the bumper and chewed up the oil pan. The oil poured out of the bottom of the truck. Then Conrad lumbered over the stack of rocks and onto the rocky overlook, where Eric and I watched the sheep in the valley. Perhaps he looked back and saw his truck waiting for him. Perhaps he saw the sheep too and said "amazing!" just as Eric had. Then Conrad pulled out a pistol from his pocket and placed it in his mouth. His heart beat violently. Don't ask where he got the pistol. I don't know, I don't presume to guess about such things. Maybe he always had one. I can imagine the gunshot exploded and all confusion being perfectly clear. He felt himself crash against the metal, fur flying in a large cap, twirling like a Frisbee and landing in a bloody distance yonder. I think Conrad would have liked to have felt the black ravens released from his brain, flapping into the open valley, and spreading out in all directions. Finally.

At the funeral, Ma was not dressed in lavender, but in black. For the reception afterwards the ladies made what I liked: enchiladas, rice and beans, lasagna. The ladies even tried to make what Eric liked: vegetarian meatloaf with bulgur and Japanese tofu salad.

I was alone with Eric in my mother's bedroom as we removed our jackets after the burial. I wanted to grab my son, hold him close forever and not let go, be a smother mother, make him small again, tell him that he is on the right track and that sons don't have to be like their fathers. Finally, I snatched him by the head and plunged a kiss on his topknot. "Don't leave me," I whispered, keeping my mouth to his head. I was holding him up, just by his fragile head, the rest of his body struggling with its own gravity.

KATHLEEN DE AZEVEDO

I let go and took his hand. Eric was dry-eyed.

"You can cry, you know. At funerals it's permitted."

"I made peace with Buddha," Eric shrugged.

I smoothed his hair back, I wanted to say something that would be meaningful to him. But I had no meaning myself. Instead, I took his hand to lead him down the stairs. The people looked up and applauded, like they did for my wedding. I held up my hand. "Please. No ceremony. Let's eat."

The ladies moved sadly toward the table, which groaned with food and a strange flower arrangement of manzanita and some dried desert weed thing. The tablecloth was a bright serape, and oh, people might say, what kind of funeral decoration is this? But I liked it. Conrad never liked bright Mexican things like this. It was strange to be in my mother's house with no music, no new boyfriend or lounge lizard to display. The women's pumps clumped on the kitchen floor like a herd of restless sheep. They were waiting for someone to tell them what to do, what to say in this situation. They didn't know if I loved my husband, felt guilty or what. I didn't even know myself, so how could I blame them? Someone handed me a beer. That's all they could do. They smiled wordlessly, and stroked my upper arm and hugged me. I meandered over to my mother's record player. Funerals didn't suit my mother. Now I wanted to see people in love, the way I did when I usually came over here. I fingered through the records, slipped the black disk out from the cover, and placed it on the record player. The music was a light cha-cha-cha.

The women turned, surprised. I smiled. "You guys dance. Why not."

The women looked at each other, their eyebrows made up so a pencil line contained all their stray hairs, their lipstick catching the red of urgency. The music cocked their ears, and they rubbed their feet on the floor not quite wanting to, but couldn't help it. Two ladies stepped away and saw Eric with a small glass of beer but thought what the hell, he's been through a lot. One by one, the women took each other by the hand and began dancing. They were in dark funeral colors, but I imagined them in violets and yellows and batiks. Someone took my hand. It was Ma's boyfriend, the Hidalgo I had met at a party before. Except now, instead of wearing white, he was in a shiny black suit. I saw the small string mustache and wondered how he could be so patient as to clip his mustache like that. "Please, Celia," he said, "let's dance." I shot a look at Ma, who nodded in approval. I put down my beer bottle. The Hidalgo took me and whirled me onto the dance floor. His hand touched my back lightly, but it could move me anywhere, the tips of his fingers played with the small, subconscious nerve endings of my lower back. His mouth slipped near my ear and whispered, "Remember how I said that I didn't want you to read my cards, that I'd rather face disaster when it came?"

"I'm sure you do very well in the face of disaster," I said as I leaned my head on his shoulder. I shouldn't have had that beer.

"You do well too." He played with my hair and smoothed his hand down my back. The music brought everyone to the dance floor. They were almost waltzing, the generous hips swayed to the music. The Hidalgo gathered me closer, and I realized I hadn't been held this tight before, not even by Conrad. I noticed the whiteness of the Hidalgo's ponytail and the many rings on his thin brown fingers. He had many songs to sing about love, and he sang them. *Come to me, oh you who are tossed, come in the madrugada, together we are lost.* You would think he'd not sing those kinds of songs being in the situation we were in. But he sang them in my ear, unabashedly. I started to cry. I leaned my forehead hard on his shoulder and tears gleamed on the silk threads of his suit. He rocked me, shushing gently. Maybe I cried for myself and for Eric. Or for Conrad and how he died, or for how little there was in our marriage. *Llora!* the Hidalgo urged, *cry, cry out all the sadness! You are never more alive than you are today!*

HERMANO

Alan Elyshevitz

WHILE RUTHIE KEPT BARKING, the wind kept blowing, kicking up a dust storm that forced motorists into Sandoval's Trading Post. Whenever a customer left the store, Maury had to come out from behind the counter and latch the door to keep it from flying open. All morning long, he lumbered from his stool to the door and back again in a ritual of tedious commerce, of greetings and farewells.

Around noon, Felipe Alvarez showed up. "Good day, *hermano*. How's business?"

"Picking up, Felipe." Maury took a slab of beef jerky from a plastic jar, tore it in two, and gave half to Alvarez.

"Thanks. I've got a craving for salt today."

"Have something to wash it down," Maury offered.

Alvarez rubbed the stubble on his wrinkled face, then selected an orange pop from the cooler and managed to twist the cap off despite the arthritis in his ravaged hands.

Another customer knocked. An egg-shaped man whose thin brown hair fluttered about his forehead and ears.

"It's bad out there," he said as Maury let him in.

"Usually is."

The man bought a soda pop and took long noisy gulps among the aisles of canned goods, paper products, and junk food. Now and

From *Red Rock Review.*

then he glanced at Maury, who had returned to his stool behind the counter. While Alvarez kept an eye on the stranger and gnawed on his jerky, Maury listened to Ruthie barking. He worried about his lawn chair out in the yard. He imagined the wind hoisting it over the fence and into the highway, causing an accident.

"Your dog barks like crazy out there," Alvarez said.

"Customers get out of their cars and talk cute to her," Maury said. "It takes her a while to settle down. Ruthie hates to be patronized."

"Me too." Alvarez smiled. His teeth were big and bright, the only parts of his body that seemed ageless and well-maintained. "It's like when the tourists talk slow to me because they think I don't speak English well. You know the kind. Archaeologists. Anthropologists. Students and professors. Those fools wear shorts, and no hats. They think the petroglyphs at Torpedo Creek *mean* something." Though he was a competent local historian, Alvarez liked to play devil's advocate.

"They must mean *something*, Felipe."

"Pretty pictures, pretty shapes. The Indians made them to break the monotony."

"People write books about them," Maury said. "Experts."

Alvarez rubbed a thumb and forefinger together. "For money, that's all."

The stranger continued to linger in the aisles, examining the disordered shelves and rearranging cans like a stock clerk.

Maury's back ached. He shifted on the stool. "The Indians must be squirming in their graves."

"We're standing on them," said Alvarez. "The whole damn state is one big Indian graveyard."

Maury's shoulders twitched.

"Don't feel bad, *hermano*. It was Coronado who destroyed them. And the damn missionaries. I don't trust those new ones either, those evangelists down the road."

"They don't bother anyone." But Maury did wonder sometimes about the mysterious Protestant mission that had opened several years ago to serve local laborers and poor folk in a compound of adobe dwellings behind an imposing aluminum fence. "They don't bother me, anyway."

Maury followed Alvarez's gaze to the stranger. The man was handling tins of soup, beans, and peaches, turning them over as if looking for price tags. He scrutinized packages of flashlight batteries, comparing brands. He squeezed bags of pretzels and tortilla chips as if checking whether the seals were intact.

"Who is he?" Alvarez whispered, leaning across the counter.

Maury shrugged.

Stretching his arms, Alvarez groaned like a man awakening from a satisfying sleep. "I better get going. I have to testify at the County Commission for Land Development. You know how they ask old-timers like me to give a historical perspective. Some lawyer named Kruger is twisting the Commission's arm to let somebody do something near Torpedo Creek. Same old story. They say this Kruger plays hardball."

"Good luck."

"I don't need luck," Alvarez said. "I don't care who wins. I just like to testify. It's the only time people have to sit still and listen to me. Why don't you come? Close up early and watch the show."

Maury declined.

Alvarez removed another bottle from the cooler and winced as he twisted the cap off his pop. "You used to be a real dynamo. In the old days you left your fingerprints on everything."

"I'm slowing down, Felipe." As if to prove the point, Maury shuffled to the door.

Alvarez lowered his voice in case the stranger was listening in. "You still grieve for my sister, but you won't talk about it. It's bad, *hermano*."

Maury watched him walk to his car. The wind had died down. When Ruthie saw Alvarez, she barked furiously, sprinting back and forth at the base of the chain-link fence, her short legs churning, ears flapping. Alvarez did not say a word to her. He wouldn't even glance in Ruthie's direction.

Finally the stranger made his shopping selections: large bags of rice and lima beans, along with several boxes of macaroni. He could barely carry it all in his arms.

"You need a basket?" Maury called out from behind the counter.

The man looked up and grinned as if the suggestion was ridiculous. "No thanks, Mr. Sandoval, I can manage."

"You know me?"

"Everyone does." He waddled over and let his groceries fall on the counter. His body was compact, his face clean-shaven, boyish. Maury noticed the amateurish quality of his haircut, his uneven bangs and asymmetrical sideburns. He imagined the man trimming it himself in front of a bathroom mirror.

"You must have quite a family . . . Mr. . . . ?"

"Call me George."

They shook hands. George's palm was coarse, like that of a miner or rancher, but his manner was benign and confident, like that of a schoolteacher or, Maury thought, a real estate agent.

"You have children?" Maury asked.

George's smile grew. "A large extended family, you might say."

"You've cleaned me out," Maury said. "Now I'll have to order more of everything." Though George was still smiling, Maury sensed that he had not taken this as a joke. "You're new to this area."

"Compared to you, Mr. Sandoval."

"Funny I've never seen you before."

George extracted a wallet from his back pocket. "We keep to ourselves."

Maury bagged the groceries, tallied the bill on the register, and handed over change from a fifty. Lifting a bag in each arm, George staggered to the door.

"Wait," Maury said, "I'll get that for you."

"You live in that trailer?" George asked.

"It's a mobile home."

"What's the difference?"

"A trailer is mobile, a mobile home isn't. I use the Cadillac to get around."

George ignored the witticism. "You're out here by yourself. How long has it been?"

"A year, give or take."

While Maury held the door open, George fidgeted with his bundles. One of the bags had begun to slip, so he boosted it with his knee.

"When did Mrs. Sandoval pass away?"

Maury hesitated. "Do I know you, George?"

George shook his head. "No, you don't, but this is a small community."

"It's a large community," said Maury. "There just aren't many people."

"But it's easy to tell when one of us has gone."

All afternoon, customers came and went, and Ruthie barked when they jabbered at her. Maury served them perfunctorily. When the last of the stragglers had gone, he daydreamed about the alternatives his considerable savings could buy if he weren't so frugal and lethargic: travel to exotic countries, a ranch with a few docile sheep, female companionship. He suspected that the woman from the parcel-delivery service, buxom and shapely even in her khaki uniform, was attracted to him.

Around seven, when Ruthie keened for dinner, he closed the store. Out in the yard his lawn chair had been impaled on the fence by the wind and hung there as if shot during an escape attempt. He pulled the chair down and set it beneath the awning above his front door, while Ruthie alternately attacked and evaded his feet. After his wife's death, Maury had retired from real estate, sold his oversized house, and bought the Trading Post and mobile home, where he befriended this obstinate mutt that refused to leave the property. Perhaps the dog had been abandoned by the previous owner. Maury had no great love for pets, but Ruthie's recalcitrance impressed him, and he soon got used to her. After a while he got used to everything.

"Okay, little girl. Supper time."

Ruthie gazed at him with opaque brown eyes. He stooped to caress her ears. They were the color of adobe, the texture of a shag carpet. She licked his wrist.

In the kitchenette, he scrambled eggs for himself on the grease-coated stove, in the same tarnished frying pan his wife had used every weekend to cook up huevos rancheros. The eggs separated into dry yellow clumps. He added salsa from a jar and ate his meal while staring out the window at the cracked chalky earth of his yard.

Beyond his yellow Cadillac, on the other side of the road, sagebrush had begun to fade into the landscape like animals with natural camouflage. The setting sun glowed red as if it were a colossal dying star.

Maury wondered whether Alvarez was right. Did the petroglyphs at Torpedo Creek represent anything real? Herons. That's how they had appeared to Ruth—Felipe's sister, Maury's wife—the last time she and Maury had visited the creek. *They really are amazing,* she had said, marveling at the ancient stick-figure paintings on the boulders. *Can you imagine herons out here?* Ruth knelt by the trickling creek, which had shrunk to a pitiful stream during a recent draught. Much of the red-clay bed was visible, and cottonwoods and yellowing shrubs on the banks seemed as fragile and dry as burnt matchsticks. She dipped her hands into the water. She was wearing a loose cotton housedress—red and tan, with a geometrical Indian design—and Maury envisioned her as a tribal woman washing clothes by hand. She walked across the creek on a row of loose stones. *What a good idea, coming here,* she shouted. Her enthusiasm took Maury by surprise. *It's been years. I feel like a girl.* He forced a smile. *You look like a girl.* But Ruth's age was apparent. She was heavy. She was clumsy. She stumbled on the precarious stones. Maury prepared himself to lunge at any moment, to reach out from the bank and rescue her. *We should do this more often,* she said. He had felt suddenly ill then, sick with the kind of foreboding he experienced whenever a thunderstorm was in the offing. But the sky, as usual, was generously blue. The storm was elsewhere—upheaval of a different kind—slightly beyond the horizon of time.

Sundown at Sandoval's Trading Post was a time of deep silence and solitude relieved only by Ruthie's scratching at the door. Maury let her in. He sat in the living room, on the only comfortable chair he owned, reading the newspaper with the dog on his lap. An hour later, he prodded her to leap to the floor. Then he got up, went to the bathroom to brush his teeth, and undressed for bed.

In the black void of the bedroom, he stretched out on the left half of the mattress. This was a habit he couldn't break—leaving

ALAN ELYSHEVITZ

space for his wife. Through his slumber he felt the temperature plummeting, the dry desert air turning suddenly cold. He pulled a blanket up to his shoulders and reached for a body that wasn't there. He recalled the last time he and Ruth had made love, in the midst of a quarrel in their majestic bedroom in the big house on the rim of a mesa, an adobe fortress he had built for her with the profits of his lucrative real estate business. Maury caressed her ample waist beneath the well-worn fabric of her nightgown. Running his hand along the familiar striations of her rib cage, he was stirred by tenderness and comfortable lust, even as she lamented. *Sometimes I think our marriage is part of a deal you made with Felipe, to get a share of our family property. All business, no love. I know it's horrible to feel that way*—Then she began to sob. *That's insane, Ruth. Don't be*—He stopped himself from calling her a fool and pressed her face to his shoulder, aware that strong emotion—any strong emotion—increased her receptiveness to sex. She sobbed as he entered her. She sobbed as he ejaculated. She sobbed until she fell asleep on his arm and his fingers went numb, leaving him awake to ponder the enigma of female hormones. When Ruth opened her eyes the next morning, she yawned luxuriously, smiled at him and said, *I love waking up with a man in my bed.*

Some persistent and vaguely threatening sound caused him to imagine that someone was trying to break into his mobile home. But it was only Ruthie pawing at the bedroom door. Too tired to get up and let her in, he fell asleep. His last thought of the night concerned the flimsiness of this place—this house on blocks, this purgatorial cell—how it insulated him from nothing at all.

A long, slow day at the Trading Post. Alvarez had not visited him, nor Ramirez from the auto repair shop, nor Montoya from Maury's old real estate office, nor the woman from the parcel-delivery service. The only acquaintance who came by, in the late afternoon, was the last person he wanted to see. When he responded to a sharp-knuckled rap on the door, there she was: Isabella. For years she had been his wife's best friend. She stood stiffly in the doorway, wearing, as always, a plain brown dress, nearly black, reminiscent of a nun's habit. Her dense eyebrows and sun-cracked lips gave her an air of disapproval. Though she was younger than Maury by at least five years, he thought of her as a relic from an older generation. Privately he referred to her as "Walking Woe."

"It's been twenty-three months," Isabella rebuked him.

"I'm aware of that." Maury stepped aside to let her in.

She strutted toward the counter and looked around. "This place is filthy."

Maury did his best to hold his temper. At Ruth's funeral, Isabella was the person he had leaned on as he wept tears of sorrow and relief, despising himself for the latter.

"Two years," she said.

"Twenty-three months."

"Don't you think it's time for a proper memorial? Something public, something for the community."

"What do you suggest?"

"A school, for instance. You could finance a new elementary school and have it named after her," she said. "Even better, a hospital. To the best of my knowledge, you've never been in a hospital."

"Only once. And once was enough." Maury recalled his wife in an institutional bed, her ravaged face like a plaster cast. Her skin was parched, her hands swollen like prickly pear cacti, her chest collapsed. Her voice, degraded by medication, could manage only one audible sentence: *I've finally lost that extra weight.* After that visit he couldn't go back.

"The Ruth Sandoval Memorial Cancer Center." Isabella tried the title for sound. She seemed to like it. "You can afford to build a geriatrics wing, at the very least. The way you live now, you can afford an entire medical facility."

"Each of us grieves differently, Isabella."

"Look at this dirt everywhere," she said, pacing through the aisles where dust balls scattered in her wake. "Appalling. You may as well live outdoors with the lizards and jackrabbits. Ruth kept you human. Her memory deserves more from you than this. Her influential husband has become a grocer. Your wife would be horrified."

"Her brother doesn't seem to mind."

"Felipe?" she said. "That man is a barbarian. He had his father cremated, did you know that? He wanted to forget the old patriarch, obliterate him. He scattered the ashes from the top of a butte so the wind would take them as far away as possible. For all anybody knows, they landed in the Gulf of Mexico."

"He's family, Isabella, you're not." Instantly Maury regretted saying this.

"I view that as a positive attribute," she said. "Because I'm not a relation I can see things clearly. Mauricio, I believe you've lost your mind. What were you thinking, naming that mongrel after your wife?"

"It was the first name that came to mind, so I stuck with it."

Out in the yard Ruthie began to whimper as if she had overheard and understood what they were saying. She was hungry, which gave Maury an excuse to close early.

"We'll talk about this another time," Isabella said. A wraith of tenderness, of pity, appeared in her eyes, just for a moment, but it softened him.

"Take care of yourself, Isabella."

Ruthie yelped as Isabella marched with exaggerated dignity to her station wagon, a beige-and-gray monstrosity that evoked painful memories. During the last several months of her life, before the hospital, Ruth had gone out with Isabella every Friday evening. They had joined some sort of women's club, she said. Deep down Maury didn't believe her, but it was good to see her active again. A positive sign, he told himself. Ruth had begun to lose weight. None of her clothes fit. A simple trip from the bedroom to the bathroom became an ordeal. Still, she insisted on going out one night a week to the "women's club." Whenever Isabella came to pick her up in the station wagon, Maury assisted his wife to the car. Neither he nor Ruth said a word at these times. It was a ceremony of silence. From then on, they occupied separate realms: Maury was actively engaged in daily life, the dry land solid and certain beneath his feet, while Ruth resided offshore in a kind of undersea world of impending death. They talked less and less. They seldom touched. Slowly but surely Maury forgot the feel of her body.

He closed up for the evening. In the yard he saw that his lawn chair was leaning against the fence. He dragged the chair back to its place beneath the awning, then fetched a ten-pound bag of dog food from the house and knelt to pour some into Ruthie's dish. He heard a vehicle pull up to the Trading Post. A car door slammed. Maury did not turn around. While Ruthie licked his hand, he murmured endearments to her.

"What's her name?"

Maury hadn't noticed George approaching and was embarrassed to be caught talking to the dog. "Cleo," he lied. His visitor was carrying a leather briefcase. It looked new. It looked expensive. Maury stood and hugged the bag of dog food in the same way that the other man had embraced his groceries the day before. Ruthie gobbled up her dinner, her long ears draped over the plastic dish.

"Mr. Sandoval," George said. "We need to have a conversation." Though Maury didn't want to talk, he could think of no way to politely refuse. He set the bag down at his feet. Ruthie, having emptied her dish, attacked the bag but could not tear it open. "Can we go inside?"

The kitchenette was too cramped for guests. There was no table, just a single green vinyl chair against the wall, next to an empty spice rack. Maury insisted that George take the seat. "You want some . . ." In vain Maury rifled through his space-saving refrigerator for an alternative to instant coffee. " . . . coffee?"

"Mr. Sandoval," George said, "I knew your wife. We all admired her. All of us at the mission."

Maury nearly dropped the little pot of water before placing it on the stove. He turned the burner on, then turned to face George. "So you're not a woman, and there's no women's club."

"I beg your pardon?"

"Who is *we?*"

"My staff and I," George said. "And our parishioners, of course. Retirees without pensions, mainly. Shepherds, miners, hired help."

"Catholics?"

"Very much so."

"And you?"

George looked him in the eye. "Flexible."

The water began to boil. Maury poured it into a mug, dissolving the deep-brown crystals. "What exactly do you want from me?"

George removed a pair of reading glasses from the breast pocket of his clean white shirt and put them on. They made him look like an ordinary clerk. He unlatched the briefcase and removed a document. "Your signature," he said. "Read this carefully. Take your time."

It was an endowment of several thousand dollars described as "a gift from the Sandoval family." Maury recognized his wife's timid signature at the bottom of the page; the line reserved for his own was blank. Her name written in her own hand made him see her face clearly in his mind.

"This endowment only recently came to light," said George. "Somehow it was misplaced by our attorney's office."

"You've got your own lawyer?"

"Mr. Kruger is a member," George said. "He offers us his expertise for a pittance."

"Do you really think I'm going to sign this?" said Maury. Impassively George sipped his coffee. "Yesterday you came to the Trading Post to see me, am I right? But you didn't want to deliver your pitch in front of Felipe. When he left, you decided to feel me out and come back today for the hard sell."

"We needed supplies."

"Why don't I believe you?"

George shrugged. "You're a skeptical man."

"And you," said Maury, "are a clever one. How do you keep your mission afloat? You fleece your flock?"

"The mission survives by the grace of God," George said. "Financial solvency is a secondary matter."

Maury grunted. "You mean, a secular matter."

"Mr. Sandoval, I take my calling seriously." George drew a deep breath. He placed the mug on the spice rack and his palms on the briefcase. "Let me be direct with you. You're a businessman. Think of this endowment as payment for services rendered."

"You've done me no service."

George pulled something else from the briefcase. An enlarged color photograph, a posed group portrait of everyone at the mission: George, his staff, and especially his parishioners, who could be recognized by their haggard, elderly, smiling faces. Near the center of the group stood Ruth, gaunt and sickly, yet beaming as if she had just won a medal.

"Strictly speaking, the mission is not a nursing home," George said. "Still, we have to be practical. We provide a wide variety of services to the indigent. Many of our members are alone in the world. No family. No support, financial or otherwise. Our resources have to come from somewhere. Ruth understood that. She wanted to help. Specifically, she wanted *you* to help. To honor her memory. Notice anything odd about the picture?" Maury didn't know what to say. "Your wife looks happy, doesn't she? In her condition, a minor miracle. You can't put a price on that."

"But you have put a price on it."

"Ruth Sandoval was a beautiful soul," George said. "We intend to use this endowment for a beautiful purpose."

"Attorney fees," Maury muttered.

George looked at him with a neutral expression on his youthful face. He folded his glasses and inserted them into his shirt pocket. "Good-bye, Mr. Sandoval." He got up to leave. "Think it over. And keep the picture. I have the negative."

As soon as George had gone, Maury felt like a patient who had just heard a diagnosis he didn't understand but had failed to question. He followed the man outside. The air felt as warm as freshly baked bread. George stood by his pickup truck with his arms folded, looking at the desert, looking at the sky.

"A magnificent landscape," he said. "As a native of the area, it must seem commonplace to you, but I'm from Tennessee originally. Last week I took my first trip to Torpedo Creek. It's so nearby, I should have made the effort long ago. The petroglyphs are remarkable, a singular connection to the past. Is that kind of thing important to you?"

"Yes." In fact Maury had never asked himself the question.

"I'm part Cherokee," George said. "On my mother's side."

"You look German."

George grinned. "That's my father's heritage. Merchants and missionaries for three hundred years. Supposedly one of my ancestors met the czar."

George opened the driver's-side door of his truck.

"She never told me," Maury said. "You were her secret."

"Let me show you the mission sometime. Ruth would have wanted that." Maury hesitated. "Don't worry, Mr. Sandoval, no one will try to convert you."

"I'll think about it."

"Our practice is for men to address one another as 'brother,'" George said. "May I call you that?"

"I'm not a member."

"That, Mr. Sandoval, is irrelevant." George climbed into the truck but left the door open. "One of these days you'll have to tell me about your background. My guess is that a successful man like you has conquistador blood in his veins."

George scanned the terrain. As the sun went down, tufts of flora across the road began to lose their color. "Look where you are." He raised his hand as if revealing the entire world to Maury. "Look where you've placed yourself."

The setting sun blinded Maury, so he used the photograph as a visor. Here was the lifeless soil of his yard, and his mobile home like a tugboat run aground. Squinting, he gazed across the desert in the direction of Torpedo Creek, which had been running languidly for generations, feeding a few drops of water to all the arroyos in the county, keeping everyone barely alive for a time. First the Indians, then the Spaniards, now George's ministry.

"Here I am," Maury said. "So where is that?"

George lowered his arm. "Exile, Mr. Sandoval."

As the sun set, Maury sped westward in his Cadillac. Nerves and intuition were driving him. He ended up twenty miles from home, at Torpedo Creek. Despite a twinge in his lower back, he ambled down the tourist access trail—the same trail he and Ruth had casually strolled along two years before. He arrived at the shady cluster of boulders where the petroglyphs could be found. They were difficult to see, and he hadn't brought a flashlight. Breathing heavily, he moved so close to the cool, rough stone that his breath rebounded and warmed his face. Even then he could barely make out the primitive art. To Maury the drawings resembled neither an alphabet nor images. They were simple streaks of oil, abstractions devised by an alien mind. As ephemeral as heat waves rising from the desert, their meaning eluded him.

The air was chilly in the midst of the boulders. He emerged into the last daylight washing over the meager creek. The row of loose stones that his wife had traversed was still there, bisecting the stream like remnants of a collapsed bridge. He thrust his hand into the water and retrieved one of the smaller stones, cradling it in his palm as if it were an injured animal. He decided to go to the cemetery soon—he hadn't been there in months—and lay the stone on Ruth's grave, an ornament only she would comprehend. Out of the corner of his eye, he glimpsed a large bird alighting in the brush on the opposite bank, then taking quickly to the sky. The winged silhouette glided in the twilight. Maury wanted to believe it was a heron, though it was probably a hawk.

LOOKING FOR EIGHT

Marcela Fuentes

SMALL ENOUGH TO PULL UP *in a plastic milk crate by a rope slung across a tree limb, but you didn't wear those blue-footed pajamas anymore. You insisted on taking the first turn in our makeshift elevator, because I was a girl and the firstborn, unfair in your baby chauvinist eyes. An old rope and a very tall pecan tree, so my reasoning to test my weight on it seemed appropriate; I was heavier. But I wanted to make you happy.*

I can still see your face peeking down at me, as I hoisted you higher and higher into the air, watching me, not smiling but serious, afraid but determined that yours would be the first glory.

You almost made the tree. I could see the leaves on the small offshoots from the limb start to touch your head, hesitantly, as though they couldn't decide whether or not to claim you. And then the rope snapped, and it didn't matter whether or not the leaves wanted you. Even now, I can't remember seeing your descent, whether you screamed or even changed expression. You must have been looking at me, perhaps that's why I refuse to recall. That's where my memory stops, the sound stops, the bright day ends there and only begins again after you are fallen.

I saw you beneath the pecan tree, between two roots like giant, veined wings sprouting from your shoulders. The ground hard-packed,

From *Indiana Review*.

pale dirt and you were wearing your gray Batman T-shirt, which I realized in that moment almost matched the color of our grassless yard. Your eyes were open, staring straight up through the branches, past the leaves that left speckled shadows across your face.

A star-like wound, a little red mouth, blood flowing from your forehead. You weren't crying.

I knew then, when you bled serenely into the dusty earth, that you could die. That at any instant, my brother could be taken from me forever. And so I began my guardianship in earnest.

Lorenzo was calling from a payphone again, probably at a gas station. Alma could hear wind scraping against the receiver when he said hello.

"Hey," she said. "You still in Tampa?"

"I'm in San Antonio."

"When did you get here?"

"'Bout twenty minutes. How do I get to your house?"

Alma gave him directions, then went out to the porch to wait. She'd forgotten to replace the light and didn't want Lorenzo to miss the house number in the dark. He had called her from Cheyenne a few weeks ago about a rodeo in Tampa.

Lorenzo pulled up in a dented Chevy S-10 with Wyoming plates. Dry, white mud was spattered across the bumper. It wasn't his, or at least, it was not the truck he had driven away in eight months ago.

Alma stood up as Lorenzo crossed the broken sidewalk. He was much browner than the last time she had seen him. Thinner too. "Where'd you get the truck?"

"Borrowed it. Mine's in the shop." Lorenzo hugged her, his cotton T-shirt warm and smelling of sunflower seeds. She gestured toward a patio chair, but he shook his head.

"No, I can't stay—I'm going to Del Rio." He stuffed his hands in his pockets. "Super Bull's this Saturday. If I place in the top three I might qualify for the San Antonio Stock Show and Rodeo."

She knew there were a few rodeos in south Texas scheduled in the next two weeks. Mostly smalltime stuff, like the one in Del Rio,

MARCELA FUENTES

but riders who hadn't had much luck might be inclined to improve their scores for the pro circuit. She guessed Lorenzo wasn't having much luck.

"Come see me ride?" he asked.

She looked up at Lorenzo. A thin scratch ran high across his left cheek, somewhere between fresh and healed. And there, just at the hairline above his left eye, a faint mark, visible only because she knew it was there. She thought of a rider she had seen at the rodeo two years before. She had seen a rank bull deliberately shift the rider forward and throw its head back, into the rider's face. The rider had crumpled like a scrap of paper in a fist, and slipped off, flapping limply against the bull while it dragged him through the dirt because his hand was caught in the rope. Bullfighters had to corner the animal in order to pry the rider's fingers loose. Every bone in the man's face had been broken.

"I wasn't planning on going home this weekend," she said.

"It's only two hours away. You could drive down Saturday morning."

"Does Mom know you're coming?"

Lorenzo shrugged. "I've got a place to stay. I just wanted to know if you'd be there."

When I drive up to the house, I can see your makeshift bull at the far end of the field beside the barn, lonesome as an overturned tricycle. From a distance, I can tell that the springs are sagging and the barrel hangs off balance, close to the ground. Weeds sprout around the posts and the barrel has grown rust spots. But I'm the only one who gets close enough to look. Mom never goes into the field, and this year Dad planted his alfalfa at the other end, opposite the barn.

It's a ghost in the background of every visit, the undertone of conversation; when I go home, they want news. Mom prods and prods, jealous because you don't call her, and if I haven't heard from you, lectures me about going out too much—I might be missing your calls. I end up repeating what you said last time, and she worries every word like a terrier, looking for significance. I don't tell her that you mostly call when I'm at work, that all you leave on my answering machine are the names of cities. She doesn't ask when Dad's around, but I'm sure she gives her own reports after I'm gone. He hasn't said your name since you left, but he hasn't taken apart your practice bull either.

He wouldn't help you build it, so I did, though I wasn't very good at holding up the posts while you packed in the dirt. After we finished, you spray painted AINT SKEERT *in red across one end of the barrel, and teased me into trying it out. Keep your arm slack, you said, tying my fist in the bull rope, or you'll lose your balance. But when you started shaking the springs my legs weren't enough to hold that lurching barrel and I couldn't keep my arm from freezing. I fell off every time.*

Sometimes at night, after they fall asleep, I go out and sit on the barrel. It's so low that my feet almost touch the ground, and if I rub my finger across AINT SKEERT *the paint flakes off. If I bounce on it, the broken springs creak and flounder. This old barrel is tame. It can't buck anymore, it can't spin and it won't chase me if I fall. It's held up by car springs and wood. It's a toy, like a trampoline, not a study guide.*

You ain't scared. But I am.

"I cried a lot when I was pregnant with Lorenzo." Alma had only been home an hour, and already her mother, Genevieve, had started her monologue of theories about her son. She had somehow managed to work herself into the idea that Alma had enough objectivity not to mind.

Combing her hair before the bathroom vanity, Genevieve was short enough so that Alma could stand behind her, watching, and see both their faces. Alma's mother was much smaller and lighter skinned; Alma felt like a large brown moth hovering over her.

The brush made slow, quiet strokes. Genevieve flipped her hair back and the ends grazed Alma's face. Genevieve's face, light as cream, trembled on the edge of remembered pain: her eyes shiny and round, full of tears, her mouth gathered tight.

"Your Dad was already getting really bad. You know he left me twice before Lorenzo was even born? Twice in nine months. I don't know why I kept letting him come back, I was so stupid."

She made the brushstrokes shorter and harder, dragging the bristles against her scalp, as though to punish herself. "Things like that can affect the baby. I think that's why Lorenzo is very insecure. Every once in a while, he needs to touch and know you're there."

Alma tried to catch her mother's eyes in the mirror. "Are you going to watch him ride tomorrow?"

"No." Genevieve set the brush on the counter. "Your father would have a fit. You go, *mi'ja*, you like rodeos." She began sorting through her jewelry box for earrings.

"That's why I came home this weekend."

Genevieve hugged her, so small that Alma could rest her cheek on Genevieve's head. "God gave me a girl first because he knew I needed you."

Pigtailed and in red corduroy, I stood beside her bed watching her cry. Just after Christmas, I remember, because I kept finding strands of gold tinsel in the carpet. I held some, my hands on the comforter, hoping to show her how beautiful it was, and draw her away from wherever she was. Her eyes were open, itchy-red and puffed, but ignoring me. So I looked at her stomach, where her shirt had pulled away from the waistband. This is how I first saw you. Screened by a light blue blouse and the elastic waist of a pair of warmers, a lump in the middle of her, smooth and round and alive beneath the bland anonymity of her skin. I touched you, my hand small and brown against the pale swell of her belly, and you felt like an eyeball beneath a closed lid.

"That's your brother," she said, "and it's your job to take care of him because I don't know who else is going to do it." Her eyes were angry and I dropped my hand.

Little tadpole, silent, eyeless, breathing liquid in a world as dark as the inside of a closed mouth. How was it there, feeling the rising tide of an unnamed anger, the tremors of your weeping universe, listening to sobbing while you slept and waited out your months of cell division? Tears slipped into your umbilical cord, shedding into the pocket of your belly-to-be so that they grew with you and when you were born, stayed.

You must have heard them when I did not. Did he hurt you when he hurt her? He must have. The memory of rage before you were born. Is that what drives you to look for violence, to let it skin your lips back over your teeth?

Lorenzo could sit in a group of men and fit into the pattern of caps and knuckles and heavy boots. His voice was the last heard, his figure blended easily into the backdrop of maleness, and when he laughed, his face would close over, a generic reproduction of a laughing man. It was easy to look past him and not notice.

Still, Alma immediately picked Lorenzo out among the other smallish, whip-thin cowboys climbing and hopping from the chutes or sitting on the rails around the arena. He stood balanced on the railing of the pens, one hand gripping the big red pipe of the gate hinge, watching the bulls.

The crowd murmured restlessly, unhappy because the bull in the first chute lay down when the rider straddled him. Rodeo bullfighters in oversized Levi's cutoffs and suspenders tumbled into the arena, jostling each other. One, setting up a dummy in the middle of the ring, began bantering with the announcer. Like the rest of the bullfighters, he wore high-dollar athletic shoes.

The attendants got the animal up finally, by poking it in the eye with a salt stick. The bull lunged at the chute gate, thudding hard. Its rider settled himself and gave a curt nod. The gate swung open.

It amazed Alma how a stubby-legged creature weighing about as much as a small car could move like a cat and leap four feet in the air. This one had a brindle hide and small, round-tipped horns. The rider pitched back and forth, limbs flailing like a cloth marionette. Two seconds. The bull spun in a tight circle then broke hard to the left, swinging the rider sideways, pulling him off balance. Five seconds. It leaped again to the left, twisting its body so that its hindquarters shot left, forequarters pointed right. The rider slapped into the arena railing. Six seconds. Two bullfighters pulled him up and half-walked, half-dragged him from the arena.

"C'mon y'all and give this cowboy his due," the announcer chided them. The audience clapped respectfully.

The bull trotted around the arena, thrilling the crowd by goring the dummy and grinding it into the dirt before being chased back to the pens.

Two and a half hours after the riding began, only seven riders out of twenty-five had completed all three of their rides. Lorenzo had made eight each go-round and taken second place. Alma waited in the bleachers long after it was over, and he finally appeared near the pens. She knew he was hurting when he opened the gate and shuffled through rather than vaulting over it. Crossing the arena, he was a tiny scrap of a boy, his chaps stirring up dust around his boots. Alma stood up as he reached her side of the railings and began climbing them slowly.

"You are one dirty hombre. Ready to go?"

"Yeah." A stripe of clean brown skin lay over the ridge of his eyebrows when he took his hat off.

"I saw that bull step on you when you jumped off."

He grinned. "Stomped me right in the ass."

"You okay?" asked Alma as they left the fair grounds.

"My right cheek is still numb."

They had come in his truck, but Lorenzo asked her to drive back. He fiddled with the tuner as they pulled onto the street and found a scratchy AM station playing Patsy Cline.

"I qualified for PBR," he said quietly. The radio light made a curious shadow pattern across his face. "You gonna come?"

Alma didn't want to answer, but he kept looking at her. "Yeah. I'll be there."

In the darkness of the cab, she peeked at him. There was a clot of dirt clinging to the hair above his ear. "Aren't you ever scared?"

"I guess." He settled himself against the seat.

"I get scared," said Alma, "I don't know how you do it."

"You have to be quick and you have to pray," he said simply.

"You're telling me you're up on that thing praying? That's what you're doing the whole time?"

"Hell, yes. What else would I be doing?"

There's a photograph I have of you and me; I must be in first grade; Mother bought me those wide-leg, plaid pants that year, and you are one or so; you are wearing square, white infant shoes that make your feet look like tiny hooves. I'm feeding you something and your face is mashed into my palm, your arms stiffly away from your sides. Was it candy? I can't remember, but anytime I gave you something edible you never used your fingers. You would press your face into my palm and when you bent I could see light-brown baby curls kicking up at the base of your head. Your mouth sometimes plucked at my skin, but mostly I would feel your chin, small and hard as a pebble, digging in—not enough to hurt, but enough for you to hang on. You would teeter, elbows crooked like baby bird wings, back and forth between your feet and my hand. And I would hold as still as I could, balancing you in the center of my palm. You never reached out to steady yourself, safe in the perfect truth that as long as I was holding you, you would never fall.

Freeman Coliseum smelled like sausage wraps and beer. Alma had bought a good seat, fifth row, close enough for her to smell arena dust. She twisted uncomfortably; already the arena was hot and loud with overhead music and the rumblings of the crowd. The announcer kept teasing the audience, and when the lights went out, there was a massive roar in the darkness.

"All right, San Antone, y'all ready t'see some bull ridin'?"

Blue and white spotlights swirled over the arena as the announcer made the introductions. There were forty cowboys, all about the same size and shape, hidden under hats and fringed leather chaps. Alma waited through a dozen or so before the announcer got to him.

"From Del Rio, Texas, number sixteen . . . *Lorenzo Ybarra!*"

MARCELA FUENTES

The spotlight caught him. Lorenzo looked short and anonymous, like a gunslinger with his black chaps strapped low around his hips. He lifted his hat at the crowd, blinking against the hard light. People around her cheered. The white competitor flag taped to his safety vest fluttering as he trotted across the arena.

When the lights came on again, Alma sat back in her seat and shut her eyes. The announcer called out the first go-round. It wasn't Lorenzo, and neither was the next. By the time the fourth rider had gone, it was a game to see how long she could keep her eyes closed. Alma counted the riders, counted the seconds. Two and five, then three. His name was not called. A swift thrashing in the chute, cowboys hollering. Seven and four. And still nothing. The dust thickened in her nostrils. An eight. She heard spectators screaming, the announcer chipper as an auctioneer, "Folks, we got a score on the board! Eighty-nine and a half points for number twenty-two, Blake Kelly! Eighty-nine and a half on Jim Jam!" And beneath everything, the low whine of the eight-second buzzer.

"Number sixteen, Lorenzo Ybarra, ridin' Gas Hog from the Bad Company stockyards."

Alma opened her eyes. They were strapping him in. Two rows down, a man could not find number sixteen's stats and the woman next to him pointed them out on the program. Lorenzo bobbled, trying to get settled, one hand knuckled on the top bar of the chute.

She saw the brim of his hat dip once, and the gate swung wide. A pale yellow bull surged into the arena, flinging Lorenzo along its back like a banner in the wind. Alma let out her breath when he made it through the first hard spin. He clung there, his chaps flapping away from his knees like fringed wings. The force of the bull's landing wrenched him forward. The bull made three short hops, gathering momentum, and snapped him around. Lorenzo let it, riding out each leap and spin like a fishing bobber in a fast eddy. He lost his hat, and Alma saw his face under the harsh lights, clamped down upon itself, eyes nothing but black slashes, his silver mouthguard flashing every time his head jerked. She began to know how many prayers could fit inside the sound of the buzzer. She stood up slowly, watching the jolting line of his shoulders and finding there a violent rhythm.

"C'mon, Lorenzo! Come on!" she screamed, fists drawn tightly against her sides, "Stay on! Don't you fall! Damn you, don't you dare fall!"

Beneath the announcer's balcony, the clock hit six and half seconds. And still Lorenzo hung on, loose as a rag, balancing on the palm of his hand.

DEAD MAN'S NAIL

Dennis Fulgoni

AUGUST, THE SUN LIKE A WHIP. You fill the Hefty bag with hose water. The poor man's Jacuzzi. Filling a Hefty bag with hose water is not an easy thing. You grip one end and water fills the bag. The more it fills, the harder it is to keep the bag upright. An act requiring great skill and dexterity, you tell yourself.

You're waiting for your best friend, Pablo Perez, to call. His father's recently put in a pool, and you're hoping for an invite. It's already past noon, and no call, so the poor man's Jacuzzi becomes your sanctuary, your oasis, on a hot afternoon.

The best way to get inside the poor man's Jacuzzi, once the bag is filled, is to stick one leg in while holding the bag simultaneously, and then, and this is the hard part, to swiftly stick your other leg in without too much water spilling out. Cars drive by, people stick their heads out their windows, watch the pathetic kid sitting in the trash bag, laugh. You think these people are retards and assholes, and that makes you feel better.

You have a dead man's nail. A few months ago, the nail on your index finger fell off after you'd smashed it with a hammer in shop class. The class was building birdhouses. You were excited, because you and Pablo shoot birds with slingshots. During the final parts of construction, you got cocky and pounded the nail too hard. But

From *Colorado Review*.

you missed the intended nail and hit your fingernail instead. Blood pooled on the worktable. The teacher, a man named Jones, yelled: "Goddamn it! Get that hand under the faucet!" Someone's always yelling at you: your parents, your teachers, your neighbors. You thought you saw bone under the stream of water. You found out later it was just the nail, which hung on the finger by a sinew of flesh. Mr. Jones wrapped the finger in gauze, sent you to the nurse, who said, "You're going to lose this nail. Don't worry, a new one will grow back. That's the wonderful thing about the human body, its resilience." But a new one never did grow back. Instead, something that looked like hamburger meat grew back. Your mother took you to Kaiser Permanente on Edgemont, and the doctor said, "The nail plate's damaged. We'll have to graft a new nail on there for you." And they did. But little did you know then that the nail plate would come from a cadaver in the morgue. Apparently, lots of people who lose their nail plates end up with a dead man's nail. The guy sitting next to you at the Burger King might be part corpse and you'd never know it.

The nail still hasn't taken, not completely. Things are tenuous. You sit in the Hefty bag and stare at the nail. It looks pretty much the same as your other nails, only shorter. It forms a half moon next to your skin. It has a nice sheen. You imagine the coroner polishing your nail plate in a little dish. You imagine him being persnickety about the nail, peering at it under a magnifying glass. *Ah, what a pretty dead man's nail,* this coroner thinks. Of course you're proud of the nail. It's your distinguishing feature. You show it to people in line at the market, teachers, and kids at school. The boys think it's cool and the girls think it's gross. You're glad you're a boy.

You hear the distant ringing of the kitchen phone. You play this game with yourself where you try to guess who's calling by the sound of the ring. You've gotten pretty good at it, although you can never really hear a distinction in the rings. When your mother opens the kitchen window and yells, "Pablo's on the phone!" you're not surprised. You dump out the water from the poor man's Jacuzzi. Ants scatter in the grass. You love the way they look so helpless, drowning, you in control. If you could, you'd drown bigger things. Not dogs or cats—you're not a psychopath—but maybe squirrels or opossum. You wad up the Hefty bag and walk inside, dragging it behind you. Your mom leaves the receiver lying on the kitchen counter. The TV is on in the next room, playing one of her soap operas. You hate those things. The lighting is always strange, and you get this weird sensation watching them like you have a fever. "Pablo," you say.

"Get your ass over here," Pablo says.

"What's up?" You try to sound nonchalant, as if you haven't been waiting all afternoon for his call.

"Eric Manheart is going to jump off the roof!" Eric Manheart is Pablo's sister's boyfriend.

You think about this for a moment but don't say anything.

"Some of my sister's friends from Eagle Rock High are over," Pablo says. "Everyone's gonna watch." Eagle Rock High is the school Pablo's sister, Delores, attends. You're due to attend there in two years, as is Pablo. The idea is exciting and scary. You try to imagine the kinds of friends you know Delores has—long-haired stoners with skinny rock star bodies—sitting around the pool watching Eric Manheart jump off the roof. Eric is a stoner and a surfer too. You were a stoner once for about fifteen minutes, but the smoke felt like somebody scraping the inside of your lungs with a scalpel, and being high was like the lighting in your mother's soap operas, so you quit.

Eric has long brown hair and wears a gold chain with a naked woman pendant around his neck. His torso is thinner than your father's thigh. He seems like a brave guy, someone you could see jumping off the roof into Pablo's swimming pool. You've heard stories of him telling off teachers and beating up his own father. When you think of beating up your own father, the thought seems fantastical. But you believe every word of it. If Eric says he's going to jump off the roof, you have every reason to believe that he's telling the truth.

"Be right over," you say.

Your mother walks into the kitchen drinking a club soda. "What the hell are you doing with that bag?" She burps into her hand.

"Goddamn it, look what you did to the floor!" There is a thick line of water on the living room floor. "Sorry," you say, grabbing a towel from the pantry, and walk out the front door.

Pablo has a funny thing about towels. You always have to bring your own. He's afraid he'll get your germs. But bringing your own towel is a small price to pay for spending the afternoon at Pablo's. There's the pool to swim in, there's Eric's daredevil feat, and there's Delores. Delores is so beautiful you can barely form words when you speak to her. She has almond eyes, thick lashes, dark skin, and the most luscious ass you've ever seen. She favors a yellow bathing suit with the word *Smokin'* on the butt. You nudge Pablo whenever she walks by, but he only rolls his eyes and says, "Slut." Nothing seems slutty about Delores to you. After all, she's only dated Eric, at least to your knowledge. She treats you with either indifference or disdain. Still, you've made it a mission to date her before you die.

You walk down the street, the concrete hot under your feet. You hop from foot to foot, and then decide to walk the front lawns up the block to Pablo's house. Your neighborhood is officially known as Sagamore Park, but everyone just says Eagle Rock. Eagle Rock is named for a big rock off the side of the freeway that's supposed to look like an eagle but actually looks like an enormous brown egg. The rock gives people in the community an unwarranted sense of pride, like they belong to something bigger than themselves. People drive around with "I Love Eagle Rock!" bumper stickers on their cars. Even though you criticize this behavior in the residents of Eagle Rock, you go to Eagle Rock High School football games wearing an Eagles T-shirt and singing along with Queen: "*We will, we will rock you!*"

The houses in Eagle Rock were built in the twenties, and no two look the same. You ate dinner once at your friend Doug Hiurra's house in the neighboring city of Glendale, and every fourth house there was identical. Doug tells you it's cool because when he visits his friends in the neighborhood he always knows exactly where to find the bathroom.

Pablo's house is the most unique of all. His father is a photographer for magazines like *Time* and *National Geographic*. He once took an impromptu photograph of you with a Dodgers baseball cap sitting sideways on your head. The photo won first prize in the local paper, the *Eagle Rock Sentinel*. Pablo's father took you to McDonald's to celebrate. Pablo's mother is a traveling nurse. She's assigned to various hospitals throughout the state which need her to fill empty slots. Sometimes she's gone for months at a time. Your father works at Eagle Rock Lumber. Your mother is a stay-at-home and does nothing.

Pablo's parents are never home. Their house is a giant playground for Pablo and Delores. You hardly ever hear adult voices when you visit. It's like being in a *Peanuts* cartoon. The Perezes paint their house a different color every few years. Now it's black as your father's coffee. You've never seen a black house before. Your mother calls it tacky, but you think it looks haunted. You once tried to convince your parents to paint your house the same color. "Why not," your father sneered. "We can sell the Toyota and get a hearse, too." You've decided your parents are jealous, unhappy people with very little imagination.

As you approach Pablo's house, you hear voices in the backyard. Pablo's father has constructed a huge redwood fence around the pool, so all you can see from the street is the top of the slide and occasionally water shooting up when somebody cannonballs. You walk up to the gate and look inside. It's hard to get a good look through the slats. You hear Delores's voice: "Pablo, get off that fucking thing!" But you can't see Pablo and can only guess he's taken Delores's inflatable raft again and is trying to surf on it. You can smell the chlorine, and want to be inside that water really badly. "Hey, Pablo, it's me!" you shout. When you don't get an answer, you start to slap at the fence with the palm of your hand. Then you see Pablo's fat belly as he comes towards the fence to let you in.

"You're just in time," he says. Pablo has buck teeth and fat, puffy cheeks. He often has a bewildered expression on his face. He pulls the gate open and you walk inside, stepping over a crushed Budweiser can. You look closely at the can and see that it's been turned into a bong. A small dent has been made at the top, and tiny holes have been poked into the aluminum.

A red-haired guy is standing in the shallow end of the pool. His hair is long, wet, and slicked back. You don't recognize him, but you figure he's probably one of Eric or Delores's friends. He moves around the shallow end of the pool slowly, resting his palms on the surface of the water, like the pictures of Jesus you've seen in the Bible study books at Verdugo Chapel, where your mother makes you go to Sunday school. The red-haired guy moves around the pool, and when he turns to face you, you lift your hand in a wave, but he ignores you and you wish you wouldn't have done that. You look around for Delores, hoping she hasn't seen you being snubbed, but she isn't anywhere around. Pablo puts his face close to you, as he has a bad habit of doing. You smell peanut butter on his breath. Pablo's breath usually smells like salami or chocolate or tuna. "Eric's in the kitchen, having a few beers for preparation. He's gonna jump for sure. I'm getting my seat ready on the patio." On the patio, four deck chairs are lined up in a row, concert style.

You look at the roof. Pablo has a two-story, Spanish-style house. The tiles up there have always looked a little unsteady to you. In fact, you can see a couple hanging over the edge. You wonder how somebody could actually get a running start on those tiles. The horizontal distance between the roof and the pool is about seven feet, and the roof looks about thirty feet high. If Eric misses, he's going to die. You know that for sure. If he makes it into the deep end of the pool, he may still die. You know the pool is only nine feet deep—you dive down to the bottom all the time to collect the colored pool rings—and you've hit your feet on the bottom of that pool several times when jumping off the diving board, which is only about two feet over the water. Of course you'd bounced and jumped but still you couldn't have gotten higher than eight feet maximum. You imagine Eric flying off the roof and landing on his head, his skull cracking open, brains oozing out on the concrete. You imagine Delores crying and you consoling her, taking her in your arms and telling her, "It's okay, it's okay," the way you've seen men do in the movies when comforting their lovers.

Pablo grabs your hand and looks at the dead man's nail. "That is so bitching," he says. "Hey, check it out, Ted!" he calls to the red-haired guy. "This guy's got a fucking corpse fingernail and shit."

Ted looks at you with a puzzled expression. "Come here, little man," he says. You notice now that he's got freckles all over his face, neck, and shoulders. You walk over to the edge of the pool, holding your hand out stupidly like an old woman asking for help getting out of a car. You put it in front of his face. His eyes, which are bloodshot, widen. "What the fuck is that?" he says, looking at your nail.

"I told you," Pablo says. "It's a dead man's nail. He got that off a corpse in the morgue."

Ted's thin pink lips spread into a grin. "Fucking A," he says, seeming to need no more explanation about how you got a corpse's nail on your finger.

You try to explain, even though it's not necessary. You ramble on about birdhouses and Mr. Jones, and the school nurse and the doctor, but Ted has already gone back to pacing in the shallow end of the pool and you want to kick yourself for being such a blabbering idiot.

Pablo cannonballs into the pool. When Pablo cannonballs it's a serious matter. Cool water sprays across the backyard, showering the lemon tree on the patio. Water lands on your arm. It's crisp and cool and makes you think of the first moment you'll jump in the pool. "Pablo!" Delores calls from an upstairs window, her bedroom window. "Get your fat ass out of the pool! I told you no more splashing!"

"Fuck off!" Pablo says, gurgling water.

"Watch your fucking mouth," Delores says, and shuts the window.

You decide to go for a quick swim before the big event.

Pablo's pool is clean. A pool man comes twice a month, checks the chemicals, and puts in chlorine and acid. The water is clear blue, transparent. You take a swimming mask from the side of the pool, slip it over your face, and slide into the pool. Underwater, everything is peaceful. You can see everything clearly. You see Ted's naked legs. You see the thin, red hair dancing in the water like the tentacles of a jellyfish. You see the bottom of the pool, tiny particles of dirt resting on the smooth, curved floor. You swim around, holding your breath. Your old record is one and a half minutes. You swim towards the deep end, where you see a quarter resting near the drain. You dive down, arms outstretched, as if you are bending to pick up a baby. The further down you get, the more your ears hurt, the water pressure coming down on you like a ton of weight. You grab the quarter and make your way back up to the surface. When you emerge, you reconsider Eric's prospects for jumping off the roof. True, it's only nine feet deep on this end of the pool, but it's a long nine feet. You tilt your head to one side and pound on your ear, then tilt your head to the other side and repeat. Water trickles out of your ear, worm-like and slithering. You take off the mask and stare up at the roof again. It seems so high from here, as if you were looking at the top of a skyscraper. You've always been afraid of heights. Pablo comes out of the back door laughing, his fat body like a giant burnt marshmallow. He's stuffing his face again, this time a hardboiled egg. He takes a bite, stares at you in the pool, and says, "Just about time."

You have to pee. You could pee in the pool, but you know Pablo's father has put in a chemical that will turn your pee a different color, so that everybody knows what a pig you are. You dry off and walk inside. The house is cool and dark. The bathroom is on the bottom floor, near the den. Pablo's father's photographs hang in the den: cacti, rock formations, portraits of old wrinkled men and women in the desert. You look for your own photograph, the one of you in the Dodger cap that won first prize. It used to hang in this room, but in its place is a picture of a fat woman doing the limbo. You feel a little hurt, but then again, maybe Pablo's father has put the picture somewhere else in the house. After you visit the bathroom, you go into the kitchen to get a snack. You find Eric Manheart leaning against the kitchen counter, drinking a beer. He's shirtless, but he's wearing Van's tennis shoes, although the laces are untied. His hair hangs long past his shoulders, and his red swim trunks rest just below his hips. You see a thin line of hair running from the bottom of his belly button and disappearing into his shorts. Pablo has told you this is called a whoopee line. There's something disgusting and intriguing about it. You can't take your eyes off it. Eric Manheart is guzzling his beer and doesn't notice you standing at the entrance to the kitchen. You walk over and open the refrigerator. Inside are all kinds of good things to eat: Jell-O, lunch meat, cheese, Coke. Your own refrigerator is stocked with vegetables and Arm & Hammer baking soda. You wish you lived at the Perez house.

You decide on a piece of cheese. As you bite into it, you look at Eric again. But he's looking out the kitchen window. You look at the curve of his neck and see for the first time how his neck looks like a girl's neck: long, slender, and gracefully curved. His entire body looks like that. Everything seems to bend in a curved formation, like the bottom of Pablo's pool. You stuff the rest of the cheese into your mouth and lick your fingers.

"Gonna jump off the roof," Eric says.

You look up, but Eric is still looking out the kitchen window.

"Gonna jump off the roof," he says again, and then glancing over at you, he takes a long swig of his beer and crushes the empty can in his hand. The sound of folding aluminum rings in the kitchen.

"When?" you ask.

"Couple minutes," he says. He doesn't sound scared, more confused. He seems like a man about to be sentenced to death for something he hasn't done.

"I've got a dead man's nail," you say.

Eric looks out the window again, crosses his arms.

You're hoping he wants to see it, but he doesn't seem the least bit interested. You look at your nail. From the pool water, your index finger is all wrinkled, like a raisin.

"Delores dared me," Eric says. It hasn't occurred to you that this is a dare. You'd just thought that a guy like Eric Manheart was always proving himself, not to the world, but to himself. The thought that Delores has dared Eric to jump off the roof makes the whole thing more exciting somehow. You wonder what you'd do if she asked you to do the same thing.

Eric stands up straight, then scratches his forehead. You try to see if he is shaking, but he looks perfectly calm. He throws his beer can in the sink. It clinks around like a hubcap come loose from a car. Eric walks across the kitchen in an old-maidish sort of way. You catch a whiff of marijuana about him.

You should go outside now. You should get a seat in one of the lawn chairs, pop open a cold Coke, and watch Eric fall to his death. But you don't do this. Instead, you follow Eric through the den, the living room, and the back hallway. Wooden stairs lead up to the second story. Again, the walls along the staircase are lined with photographs. You look in vain for your photo. But it's just more rock formations and desert landscapes. Eric walks in front of you, slowly, each step a laborious undertaking, or so it looks. You try to walk quietly, so that he doesn't hear you, but the steps are creaking under your feet. When Eric gets to the last two steps, he leaps up them. You try to do the same, but slip on the second-to-last-step and fall face-first onto the carpet in the hallway. The carpet burns your cheek like a slap. Eric doesn't even notice. He's already at Delores's bedroom doorway.

"Hey, Baby," Delores's voice sings. From the floor, you watch her come out of the bedroom and give Eric a big kiss on the mouth. She's wearing the yellow bathing suit. Her dark brown breasts push out against the top of her suit like eight-balls. She hugs Eric around the waist, then looks over his shoulder at you lying on the floor. You feel blood rush to your face. "What the hell are you doing?" she asks you. You do a push-up, rise to your feet. "Looking for Pablo," you say.

"Pablo's in the pool," Delores says. She looks you up and down like you're some stray animal that had died under her refrigerator.

"Oh," you say.

Delores turns to Eric, takes his face in her beautiful, dark hands. Her slim fingers are like ripples of muddy water, caressing his face. "You ready, baby?" she says, as if they were going to the movies.

"Yeah," Eric says.

"Okay, I'm going downstairs," Delores says. "I'll be cheering for you. You can do it," she says.

She walks by you, that great ass shaking, the *Smokin'* insignia bobbing back and forth as she heads down the stairs. You stare at the back of her thighs and wonder if you should follow her or not. But something makes you stay. Eric walks past you and into the master bedroom, where Pablo's parents sleep. He opens the door and walks inside. You follow. The room smells like cinnamon. The master bedroom leads to the balcony. You know this because you and Pablo sometimes throw lemons at cars from the balcony. Eric opens the balcony door and walks out. In order to get on the roof, he has to do a pull-up, grabbing hold of the Spanish tiles. He does this without hesitation. You walk over to the edge of the balcony. Near the wall is a cardboard box. You open it and see all kinds of trash: old newspapers, magazines, and crumpled-up photographs Pablo's father has obviously intended to throw away. You pick through a few and find your picture. You stare at your face, the Dodgers cap, the gap between your front teeth. The picture is covered with dust. You tear it up and drop the pieces off the balcony. You watch them flutter to the ground like feathers. Then you do a pull-up and follow Eric onto the roof.

Once you're on the roof, you see that Eric is walking slowly from tile to tile. You can see everything from the rooftop: all the houses, the streetlights, even the Golden Jug liquor store down the block. The wind feels stronger up here. You see clouds moving across the sky at an incredible speed like herds of animals—buffalo, deer, lions. You see your house. The roof is pale green, like a giant dollar bill. You imagine your mother watching her soap operas, and you feel depressed, imagining her looking at the handsome tall men—nothing like your father—in their business suits and styled hair. You imagine your mother drinking her club soda, burping into the empty den.

Eric is standing at the edge of the roof now. He's looking over the edge. He doesn't look afraid. To your surprise, he sits down on the edge of the roof. His legs are dangling off the side. You hear an occasional tiny voice calling to him from the backyard: "Come on, Eric, what are you waiting for?" Eric picks up a stray chip of tile, cocks his arm back, and tosses it off the side of the roof. Not in a hostile way—he's obviously not trying to hit anybody—more like he's just throwing rocks, sheepishly, into a lake he's sitting by. You listen for a splash from the pool, but none comes.

You shift your weight, and when you do, a tile cracks under your foot. It's a sharp, quick sound, like the breaking of a bone. Eric turns around and sees you standing behind him. He doesn't seem surprised. He moves the hair from his face and runs some strands behind his ear. "They want me to jump," he says.

"I know," you say, crossing your arms. "Are you going to?" It occurs to you for the first time that you want him to say no, to chicken out. You want him to be small in the eyes of the people watching from the patio, especially Delores.

"What's it feel like having a dead man's nail?"

You look at your nail in the bright sunlight. For some reason, the angle of the sun, maybe, it looks pink now. You're surprised that Eric is asking you this, as you hadn't thought he'd been listening in the kitchen. "Doesn't feel like anything," you say, and you realize that this is the truth. It feels just the same as it did when you had your own nail. Sure, the tip, where the nail is yet to grow in, is a little tender, but other than that it feels exactly the same.

"Come on, Eric, we don't have all day, honey!" Delores calls.

You could jump yourself right now and make Eric look like a total pussy in front of everyone. But you haven't even glanced over the edge yet. And you know if you do, you won't do it.

"We read in biology class about transplants," Eric says. "People getting livers, kidneys, hearts, even eyeballs from the dead."

You've heard of these transplants too. But you'd never heard of a person getting a corpse's nail, which makes your transplant seem special.

"This one guy, he got a corpse's ear. His crazy bitch of a wife cut his old one off. So he gets this guy's ear, and he swears he can hear things he'd never heard before."

This sounds ludicrous. You know that the ear is really the same thing as a cupped hand. It's just there to catch the sound waves. But still, the idea is interesting, and you lean in a little as he finishes the story.

"He started hearing God talking to him. The guy who'd donated his ear to science was a minister or some shit. And now this guy said he could hear God telling him things like: *Judge not, lest you be judged; Covet not ye neighbor's wife.* All this shit. Can you imagine?"

You wonder if maybe the guy who donated his nail to you was a famous electric guitarist.

"When I die," Eric says, "I won't donate anything. I don't want my consciousness and shit walking around in some fucking asshole's body. No offense."

Eric stands up. "I'm not going to do it," he says, brushing off his butt with the back of his hand. He wobbles for a second, nearly teetering, and you consider the possibility of pushing him off the roof. You could do it. You could get away with it. Nobody would ever figure it out. But you don't do anything but stand there and stare at him.

"I'm going down and drink another beer," Eric says. "I don't need this shit."

You hear Pablo call, "Oh, man, what a chickenshit!" And then everything is silent down there.

Eric walks across the roof casually, as if he's walking out of a room where the conversation is not to his liking. You watch him go the length of the roof, his head bent forward, as he steps from Spanish tile to Spanish tile. Eventually he gets to the other side of the roof, sits down on the edge, and lowers himself back onto the balcony.

Now that he's gone, the roof seems larger and more frightening. It's like the sensation you get when you go into the ocean by yourself. It seems as if unlimited possibilities of peril have opened up now that you're alone on the roof. You look around the neighborhood again, and this time you see something you hadn't before: a man is standing on the roof about four houses down. You calculate this to be the house of Mr. Basin. You watch him pacing back and forth on the roof. He bends over, picks something off the roof, like a man pulling weeds, and tosses it aside. He stands by the air vent on the top of the roof, and knocks twice on the aluminum surface. But you can't hear the knocking, only see it, and you're reminded of being under the water with the mask on, no sound, but everything perfectly clear. The top of the roof is like this. It makes everything perfectly clear and crisp, like looking through freshly washed windows. Suddenly, Mr. Basin lifts one leg in the air and holds his hands out at his side, like the Karate Kid. You laugh. Of course he thinks no one can see him. He balances like this for a time, then lowers his leg and arms, does a couple of karate chops, and walks back to the ladder that is leaning against the side of the house. You walk over to the edge of the roof, the side looking over into Pablo's backyard. The drop is not as bad as you'd imagined. Eric is down there, talking to everyone. Ted says, "You chickenshit." Delores laughs. It's not a mean laugh, more like a pretty, joking laugh. You'd have thought she'd be upset with Eric. But now you can see it was all a joke, and she doesn't seem upset at all. You can't believe it. You watch Pablo get out of the shallow end of the pool. He dries off with a towel and says, "I would have done it."

Delores laughs harder. "You'd can't even get on the roof, fatso!"

You back away from the edge. The wind has picked up a little, causing you to feel unsteady. You think about how easy it was for Eric to back down. You had expected something else entirely. Had you backed down like that, everyone would have railed you. It pisses you off. You know what you have to do. You hadn't known it until this second, but now it seems perfectly clear. You get set in the starting position, your knees bent and your hands on the hot tiles. You push off, and just like that you're running towards the edge of the roof, determined to leap as far as you can. When you get to the edge, you push off, and the next thing you know you're in the air.

Of course you've heard that when people have a near-death experience, they see their life flash before their eyes. But as you plummet toward the pool, you see your death. You see your lifeless body lying on a stainless-steel table, as men in white coats pull off your nail plates with pliers. They talk to each other. "Hey, this is a good one" or "This boy obviously got his fair share of calcium." Just before you hit the water—head-first, as you've spun around in midair— you yell out Delores's name, which comes out sounding like *Tortes*. As you rocket down through the water, it rushes up your nostrils. You push your hand out to avoid hitting your head against the bottom of the pool. Your hands pound against the concrete on the bottom of the pool, but you push up and swim toward the top. When you emerge, you imagine the cheers and the cries from all those people who watched Eric chicken out and you jump. But once you've gotten your bearings, you realize there's no clapping, no cheering, nothing. You wipe your eyes in disbelief, look around 360 degrees, but the entire yard is empty except for Ted. He's sitting in a lawn chair, eyes closed, the crushed Budweiser bong lying on his lap. You swim over to the loveseat and sit for a minute, your heart thrashing in your chest. After a while, you step out of the pool and grab your towel. You look at your swimsuit and see that it's turned pink. It takes a second for the color change to register. You look at the pool and see a cloud of blood near the love seat. You panic, examining your arms and legs, pulling out the waistband of your bathing suit, peering inside to see what the damage is. But then it occurs to you that there is no damage. You've simply urinated, and the agent Pablo's father has put in to trap would be pool pigs will give you away to everyone. You try to think of a way to conceal the red chemical cloud. You decide to jump back inside the pool and splash around.

You're at the edge of the pool, about to jump in, when you hear scattered clapping coming from Ted. He's clapping very slowly and nodding his head. "Fucking beautiful, Man," he says, and then lifts the Budweiser can to his lips, strikes a match on the patio, and starts lighting his bowl. He holds the smoke in for a moment, his throat crackling, then releases the smoke slowly. "You fucking flew off that motherfucker, Man." You feel proud. There was a witness after all, even if he is stoned.

Pablo walks out the back door, holding a Ding Dong in his hand. The swim mask hangs around his neck.

"Hey," you say. "I got to go."

"You just got here."

"My mom said to be back by four." You have no idea what time it is, but it feels like days have gone by.

Pablo stuffs the entire Ding Dong in his mouth. Then he looks at the pool and nearly chokes. "Hey, you fucking pissed in the pool!" he screams, pointing to the blood red cloud.

"I did not."

Delores walks outside. The yellow bathing suit is skimpy around her crotch, and you see two or three stray pubic hairs. You stare for a moment, trying not to, until she notices, and narrows her eyes at you. "Take a picture," she says.

"This guy peed in the pool, look!" Pablo shouts. He points again to the red cloud, laughing.

"I jumped off the fucking roof!" you yell, although the declaration sounds like a lie, under the circumstances.

"Sure you did," Pablo says.

You look at Ted in the lawn chair. His eyes are closed again, his body slumped over. It looks as if he's passed out. "He saw it," you say.

Pablo says, "Whatever, bed-wetter."

You grab your towel and are determined to leave and never come back. But as you're reaching for your towel, you notice something funny about your hand. You do a double-take. You realize the dead man's nail is gone.

"Hand me the mask," you tell Pablo. You take the mask from around Pablo's neck. You secure it over your face, and then dive down into the pool. Your hand stings once it hits the water, but you don't care. You dive down to the bottom, through the cloud of red, until you come to the drain. You search around for a while, bits and pieces of small rock, but no nail. Then, just as you're about to swim back to the top for air, you see it, floating like a tiny fish right in front of your face. You swipe at it, but miss, and the nail floats around your face. You swipe at it again, clutch it in your hand, and swim back up through the red cloud until you reach the surface. When you emerge, Eric is outside too, and Delores is sitting on his lap, brushing the hair from his eyes, her tan legs crossed. You step out of the pool, holding your dead man's nail.

"Look, honey," she tells Eric. "It's the pool pisser." Then she turns and gives Eric a big kiss, all tongue.

You grab your towel again and head for the gate. You walk outside into the neighborhood. The concrete has cooled down considerably, and you should be able to walk all the way home without using the lawns. But you don't walk. You run. When you get within twenty feet or so of your house, you look down at the dead man's nail in your hand. It looks so tiny, so insignificant, but you hold onto it anyway.

FOOD STAMP

Anna Green

NANETTE RIOS LEADS HER THREE KIDS down the frozen food aisle of Thriftee's, their arms locked together like a chain of plastic Barrel Monkeys. I pretend not to see her, but I know she sees me. In Nowhere, Arizona, everybody sees everyone. Welfare moms see Mormon moms. Whiteys see Mexicans. Skinny people see fatsos. Can't ignore a damn soul around here.

Nanette and I haven't talked since the day she swiped a ten-dollar food stamp from me almost two months ago, not that I'm counting. My dad sometimes steals from me. Nothing burns me up more than thieves. Especially a grown employed man taking food stamps from his daughter and grandkid. The other day, I caught him fishing them out of my purse with a look in his eye like he just won the welfare lottery. Worst of it, I know he's not using them for food. He cashes them around town to get smokes and booze. It's easy. Just go into a store, buy a twenty-five-cent gum, then you got real money in change.

I get $260 a month. Only money I have to get groceries for Katrina. She has a disability. Not like a retard. She eats a lot. Barely ten, but she weighs 123 pounds. Child obesity, the doctors say. I've tried to put her on a zillion diets. Nothing works. Of course, the kids at school are mean to her. One time, I nearly ran over a

From *Alligator Juniper.*

boy with my Regal for yelling, "Fatty Katty, Fatty Katty." I would have done it too if Katrina hadn't tugged on the steering wheel with a chocolate-stained hand.

Today in Thriftee's, I walk down the aisle searching for some frozen meals. I toss a few macaroni dinners in my cart, then glance over at Nanette, who now has put some of her kids in a basket. Her oldest, Cleo, waves at my girl Katrina, who waves back and rips open the box of Fudgesicles from my basket.

This whole situation makes me sad. But what can I do? Until the theft, Nanette had been my best friend. During eighth grade, I moved to town after my dad got on at the copper mines. Nanette was the only person who wanted to hang out with me, the new white kid. She sat by me in Arizona History and we became friends easy as that. She thought I was cool because she heard me say *chupame* to Mr. Oilster, who'd shushed me for sharpening my pencil. Nan and I went through most of school together, got pregnant around the same time, and raised our first daughters together. Now—what a shame—we can't even talk to each other in the store.

I'm not a tight ass, really. When you're a single mom with no job, you keep track of every cent. That's what gets me about Nanette. She knows it's tough to find work in Nowhere. How hard it is to get a man worth a shit. I had put that ten-dollar food stamp in the console of my Regal and even wrote *For Welfare Moms Only* on it to keep my dad away. That bill must have sat there for a month. Then I gave Nanette a ride to the store for burger meat and buns. She snatched it right in front of me. "Call ya later," she said.

I never heard from her again.

Fine way to treat a friend after all the babysitting I've done for her. With three kids, Nanette gets stressed out. I've seen her whomp the daylights out of the little ones, so I used to let them come over and stay with me and Katrina, just to give Nanette a night off. Like a big slumber party. Katrina loves the kids. She and Cleo end up doing most of the work. They feed the babies macaroni and Popsicles, change the bed when they pee, and sing that annoying Barney song: *I love you, you love me. We're best friends like friends should be . . .*

ANNA GREEN

Katrina knows more than I give her credit. She said to me the other day, "Mama, why don't you ask for the monies back? I miss Cleo and you miss Nanette." I softened. Nanette and Cleo are two people out of the whole town who are nice to Katrina. They love her just the way she is. The thought almost made me want to pick up the phone. But then I remembered seeing Nanette out at the bar with her other friends, *cholas* from high school. She had money to go drinking at the Cactus Club, but she couldn't slap me ten bucks. I watched her pay for her drinks with a twenty-dollar bill. She waved it around like it was an American flag. After that, I went to piss, and when I got back to my table, there was a Bud Light waiting for me. I asked the waitress who sent it, but she said it was from "a friend." Feeble ass-kissing if you ask me.

When I catch my dad stealing, it's different. He lets me and Katrina live at his apartment in a skanky part of town called Little Hollywood. Four years ago, he lost his job with Phelps-Dodge because of his drinking, and now he can barely keep odd jobs around town. He screws our downstairs neighbor Marla, a nasty lady with jacked-up teeth. She's white trash if I ever saw it, six kids to boot. But she gives him whatever he wants. Last time I caught him stealing, I said, "Dad, why don't you get some stamps from your woman if you're so hard up?"

"She won't talk to me," he said. "And she *ain't* my woman."

I never saw one block of cheese or a gallon of milk that week. Of course, there're plenty of times like that. Too many to count.

Katrina said not long ago, "Mama, you got to tell hims not to eat all our food. I get so hungry."

"Baby," I said. "We have to live here. If I started a big fight and he kicked us out, where would we go?"

"Nanette's," she said.

Oh sure, I thought. From one thief to another.

We stroll down another aisle. I grab twenty bags of ramen noodles. Katrina twirls around, holding her naked Fudgesicle stick above her head like a magic wand. "Zap," she says. "I'm skinny. Zap, Mama, you're rich."

"Zap," I say. "Nanette's gonzo."

Down aisle 6, I bump into Deirdre Johnson, a nice Mormon girl who teaches my GED class. In her cart sit two blonde toddlers with perfectly trimmed bangs and chubby apple cheeks. Deirdre's a talker, so she tells me first thing about her research at the genealogical center. She finally found some records for her great-great-great-great-grandfather on her mother's side. Zedediah somebody or other. She's so excited about it that I feel a bit sorry for her. Doesn't she have anything more important to do than look up a bunch of dead relatives who—if alive—would knock on her door and ask to borrow some money? Then I think about the time in high school that Nanette and I spraypainted a pentagram on that genealogical building, just to scare the Mormon kids around town for fun. Deirdre's sweet smile makes me feel a little guilty.

I'm about to interrupt Deirdre to ask her if she could help me pick classes for community college next semester when I see Nanette come towards us. She parks her kids next to the soups, and then squishes her butt between our carts so she can grab a can. "Excuse *moi*," she says.

I keep my focus on Deirdre while she's talking away, and out of the corner of my eye, I swear I see Nanette put her hand near my purse that's dangling by my hip. I can't give her the satisfaction that I notice her, so I don't move a muscle. But the more I think about it, the more it bugs me. Finally, I'm rattled enough that I throw my bag on top of the groceries and push my cart away from Deirdre, who at the last second asks me to church like always. I scoot around the corner to look for Nanette, but she's gone. Katrina's the only one in the aisle, and she's busy playing with the prayer candles and the metatés on the middle shelf.

"Where'd she go?" I ask.

"Who?" says Katrina.

"You know."

"Why do you care if you aren't friends no more?"

"It's complicated, sister. I can't explain it right now."

"Seems easy to me. Just say you're sorry."

Sorry? Sorry that *she* stole from *me*? And tried to do it again before my very eyes? If Nanette did try to stick her hand in my purse, then she wants a confrontation, but Katrina's right, why do I care? I'm not going to give it to her. Besides, I've seen Nanette fight, and let me tell you, she is mean.

One night we were at the Cactus Club, and a woman who Nanette's ex-husband once cheated with was *cumbia*-ing on the dance floor. Nanette and I sat at a table by the DJ booth, sipping beers, smoking an occasional cigarette. We were playing the betting game, which we do sometimes when we're bored. We bet change or food stamps on dares we may or may not go through with. I had said, "Bet you ten bucks you won't go up to that biyatch and knock her lights out." Nanette tied her hair back, headed towards the dance floor like a marine, plowing bodies out of the way. She yanked that lady by her nappy hair and wham, bam, beat the blue Jesus right out of her. We got kicked out of the club, but it was worth it. Later, Nanette said she didn't remember it clearly. That sometimes she blocks things from her mind. Maybe that's what happened with the food stamp. She stole it. Removed it from her memory entirely.

The other week my dad heard me grumbling about Nanette. He said, "That's what you two get for hanging around Mexicans. I'm glad you're not speaking. Now those little beanheads won't stay here anymore, stickying up the place with those dirty hands. Man, Mexican kids are the drooliest little bastards on the planet."

I nearly threw one of Katrina's naked Barbies at his head. I wanted to scream that he was a sorry-ass hypocrite since he never did any cleaning and was pretty disgusting himself. Of course, I can't talk to him that way now, but once I get my GED and eventually snag a job at one of the prisons, I won't have to speak to him unless I want to.

I don't have people to talk to since Nanette stole from me. Sometimes I miss hearing her say, "What up, *pendeja?*" No one else swears at me in Spanish. I try to get Katrina to say some bad words like *puta* just to make me laugh, but she refuses. She knows what they mean. She's getting big—not just fat, but grown up. She's at that age where she doesn't want to be around me as much. She's embarrassed we use food stamps. Last month when we were at the Conoco, she got a sudden hunger. I pulled out a stamp to give her for a candy and she dove in the back seat. Well, more of a roll-plop. The car bounced up and down like a boat skipping waves.

I can't blame her for hiding. People stare at Katrina everywhere we go.

Now Katrina follows me down aisle 8 of Thriftee's, the cereal rack. All I can think about is Nanette, wonder how she could have done this to our friendship. Maybe she wants me to pick a fight with her.

A couple of middle school girls with matching Bulldog T-shirts stop at the end of the aisle and point at Katrina.

Ba-boom, Bertha, boom-boom, one sings.

I glare first, thinking that might scare them off, but they all chime in. Without a thought in my head, I aim my cart and run as fast as I can, even though the basket is close to full. I push it hard, Katrina wobbling behind me yelling, "Mama, get back here, damn it."

Those girls look dumbfounded. I am point two seconds away from ramming into them before they scatter. Once they're out of the way, I can't stop the momentum of the ride and fly smack into the cart of my dad's girlfriend Marla.

She jumps back from her basket, ass first into the packaged chorizo. "Shitfire," she says. "What's your problem?"

"Uh . . . racing. Me and the kid."

Katrina comes huffing behind me. "Sheesh, mama, you gotta quit trying to run peoples over."

Marla eyes me suspicious-like. "Your dad send you to kick my ass?" She hops out of the freezer, wiping the ice shavings off her back. "I told him I was filing a complaint with the cops. You got issues with me, girlie, let's take it outside."

"I don't want to fight you, Marla," I say, even though I can imagine the pleasure I'd get from knocking out those blackened teeth. "What happened with my dad?"

"Son of a bitch owes me two hundred dollars is what. Now I don't have nothing to feed my kids. Do you have one of them new EBT food cards yet?"

"No, we still have stamps."

"Perfect. I'll take whatever you got."

"Marla, we have to eat too."

She looks Katrina up and down. "Ya'll don't look bad off to me."

I reach into my pocket, pull out my wad. "I can't give you more than twenty."

"Give me forty and I'll drop the complaint against your dad. He's doing jail time if it goes my way."

Katrina's eyes almost pop out of her head when she hears that. "I don't want Grampa to go to jail. Give it to hers, Mama."

After I hand her the forty in a crumpled ball, she rolls her basket away without a word.

I make Katrina put back some of the milks, cheeses, the open box of Fudgesicles, and a couple other items. She whines but does as she's told.

We get in line. Put our food on the belt. The cashier is Mandy Peterson, who in high school used to be Ms. Thang. Cheerleader. Ding-dong.

Soon as I pull out the food stamps, Katrina bolts out the door.

The total comes out to be $235.62.

I have only $220.

I pretend for a moment everything is cool. Flip through my bills. Maybe Mandy is still as stupid as she was in school. I hand her the goods.

"This is not enough," she says.

I reach into my pockets. "I had $260 in there, you sure?"

I can tell the line behind me is growing, but I don't turn around.

"You want to put some things back? Are you Lucy from class of '88? I remember you, pregnant our senior year. Was that your girl who ran out?"

I'm about ready to scrap the whole thing and hit the door just like Katrina. Go to Safeway and start all over when I hear a voice say, "Look in your purse, *pendeja*." Nanette, two carts behind me, smiles. I open the front pocket and find twenty bucks of real money; the top bill has *For Welfare Mothers Only* written on it.

After I pay, I wait for Nanette in front of the store.

She hauls her stuff outside, kids hanging off the cart. "Couldn't stand for that Mandy to make you look bad." She plugs her nose and repeats, "Are you Lucy from class of '88?"

The kids pop off the basket and run to hug Katrina. They jump all over her. Cleo on her back, the little ones on her front, she carries them through the parking lot.

"Thanks for the save," I say. "But where you been? No call."

"My phone hasn't been ringing either." She raises one of her penciled-on eyebrows.

"Nan, you took money from me, then disappeared. I don't like that."

"You squelched on our bet. I don't like *that*."

"What? From the bar that night?"

"I fought that lady on our bet, 'member? Or did you conveniently forget?"

I can tell by the way she has her boobs stuck out that she is in preflight pose. "Are you starting shit with me, Nan?"

"Yeah. I mean, I just paid you back big time and you're out here giving me attitude."

"That bet was a joke. You knew that."

She steps closer. "I don't joke when it comes to money, girl— even with you."

"Well, you don't scare me," I say. "So you can quit with the Mexican standoff."

In a second Nanette rushes me the way she had nabbed that lady in the bar. I kick her in the ankle to push her off balance, but she grabs me by the hair and yanks my head to the ground fast. She pins my face on the hot black concrete. All I can see at that moment is Katrina in the parking lot spinning the kids around. I think how sideways Katrina doesn't look that fat. She could pass for hefty or even tubby.

"If our babies weren't here," Nanette says, "I would have already pounded your white ass, so listen to me. We been friends a long time. I don't want stupid shit like this to come between us. When you get up, we cool."

She releases my hair. A bag boy with a tattoo of a cross on his neck runs over. "You all right, ma'am? Need five-o?"

"No cops." I pick myself off the ground, pull a flattened cigarette butt out of my hair.

Katrina and the kids surround me. "Mama, you okay? Did you fall?"

"Sort of."

"Clumsy girl," Nanette says coolly. She licks her thumb and wipes some tar off my forehead.

I remember the time Nanette wanted to fight me in high school because she found out I was going with Fernando Duran, the guy she had wanted since eighth grade. She had stayed pissed for a month and yelled SLUT at me whenever we passed in the hallways. But the day after Fernando dumped me for another girl, and the whole school was buzzing with the news, she was at my locker with a note that said, "Let's due lunch."

Some part of me wants to grab Nanette by her highlighted hair and slap her for being such a good and bad friend.

"Katrina, see if Cleo and the little ones want to spend the night with us."

She gawks at me for a moment. "Is it okay with Nanette?"

"For real," Nanette says. "I need a night to watch my *telenovelas* in peace or else I'm going to get CPS called on me for child-shaking."

Katrina jumps half a foot off the ground. "Yippees!"

I lead the kids to the car, where Katrina takes over by buckling up babies and helping with groceries. Soon after, Nanette speeds out of the parking lot in her faded Taurus. The screech of her wheels against the pavement sounds like *Seeeeya*.

On the drive home to Little Hollywood, the girls sing the Barney song, but with silly words. *I love crackers, you love cheese . . . we're best snacks like snacks should be . . .* They act so excited, they can't stop squealing between verses. I try not to laugh, but give in after they rhyme *mommy* with *salami*. As we get closer to our street, the girls settle down, so I make one last stop at the Circle K. I have enough change to buy the squirts some Nerds and Sweet Tart candies, just in time for when my dad gets off work.

GUADALUPE AND THE TAXMAN

Donald Lucio Hurd

THOUGH GUADALUPE LOPEZ had brought more than a hundred children into the world, she had never had any of her own. She had been married once, when she was in her early twenties, but her husband died or ran off with another woman, depending on what story she felt like telling.

As a girl she had been wild, running through the streets of Espantosa like a *gallina sin cabeza*. She was famous for eating dirt and making pets of unusual creatures (possums, frogs, even a polecat). After the death of her father, her mother never left the house except at night when she would wander through the streets wailing like la Llorona.

When Guadalupe's mother died, it was several weeks before the body was discovered. Neighbors noticed a foul smell and investigated. What they saw when they kicked down the door took their breath away. There was decaying food everywhere, and piles of feces in the corners of every room. When they opened the door to the bedroom, they got another shock. The body was on the bed and badly decomposed. Piled around the bed were hundreds of pairs of men's shoes.

The missing shoes had long been a mystery in Espantosa. Nearly every man in town had lost several pairs, and until then no one had been able to explain their disappearance.

From *Southwestern American Literature*.

"Those are my workboots," said Hector Mendoza, Melchor's grandfather. "Jesus."

They found Guadalupe huddled in a closet, clutching a ragged doll. She was filthy and looked up at them like a feral animal.

Guadalupe was taken in by her Great-Aunt Hortencia, who tamed the girl and, it was rumored, taught her the ways of the *curandera*. Though she would never learn to read or write, Guadalupe would come to have an encyclopedic knowledge of local horticulture. She assisted her aunt in delivering babies and eventually took over the job completely.

It was Hortencia who first taught Guadalupe the secret of transforming her heart so that it beat like a rabbit's or fluttered in her chest like that of a hummingbird. In time, she learned what it was to soar in the sky like a hawk or burrow in the blind, dark earth like a worm. Through Hortencia, Guadalupe discovered the animal within her.

It was during this time that the legend of *la Lechuza* was born. People claimed to have seen an enormous owl flying over the darkened waters of the Espantosa on moonless nights. Some said its wings spanned more than six feet and that anyone who heard its call would suffer some misfortune.

When her great-aunt died, Guadalupe moved back into her mother's house. Though her wild days were behind her, she continued to inspire all kinds of stories, and was almost as popular a bedtime threat as Sammy the Smiling Goat *Chupacabra*. Most of the townspeople treated Guadalupe with a mixture of fear and respect.

Without a doubt Guadalupe's most famous deed was the time she put the evil eye on Howard Meeks, the county tax assessor.

Meeks had only been on the job for a week when he learned that Guadalupe's house was in arrears and had been so for a ridiculously long time.

"You mean no one has collected taxes on that house in eighteen years?" Meeks asked his assistant, Henry Arispe.

"It's not that easy," Henry explained. "The owner is a crazy woman named Guadalupe Lopez. People say she's a *curandera*. A witch." Meeks rolled his eyes. Henry continued. "Getting her outta that house is no easy matter."

"Serve her with papers," said Meeks.

"Been done."

"Listen," said Meeks, growing impatient, "that house belongs to the county. Have the constable evict her and put a lock on it."

"Also been done."

"And?"

"She just breaks the lock and goes back inside."

"Christ!"

"The problem is, it's our house. The county's, I mean. But it's not like we can actually do anything with it. It would never sell."

"Why not?"

Henry lit a cigarette as Meeks frowned. It was one of Henry's habits, like extended lunches, that Meeks meant to change, and soon.

"You been there yet?" Henry asked, blowing smoke in the general direction of his boss. "Well, *when* you go there, you'll see."

The next day Meeks went to Espantosa. He pulled up at Bill French's gas station in his car with the Tax Assessor insignia on the door panel. French took one look at the logo and began to sweat.

"I'm looking for Cerralvo Street," he told French.

Like most people in Espantosa, Bill French was behind in his taxes, so he was understandably relieved when he discovered the assessor was not coming to see *him*. On the other hand, he couldn't help feeling sorry for the poor son of a bitch who was in trouble.

"Cevallo Street?" said French scratching his chin.

"Cerralvo," Meeks corrected him.

"Never heard of it."

Meeks looked at him over the top of his glasses. "What? You can't tell me in a town this size . . ."

"Hell, boss, half the streets around here got no signs. You might have a name on a map . . ."

"But how do you get around, then?"

French laughed softly, sizing up his customer quickly and dismissing him as a college-educated idiot. "Well, let's see," he drawled. "I guess we get around 'cause we lived here all our lives."

Meeks sighed. "I'm looking for a woman named Guadalupe Lopez. Her house."

"Why didn't you say so in the first place?" French proceeded to give the assessor directions while Meeks listened patiently. "And don't forget," he added as Meeks climbed back into his car, "if you pass the water tower, you've gone too far."

"The water tower," Meeks nodded.

As soon as the tax assessor pulled away, Meeks went inside and phoned Dottie Price. Guadalupe didn't have a phone, but Dottie lived just down the street.

"Dottie," he said, "there's a tax assessor in town." Dottie gasped and almost dropped the phone. "Now settle down. He's after Guadalupe. You better send someone over there to warn her. I sent him on a wild goose chase. With any luck he's already lost."

Meeks *was* lost. He had been driving for a quarter of an hour and had not even managed to find the water tower, which would have at least given him a point of reference. Driving slowly down the road in his Crown Victoria, he spotted a teenage boy and pulled over. He motioned the boy to his car.

"You know where Guadalupe Lopez lives?" he asked.

"Qué?" said the boy, leaning in the car window and enjoying the blast of cool air.

"Do you speak English?"

"Sí," said the boy, grinning.

"Can you tell me where the water tower is?"

"Qué?"

"Damn it," said Meeks. He rolled up his window and pulled away.

"Dumbass," said the boy. At that moment his mother poked her head out of the screen door and asked who was in that big shiny car.

"Just some *pendejo*. He's looking for the water tower," the boy grinned.

"We don't have a water tower," said the boy's mother.

"Like I said, he's a *pendejo*."

Meeks drove around Espantosa for the better part of an hour. He would never have imagined it would be so hard to find one house in such a small town. The problem was that Espantosa was spread out over a fairly large area, with long expanses of unused land between clusters of houses. Also, the map he had was hopelessly out of date. Streets that were indicated on the map no longer existed, and streets that did exist were not on the map.

In desperation, he pulled next to a ramshackle row of houses and asked a barefooted ten-year-old girl who was playing marbles with bottle caps in her sandy front yard if she knew where he could find Guadalupe Lopez. The girl looked up at him and pointed to the house next door.

The tax assessor looked over at the house and gasped. He knew now what Henry meant. The house was in terrible condition, with missing shingles on the roof and a lopsided porch that looked like it might topple in the slightest breeze. One window was covered with plywood and holes in the siding had been patched with two-by-fours.

"This is not a house," Meeks muttered, "it's an accident waiting to happen."

He walked up the gravel path and nearly turned his ankle on a pothole the size of a dinner plate. He stepped gingerly onto the porch, feeling the wood sag beneath his weight. He knocked on the front door.

There was no answer. He knocked again. Then he tried the doorknob, but it was locked. He reached into his briefcase and took out some tools and began to work the lock. Unlike the rest of the house, the lock proved surprisingly sound. Finally, he put a large screwdriver against the doorjamb and began to chip away at it. Then the door opened.

"What the hell are you doing?" The woman in the doorway was an imposing figure. She was tall and heavy, with beefy forearms that would have been the envy of any sailor. Her hair was a wild tangle of black-and-gray curls. She had an enormous mole on the left side of her face from which sprouted three long, black hairs. "This is my house!" she shouted.

Meeks, a tall, slight man, recoiled involuntarily. Collecting himself he stammered, "No, no, this house belongs to the county."

"The hell you say! Get out of here, you *cabrón* pig, before I break your scrawny neck."

"Madam . . ."

"What's that?" Guadalupe moved forward menacingly. "What did you call me? You think I'm a whore?"

"Uh, Miss, you cannot threaten a county official. I have the authority . . ."

"You don't have shit. Now get off my porch before I get my shotgun."

Meeks, who had been cowering unawares, straightened up and squared his puny shoulders. "All right, but I'll be back."

"You better bring an army with you, you son of a bitch!"

Meeks collected his tools and turned to leave. He was surprised to see the entire scene had been played out before an audience of Guadalupe's neighbors and other interested parties. Even Bill French was there, leaning on the front of his pickup. He'd closed the shop just for the occasion. The spectators applauded and cheered as the tax assessor walked back to his big, shiny Crown Victoria with the county insignia on the door panel.

When he got back to the office, Henry was sitting in front of a file cabinet smoking a cigarette and dropping ash onto the records.

"Put that cigarette out!" Meeks bellowed.

Henry complied, dropping his cigarette into a Coke can. "How'd it go?"

"That house," said Meeks through clenched teeth, "belongs to the county."

"Sure," Henry said agreeably. And as he watched his boss walk into his office and slam the door, he added under his breath, "But what are we gonna do with it?"

The next day Meeks woke up with a hacking cough. He went to work, but by noon it was clear he was in no condition to be there.

"Get on the phone to the constable and have him serve papers on that woman," he told Henry between coughs.

"Sure," said Henry, "but I told you, it's been done."

"We're gonna do it again." Meeks wiped his mouth with a handkerchief. He looked down at it and gasped. It was black.

Meeks did not go to work the next day, or the day after. He spent most of his time in bed, sweating and shivering and coughing out his lungs. On the third day of his illness he woke up in the middle of the night and was shaken by a coughing fit so intense he almost passed out. By this time, he felt like he had swallowed a box of needles every time he took a breath. The next morning he slowly and painfully dressed and drove himself down to the doctor's office.

The doctor, a young kid just out of medical school, examined Meeks carefully. He asked his patient to breathe deeply as he listened to his chest, but this prompted a coughing fit so intense the doctor feared he might lose him on the spot. When the fit finally subsided, Meeks wiped his mouth with a Kleenex and showed it to the physician. It was stained with a dark, sticky mucus.

"Give me a minute," said the young medico. "Try to relax."

A few minutes later, the doctor returned. Meeks looked up at him weakly. "Mr. Meeks, have you ever worked in or around a coal mine?" he asked.

"What . . . the . . . hell?" Meeks whispered hoarsely.

"Well, the thing is, as near as I can figure, and I'm no expert on this condition . . ."

Meeks waved his hand limply. "Just . . . give it . . . to me . . . straight."

"All right. Near as I can figure, you're suffering from all the symptoms of black lung disease. Only thing is, I can't figure how you ever contracted it in the middle of South Texas."

When word got around Espantosa what had happened to the tax assessor, people shook their heads and muttered, not without sympathy, "She's put a hex on that poor bastard." Their sympathy did not, however, prevent many locals from starting a pool betting on just when the assessor would kick the bucket.

When Henry learned of his boss's condition, he told his wife, "That old witch has put a hex on the dumb bastard."

His wife, Tina, who was standing at the sink snapping the ends off a colander of Kentucky wonder beans, said over her shoulder, "Well, you told that *pendejo* shithead not to go around bothering that woman. He should have listened to you." Tina harbored the conviction, not unfounded, that her husband was worth ten of his boss. When the position came open, she had insisted Henry interview for it, though he protested it was a waste of time.

"No Mexican is ever gonna be made tax assessor in this county," he explained.

That he had been proved right did little to appease his wife's anger over his lack of ambition.

Now, as he looked at her from behind, admiring her slim shoulders, the beauty of her ass, Henry got up from the table and kissed the back of her neck, whispering soft indecencies into her ear.

Tina leaned back and sighed and he reached around and cupped her breasts.

"Men!" said Tina, tossing a wonder bean at her husband over her shoulder.

A half hour later, as they lay in bed together, Henry lit a cigarette and said to his wife, "Just the same, I better see what I can do to help the poor bastard."

The next morning, Henry drove to Espantosa in his old Chevy pickup, wisely leaving his own county car with the tax assessor insignia on the door panel at the office.

He drove straight to Guadalupe's house and knocked on the door. She answered in her bathrobe, took one look at Henry, and smiled.

"How's your boss these days?" she asked.

"I think you know how he is, ma'am," said Henry. "I doubt he's gonna last long."

"It's his own fault," Guadalupe said.

"I know that. But the thing is, ma'am, he's right. This house belongs to the county."

Guadalupe crossed her arms across her ample bosom and glared. "You better be careful," she said. "What your boss has might be catching."

"Yes, ma'am, I know it," said Henry. "But that don't change the fact that this is not your house. But I have an idea."

"I'm listening."

"Well, if this is the county's house, and it is, then we can do anything we want with it. We can sell it . . ."

"No way, *pendejo.*"

"Or," Henry continued, "we can auction it off."

"You don't look so good," said Guadalupe. "I think maybe you already caught that disease. Maybe you should go home and get into bed."

"Now listen," Henry added hastily. "If we auction off this house, we're bound to accept the highest bid. That's the law." Henry licked his lips. "So here's the deal. I'm ready to auction this house off right now, right here. We'll waive the public notice."

Guadalupe looked at him suspiciously. "Is this some kind of trick?"

"No, ma'am." Henry looked over his shoulder. "And it seems like you might be the only bidder. So, if you care to start the bidding . . ."

"How much?"

"How much do you have on you?" said Henry.

Guadalupe went into the house and came back a moment later with a tin coffee can. She looked inside and hastily counted the bills. "Forty-six dollars," she said.

Henry swallowed hard. He announced to the thin air, "I am bid forty-six dollars. Is there another bid?" The two of them looked up and down the empty street. "Forty-six dollars going once, twice, three times," said Henry loudly. "Sold! For forty-six dollars." He took some forms out his pocket and filled them out, stamped them with the seal, and handed the carbon to Guadalupe. "Congratulations, ma'am. You are the proud owner of this, um, unique fixer-upper."

Guadalupe handed Henry a wad of bills. "Tell your boss I think his condition might improve," she said, smiling grimly. Then she added, "Your boss ain't gonna like this. You tell him, he gives you any trouble he's gonna get the goddamn plague next time."

When Henry got back to his car he looked down at the wad of bills. He counted it. It was twenty-eight dollars.

A few days later, when Meeks's condition disappeared as mysteriously as it had arrived, he returned to work. Henry told him about the auction.

"Who authorized an auction?"

"Well, it was our house," Henry explained.

Meeks, still weak from his ordeal, nodded impatiently. "Okay, okay," he muttered. "How much did we get?"

"Forty-six dollars," said Henry, handing his boss the paperwork.

"*What?*" Meeks shouted, then doubled over with pain. His chest was still on the mend. "How . . ." he gasped, "did . . . we get . . . so little?"

"Well, as you know, real estate values in that area are pretty depressed."

"Yeah . . . but still. How . . . many . . . bidders?"

"Oh, a bunch a folk showed up. But as you know, economic conditions in that area are pretty depressed."

Meeks nodded vaguely and walked unsteadily toward his office. When he was sitting in his chair, he looked down at the paperwork Henry had given him. He read the name of the purchaser and went red in the face.

Henry was not sorry that he had saved his boss's life, even if he got no thanks for it. The only thing that really pissed him off was that it had cost him eighteen dollars out of his own pocket to do it.

Guadalupe's defeat of the taxman cemented her reputation as a *bruja*. Though the people of Espantosa feared her more than ever, they also consulted her in droves.

"Guadalupe, help me with my no-good husband who's cheating on me. Cast a spell on him and make his *ganas* drop off."

Or . . .

"Guadalupe, make my boss get off my back. Cast a spell on him and make his dick shrivel up like a dead snake."

Or . . .

"Guadalupe, I got a ticket for speeding. Cast a spell on that no-good Smokey the Bear and turn his dick into a rattlesnake to bite him on his ass."

Though Guadalupe never succeeded in making anyone's *ganas* disappear, or in turning anyone's penis into a snake, living or dead, she was nevertheless credited with every disaster that befell people in Espantosa. When Fent Hurley's roof was lifted off his house by a twister, people said he must have pissed off Guadalupe. When Benny Cantu developed cancer, everyone attributed it to the fact that he had once shot the finger at Guadalupe. No matter that this event occurred when Benny was still a teenager. "That *bruja*," people said, "has a long memory."

Even now, whenever Guadalupe waddled out of her house, people went out of their way to be polite to her. And they still consulted her, though the old woman was hard of hearing and they had to shout their requests.

"Guadalupe," someone would say at the top of his lungs, "my stinking whore of a wife is sleeping around!"

"Who's coming around?"

"My wife is sleeping around again! That bitch is fucking everything in sight!"

"Ah," Guadalupe would say, nodding her head.

AT THE POWWOW HOTEL

Toni Jensen

WHEN THE CORNFIELD ARRIVED, I was standing in our hotel's kitchen, starting Lester's birthday cake. It was raining outside, foggy, too, for the sixth day in a row, and there was flour all over my blue jeans. I was trying to figure out what the book meant by *sift*. Lester had been outside by the canyon all morning, inspecting bugs or digging holes or looking into the sky. But then he was in the kitchen, looking up at me, saying, Dad, it's here, his hand on the dish towel I'd tied around my waist. Lester had only spoken about ten words since his mother died last month, so I put down the flour and followed.

We live in West Texas on a three-hundred-acre cotton farm at the edge of Blanco Canyon. We own the Blanco Canyon Hotel, all twelve rooms, though everybody in town calls it the Powwow Hotel on account of Lester and me being Indians, Blackfoot, more specifically. My wife Charlene, she was Indian, too, Comanche, from around here. There had never been a powwow out here to any of our knowledge, but that's just how people are in West Texas—what they know about Indians involves the Texas Rangers, powwows, or pictures of Quanah Parker they've seen in bars and restaurants, way in the back by the bathrooms. We were never sure whether to ignore the joke or to capitalize on it, to change our name and market ourselves that way. We talked about it, Charlene and me, laughed over it.

From *Nimrod*.

But there hadn't been much laughing lately, with it being just Lester and me, with Lester not talking and getting picked on at school for it. This kid had said, Hey, Lester, I hear your mom died. I thought all you Indians were extinct already? And then, according to his teacher, most of the other boys in the class laughed. She said the kid who said it was a bully, that the other kids were afraid. But I said when I was in school, fourth grade was when kids started to get mean, that I couldn't imagine things now being too much different.

It was late fall, just before Thanksgiving, and most everybody had their cotton in, except for a few late fools who now were having to wait out the rain. Out here, where we live, it's four miles to the nearest neighbor and nine miles in to Crosbyton, the nearest town. It was a record rain year according to the papers and the blond girls with big smiles on the TV. Lester followed the weather on the Internet, had been writing in his journal about the rain—how we were over five inches for the month, how the conditions might be right.

Lester was supposed to be using the journal to write down how he felt, what with his mother being gone and his not talking much. But mostly he wrote about the weather here in Texas, and north of here, all the way up to Canada. It worried me, this obsession, because the only jobs I knew of where you got paid to think about weather were on the TV, and they involved being smiley and blonde and a girl.

Lester still had a hold of the dish towel, was pulling me toward the western side of the property to the grassy area in between the canyon and the biggest cotton field. He stopped about twenty feet shy of the grass, his face turned up to mine, his eyes the size of silver dollars. At first I thought the grass had gone crazy, what with all the rain. But then, through the thick fog, I saw something waving above my head, something tall and green but not like grass. I stepped forward, kept stepping forward though my heart stuttered and my throat went dry. I kept stepping forward until I was in the middle of it, touching its rough edges, stalks towering over me, next to me, short ones, too, some only knee-high. I was standing in the middle of it, breathing in the new smell—green and raw and still like dirt, somehow—when I felt his hand, on my arm this time.

Dad, Lester said, they're going to be here soon.

And he led me back out of the corn to the hotel, and we started to prepare.

The first carload of Indians arrived two hours after the cornfield. Lester and I had spent the time making beds and sweeping floors, clearing the dust off everything as best we could. November was never a busy tourist month, not like May or June, and we hadn't had any guests since Charlene died, since the rain started turning the caliche road into wet cement. The whole time Lester talked about the cornfield—how it had started showing up in Canada, on the re-serve north of Selkirk last spring, how it had been traveling south ever since, how along the way, Indians had been following.

How come I haven't heard about this? I said.

Lester rolled his eyes, which were still large, almost all dark pupil, and he shook his head at me. His dark brown hair fell into his face, and he pushed it behind his ears, all business. Dad, he said, you only read the Lubbock paper. He snickered. And you watch the local news.

We went into his room then, and looked at his computer for a while, and he showed me the places where people were talking about the corn.

The meteorologists, the scientists, the ones who believe it exists, say it's global warming, Lester said. That it's all the rain bringing it.

I nodded like I understood.

But a lot of scientists say it's just an Indian trick, Lester said.

I nodded again. This I understood. And what are the Indians say-ing? I said.

A car honked out in the lane. We looked out the window, found an old Buick, its tires caked with the cement-like caliche, its side splattered. Five people were pulling themselves from the car, stretch-ing and laughing and moving toward the corn.

Lester was already at the door when he turned to me.

Dad, he said, you can ask them yourself.

The first family, the Jenkins family, were from Alberta, from the Blood Reserve, and they had been following the corn since the beginning. Melvin Sr. knew my uncle Jack, who I was named after, and we shook hands out in the muck of the caliche lane, grinning at each other, then looking down at our feet, then back up at the corn.

It's something, Melvin said. He hitched his pants back up to the middle of his belly and rubbed the top of his head. He wore a buzz cut, ex-military, maybe, and his nose looked like it had been broken at least three times. He was well over six feet, a half foot taller than me, but standing next to him didn't make me feel short. It made me feel like I should stretch a little, should try to be taller.

Yes, I said, it's something.

I wished Charlene was here. She was the one who knew how to talk to people. Lester and me were a little pitiful that way, although today Lester seemed to be doing better than I was. He was over in the corn with Melvin Jr., and even through the rain, the next car pulling up, honking, I could hear them laughing.

After the Jenkins family, the cars came one behind another, and pickup trucks, too, and then the news crews, of course, and the anthropologists. The last anthropologist's old truck bogged down in the caliche half a mile in, and carloads of Indians drove by, honking and waving, leaning out their windows to take pictures, yelling, Don't worry, we'll document it for you. But somebody picked the guy up, eventually. He was here in time for dinner, for the extra place we'd set at the picnic table.

By dinnertime, the rain had finally calmed down to a drizzle. Later it would stop altogether. Almost everybody had brought their own food, and those who hadn't were fed by Lester and me or by someone else who'd brought enough. Some Lakota named Artichoker flipped hotdogs and hamburgers on the grills, which had been set up under the tallest sycamore. The Jenkins family helped pass out paper plates, and a group of middle-aged and old women had taken over the kitchen inside. Someone had finished Lester's cake, and a big group gathered around, singing, and Lester blew out all ten candles in one try, which seemed like good luck.

Our neighbor Tom Miller drove the four miles over from his place and brought an extra picnic table. He worked in town at the school, but he also worked part-time for the *Crosby County News and Chronicle*. He brought along a notebook, but his camera was broken.

Shit, he said. He ran his hand through his gray-blonde hair and stared. I didn't know there were this many Indians.

He was so busy looking at all of us that I wasn't sure the corn-field ever registered, not really. He went around interviewing people, asking just a few questions at a time, mostly where were they from and what did they think of Crosby County, of our fair state?

I was busy running around with a garbage bag, picking up Coke cans and paper plates, when I saw Tom trying to back his truck down the lane through all the chaos. He rolled down his window when I came over.

I suppose your competition will be here soon, I said.

Doubt it, Tom said.

Oh?

I called it in, Tom said, tried to stir up some interest, but the Lubbock editor said he didn't think their readers were much interested in Indians. Indians or corn.

Oh, I said. Well.

Good for business, though, Tom said, gesturing at the crowd.

Yeah, I said, good for business.

He thumped the side of the truck with his hand, gave a little wave, and weaved his way down the lane.

The stars came out thick, with the canyon underneath, and those who were going to be sleeping outside joked they had the better lodging, the room with a view. The twelve rooms inside were taken up by the Jenkins family and the Artichokers, another Lakota family called Blackbonnet, some Anishinaabe named Bairnd, a Pima woman named Smith, a Laguna Pueblo called LaLee, some Navajo named Richardson, a Cherokee family called Jones, two Hualapai newlyweds named Whatonome, a Choctaw named Byrd, and the anthropologist, Becker, who'd called ahead from his broken-down truck and snagged the last room.

On the back porch, a Navajo and an Aguna Pueblo were talking about why the corn had skipped them, had set its course east of their tribes.

We're from corn tribes, right? the Navajo said.

I know, said the Laguna Pueblo, shaking her head. Maybe it'll change course, come our way next.

This was the favorite conversation, of course, predicting where the corn would go next or guessing how long it might stay. According to the Jenkins family, its average stay in one place was only forty-eight hours. Just like the average hotel visitor. Just like the time between Charlene's diagnosis and her death.

Melvin Sr. and I took over the porch after the women from Arizona went inside, and we sat on opposite sides of the porch swing, letting it move a little but not too much, looking out at the people setting up their tents in front of the corn, the canyon. I couldn't see the corn that well, but I could hear people moving through it, the rustling of them against the stalks like candy wrappers being opened, a good sound, full of expectations. There were even some people with bedrolls and sleeping bags who liked to sleep in the cornfield itself, right there with the itchy stalks and that bright green smell.

I'd been thinking about what Melvin had said—only forty-eight hours—thinking about Lester, who was in his room playing with Melvin, Jr. I'd been wondering if there was any way to prepare for it leaving.

Melvin, I said, is there any way to know? To know when it'll be gone?

Nobody ever sees it, he said. People have tried, but it always goes at night, comes to the new place before dawn.

Angela, Melvin's wife, came out of the kitchen, bringing the smells of coffee and baking bread with her.

Those boys are going to want to sleep in the corn, she said. That all right with you?

She was asking me, but she was smiling at Melvin, her arm moving up and down his back. I looked away. Over in the cornfield, flashlights blinked and flickered. The scientists were examining its root system, Melvin had said, trying to figure out how it attached and detached.

Sure, I said, that's fine. I'll go tell them.

When I walked through the kitchen, the women were cleaning up. They got quiet for a moment, the hum dying down, and all I could hear was the whir and hiss of the big coffee pots. The smells of coffee and soup and baking bread were making my mouth and eyes water, even though I was full. It hadn't smelled like that in our house in a long time. Charlene had only been gone a month, but she hadn't been herself, hadn't been cooking for a long time before the doctors said it out loud, cancer, before the last quick days and the long quiet after. I realized I was just standing there staring, that I was making the women nervous, so I passed through, and they started up their talking again, and everything sounded right.

Lester and Melvin Jr. were in Lester's room, studying the computer, their heads together, talking soft.

Lester, I said, it'll be time for bed soon.

He turned around fast, startled, but he still smiled at me. He and Melvin exchanged a look, and Melvin grinned.

Okay, Dad, Lester said. That's fine.

He and Melvin were laughing when I backed out of the doorway, and I had the feeling they were laughing at me, something I'd done or said that I didn't know about, but that was fine with me. Any kind of laughing was fine with me.

The next morning rose bright and clear, and by the time I was up, the women had taken over the kitchen again, or maybe they'd never left. Either way, they were fixing cereal bowls for the boys when I came downstairs, and I carried the bowls out to the cornfield, calling Lester's name as I went. He and Melvin Jr. were lying face-down in between rows of corn, examining the roots with a magnifying glass. When they rose, they looked serious.

What do you think? Lester asked.

I opened my mouth, but then I could see he was talking to Melvin Jr., so I shut it again.

You might be right, Melvin said.

No, Lester said. No, no, no, no, no.

And he was off, running past me and the cereal bowls, the corn fronds opening for him, then closing behind.

I found him in his room, clicking away on the computer, his eyes narrow and tight, his mouth a line there'd be no arguing with.

Hey, I said. I set down his cereal bowl. It's going to get all mushy.

He ignored me like I figured he would, and for the thousandth time, I wished for his mother. Charlene knew how to joke him out of his moods, knew when to back off or step forward. I had retreated to a space halfway between Lester and the door.

Lester, I said. What's—

Go, he said. Just go.

After breakfast was served and the sheets put in the washer, I cornered Melvin Jr., who was bouncing a superball off the side of the house.

They've moved a sixteenth of an inch, Melvin said.

What? I said.

The roots, he said, they're starting to move.

Lester spent the day in his room on the computer, tracking the weather patterns, praying for rain. The sun here was so bright, the paler Indians were applying sunscreen, the blondes in particular. A group of teenagers played hackysack, another tossed around a Frisbee, and a large group of Choctaws started a game of softball that went on past lunchtime and only ended after dinner when the sun started setting, sinking red and orange and yellow into the canyon.

I was on my way into Lester's room with a plate of hotdogs when I saw Angela in the doorway. I stepped around the corner, leaned into the wall, trying to hear, but I couldn't. It wasn't long, though, before the two of them came out, Lester looking less angry, holding a hotdog in one hand, his magnifying glass in the other. And it was then that I heard it: drums starting up low, voices rising alongside the drums.

By the time I weaved through the women in the kitchen and got back outside, the dancing had started. No one was in costume—no spare room in the cars, I guess—but everyone was moving anyway. Old women stepped forward in time with the music, their hands clutched to their chests, though few held fans or shawls, and some had their hands hanging down, keeping the rhythm at their sides. Teenage boys and girls were leaping and falling in blue jeans and T-shirts, the drummers speeding up or slowing down, trying to make the showoffs miss a step.

Melvin nodded to me, and I went over to the edge of the circle, stood next to him.

Say hi to Uncle Jack for me, I said.

Sure, he said. Anything else?

Tell him he missed it, I said. Tell him he missed a hell of a show.

Lester was across the circle from us with Melvin Jr., and beyond them some people were packing up already, anticipating the morning. Angela finished up in the kitchen and made her way over to us. Some teenagers at the edge of the circle were drinking from liters of Mountain Dew, sliding little pills into the sides of their mouths like no one could see if they did it that way.

They're trying to stay up, Angela said. Trying to stay up to catch it moving.

I leaned forward and turned my head a little, listening for the corn, but there were only the sounds of the drums and the laughing and the feet pounding. I leaned forward further, squinting, but it was too dark, and I couldn't make out where our yard stopped and the cornfield began. I could still smell it, though, even if it was a smaller smell now, less green, less bright.

What did you say? I asked Angela. What did you tell Lester?

She sighed and looked out over the crowd. I told him this is it, she said. I told him he could wait in his room all he wanted, but that his mother wouldn't want him to miss this. So much has been taken, but I told him to look—to look at what we have.

I nodded.

And I brought a hotdog, she said. That helped.

We laughed, and Melvin joined in. Across the circle, a tall, skinny girl took Lester by the hand, and a shorter, plump one grabbed Melvin Jr.

Hey, Melvin said, look at that.

Melvin Jr. and the short girl were swept up right away, into the counterclockwise stepping, both of them keeping good time. Lester held back at first, pulling away so hard the skinny girl's arm looked like a rubber band that might snap. She started to walk away, and I held my breath. Go, I wanted to shout, go on, Lester. She was three steps away, headed toward a large boy to her left, when Lester started to move. It was slow at first, like he was having to tell his legs to go, but soon he caught up to her, was tapping her on her bony shoulder, and she was turning.

I breathed out, and I thought I heard Angela and Melvin doing the same.

Angela took Melvin's hand and pulled him a step toward the circle. Come on, she said, dance with your wife.

Lester was keeping rhythm better than I would have guessed, was matching up with the skinny girl's long strides. They moved past me, and the skinny girl leaned down to say something in Lester's ear, and Lester laughed and said something back.

In the morning, the sun would still be shining. I knew that. In the morning, a quiet was going to descend that could expand, could make that other quiet grow in a way that would bring on even more sadness. I knew that, too. But tonight there was the sound of feet, moving counterclockwise, the smell of coffee and bread and the raw greenness of the field. And tonight there were my legs, too, stiff at first, but surprising me by doing anything at all, and then there I was, part of it, moving.

TONI JENSEN

THE FIFTH DAUGHTER

Charles Kemnitz

Radon is the fifth daughter in the radioactive decay chain of Uranium-238.
—Phase II-Title I Engineering Assessment of Inactive Uranium Mill Tailings

AT THE BOTTOM OF THE HOOP CANYON, the Tingling Woman waits patiently in the dancing heat for Doll or Chinli to appear next to the piñon log that props open the broken door of their federal house. The air conditioning in her pickup swirls smoke away from her face as her cigarette burns down. Long ash falls onto her blue satin blouse when Chinli edges into the doorway. As soon as the girl's shadow touches the wind, Chinli waves a gentle greeting, then whirls and disappears inside.

Moving heavily, Ada Nadlahi climbs from the cab, brushes at her dress, flounces the pleats, and wishes that she could wear something more practical, cooler, when she tingles. Ada is, politely, a stout woman, and she begins sweating almost immediately as she waddles toward the Nilchi home. Its flimsy wooden walls will cook the interior as hot as the blazing canyon, so she resigns herself to the necessary heat and exertion. The smell of coffee greets her—she's expected and quickens her step. Her visit is serious business, not social.

She slips across the threshold and hesitates in the sudden gloom. Nobody greets her, but polite silence is expected, even from someone who doesn't follow all the traditions. No rush to utter unimportant words. She stands quietly, waiting for her eyes to adjust, then settles her bulk into a kitchen chair. It growls beneath her weight.

From *South Dakota Review.*

Doll sits across the small breakfast table, picking at a flake of Formica. She is stiff, stoic, in pain. Ada has come to tingle Doll.

A kerosene lamp, a pot of coffee, mugs, a plate of cookies, stand on the table. Chinli leans against the wall between the stove and the nearly empty water bucket. Her eyes flash resentment. They are sharp obsidian flakes. She is alert, hasn't slept well. She looks like she has been brutally awakened so that everything around her, without changing shape, has become a threat, a wild plundering of her desires.

Doll pulls over the coffee pot, pours a cup, then heaps in six spoons of sugar. Reservation coffee—thick and sweet as molasses. She passes the mug, slides the platter of cookies within reach, then fishes in a pocket for her grandfather's brooch. The silver is tarnished, beat out a hundred years ago from three Mormon silver dollars. Reluctantly, with one final caress, Doll pushes it across the table and Ada's talons snag the jewelry. Rings as big and blue as robin eggs strangle the Tingling Woman's short, thick fingers.

Comfortable in silence, Ada nibbles cookies baked from equal parts corn flour, sugar, and sheep lard. Her mother called these cookies "squaw candy"; the Mormons, more vulgar and poetic, said they tasted like "sugar tits." But those words have disappeared.

The house is oppressive. The sweat on Ada's face runnels into the corners of her mouth while she eats. Sugar and salt. Life's essentials. After each cookie, she picks crumbs from the littered formica, sucks each finger clean, then leans forward. Her squash blossom necklace and concho belt jangle musically, tolling against the table's edge. Ada Nadlahi wears her Tingling Woman status in the fashion of her dress, her silver, the cast in her eye.

The notes of the Tingling Woman's wealth grate inside Chinli's neck bones. She pushes away from the wall and takes three deliberate steps across the kitchen, turns her back and walks to the end of the hall. She shoves aside a blanket that curtains her bedroom. Rusty springs screech beneath a bare mattress.

The Tingler pushes her chair back from the table, then lumbers to her feet. A groan trickles from her gaping mouth. She pauses to catch her breath, her knuckles resting on the tabletop, then she rises

CHARLES KEMNITZ

and lights a cigarette. Smoke rings float to the ceiling and seep through cracks in the walls. Ada stares past Doll to the swaying blanket and cups the heavy brooch in her paw.

Doll will not look into the Tingling Woman's eyes. On the reservation eye contact is not only impolite, it is genetically impossible. The Ute raise their children to respect elders by lowering their gazes and voices to the earth. To stare into an aunt's or uncle's face is the rudest insult. Waiting, Doll rearranges the coffee pot and mugs and empty plate into a still life. Patiently, she squares her shoulders.

Ada smokes. Her hands begin tingling.

"I've been weak and feverish. My skin smells in the morning," Doll explains to the space between them.

Ada's arms float up until her hands hover like two nervous hummingbirds. The cigarette flutters between her lips. She caresses her new brooch. She shelters the jewelry in one palm, then pulls her arms down and plants her fists on her hips. Her smoke and breath tremble. Her necklace and belt tinkle like silver sheep bells in the distance.

"It might not be the Poison," the Tingler says.

Doll nods and narrows her eyes.

"I wouldn't have called you out here, Ada, but you know how the hospital is. We make the trip and nothing is wrong, next time it gets harder to see the doctor."

The Tingling Woman tugs a red bandana from her sleeve and wraps the brooch. She slips it into a pocket, then touches her fingers together. Her knuckles crack; piñon nuts crushed between hammer stones.

"Yes. That's a bad place. This is better. I will tell you, then you will know what to say to that doctor."

Doll smiles. She straightens against the back of her chair.

"Chinli tells me I should go to the doctors. But I want to do things the right way, even if it costs me my grandfather's silver."

"We're old friends. That's what I came for."

Ada spreads one hand on the table and wills it to stillness.

Doll blinks crazily. The smells of coffee and cigarette and every sickness on the reservation leak from the Tingler's pores. She pushes herself up and stumbles against the chair. She shuffles down the hallway.

When Ada enters the bedroom, Doll lies on her back on her cot, breathing shallow in an attempt to control her fear. Ada kneels beside Doll's bed and grasps her medicine bundle in her left hand—gently. It can injure both of them if misused. Her sagging stomach and breasts rest against Doll's knees and the mattress. Palm down, she spreads her right hand over Doll's skin, carefully avoiding contact. When her hand passes over whatever bad thing has possessed Doll, the sickness will flow through Ada into the leather bundle, and when she opens the bag she will know which healing sing will restore Doll's balance, release her illness to become part of life's harmony. This is not a cure the *t'shuker'bo'in*—the white doctors—would accept.

Ada's hand tingles slightly over a rash on Doll's thighs. She shakes her head. "Nothing." Then she pulls herself down the bed to tingle Doll's pelvis and liver. Her hand trembles violently, like dragonflies flitting against a desert wind. She moans and clutches her medicine bag. Heat suffuses her body, and she flinches. She closes her eyes against the sweat pouring down her face, then sits back on her heels, exhausted, breathing heavily.

Chinli slips into her mother's room and watches from the door. She doesn't interrupt, but wants to stop the ceremony. It's a waste of her grandfather's silver. Doll could get a diagnosis and treatment for free at the Indian Hospital in Towaoc.

Doll lifts her head, a warning against her daughter's impulse. Chinli turns her face to the window.

"What is it?" Doll asks.

"Let's find out," Ada answers.

Slowly, she uncoils her left hand. Her palm is seared, beginning to blister. She opens the bag and a lump of pitchblende tumbles out.

The school bus climbs out of the canyon, turns south on the highway that arrows across the high desert plateau, and the passengers begin baking. Beyond the asphalt, irrigated fields stretch to the timbered foothills of the San Juan Mountains. Doll reaches across Chinli to open the window. The corroded aluminum sticks for a moment, then the sash crashes down and a blast of scorching, dry air feathers hair across her face. It is nine and the heat has not yet begun.

They are two of only six people on the bus. Doll and Chinli sit alone. The seat across the aisle holds a green plastic garbage bag that contains a change of clothes and a toothbrush, just in case the doctor admits Doll for the Poison. She wears a sleeveless blouse, jeans, and a pair of stained, white high-top basketball shoes. Chinli folds a blue bandana and ties it across Doll's forehead. Doll looks too old to be her mother. She is thin and sinewy, skeletal. The Poison has stripped her flesh to the bone so that her elbows and knuckles jut out sharply—weathered rocks silhouetted against the sky. She sits with her spine pressed firmly into the hard seat, holds her hands clasped together in her lap, and stares blankly at the level, green fields. This is alien country for her, but she bears the serenity of someone who has accepted her own death. By ten the heat has begun and it will get worse.

The bus stops at the new Mountain Ute reservation casino. The driver and other passengers get off to stretch and buy soda from a machine in the lobby. Nauseated, Doll goes to the washroom. She takes her shirt off, splashes herself with water, and stands in front of the mirror until it is time to go. When she comes back to her seat, Chinli has unpacked their lunch. A chunk of cheese, two squares of cornbread, and two Blue Bead cookies. While they eat, the bus turns toward the town and pulls into the hospital parking lot. Doll runs her fingers through Chinli's hair, straightening it. Doll takes off the bandana, wipes the sweat from her neck, then stuffs it in her back pocket. They follow the others into the blank stone building. A dry, moaning wind chases them down a long, antiseptic corridor to the crowded waiting room. Doll stands in line at the water fountain, then drinks until her stomach sloshes. It will be a long afternoon and evening, then the drive back to the mouth of her canyon and the strenuous hike home.

Chinli stuffs the trash bag beneath a wooden chair. The wall behind her is all window and sun reflected off the cars and pickups in the parking lot. She wears a blue flannel shirt and jeans and red basketball shoes. Her hair falls free but lanky because she hasn't washed in more than a week, too occupied with her mother to lug water from the spring. She sits near the window where she can see who comes and goes without looking directly at any of the aunts and uncles waiting for bad news from the nurses and doctor.

Doll checks in with the receptionist. Her one o'clock appointment has been postponed until two. She returns to sit beside her daughter. A single electric fan in the corner swirls the air sluggishly. Doll scratches her fingernails against the chair.

An hour later, the door leading from the waiting room into the clinic opens, noiselessly, and a plump, young nurse appears, with very pale skin and hair the color of fire. Her eyes seem too small behind her thick glasses.

"Are you Doltsoi Nilchi?" she asks the first woman she sees.

The woman glances down, then whispers "*Nda.*"

"No," the nurse repeats, peering at the patients sitting stoically in the waiting room.

Chinli and Doll stand, then follow the nurse into a room that smells like decaying flowers. Doll sits on an examination table, while the nurse records her temperature, blood pressure, and pulse. The room is oppressively sterile and there's no place else to sit, so Chinli remains standing, the trash bag dangling from her hands. The nurse asks questions, checking off boxes on a form, then tells Doll to take off her clothes and wait. When she leaves, Chinli stuffs Doll's clothes into the bag and perches beside her.

"All right?" she asks.

Doll smiles for the first time that day.

After half an hour the doctor comes in, wiping her brow with the sleeve of her lab coat.

"Hello. I'm Dr. Merritt. And you are Mrs. Nilchi?" the doctor asks.

She stares at Chinli, then to Doll; neither responds. Finally, the doctor rummages in a drawer beneath the table and hands Doll a green paper gown. Doll slips into it and Chinli ties it back. After checking temperature and blood pressure and pulse, after reviewing Doll's medical history, the doctor shakes her head.

"What seems to be the problem?" she asks.

"It's the Poison," Doll answers.

The doctor scribbles a note.

"How do you know?"

"The Tingling Woman came."

"Who?"

"Ada Nadlahi."

The doctor still does not understand.

"Ada. She came and tingled me," Doll explains patiently, as if to a child. "I have the Poison. It's in my blood."

Doll stares back with quiet determination until the doctor looks away, lowers her head, and begins to write again. Half a page, then she places the clipboard and pen precisely in the center of the counter running along one wall, pulls on rubber gloves, and from behind, slips her hands beneath Doll's arms.

During the examination, Chinli watches her mother's face. Doll winces every time the doctor touches her.

"Your liver and spleen are tender," the doctor says at the conclusion of her examination. "How long have you had this rash on your legs?"

"A week," Doll answers.

"Fever? Fatigue?"

"Yes."

"Any unusual bruising or bleeding?"

"No."

Dr. Merritt picks up the medical form. "How old are you?" she asks Doll.

"Almost sixty."

"Well, it could just be anemia. Common for a woman your age. We'll run a few tests to make sure," she says without conviction. Experience has made her pessimistic. Ute only come to Indian Health Services when illness has almost run its course. If Doll has finally developed cancer from breathing the radon in the old uranium mines, then she's probably already dying.

Dr. Merritt shoves the form and a pen at Doll. "Sign here," she says.

The nurses don't call the aunts and uncles into a private room, just walk up to them and announce the sickness so everyone knows. Already, after waiting three hours, Chinli has heard that two young girls hit by a drunk along the highway have died. Dr. Merritt comes herself, she doesn't send a nurse, and Chinli's pulse quickens, but she stares unrelentingly because the Tingling Woman has already given her the bad news. Dr. Merritt glances at her watch, a cheap digital that can be purchased on a whim while waiting for the cashier at Wal-Mart. Obviously, the doctor isn't trying to impress her patients and is unimpressed by them.

"She has acute myelogenous leukemia. Her spleen and liver are involved. The rash on her legs tipped me off. It's a condition called thrombocytopenia. The rash is actually pinprick bleeding beneath the skin. Does she have any brothers or sisters?"

"No. The others died when she was young."

"Well, she needs a bone marrow transplant. She needs to go to Albuquerque, Denver, or Salt Lake. This type of leukemia is always fatal without a suitable marrow donor. You need to be tested, and if you aren't a match, the big medical centers have databases."

"She won't go," Chinli says.

"Then take her home. Make her last days comfortable. You can expect loss of appetite and weight, night sweats, lots of pain. We'll try to control the pain with morphine when the time comes. She's getting dressed."

"How long?"

"At this stage? A few weeks. Maybe three months. Listen, if she won't go for a transplant, then it's too late. There's nothing more I can do for her, and I've got other patients."

Chinli rolls from bed. A light, clear and violet as any dream, streams through her window. She sweeps aside the blanket and walks down the hall to the kitchen. Doll sits at the table, a silhouette in the doorway open to the coming dawn. Chinli isn't surprised. Her mother never sleeps when she's working on a new blanket. Doll lifts her head to greet her daughter. She's been up all night at her dye pot. Ropes of yarn, corn-tassel yellow, dripping wet, loop from two wire hangers above the stove. The dye sizzles onto the stove and spatters onto the floor. The searing vinegar and sheep urine her mother uses to dissolve crushed ocher lodges acrid in the roof of Chinli's mouth. She scrubs her nose with the back of her hand to keep from sneezing, then shoves a stick of piñon into the stove and puts on a pot of water. When it steams, she throws in two handfuls of coffee, smells to test the strength, then tosses in another measure for the pot. She cracks a small egg and adds the white and shell to bind and settle the grounds, then hands her mother the yolk in half a shell, and Doll drinks it down.

Chinli slept restlessly and woke leeched out. She runs a strand of yarn between her thumb and fingers. Her skin dyes the color of her mother's jaundiced skin.

"You know better," Doll reprimands gently. "I'll have to cut that out now."

"Sorry."

"No, you're not," Doll chides.

"You're angry."

"I've decided to put some yellow in my blanket."

"I like yellow."

"I think frogs."

"What?"

"The Emergence Lake and a yellow frog for one of the guardians."

"A chant weave? You've never made one."

"I'll make this one."

"That would be perfect, Mother."

After coffee, Chinli walks into the dawn and pauses for a moment, as always awed by the pink and mauve cliffs that surround her home. Tailings from one of the dog-hole uranium mines spills into the top of the arroyo, a cancer on the canyon's beauty.

Chinli calls the sheep and they follow her down the arroyo to graze.

Alone, Doll pours herself a cup of coffee and fills it with sugar. Then she follows her daughter outside. As the sun drops into the canyon and drives off night's chill, devils begin to spin and dance around the house. She crosses to her loom and kneels, drinking in her blanket.

Despite her gentleness with Chinli, Doll is angry. Not about the ruined yarn, but for her own illness. She knows it has something to do with the uranium mining on the reservation when she was a girl. The Poison got into her blood, and now it is killing her.

Doll sits back on her heels, places her palms flat against her thighs, tilts her head, and follows the sun through closed eyelids. She crosses her legs and contemplates the loom. She cannot weave again until her heart calms, or she will ruin the design. Instead, she searches out any imperfection. Her shoulders knot. Doll sways, and follows the threads forward to the time of her death.

After waiting patiently for a few hours, she steals back into her house. The skeins above the stove have dried. The yarn is vibrant. She takes it down, drapes it over her arm, and plods back to her work. The willow ramada casts bands of shadow across the blanket. She hangs the skeins from a twig. An early hummingbird flits around the yellow yarn, seeking nectar. This is the Emergence Path. She resets the loom, straightens the warp threads, tamps tight yesterday's last woof, winds and arranges her shuttles, then throws the first strand that will stitch a yellow frog into her last blanket.

Chinli pushes the sheep up the arroyo, into the corral, then jogs to the outhouse. Afterward, she rummages in the kitchen for another cup of coffee. She crosses the dusty plaza and sits against a post next to her mother. The wood is worn smooth after years blasted by desiccating winds. She spins the mug in her hands, but can't drink.

"You've been crying," Doll says.

"You're to blame. Why don't you get mad at me anymore?"

Doll catches her shuttle. "Look at my frog."

Chinli remains motionless, then dumps the coffee between her feet. "It's a beautiful frog, Mother. You worked hard to finish so much while I was gone."

"It will be from the Chal Chant," Doll says.

Four frogs—*chal*—stand guard over the dark waters of Emergence Lake; lightning radiates to the four corners. Chinli studies the one her mother has woven. It is exactly like the frogs at the seep, splayed out, as if leaping into the water, ready to kick as soon as it enters the pool.

"A blanket like this, it's for a gallery or a museum," Chinli asserts.

"This one is for me."

"I know, Mother."

"Let me clean your hair today," Chinli offers.

"Okay. Yes. That'd be good." Doll smiles. She has not slept well for two weeks, not since the visit to the hospital. She has replaced exhaustion with weaving. She leans back from her loom and folds her hands on her thighs.

Chinli moves closer to her mother, pulls her fingers through Doll's hair. The white sun ignites rainbows in the blackness fanning across her shoulders. Chinli takes a wool card, the teeth widely spaced, and tugs against the knots, then she washes Doll's hair with sand and a cup of water.

"Now, let me do yours while mine dries," Doll says.

"You're too weak," Chinli protests.

Doll puts aside the yellow yarn and begins weaving in black. She works silently while the sun dips below the cliffs and throws the canyon into shadow. She continues weaving into the dark with the speed and precision of a master, hardly moving any joint in her body except her gnarled hands. The shuttles fly and the blanket becomes more, creeping closer to its end. Doll's face glows with pain. She avoids her daughter's eyes, thinking, *My skin is becoming immaterial.*

Doll feels her way through the darkness, pulling on her jeans and T-shirt, then slips into a pair of old high-top All-Stars. She ties the laces by feel, becoming a desert snake, an imagined hiss of motion across the floor. The small key she wears around her neck scrapes against the lock on her jewelry box until the latch springs and the top pops open. Her mother's squash blossom necklace chimes when she lifts it out and drapes it around her neck. The Poison gives off some powerful radiation. She has just decided to climb to the seep with yellow frogs. The Poison has given her the power to walk through cracks in the canyon walls.

She shuffles to the outhouse hanging above the arroyo. The dawn wind whispers, barely audible, and the dark odors of frightened sheep milling in the fold, agitated, trundling in endless circles fill the air.

We must have had a coyote last night, she says to herself. Doll turns her back on the sheep and walks down the canyon. She wishes things could be the way they were before Ada's diagnosis.

An hour later, she comes upon the confluence with Yellowjacket Canyon and turns toward Ismay's trading post. Halfway up the wash she stops to rest in the shade beneath a plum tree planted when she was a girl. High clouds scud through gnarled branches overburdened with nearly ripe fruit.

She picks half a dozen plums, eats two, and tucks the rest in her pockets. Juice runs down her chin and stains her T-shirt. She leaves the shade and climbs out of the wash to the sloping talus at the foot of the mesa, where she leans her head against the searing black basalt, heaving and panting. Nausea churns her stomach and bile crawls up the back of her throat, then she vomits, spewing rancid coffee and putrid fruit down her chest, soaking her jeans and shoes. When the spasms pass, she slips between two boulders into a slot canyon and chill shadows.

Sometimes the stone walls narrow to the point that she must turn sideways, and even then her breath is squeezed from her chest as she forces her way farther up the mesa. Halfway to the seep with yellow frogs, Doll boosts herself onto a ledge and props one hand against the stone and bows her head on her arm, sucks in deep drafts of air. Sweat stings the corners of her eyes. Not from exertion. From the Poison. She feels life draining out of her. It is, amazingly, a cleansing.

She eats another plum to quench her parched tongue, then sucks on the stone and swallows her own spit. Above her, clouds tumble down the narrow river of sky like whitewater. Pollen from flowering yucca flows off the mesa top and drifts onto her hair and shoulders. The glittering specks remind her that if she's caught in a cloudburst, the canyon will fill with flash flood and she'll drown.

The seep is one of those rare, sheltered places in the desert where water bubbles up slowly, only a few gallons a day, barely enough to balance evaporation for most of the year. It is a shallow pool about thirty feet across, shimmering at the bottom of a sixty-foot sinkhole drilled into the heart of the mesa by eons of swirling snow melt and violent summer storms. Its surface reflects the noon sun and is frothed with frog spawn. The little yellow frogs lurk at the water's edge, silent and waiting, petrified by Doll's appearance into brilliant rock art, their desperate reproduction interrupted.

The basin of the seep is filled with turquoise beads, silver conches, pottery shards, obsidian arrowheads and knives, clay figures of *chal,* children's dolls. The green dome of a Navajo willow, stunted by the shallow soil, weeps into the pool. Strips of dyed deerskin, bright swatches of velvet, old hats and boots hang from its branches. This is one of many hidden medicine springs where Mountain Ute women who have lived beyond their periods once came to die. It is a sacred politeness—better than growing very old and being doomed to life in a snakeskin.

Doll hobbles across the sandy floor and slumps onto a pile of stone slabs beneath the tree. This is where she wants her grave when she dies. She might weather three or four seasons under these stones, but the ebb and flow of water rushing off the mesa will eventually wash her bones away. Doll lies on her grave and stares at the reflection of clouds scudding across the water. The sun arches above the well's mouth and shadows sweep down the walls. The willow branches rub against each other, creaking gently. Around the seep, the frogs begin croaking again.

Finally, an afternoon monsoon bursts across the mesa. Doll turns her face into the rain. She could shelter beneath the overhang, but doesn't move. Instead, the rain washes her clean, soaks her skin, carries away the foul smells of her illness. Lightning stabs the mesa overhead and thunder pounds the surface of the seep. A drumhead. It deafens her. Water rushes down the walls, filling the well until the seep laps her heels and rushes turbulent and muddy over the spillway. The narrow mouth of the slot canyon swallows the flood and almost an entire generation of unborn frogs. For a moment, with the Poison bursting into flame, Doll wishes that she'd been wedged at the tightest point where rock emptied her lungs. After the squall passes, after rain and thunder and lightning move onto the high desert and become a distant, rumbling echo, Doll crawls to a dead fire inside a shallow cave, shoves her hands into the cold ash, pulls them out, empty and white, and peers between her fingers.

Her daughter faces her from across the seep. Chinli is in shadow, darkly silhouetted against the pale sandstone. She glides silently across to Doll and drops a handful of kindling beside the fire pit. The sticks hit the ground, snap. Her daughter wears clean shoes and dry jeans, even though she must have climbed through diminishing flood.

"Hey, Daughter."

"Mother." Chinli swipes her hands on her thighs, shoves them into her pockets. The sun slips beyond the mouth of the well and shadows darken the slabs of fallen mesa. "You stayed out in the storm," Chinli observes.

Before answering, Doll contemplates her ash-white hands.

"I'm asking, why didn't you come out of the storm?" her daughter repeats, reaching for twigs to start a fire. She digs a lighter out of her pocket, kneels, and holds the flame in the hollow beneath the tinder. Dry leaves catch, and the two of them stare into the flames. Chinli unties the blue bandana around her neck, shakes it out, hands it across the fire, then rocks back on her heels, the way she studies one of Doll's blankets unfinished in the loom.

Doll wipes ash off her hands, then twirls the neckerchief into a tight rope and hands it back. Her daughter wraps it around her neck and ties a loose knot at the hollow of her throat. The two of them hold a duration of silence and politely look away. Doll gazes up the well into the bright sky filled with gyring clouds. Vertigo weaves its net of unbalance and she turns away. Her daughter flickers in Doll's peripheral vision next to the fire.

The frogs fall silent for a moment, then croak a thousand identical notes.

Chinli nods her head as she shreds a willow leaf and flicks the debris into the flames. They flare—shooting stars.

Doll raises an eyebrow and stretches the silence.

"Last night you had a fever. Do you feel better?" Chinli asks.

"It wasn't fever. You worry too much. Besides, there's nothing you can do."

"The Poison is shrinking you. It's as if you're already dead."

Doll pays no attention to her daughter but gazes into the embers. She passes the tinkling necklace through the fire.

"You're thinking you have no inheritance," Doll says. "It'll be all right."

Slowly, then, she rises and begins dancing. A shuffling circle. Chanting. Hunched over, Chinli fastens the squash blossoms around her neck. A few minutes later Doll's song turns into an uncontrollable cough, then her spine collapses and she slumps next to the wall. When she recovers, she stares at her daughter.

Chinli squirms. Her mother's look isn't natural. She tosses another branch on the fire. The sparks fly. One lands on her shirt, but she doesn't bother to brush it away and it burns a pinprick, scorches her skin. She waits patiently until the ember dies, then clutches the necklace in her hands.

"Have you come to take me home?" Doll asks.

"No. Just to find you."

Doll rolls onto her back, throws her gaze to the scudding stars. "I planned to stay here forever."

Chinli's head snaps up and for one moment she stares rudely into her mother's black eyes, shimmering unsubstantial, a reflection at the bottom of the well. Doll's eyes catch fire with an intensity that consumes Chinli's heart.

"I know," Chinli answers.

Doll pushes to her feet. She walks to the spillway. The frogs croak, uninterrupted, as if she is a ghost passing over the sand and stone. She lowers herself into the slot canyon. When Chinli crawls out of the cave, the frogs fall silent. She peers into the bowl of the seep. It is utterly empty.

WHAT I NEVER SAID

Elmo Lum

THIS WAS US: me and my father, my brother and my other brother, Franny, who was the dog, and my mother before she passed on. This was back in our family days, in the years we were traveling. Back when us five drove crammed in a van, traveling state to state, every day a new place and a new camp.

I was maybe eleven and my brothers both seventeen. That year we were in the West, which is how my mother called it. The season was spring and we were driving the desert states, solo on the road, orange with the morning. With my father at the wheel and my mother still dozing, us brothers still packing from when we broke camp.

We were in the state of billboards. It was billboard after billboard along the length of the highway, advertising the highway west. They proclaimed gas, food, and souvenirs. They called for stopping and gave the miles away. Some read *Authentic.* Some read *Mexican.* All of them read *Exit.*

"Don't wake me, it's garish," my mother said.

"I just need you to tell me how you feel," said my father.

"I'm sleepy."

"You know it's important that you tell me how you feel."

"I'll feel better if I can sleep."

From *New England Review.*

"You've been sleeping all night. How much sleep can one person get?"

"I won't find out unless I sleep."

"Tassie. Tassie?"

"Dean, stop it."

"This is important."

"I feel fine, all right? I feel fine. Now let me sleep."

The light was turning hard outside. The sky was sharp and the shadows were sharp on the mountains in the distance on either side. The desert was coloring. The sun was up, the morning turning warm.

We were dusty. It was day three in the desert.

Us brothers got the tent packed; up front our mother woke. She stretched, arching, yawning, holding a palm against the morning.

She said, "You'd think they'd have stopped by now."

She meant the billboards.

She said, "How are you boys back there?"

We said we were fine.

She said, "Is Franny drinking enough?"

We said that she was. These were our orders when we were driving through the desert, to keep from dehydrating the dog.

"God, I hate the desert," my mother said.

It turned an oven in the van. The windows were all open but the highway wind was hot. Which wasn't much for changing the air we had in back. Us brothers were growing sticky. Franny was throbbing on the floor. My mother was mopping her face with her hands, then wiping her hands, then mopping her face again.

"The desert was whose idea," my mother said.

"Try this in the summer, if you think this is bad," said my father.

"This is torture."

"This is the fastest way. You want to go see the coast, let's go see the coast, but this is the fastest way."

"We could have driven a better way."

"There's nothing but desert between us and Idaho. That's a country away. Do you want to drive a country out of our way?"

"This is torture."

"Boys, get some water up for your mother."

We passed up a plastic jug.

"Drink some water, Tassie."

My mother took the jug and tilted the water over her head.

"Jesus, you're getting the seat all wet."

"It'll dry, Dean."

"Are you sure you're feeling all right?"

"I'll be fine, Dean, all right?"

"Drink some water."

"Dean, I'm fine."

"You made a promise, Tassie."

"You want me to drink the water? Will you stop if I drink the water? I'll drink the water." She upended the jug over her mouth and started swallowing. She swallowed, lips round, the water pouring down the corners, down her front, eyes wide on my father all the way.

"Jesus, Tassie, the seat."

"The seat'll be fine, Dean. Trust me."

Lunch was fast food when we stopped to fill up gas. We ate it out of paper sitting at a table that wouldn't move. My father picked the table because it had a clear view of the van. We always ate in clear view of the van. The van was everything we had, my father said.

It was easy in the restaurant to breathe. The air was cool and the seats were cool. We were drying off in there. I was cold. I was having myself a milkshake I almost couldn't suck through the straw. My brothers were grinding ice in their teeth a table away. My father was dipping fries, twice at a time, in the ketchup on the paper on the tray. My mother held her eyes closed, her hamburger minus one bite. There was nobody else there in there.

My father said, "Tassie, you should eat."

My mother said, "I don't have the appetite."

"You've barely touched your food."

"You can have it, if you want it. Do you want it?"

"Tassie, it's your food. Eat your food."

"Be a good boy," my mother said, "be a good boy and check on Franny."

I took my father's keys. It was searing outside. I let Franny out and got her bowl from inside. It was dry. I filled it from a jug and left it on the asphalt, on the side where the van had some shade. Franny was already there, panting. She lapped from the bowl. I sucked from my milkshake. The cup was going wet and soft in my hand.

My mother came out, her palms against her head. My father came out after, saying, "You made a promise."

My mother said, "God, not now."

"Listen, Tassie. You made a promise."

"Don't remind me." She pulled open the van door and climbed inside the van. She cranked the window down and slammed the door.

My brothers each came out, their cups topless in their hands.

"Get in the van," my father said. "And get that dog in."

The van was worse for sitting still. The air was a fever, worse even than outside. I felt dull. Franny lay on the floor and my brothers both sprawled in back. I sat up front, close up for the air, hot as it was, and the view, such as it was. Where a desert lake shimmered, then disappeared, then shimmered on the desert again.

"My kingdom for a lake," my mother said.

The country was turned to cholla. They spread clustered and blond down the slope of the hills. They covered the flats in furry clumps. Up against the highway fence they crowded through the wire, growing from the shoulder in sprouts. Here and there, at the edge of the asphalt, lay a dry one run over, grown too near.

The slopes grew closer. On the side with the sun they grew brighter and paler, on the shaded side steeper with rocks. I spotted over the top the day's first clouds. They were wisps and streaks, milky and thin, but clouds in the marble blue sky.

My mother was sopping. She was wiping her face with her shirt already soaked. She wiped her arms and craned her neck to wipe her throat. She rolled her sleeves up past her shoulders. She was bright. The sun through the windshield had my mother squinting.

"This is torture," my mother said.

"Going to the coast was your idea."

"If I thought going to the coast was torture I would have told you something else."

My mother nudged my arm; it was with the water jug. I took it and uncapped it and drank straight from it. The water was warm. It tasted salty from the corners of my mouth. I capped it back. I lay back. The van was loud. The engine was thrumming and the wind was roaring through the windows. It was dim or seemed dim down on the floor where I was.

I grew asleep or close to sleep in the heat. Lying on the van floor, dreaming of the restaurant. Which was such pure silence against the noise of highway driving. Where I'd heard my father chew. Where I'd heard Spanish behind the counter. Where when the man came by, pushing the mop against the tile, I'd heard that, too.

Franny had her eyes closed, running in her dreams. My brothers sat in back, playing cards. I drank some more warm water. My mother's hand hung asleep. I felt a turn to the van and sat up. My brothers both looked up. We were turning off the road, onto a solitary overpass, one building standing there.

"Van overheating," my father said.

The sun was pounding. Franny dropped to her spot down under the shade of the van. My father pushed the hood up holding towels against the heat. Waves blurred off the engine.

"Let's go inside," my mother said. "Dean, we'll be inside."

The door tinkled when we came in. Before us the room was cool and dim. From the back of the store I heard a television. A woman appeared there, coming from a doorway. She called out, "How are you all folks today?"

"Fine," my mother said. "Little van trouble."

"You got trouble with your van? I'll get Tom to take a look. Tom!"

"It's nothing, it's just that it's hot. The engine's overheated, that's all."

"We'll get you some water. Tom!"

A man came from the door, bald and red. "What's this about car trouble?"

"They got their engine overheated."

"I'll get some water."

"It's a scorcher," the woman said.

I watched bald Tom through the window, hauling a jug. He and my father shook hands at the van. They ducked down together, bent into the engine, poking down inside, bald Tom shaking his head. He pointed to the store. He and my father rang the bell through the front.

"Still too hot," said bald Tom.

My mother leaned and pointed down the counter to the jewelry. I walked past the rocks, the amethyst and quartz. My father studied the postcards, my brothers the rattlesnake molts. My mother tried a bracelet, silver, and pointed to a necklace of turquoise.

"You all thirsty?" the woman asked. "We got water, and soda for the boys."

"I think we're fine," my mother said.

"You change your mind, you let me know."

My mother crumpled.

"Oh my Lord," the woman said.

"Tassie. Tassie, get up," my father said.

"It's fine," my mother said, "I'm fine."

"No, you're not, honey, you're worse off than you think. Tom!"

"Boys, help me with your mother."

My father got an arm under my mother and my brother the other side. Together my father and brother helped my mother out the front. I ran to get the van door and they lifted my mother in.

The woman came running. "Sir? Sir, I'm calling emergency."

My father dropped the hood shut and got in the driver's side.

"I'm fine, really," my mother called.

"Franny," called my brother. "Come on, Franny, inside."

Bald Tom came out as my father pulled away. He and the woman watched us turn down the ramp. Bald Tom had a hand to his head. We turned, my brothers and me, and watched them watch us leave.

My father was intent and speeding. The speed shook the van, skipping the van with the bumps, with the speed, the van bumping with the asphalt. My father drove faster, putting the engine in a whine. We began shaking. The fence smeared faster and blurred.

My mother screamed over the engine running high, "Dean!"

My father, leaned over at the wheel, ignored her. He kept his foot down, pressed flat to the floor. We sped faster. The chassis was rocking, the engine ran pitched. My mother pushed both hands to the dash. Franny held stiff, four legs to the floor. I stopped being able to see.

My mother screamed, "The boys!"

My father nailed the brakes and my brothers fell forward, and I fell forward, and Franny fell up front. We skidded, wheels locked, the van's tires off the road. Us going over the shoulder, gravel clattering the underside. Banging when a wheel drove down a ditch. My mother screamed and crossed her arms. A cactus slapped the hood. The van rocked and pitched and lurched still.

"You're crazy!" my mother screamed. "You're born crazy!"

My father pushed the door against the slope of the shoulder. He pulled himself out and wrenched the hood up. Us brothers jumped out from the back. My father was pacing. He was pacing, checking his watch, looking out around. We were the only human thing for miles. There was the highway, pinched in the distance, and beside it the tumbleweed fence. Beyond that grew the teeming cholla and clusters of creosote scrub.

My brothers each flung hubcaps. They kicked the same stone, a broken box, a tire peel. One brother slapped the other and the other slapped him back. They pulled off their shirts and tied them to their heads. They shrank down the road, bent with heat.

A dust devil swirled in. It swirled through the fence, over the shoulder, across the blacktop. Where it disappeared over the blacktop, and reappeared on the far shoulder, curling up dust, bent, harder to see, and gone. My brothers were gone.

My father swore. He was down on his knees, head under the bumper, his shirt stained green with antifreeze. He called, "Come here. Come see if you can get this cap."

"Dean?" my mother called. "Dean, are you all right? Boys, is your father all right?"

"I'm fine." He spat. "I can see it but I can't reach it."

I crawled down under and it was dripping down on me. I got the cap up and my father was back with a jug. He drained it down the mouth of the radiator. "Go ahead and cap it," he said.

I held the cap in a towel and turned the cap tight. My father checked the cap and dropped the hood.

"Dean, where are the boys?"

"The boys are fine."

"Dean, where are they?"

"They're fine."

"You let them wander off?"

"They're old enough. Where are they going to go to? This is the desert."

"Dean. You let them wander off."

"Is Franny in?"

"I can't believe you didn't watch your own boys."

I said that she was.

We drove down slow along the shoulder to my brothers. They pulled loose their shirt turbans and climbed back inside.

"Don't do that to me again," my mother said. "Do you know what you're doing to me?"

The billboards were gone. The cholla was gone, replaced by prickly pear. A town replaced the desert which replaced the town again. The sun was coming down. The glare grew wide; the desert turned rose.

"Camp soon," my father said.

He drove off on a dirt track cutting from the highway. It led straight to the hills and I couldn't see after that. My father slowed, riding the ruts, leaning forward and pointing. "How about there?"

"I'm sure it's fine," my mother said.

We pulled off into a gap between the cacti. My brothers grabbed the tent out and I grabbed our camp stove. My father gave a hand with the tent.

My mother called, "Don't let her into the cactus."

I followed Franny up the road. She zigzagged, lopsided, her tail not aligned with her nose. She stopped and smelled, smelled and stopped, grew stiff and alert with a noise. The desert was all noise. Everywhere, every direction, buzzed.

The stars were starting to grow with the evening. The desert grew darker, the cacti's black lobes chopping across the flats. She was invisible. There was a smear of light from the last of the dusk, then there was no light because there wasn't a moon. It was all invisible.

I called, "Franny."

The road was blank and still. It was loud; I couldn't hear. Ahead grew a blur, then bright dog eyes, then Franny running. I turned and there was light. I followed and Franny ran. My brothers were pulling sleeping bags, my mother was at the stove. My father was flat, pulling on one knee, straightening his leg, then pulling the other.

My mother sat shivering. She was stirring and shivering, holding herself with her free hand, shivering and stirring the pot. "I can do this," she was saying, "I can do this," gripping her spoon. "I'm not cold," she said, when my father brought a blanket.

This was dinner: canned soup over rice. My mother didn't take a plate.

"Tassie, please," my father said.

My mother said, "Dean, please believe me when I say I can't eat."

After eating we broke the jackets out. We didn't keep a fire and the night was turning cold. My mother took the blanket from my father. She stood up, draped, and walked into the dark. My father followed, calling, "Tassie." He disappeared. "Tassie?" He came back, leading my mother, my mother hunched and shivering, clutching at the blanket and my father's arm.

We turned in early. It was us brothers to the tent and my parents to the van. Franny, because it was cold, slept with us. We lay in the tent dark, all sleeping bag noise, each of us calling Franny for warmth.

She was up first. Her nose was wet and I unzipped the flap. She bounded out; it was ice outside. One of my brothers said, "Zip the flap, stupid."

I crawled into my clothes and shoes. The ground outside was visibly frosty. My father was squatted over the starting of a fire. He was striking a match and snapping the match head. "Your mother is," he said. "I better get your brothers up."

I struck a match from the matches my father left. I poked it lit into my father's tinder cone. I breathed; it flared; I began feeding twigs. The twigs caught and I put on branches. The creosote crackled, hot at my face. I pushed on a log from the firewood we kept.

My brothers were crowding the fire. My father was away, calling, "Franny." My brothers kept pressing on logs, covering the flames. My father said, "Boys, it's your mother."

She was lying in the van and blue.

We drove my mother farther up the hills, out off the track into the cacti. My father steered, dodging puncture from the spines. In a cleft in the hills where the shade was still dark and the frost still edged everything, he stopped and unstrapped the shovel. He dug in the shade, us three brothers watching, shivering, then taking turns digging one at a time. The others watching and not talking, the desert quiet and cold except the rasp of the shovel.

We dragged my mother by the feet from the van. It was my father to the legs, my brothers to the head. Together carrying my mother to the grave. She was too long. My father grabbed the shovel, hacking again, pebbles ringing, the shade shortening, the sky lightening, turning orange. Then my father and my brother laid my mother in. We took turns shoveling dirt over, pouring the soil over her feet and her body and her clothes.

"Her clothes," my father said.

We ransacked the van for everything that was my mother: her clothes, her shoes, her socks, her sandals, her hat, the ties for her hair, her hairbrush, her comb, her toothbrush, her jewelry, her journal and sketchbook, and her mysteries. We dropped it all on my mother, half-covered, and buried her together. My father stalked the spot, spreading pebbles with his shoes. He dragged over a run-over cactus.

At camp the fire was dead. We packed up the tent, our bags, and our things and drove down back toward the highway.

"We have to agree," my father said, "on the story. We have to do this sooner rather than later. I'm telling you this because you're old enough now, all of you, and you have a part in this, too. You're a part of this, too. So we have to agree on the story."

I began crying.

"Listen to me. I want you to listen to me. We have to pull together for this. This is important. This is very important. We have to have our story together. Will you try to pull together for this? I know this is hard. This is hard for me, too. But, listen, we have to agree."

"He's eleven," my brother said. "Leave him alone, he's eleven."

"Just trust me. Will you trust me?"

"Dad, leave him alone."

"But the story. We need to agree on the story."

"Just leave him alone," my brother said. "He's eleven and the story can wait."

A TRAGEDY WITH PIGS

Tom McWhorter

IT HAD BEEN A YEAR NOW, and today Fred was filled with a silent anger that he shared only with the pigs as he tended them. He kicked them. He wanted mostly to kick the old sow that was filled with babies, but because she was filled with babies, he could not. Because he could not kick the sow, he kicked the gilts, the females that had not yet farrowed, instead. It seemed almost as good. Maybelle, his wife, was in bed in the dark, cool house because she was not feeling well. She was not feeling well at least one day a month at this time of month every month, and it had been a year now.

It all started when his father had died. When his father had died, the pig farm was Fred's. He was no longer a pig farmer's son but a pig farmer himself. And now he could marry, now that he had a way. He needed to marry, because a pig farmer needs a wife. Growing up, Maybelle had always been there, so he took her.

That first married night she had said, "Look, Fred, you've started a little fire."

And he had. He had started it by putting a lit match in the ashtray with the grocery coupons that Maybelle had discarded from her coupon file as he awkwardly smoked his father's pipe across the kitchen table from her. It burned, and he smiled across the rising flames at her. She smiled back. He could not say whether she was

From *Madison Review*.

happy, but he knew that she had hope in what a pig farmer could give her, being a pig farmer's daughter herself. They smiled at each other across the fire and their faces lit up like the pigs' at sunrise, the pigs that Fred had known and fed at that early hour ever since he could walk, and before the flames had died, they had gone to the bedroom to make love for the first time.

So it had been a year now, and Maybelle was spending the day in bed and Fred wanted to kick the old sow full of babies, but he couldn't. So he was kicking the gilts instead, and when they would squeal, he would yell, "What the hell is wrong with you? What the *hell* is wrong with you?" But there was no answer, and he brooded and could not think straight as he worked under the hot west Texas sun and ankle deep in water and pigshit that turned dry and hard at the edges and in the barn and chaffed like flour into the hot, still air. Only it was not flour, nor dust, but pigshit, and it stuck to his sweaty skin and crusted the inside of his nose. On dry summer days, Maybelle would dust twice, but today the house would go undusted, because she was spending the day in bed. Fred couldn't quite believe being sick enough to be in bed all day at least once a month. He couldn't imagine it. But he could imagine the shame. He could understand that. He could feel it also to some degree.

Fred went into the house to get his own lunch, but by the time he got there, he did not feel hungry. So he poured himself a glass of lemonade. He had not washed his hands, so the dried pigshit dissolved in the moisture on the cold glass and ran and spread and faded. And walked back and forth from the fridge to the sink, and when he passed the table he thought it would be nice to sit down, but he didn't feel like he could, so he paced back and forth in the cool, dark air of the kitchen and smoked. He had given up his father's pipe for cigarettes, and he smoked lots of them. He smoked now only for the habit, so he didn't smoke his father's pipe anymore, just lots of cigarettes. They didn't have filters, so he smoked them down until the calluses on his fingers became hot, and then he would crush them out in the ashtray or on his dinner plate until the butts became unrecognizable piles of paper and tobacco.

He heard her move in the bedroom. She made soft mumbling sounds in her sleep. He knew it was time to go back out. He went into the bathroom to pee. On the back of the toilet, next to the crochet-covered extra roll of toilet paper, they sat. He wished she would keep them away. He picked up the box from the back of the toilet. He took out one of the packets. He felt the pad with his fingers through its paper wrapper.

They had planned the date so carefully, but about two weeks after they had married, she needed some. She approached him shyly. "I'm not going to buy them. A man shouldn't. That's a private, woman's thing," he said.

"But, Fred, I have to have them, and I'm too sick to go myself."

"I'll drive you to town, but you'll have to go in yourself."

At the time he was disappointed but not worried. It would have been so perfect, but this happened sometimes, even with pigs. No matter how scientific you were, sometimes it just didn't work out. You just had to try again the next time. That afternoon, a year ago, he had sat out on the rail fence in the shade of the barn watching the pen of sows and six-month-old gilts to see which, if any, were rutting and were ready to be put in with the boar. As he watched, he dreamed. He dreamed of the time when he would have several strong boys to share in the glory of a growing pig farm, but mostly to share in the great amount of work it would take to make such a pig farm successful. Having one son, he felt, had kept his father's business small, but then Fred's mother had been frail and died when he was a very young child. Fred's father had never gotten over it. But Maybelle was young and strong and healthy. Nothing stood in his way, Fred had thought.

So it had been a year now. Fred sat on the rail fence and watched the pen of sows and six-month-old gilts, as he did every afternoon, to see which were rutting and were ready to be put in with the boar. He looked in the pen adjacent. He looked at the old boar. Pigs were not the soft pink things people made them out to be. Fred's were the color of rust. They were round, very hard, and hairy. The boar was especially huge, a five-hundred-pound ham on four stocky legs. From behind, between the round, hard flanks, were the large and apparent testicles, like two softballs in a black leatherette sack. Fred's grandfather had said that pig balls were good eating, but then he ate roadrunners and rattlesnakes too. For Fred, there was other significance, so he turned his attention back to the pen of sows and gilts, to see which were rutting and ready.

At sunset, Fred could see a line of dark clouds lining the north-west horizon. A front could set the old sow to farrowing. She had already been working on a nest. If it rained during the night and she dropped her pigs, her nest would fill with water and the pigs would drown. He moved her into the barn, into the farrow-ing pen.

When Fred got back to the house, it was dark, and it was late. It had been one year today, and he made his bed on the couch, so he would not disturb Maybelle.

A heavy dew fell during the night and dripped from the eaves of the house and the barn; it dripped from the rails of the rail fence and made the whole air misty and diffused the light of the rising sun. The old sow was ready. She was down in the barn and heav-ing, and Maybelle was coming down the path from the house to help her. Mostly, Maybelle just watched. Pigs responded to kind-ness, and Maybelle was better at giving it. It was good to keep the old sow calm so that she would not trample her young or eat them. Once when she was young, Fred had left the old sow to farrow alone. He had found half of her litter dead without a mark. The next time, he was careful to watch her. Some of the pigs' snouts were catching behind the sow's vulva, and when she would bear down, she would snap their necks. Sometimes Maybelle had to reach down and free the little snout now, and the pig would pop right out. Fred saw to the feeding while Maybelle midwifed; it was better that way, he thought.

One of the new pigs was small and quite poor. It happened that way sometimes when there were ten or twelve pigs to a litter. And since you could only expect seven or eight of them, the healthy ones, to make it to three weeks, there was no sense in wasting effort on a poor one. Fred knew that Maybelle was acquainted with this, and couldn't figure why she was acting crazy this time.

"Maybelle, please give me the pig."

She held it closer. She did not move or answer. She held it closer. Fred could see no sense in this and became angry. He took the knife from his pocket and cut the pig's throat in Maybelle's arms, spilling blood down the front of her kitchen apron. She did not move or struggle. Fred stepped back. She dropped the pig to her side, still holding the twitching body by one twisted leg. She opened her mouth as if to say something, but all that came out was a grunt. She dropped the pig in the straw, turned, and ran to the house. Fred stood there for a long time before following her. Her clothes were in water in the kitchen sink. She was in the bathroom washing the blood and tears from her face. Fred held her; he reached inside her terrycloth robe and touched a breast with his rough pig-farmer's hand. He took her to the bedroom.

After, she spoke first.

"Maybe this time."

"We both know better."

"We could see a doctor," she said. "I want to see a doctor."

"What good is a doctor?"

"He could tell us."

"What?"

"I want to see a doctor."

Fred already knew. Even though he was not a man of God, he had read about it in the Bible. He had read about it in the Bible, and he was not a man of God, so he had no hope, so they went to see the doctor, because she wanted to.

Maybelle made the plans and the phone calls. Fred arranged for the neighbor's son to see to the feeding for the two days that they would be gone. Early one morning, they got into the pickup and drove away from the little white clapboard house that Fred's father had left to him. They drove through the fields that were just fertile enough to produce feed for the pigs. The houses became denser and denser until they formed a little knot of existence known as Rochester around the intersection of the two main roads that crossed in the town. The gas station was here, and Fred stopped to fill up. Maybelle walked to the grocery store in the next block. Fred waited for her to return to the pickup. She came out of the store with a sack of goodies for the trip.

Two weeks after they were married, he had brought her here. He had waited in the pickup for her. A few minutes later, she had come out of the store with them in her hand—no sack. He had never seen them before, but he knew what they were. He had slumped down in the pickup, hoping no one was watching, and had driven away quickly.

Now it had been a year. They headed southeast on farm-to-market roads toward Haskell. As they turned east there onto 380, Maybelle got out the map; neither of them had ever come this far.

Fred had a hamburger in a stand two hundred miles from home. The doctor's secretary had asked Maybelle not to eat. They found the clinic with the help of a stranger. Fred left Maybelle at the steps and drove off, intending to find some farm stores that he had been told about. He got two blocks and suddenly felt alone and lost in the big city. He pulled over at a park and, for four hours, sat and worried about the farm and the pigs. He thought about the old sow and her litter. It had been two weeks, and they had not lost one, except the runt on the first day. Yesterday he had put two gilts in with the boar.

Maybelle was waiting on the steps. They didn't talk. They ate at Denny's and stayed at the Motel 6 next door.

"The doctor said I should bring my husband when I come back this afternoon."

"What for?"

"The doctor says that he likes to talk to the husband and wife about this."

"Maybelle, this is a private, woman's thing."

"Fred, please."

The office smelled like their bathroom right after Maybelle would clean it. Everything was white and silver. Paper, glass, and chrome. The doctor sat casually on his desk in front of an open window that let in the afternoon sun and made Fred squint to see. He asked Fred about pigs. Fred answered curtly.

"Fred, there's nothing wrong with your wife. I would like you to return for some tests, but there's the possibility that there's nothing wrong on either part, but if there is, there are lots of things that can be done, and ultimately, your wife can have a baby, so there are even more alternatives beyond . . ."

Maybelle reached across and touched his hand, and the doctor kept talking and talking, but Fred could not hear him, because he kept talking and talking but wasn't saying anything.

The doctor was talking, but Fred had suddenly remembered how his father had told him as a child about a neighboring farmer who had been eaten by his boar. Fred had always been impressed by the story and had always respected his own boar. That's why Fred had never kicked him like he wanted to now.

OLD BORDER ROAD

S. G. Miller

THE KNOCK CAME at the wrong time. He said to open up and I tried to lie still enough not to be there. But my heartbeat beat so loud I was afraid it would give me away, even with him out there and me in here. The knocking kept on. It's me, he said. He said, I know you know who this is. His words were slurred, but I knew who this is was.

It was a knock on the door I had wished for.

I didn't answer it. I had a retainer in my mouth and pin curls in my hair and school in the morning. Son said he knew I could hear him and I cupped my hands on my chest to quiet me down. Finally, the knocking stopped and there was nothing but the sound of the wind gusting the dust up out in the empty lot. I got up from the bed and made my way in the dark to the door and opened it. He turned around on his way to his truck and I said come back and come in.

Son had never been in my trailer, though I had been in his pickup truck once. That was down in Mexico, where he had offered me a ride back over the border. He lived on this side, our side, down on Old Border Road, and he showed me the old adobe house on the way to him taking me to my trailer. That's where I live, he says, and then he reaches over and pulls the back string of my halter top so he can watch it fall off. We get to the trailer and I tell him this is where I live and maybe I will see him again someday.

From *Prairie Schooner*.

The wedding was big and mostly his people. I wore my mother's wedding dress and didn't notice the stain on it until it was too late. Just try to smile, someone said, and carry your bouquet lower, more like this, and no one will ever know what's there. We're on our way to the church, with the satin train of the dress spread across the entire backseat of the station wagon, and this feeling comes on over inside me that what I'm about to do is wrong: it's like the start and run of a stain, and I look down and see the black I've put on my eyelashes falling in drops on the lap of my dress. But there is no going home I know to go home to.

Son and I left for the coast after the wedding and we drove nights and days up the interstate that runs border to border, south to north, darker to lighter, to a place I had called where I was from. We had this idea to show my father the two of us married, and we surprised him, arriving at the cabin with our truck still chalked with sentences to live by. My father shook Son's hand and patted me on the back and after drinks and the things you are supposed to say on occasions of this kind, for example, how happy he is, my father says, that I am in someone's good hands, and he shakes Son's hand once more and gives me one more pat on the back. Well, I suppose that is that, I said to Son, and I put my head out the window of the pickup truck to wave good-bye and saw my father closing the door and turning the lights in the cabin out. Son turned the truck around and we started that night for the long drive back along the coast, down to Old Border Road. Then we settled into the start of a dry spell that had people talking and scared and seemed to be without history or end.

We turned onto Old Border Road in the rising haze of the day with the dawn smoking up in dust and color off the horizon. A cloud of dust trailed and caught up to us in the pickup truck and it billowed in through our windows before we could roll them up fast enough. The old man's old dog rose from the mound of dust she was on the side of the road and ran over to the truck and trotted alongside us, barking that we were back, then forgetting us to chase after a small flock of dawn birds that had settled onto the field.

The old man and the old man's wife were out on the porch of the old adobe house when we pulled up in the pickup. They stood in the place they had waved us good-bye at, and now they stood there again, waiting for us and waving, as if they had never left their places in all the weeks we'd been away. Girl, you have a home here, the old man tells me, and he reaches for the suitcase in my hand. He says other things that sound right, the way my father could have said them. The old man says we will live and work together as a family and this has the old man's wife smiling and not crying now the way she had been on the day Son and I were married and driving away.

Son and I start our being married out by washing the honeymoon off the pickup and then we go inside the house to shower ourselves after. This is the first time the old man opens the door on us and we're standing in the shower stall and he's just standing there looking at us, adjusting the hat back on his head with a thumb, not even making a noise of surprise or saying a word of apology. Incest is best, is what Son says, and while he's laughing at this and going on with what he's doing, I'm thinking about if it should be funny.

Old habits, the old man's wife says. She has called us into dinner, and I stand behind a chair and see that she has set places at the table for only three people. She looks at me and realizes this too and she shakes her head and comes back to the table and fills my empty place with a knife and a plate and a fork. During our eating she's telling me about writing thank-yous to people I don't know or care to know for candleholders and butter dishes and electric mixers and all the rest of what we got just for getting married for. We should think about what other people think, she says, and who knows whether she is serious about this or not.

The old man's wife is all right. She is kind as a mother should be to me. After a time she shows me things like how to make a proper stitch to take a hem up, and how to make a casserole and bake a lemon pie, stiff whites and all, and how to make a garden grow and flower from seed. All of what I learn about being a wife I learn from the old man's wife.

All of what we have we have because of the old man. The old man has the old adobe house because of his old man. He has all the windblown acres surrounding the house that had been handed down to him too by his old man and add to that the melon shed and the toolhouse out behind the house. He has the tackroom, the corral, the pasture, the shoots. He has the pinto and the bay, the mare and the sorrel, the few livestock he hasn't yet sold or yet traded. He has the first of his debts from his lemon tree loss, a good hired man, and a returning gang of Mexicans. He has all the land that would soon be bared down to dust on us.

The old man has the watertruck and he has Son and I water the roads with it every day. Even though the watertruck stills the road dust, still the road dust gets everywhere. It coats whatever we have both inside and outside the old adobe house. We're always brushing the road dust off of our clothes and out of our hair and even from out of our teeth. We spit road dust into the sink. We blow it out of our noses. Road dust powders the animals, and what there's still left of the flowers and the old man's wife's old roses. It drifts in through the chimney, gets in beneath the doorframes, sneaks in between the screens. It gets in between everything. It coats the shelves, the dishes, the bedding. It settles between the sheets.

Every day we try to settle it.

Every day we watch it settle on us.

Son fills the watertruck up with canal water channeled in from out on the coast. I watch him lower the hose into the ditch, switch on the pump switch, and let the pump suck up the tank's fill. We stand in the shade of the tank, in the haze of the dirt and the sun, fanning ourselves with our hats, keeping our faces covered to up over our noses with bandanas. We drink our water from gallon jugs. We swallow the dust, this dust of which we are made.

We keep on down the road with the watertruck, keeping ahead of the dust to keep the dust from swallowing us. Every day we keep on going, believing, I suppose, only in the going on in us.

Son leaves me alone with the old man, even though I said to both of them I don't need to be on the back of any animal. The old man leads me out to the corral, even though I'm telling him as I'm following him, I don't want to go. The mare is hitched at the post and stands bridled and saddled and waiting for me. I look at the horse and the horse looks at me and she stamps a hoof and whorls her head and snorts. I tell the old man I don't like not knowing what's in the mind of what I've got to be riding. Girl, he says to me. He says if I don't ride don't I know I don't fit right in the family.

I get up on the horse the way the old man tells me to, afraid anyway, like he says not to be. The old man pets the horse to steady her. He pets me to steady me. He gowpens his hands for my bootstep and I step into his handhold, pulling up with the pommel, lifting into the one stirrup and up onto the saddle and he keeps hold of the bridle until I settle and then until the horse settles. He holds onto my reins for the ride out of the corral and until we are partway down the canalbank. Now hold the reins in your hands this way, Girl, he says.

The old man keeps his horse in a slow walk ahead of me, turning around and reminding me to keep my heels down and to sit deeper into my saddle. There is an awful weakening in my knees, a tremoring in my legs, a numbing tingling in my fingers. The old man breaks into a slow lope and my horse follows his lead, moving from a trot to a gallop. She rears her head back and breaks pace and is suddenly moving from a gallop to a run and I am holding tight onto the horn in a pound down the ditchbank, whipping through a ball of dust and the lost calls of the old man.

I catch the ground hard. My breath is hit out. My ears ring loud as the locust shrill. My mouth is full of dirt and I spit mud spit and try to breathe and see through the pockets of grit and light I'm in. The old man tugs me up from under both my arms and gets me standing and he handkerchiefs the dirt and the blood from my mouth. He puts the reins back into my hands. He lifts my boot to a stirrup, pushes my backside up and over, and gets me back into place in the saddle. I finger for the broken tooth chunk cutting into my tongue and yawn to make the ringing stop.

After that, we ride every day. I ride the way the old man says to ride. I ride the horses he has, the old man's bay, the wife's thoroughbred mare, Son's cutting horse, the sorrel, and the pinto. The old man teaches me dressage and gymkhana and the ways of dressing to go out riding in for each. I dress western for the barrels, English for the jumps, and I have been ruffled and glittered for him for rodeo days. I have waved a white-gloved hand in the parade.

The old man has all of us ride, even in the heat and the dust. We take the horses out of the cool stalls they are stalled in and harness and lead them, otherwise they fight not to leave their water and their shade. We ride them blindered and slow and still the horses lather up and wheeze the dust from their lungs. They champ and foam at the bit and whorl their heads when we lope them, trying to keep ahead of the brown cloud folding in on us.

We are veiled in dust, dirt-caked. We ride through arid, desert waste. We ride deep into the grit and the heat, Son holding the lead up ahead of me. We ride by sidewinders curled in the dirt in the sun. We ride by the old adobe house where cats lay baking in the shade. Prey birds fly low and peck at the burnt animals out along the road. The old man's old dog wanders off in the dust and has to be tracked and led back home.

We ride over acres of land cut and parceled by cement ditches that funnel the water in. I hold the reins of the horses, keeping them steady at the edge of the ditch and Son opens the metal traps of the water gates. The water trickles in, sulfur-smelling and murky with silt. The horses drop their heads and drink it.

The thirst never goes out of me.

My thirst is as great as all of what I don't know yet.

The old man speaks often of the days of enough water. He tells of his great team of hired men, the foreman he had to do most of the work for him, another man hired to care for the horses, a woman to teach the wife to ride English. The old man had hired a coach to show Son how to dive and win medals. There was a cook hired to feed everyone kept hungry because of the lemon picking and the melon loading and the riding and the diving that was done. There was a driver to drive the cars for the old man and the old man's wife on bridge nights and bright-lit rodeo nights.

There were so many nights to light up.

The old man's wife talks of the days there was water enough for all of the roses. There had been roses enough for a garden of roses, she says, all of them bordered and bedded in rows. There were flushes of ramblers rambling out over the fencepost and hybrid teas growing outside the kitchen window. There were weepers clinging to the porch beams.

The old man's wife is wiping the dust from her eyes. She is back from hours in town and has parked the car under the arbor of twisted vines and dead branches. A stream of dust follows her into the house and she waves it away with her handkerchief. She puts her purse and her keys on the sideboard and goes into the kitchen and pours herself a long drink of cold tea from the pitcher. She goes into her bedroom in the middle of the day and takes to months in her bed until death.

Every day the old man comes into the wife's room. He brings a solo rose in in a tall vase for her. He brings her one of the last flori-bundas and puts it open-cupped in a glass-cut bowl. He rows china cups of dried buds along the sill of the window.

Son and I roll the wife onto her side for her to see what's left of the roses the old man brings in. We stay her with pillows behind the splintery bones of her neck, in the broken low curve of her back-bone, between the bone-juts of her wasted legs. In the afternoon, we roll her to face her the other way.

At night, we can hear the wife. We can hear the old man in the room with her, in the bed with her, crushing more of her bones with all of his weight on her.

The sound of the old man opening the hard-foam box makes me shudder. The lid rubs against the box, making a thin sickening noise come out of it, making my eyes tear and my mouth water until something moves up in me faster than I can hold onto. All of what comes up splatters out in a foamy spill all over the front porch.

The old man wipes my mouth off with his handkerchief and Son and I follow him out to the garden. It takes both of the old man's hands and the strength he uses to pull the horns of a bull back to get the plastic bag to come out of the hard-foam box. The bag is heavy as some animal, nothing like the sack of light petals I imagined it as. Son and I put our hands into the bag the way the old man does and we scoop handfuls of the bonedust out from inside the bag. We spread the bonedust out in the garden the way the old man does it, the way we would scatter feed to chickens. We sprinkle the bonedust evenly among the rows and mounds and beds of the roses, all of it falling chalk-heavy out of our palms.

The old man reads aloud from the book of psalms. Then we blow the last of the bonedust ash off the flat of our hands. Son and I leave the old man sitting out by the rose garden during the heat of the day, until, he says, the rain should came to soak all the ash in. He sits with his shotgun flat across his lap, the metal of it flashing a rod of hot light in the sun. He fires into the sky, shooing all the pecking birds away. But, I suppose you could say it, he could not shoo any ghost of his wife away.

After the old man's wife dies, I ride her mare for the old man. He has me in the wife's saddle, in her riding suit and her handtooled boots. We ride down the canalbank and the old man talks to me, reminding me to use my knees and to sit tall in my saddle, telling me there will be no clucking or giddyupping.

Sometimes, the old man calls me the name of his wife.

Rose, he says.

Some nights, Son leaves me and goes out and crosses over the border. He leaves the old man's old shotgun loaded by the door and ready to shoot, though I am not sure what for. The old man's old dog lays atwitch in her dreams on the porch. The hired man is gone hours before before dark fall. The old man's wife is gone for weeks turned to months now. The moon is rubbed out of the sky by the nightdust. It is darker than dark most nights.

There is a crick in the wood of the floorboards when he comes down the hallway. There is a groan in the opening of the door when he comes into this bedroom. The bedsprings whine when the old man gets into the bed where Son should be. The old man whispers into my hair and I listen for Son. I listen for the missing sound of the engine, the rattle of loose metal, or the squeaking of a hinge. I listen for noises and voices through the adobe. I pretend to be sleeping. My breath stays even and steady, but when the old man reaches out for me to come into me, my swallowing tells I'm awake. Girl, he says.

After he leaves I stare at the wall, seeing the places where Son might be now and the faces of the women he's with. I wait for the crunching of gravel from tires outside. I wait a long time, through the long night. Then comes a stumble of boot steps on the front porch, a fumbling of keys, another crick in the wood of the floor.

My back faces the empty place that Son leaves and I lie still enough to be sleeping. Son sits on the edge of the bed and struggles to get one boot off and then the other one off. I can hear his tongue moving thickly in his mouth when he curses. I can smell the drinking on him. I can smell the women he's been with. I can feel my heart pounding loud enough to give me away.

The night quivers. I lay awake, in the gathered rub of hind legs, in the thin-pitched screech of insects, listening for scorpions pincering across walls or crawling onto our linens. A gecko skips across a crack in the adobe. Gila monsters belly their way through the grass and the weeds and the sticks. Limes swell and burst in the heat and drop from the trees. Son licks his cankered lips. The watertruck settles and pings.

My eyes are gummed shut with dust when I wake and my ears ring in the pouring morning scorch. Son is up and gone to town, gone with the old man, where the old man will sell blocks of his land off while he's eating his eggs and his biscuits and gravy.

I open the screen door into parched light and see a diamondback lay choked on the welcome mat, along with trails of dust prints trailing off the porch, the marks of the hunter-cats. I take shelter from the sun in the shade of the melon shed on my walk back to the tackroom. The old man's old dog is asleep on the concrete floor of the melon shed, where it stays almost cool in the shade. When she hears me, she gets up and shakes, and I squeeze my eyes shut at the dust that floats up from her coat. I am remembering now pieces of where I had been in the night, a lake it was, back from where I was from, and I am trying to find the place I know there to get the feelings right that I had had once. Who were those people who kept getting in my way? Why couldn't I make my way closer to the shore? I rub at my eyes and open them again and I see the hired man over under the watertruck. He is crawling out sideways, crablike on his back, and he reaches for his hat and tips it at me. Good morning, Mrs., he says, and it is strange to hear the word Mrs. when I am just turned eighteen.

You should see it here, the way the sun has blistered its way through most everything. It has eroded into the ears and the nose of the hired man, and whitened his hair right down to the roots. The sun has burnt through the paint of the watertruck, wearing the cabtop down to sand prime, down to its metal core. The heat of the sun bores through the straw of my hat, slowing my thinking down to wanting to be sleeping. The hired man lifts the hoodlid up and looks under where the engine is and thick folds of dust sift out of cracks when he does. And I fan myself with my hat and walk on past, trying to arrange the pieces of the night I have risen from.

I look out into the start of day and see nothing but barren acres of land surrounding me. A jet moves past sound and thunders up over my head, and I guess at the time it will take it to get to the next state. A pecker bird rattles on a hollowed out old saguaro, and I am shaked back again to where I am.

I shoo the crowbirds that are fence-rowed on the pasture gate with a hard kick of the post. They hover and caw above me, their angry cries rising like razors from their gulars. One swoops down and knocks the hat off my head and I snatch it up and hurry on into the tackroom, the blood running prickly feeling through my veins, my thoughts running through reasons for punishment.

It is musty and cool and dark inside. Sun filters in with the dust through the bars of the small window. I sit at the old man's old metal desk and look inside it, hoping to find something hopeful, but what am I looking for? All I find are drawers full of tools and buckles and locks. I look at the walls around me that are nailed and studded and holding stiff ropes, stirrups, bridles, reins, flourishes of headstalls and straps, harnesses and spurs, peggings of leather riggings, worn old chaps, cracked hames, and unknowable leather things. The shelves are piled full of saddle soaps and leather balms, ointments and liniments, and whatever other kind of cream that promises to heal. I open a jar up and find something inside dried to a crust in the tin.

The whiskey is already all gone from the bottle whether because of the old man or Son or both, father like Son, Son like father, who knows who drinks it up before the other one. I toss the bottle into a barrel of trash and see the paper that was weighted underneath it with the current list of rodeo events and the sums of the prizes given for winning.

Columns of sediment pour in through the door and the window when Son and the old man pull up to the corral in the pickup truck. They walk into the tackroom and stop at the doorway, as if to let their eyes adjust to the dark inside, and I walk past in between them and out to the glare of the sun, feeling my eyeballs constricting in their adjusting.

The mare stands in the pasture in the shade of a pecan tree where I have to go out and catch her for bridling with pockets of hay and barley. I lead her out of the pasture gate and into the arena and I brush and blanket her where I have hitched her at the post, not turning to look at either Son or the old man when they come out to look at me. I can feel their eyes poking through the back of my shirt, right through my skin and deeper in.

Son goes back into the tackroom and comes out carrying my saddle and I try to take it out of his arms, but he nudges me off and throws the saddle on the back of the mare. He is rough in the handling, cinching the mare up too tight again, making her backstep and choking up too hard on the bit, making her head flinch. He goes back into the tackroom for his own saddle, and I get up on the mare and ride off before he gets back to me.

Son is blowing tin cans off the fence post with the old man's old shotgun and I am wondering what kind of event this is he is practicing for. After he clears the fencepost he goes and rows empty bottles up on wired up bales of hay. After the bottles are shot off he looks around at what's next and he looks at me and then he goes and starts shooting at almost everything. He shoots at a chuckwalla scooting from field hole to field hole. He shoots at a gopher that is dropped from the jaws of one of the hunter cats, and then he turns and shoots at the cat. He shoots at a birdrunner running along the road. I run back into the tackroom, the smoke pockets drifting up over me and off into the field like blue doves.

The old man is seated at his metal desk with a pouch of tobacco and is packing the bowl of his pipe. He strikes the match on the bottom of his boot for a light and looks up at me. Girl, the old man says, you got to forget about what was. His words buzz up like the horseflies up over my head and I wave them away in the air.

Son comes into the tackroom and hands the shotgun over to the old man. The old man takes it and settles it into his lap. Get on after that rodeo dough, the old man says, and we go out like he says, as I'm wondering what is it that makes me do what he says.

I am not afraid.

Son goes over and starts tying bullhorns onto the end of a wooden horse and starts working at his rope throws. After awhile, he goes over and tosses the rope over a parceled up bail of hay. Then he starts roping anything he can find to rope. He ropes the fence posts, the legs of an old table, a rusted out barrel and keg. He ropes the bumper of the watertruck, the whole of the old man's toolbox, the post of the mailbox. He has me run from him and he runs after me, going for my head and then going for my feet. I call at him to stop and he takes the rope to the neck of the old man's old dog, choking back on the rope and making her struggle and rasp.

Just horsin', he says.

Now my habit is to ride alone, saddling the mare up every morning after Son and the old man are up and gone. This morning is like every morning here, one hard to tell from any other one in this cloudless place we live in. Tumbled up weeds spring and roll in the wind as I skirt along the canalbank, making my mind up to ride toward the hired man's place, an easy road shaded sparely with ocotillo. I ride trying to get ahead of the hot part of the day, breaking the lope of the horse down to a trot at her falter. Hot dirt gusts around me in ropes and swirls on the ground. My hands are kid-gloved, my head brimmed with a broad straw hat, the mare rib-boned with sweat and with froth. I break her into a walk and stop to take a drink and rub the dust-scum off my teeth.

The hired man's place is an old paint-blistered trailer left settled on a blown over parcel of dirt. Whirlwinds of wind brush dust against aluminum. Locusts and crickets shrill loud in the mesquite. The long bones of some animal hang dried and chime in the trees.

Around back in a slab of shade is where I spot the pickup truck parked. All of a sudden the trailer begins to pitch and rumble. There is an upset of some kind inside, followed by a spell of silence, then a thud against a wall, the running of boot steps, a tremoring, of aluminum, and the old man and Son come stumbling out the door. A shadow passes in there by the open window, a sweep of dark hair, the flicker of a limb, the pad of bare footsteps. But I never did see her.

In between the hours and days of roping, and nights spent mostly where I don't know where he is, Son is out in the watertruck. He rides along the canalbanks and the ditchbanks and the old roads, pouring the water out in tankfulls, in cargo loads, in wet tons, the waterfill ragging out in broken streams from the back of the watertruck. He drives by me, through waves of heat, and I sit on the porch and close my eyes until I know he has passed me. I hear the sound of the tank slosh, the way you can hear a river moving in it, and I rest my head in my arms and I am back on the bank of the river again, laying in the shade of tall pines. Water rushes by, water clear enough to see the glaciered rocks and colored pebbles lining the bottom of the river bed, water that is cold and sweet enough to drink.

I open my eyes and feel the thirst aching up in me in my remembering, the thirst in me even worse looking at the water in the canal flowing in front of me, knowing we can't drink it or even get in it.

We drink our water from the well the old man dug out years before out behind the melon shed. The water from the well smells of foul-smelling metals, elements that seep into the soil and spurt out rust-colored from our hoses and our pipes, the cause, we believe, to be the leach of ore or iron. The leach in the well water stains all that it touches. It stains our sinks and tubs, the food we cook, the old clothes we live in. It stains our teeth and leaves our skin metal-stinking, our hair coppered and brittle. You learn not to breath when you need to drink it. You take it in not looking and breathless.

And the cats and rabbits will lap at it.

And we will get it down, or spit it out.

The iron in the water turns the old man's bourbon dark as ink. The old man drinks his drink that way anyway, no matter the odor or the color or the taste of it. He sits out by the pool at night, his face reflected fluorescent, drinking his black drink iced with iron-colored ice.

When the pool is drained and the bourbon all gone, the old man drinks all that he can find in the old adobe house. He empties the cabinet of the party drinks. He drinks his dead wife's fine wine, her sweet cordial drinks, the flavoring she would put in her cakes. After all that he finishes up what's in the medicine cabinet, and then what's out in the tackroom, and anything else he can find anywhere else besides that.

Son's looping a rope from elbow to fist, showing me how it has to be done. The rope is stiff at the gather for the coil and you have to work it over with a sharp turn of the wrist to make it curl with a bend in it. You have to loop it high up over your head with an even swing and then you throw your aim sharp and quick.

Son says, no, like this. He makes the stiff rope work easy for him. He says up over and pull for the head. He says loop down and time for the feet. He loops the rope over the sawhorse and lands the rope under the wood legs. He tells me to wait for the tug. Now you, he says.

We leave the corral and go out to the arena in the evening cool down. Gold sun burns through the dust haze where the land meets the sky. We fill the pens up with the cows and filter them through the shoots and out of the pen and on through. Most of the cows are too hot and too dumb, so you have to hotshot them out of the pen and on into the shoots. I put the hotshot to the cow rump and let the current buzz through them and jump them ahead to the end gate.

Son gives the nod and I open the gate latch and sidestep away for the cow to burst out. The old man and Son shoot out on horseback when I throw open the gate. Son's sorrel is first to cross over the line, and he runs the horse out hard and fast ahead, looping his rope up over his head until the sorrel catches up to the cow. He tosses the rope, drops it on over the horns of the cow, and reins his horse back with a jerk, choking the rope up on the cow's neck. The cow bawls loud and its eyes bulge out, as the old man runs alongside for the heels, swinging and then looping the headed cow around the back hoof. He ties on hard and fast.

They drop out of their saddles and stand firm on the ground, letting the horses do the work for them. The horses prance backwards both ways, stretching the ropes out, stretching the cow out long and tight, stiffening it like it will hang after butchering. The cow snots and bawls in protest. Son goes over and unropes it and we go back to the shoots and do it all over again.

It is his leaving that clings to me like the dust on me, his leaving that follows me into my sleep, the words and the images distorted, right or wrong, but always worse at night. His leaving goes back into my waking. It settles into memory of what isn't or wasn't or couldn't have been, but will be because I have seen it.

I run to the front door and get there before Son does and I get a good hold of his belt loops and say all the words I know to say to make him stay. He takes my hold apart and goes out the door, not looking at me to keep from having to see what he might see, and I watch him drive away in the pickup truck, until the body of earth he leaves floating behind him disappears and is gone.

I sit with the old man's old dog on the porch step, letting my legs get chigger-bit. The old man is in the house, and no, I won't go back in, though I don't know where to go. The old man's old dog gets up and shakes and I get up and follow her. She takes us out back into the melon shed. Good dog, I say, going over to the watertruck and opening the door of it. I give her a boost up and in and she settles on the seat in front of the wheel. I settle my head on her, finding this bed a better one than my own to bed down for the night in.

The old man left the bedroom wall pocked all up with his buckshot. The blast that he left a ringing in our ears. The shot ran through all the cool dark rooms of the old adobe house. It bled from the bedroom, blew out and down along the hallway, and filled the kitchen and the parlor up. It gusted out the open windows, rose in and up the chimney, was swept beneath all the doors. The shock was rocketed way out back to the melon shed, where it went hallowing through the toolhouse. It howled down the dusty road, stirred the dust up in the dirt bare fields, and tornadoed into the wind. The blast rattled the doors of the watertruck. It pricked the ears up on the old man's old dog. It sent the hired man running. It left the Mexicans stunned.

We took all of what the old man left us.

We lived in it, slept in it, drove it, fed it, carried it.

We cared for it, all of what was left to us as it was.

There were no words left to us by the old man. There were no last words to us, no farewell he had to bid us, no message for us to carry on with us. We looked for his whys of leaving us in his pockets. We looked for some way of knowing to be pinned to the bed or dropped to the floor. We hoped for the scrawl of his hand on a mirror, a note tacked to a door, a letter cubbied somewhere in adobe. We looked through all the cool dark rooms of the old adobe house. We looked out in all the stalls, all around the corral, in the grooves of the walls of the tackroom. We went back out to the melon shed and searched from the edge of the gully. We rummaged throughout the toolhouse. We eyeballed every post beam for the old man's words posted. We picked over shelves of studs and pins and bolts for some plans for us. We swept our palms across the dashboard of the watertruck and found nothing but dust. We found nothing but an empty look in the old man's old dog's eyes.

We locked the toolhouse up.

We used the melon shed for shelter.

We cemented the swimming pool in.

In the haze of the evening we sat out in the melon shed, at the edge of the cement gully, with our legs hung over the side of it. We hung our heads looking down into the dark hole below us. We breathed in lime and clay and dust.

We looked up to a moonless sky.

We ride in the watertruck high up over the road, looking each day for more water. We ride through white-hot swells, aiming toward some watery vision ahead, arriving always to nothing but heat and dirt. We breathe into our bandanas, our sleeves, our handkerchiefs. Our voices are dirt muffled, our words all an effort, our cries gone bone dry.

Our talk gave out after the old man died. We tossed the old man's ashes into the canal and watched them spiral into the wind. The wind blew the ash back at us and into our faces, as if the old man might have had something to say after all.

Our tongues have become whitish and thick, our breath offensive and hot. Our bodies have chafed and thinned on us. What little sex we have left between us has turned sluggish and dry. We suck on lemons to get the saliva back and swallow salt tablets for salt. Our urine has turned murky and clotted, our skin sun-darkened and hard.

There is no one to call.

No break comes in the heat for days, weeks, months. Every day is dazed. Every day is heat and dust. Every day we are gauzed with worthless dirt, covered with more and more layers of dust and dust and dust, everything around us in a stage of decay or drying up.

Every day is one more day lost.

What could be done to change it?

Son gives the hired man the job of hotshotting the cow down the pen shoot and we get back out to the arena. The hired man opens the gate for us at the touch of a hat, and Son shoots out for the head of the cow, while my horse pounds behind at the heels. Son throws the rope and there is a jolt, a punch, and why is Son's horse reeling and braking? Son is suddenly all arms and legs in the air, a cartwheel spinning, going head first over the head of the horse. He makes a thick grunting sound when he hits the ground, and the sorrel topples and rolls.

The sorrel is rising up out of a cloud like a vision. It steadies itself before running off freely, leaving an eeriness in the emptiness of the saddle. I wait for Son to come up to a stand, but when the dust clears away Son is spread out on his face on the ground. I go over and roll him onto his back and see him furred thick with dirt, and he lays there, his mouth open and soundless, the breath all sucked out of him. I kick at him. Breathe, I say. He breathes. C'mon, I say. He spits dirt spit. Get up, I say. All he says is can't.

The hired man and I pick Son up and carry him out of the arena, the hired man at Son's head, me at Son's heels. Half way out of the arena we stop to rest, laying Son back in the dirt, and he moans and chokes and spits, and I cuss at him for the work he puts us through. We drag him the rest of the way out by his boots, getting him out of the arena and up into the watertruck. He is laid out straight in the cabfront, his head in my lap, his legs in the lap of the hired man. We have to perch Son's boots on the open window frame, and they poke out the door. The hired man reaches across for the wheel and drives from over Son's legs. He starts to make the turn for town and I tell him no, let's get back to the house.

We side the watertruck up to the front porch and spread a bedspread out underneath Son so we can stretcher him out of the watertruck and get him up the steps. We're dragging him across the front porch with the old man's old dog sniffing at him, and we get him through the door, sliding him across the floor and into the cool dark parlor of the old adobe house. Son lays spread out on the parlor couch, his head tipped up with a pillow I fix for him. He tips his chin down and sucks the water out of a glass I hold for him. He takes the water in too hard and starts choking it back up and spitting it out until he is crying. The old man's old dog goes up to Son and licks his hand and his fingers and he hits her with a hard closed fist.

I hit Son back, only harder.

The land is parched, earth scorched, the color dun. It is nearly a year now since rain, and when it comes, it comes hard. The rain makes it dark as night for days. When the lightning puts the power out, I light candles throughout the old adobe house, surrounding Son with flames to see him by. He lays in a deep sleep in the parlor, appearing ready for sacrifice or resurrection or something mystical or unexplainable. I walk around in damp clothes, steaming, gathering flashlights, the old man's buck-knife, duct-tape, buckets. The house swells up, you can smell it, making the doors stick, and taking all my might to open them.

The rain sprays hard as bullet pellets on the tin roof of the melon shed. Streams of water break through the burnt holes and seared grooves of the tin roof. Water seams its way into the watertruck. It pools into the cement gully, the toolhouse, the fields. The furrows of the old lemon groves brim over, uprooting and felling the spindled trees. Bared acres fill and surround the old adobe house in a delta of water and mud. The ditches swell and overflow and the canal runs as hard and quick as a great river does, taking drowned animals and pieces of equipment with it.

The rain washes away the layers and layers of dust. It washes away the caked-on sod, the crust, the decay. It washes through the gully of the melon shed, flows out over the rim of the well, out into the ditches, on through the canals. It channels all the mud and the dirt back toward the coast and further on down into Mexico.

The hired man holds Son from under both of his arms for me so I can peel the dungarees off. Son smells of sweat and urine and his flesh is red and swelled where the dungarees have chewed into him and blisters pucker around the rawed skin of the hips. I wash him. I wash his reddened chest, his bloated face, his hard and swollen belly. I brush his teeth, his hair for him. I move his legs for him and roll him over and rub horse ointment over the sores on his backside. I prop him with pillows behind his neck and back and in between his useless legs. Morning and night, I will turn him to face the other way.

He lays in the parlor in a gibber. He is made up of words you've never heard, sentences that come from a lost place or a bruised piece

S. G. MILLER

of his mind. A garble rises out of his throat, from somewhere deep inside him. I lay my hand on his arm and feel his flesh cool and sticky. I can feel death pulsing through his veins, see it seeding in the marrow, in the bulbs and the lobes. It seeps out of him with the stench that leaves from his pores.

I lay awake in my bed in the quiet ticking of the nightclock with my eyes open and gauged to the night. Son lay out in the parlor, moaning in his delirium. The old man's old dog lay in the bed next to me and she whines in her sleep. Her haunches jerk and her limbs twitch and growls roll out from low in her belly. She gives the start of barks and I pet her to break the bad dream for her.

My gaze moves steady through the room to keep my eyes from making things in front of me up. I watch for the cast shadows of strangers, for the flicker behind a shade. Night moths flutter overhead in the lamp globe, and I listen to them as they wing themselves to their deaths.

The hired man and I go out and haul away the ruin from the storm after all the water has drained off and soaked into the land. We haul the trailer wreck and all the fallen trees out. We clear the groves of broken limbs and stumps. We treat the horses' mildewed hooves. We bury drowned cats and chickens, toss limp snakes and stiff rodents from the road off into the canal. We toss everything worth nothing into the canal, not leaving time for more rot to set in. We throw the junk in and watch it bob before whatever it is or was is sunk. We watch the scrap that doesn't sink float off like a body does.

Most of the rest that's left around here, I sell to the hired man. I sell him the watertruck, the mare, the bay, the sorrel and the pinto, along with all the cows, the hotshot to poke them with, and the rest of the feed that's left. The hired man buys the saddles from me, the bridle and the reins, the ropes and the spurs. I sell him the old man's old shotgun and throw the old man's boots in for free. He takes the old man's old dog too. He hands me a rubberbanded wad of bills and I give him my father's address where he should send the rest to.

Son flails his arms at me. I force the cup between his teeth and he spits the water back out. I rub his back to get the blood to come to the surface and the flesh sloughs at my touch. He is a mottle of bleed spots. There is a yellowy paste seeping out of the cracks in his skin. My stomach rolls at the smell of him.

The air is almost delicate. The rain has drowned the wind and cleared the sky. You can see foothills miles ahead out on the horizon spread out like dormant animals of some kind. Jets rocket up above our heads, leaving the sky bannered white. Small birds nest again in the porch beams. There are stars to see at night.

The day is clear enough to bring a day back from somewhere long ago. Where was it I was? When was it I was there? The day is a place I have been, or maybe have never been, but I long to be there, wherever it is or was, in the before this, or the beyond this, in a place I know and don't know, a place clear to me and not clear at all, though anywhere but here where I am, this I know.

I drive on in the watery light and don't look back. The old man's old dog trails along side of the pickup until I turn onto Old Border Road, and then she is gone from sight. Son is on his back in the bed of the pickup truck covered over with an old tarpaulin, the ends tucked under his head and his boots to keep from coming loose. The tarpaulin billows as soon as I get onto the highway. It gets lifted into the wind and is set adrift over the road before it floats off and into the sandhills.

I pass the ghost of an old airfield and the carcass of an old airplane that lays blazing in the sun. Further on down the highway, we pass the Old Border Prison, deserted but still linked by poles and fence and barbs of looped wire. We ride through the flat land of cholla and prickly pear, on into the dunes, then up and through the foothills, passing outcrops of bubbled rocks and boulder fields that are spray-painted with Mexican names. The pickup truck climbs in a slow chug into the high country of scrub pine and sagebrush and I drive on until we get to the place where the road goes two ways.

Desert plants flower in neat patches of dirt in the lot I pull the pickup truck into. Through the wide double doors of the building I make a shapeless figure out inside and I gesture in that direction to please come toward mine. I climb into the back of the pickup

S. G. MILLER

and pick Son's head up, heavy as dead weight, and I try to get his mouth up toward the waterjug to make him take some water. He chokes and spits. I wipe his face with a bandana and then cover his face over with it and look away, waiting for the wide doors to spring open and for someone to come for us. Two men come through the door and walk our way, one old, one young, wouldn't you know it, and I stand back and let them get Son out of the pickup and I watch them wheel Son back through the doors that open and close on their own. I trail behind at the men's heels, following them into the lobby, where I stay, letting them take Son down the long hallway without me, until they turn a corner and are gone.

There are papers they put before me before leaving.

I write my name.

GOLD FIREBIRD

Peter Rock

HARNESSING THE SUN, the gold Pontiac Firebird careened across the wide desert mirages. It surfaced, distinct and glinting, and disappeared once again. Then, shimmering, it rose and veered and finally jerked to an impatient stop alongside the pumps of an isolated service station.

Kent heard the bell, the signal of the car's arrival, tires across the hoses stretched out there, fifty feet from where he stood in the open bay, under a Cutlass up on the lift. He hit the car's underside with a bent wrench he kept on hand for just that purpose, then stepped out of the shadow, through the open garage door.

He felt the blacktop through the soles of his boots. It was a dry hundred and five, at least, but he was used to it. Squinting at the familiar, smooth shape of the Firebird, he half believed he was mistaken, seeing it shine there. The driver, a woman, was the only person in the car. He could not see well, his vision obscured by the pumps; it seemed she was turning to reach into the back seat, then pulling a shirt over her head. Setting down the wrench, Kent raked his dirty fingers through his tangled gray hair. The pumps were self-serve, but sometimes he'd go days between actual conversations.

Now the Firebird, in the shadow of the overhang, was not so bright. He walked toward it, away from the building, nothing but

From *Post Road*.

desert baking in every direction. Heat made the air down low thicken and buckle, unreliable. All this he'd grown used to, out here, halfway between Reno and Vegas. Beatty was the nearest town, though few would count it.

"That car!" he shouted, approaching. "What is it, a seventy-five?"

The young woman was sitting in the Firebird with the door open, her feet out on the pavement so all he could see were her cowboy boots—black and white, heavily tooled, the heels worn down. Then, through the windshield, her wraparound sunglasses and ragged, dirty-blonde hair.

"Must be a seventy-five or six," he said, his voice lower now. "What with those headlights; those changed, around then."

When she stood up and slammed the door, he saw that she was wearing a thin yellow dress—a sheath or shift, he wasn't good with words—and in a sudden silhouette he noticed her thin, bowed legs. She looked to be in her twenties, only perhaps as old as the car she drove, and she was slightly taller than Kent. She half smiled as she stepped past him, toward the office.

"Restroom keys're hanging on the wall," he said. Watching her, he wondered if she'd been driving across the desert wearing nothing but sunglasses and cowboy boots; he imagined that sight, to see it through the windshield, oncoming, then gone before you'd even realize. By the time you recognized what you'd seen, miles would have stretched between you.

He had not been mistaken. It was a Firebird Esprit 400, all smooth lines, slippery, a rolling promise. Four hundred cubic inches, four-barrel carb—he knew it well. Circling the car, he jerked tumbleweeds from the grille, poked at the moths and desert hoppers with the squeegee now in his hand, noted the jackrabbit fur along the front bumper. He started in on the windshield, top to bottom, bug-spattered and sand-pitted; first he saw into the backseat, piled high with unfolded clothing, and then the television, sitting in the front passenger seat, its screen raked around to face the driver's side, its cord snaking toward the cigarette lighter. Three books, their covers bleached, lay on the dashboard. He felt a stab at the familiar sight of the thickest one, the Bicentennial edition of the *Guinness Book of Records;* the middle one was a Choose-Your-Own-Adventure, the title too pale to read; the last was called *Stories about Not Being Afraid of Ghosts.* The author's name looked Oriental.

Kent moved around the car. The paint was dull, but nonetheless gold, undeniably so. The big engine ticked, cooling. Rust speckled the chrome strips, but that was only visible up close. This was a vehicle, not merely transportation.

Something sticky had set along the driver's side and around the back window, making the glass hard to see through. He scrubbed at it, wet his squeegee again, scraped along the edges. He knew she was returning because the office door, opening, let out a sliver of radio music—some overproduced country and western—and then the knock of her cowboy boots' heels approached. When the knocking stopped, he turned. She stood there, ten feet away, watching him, a stick of beef jerky in her hand.

"Where you headed?" he said.

Taking off her sunglasses, squinting, she looked up and down the highway. No one was coming; no one would come. He feared she'd pay him and just take off, but she seemed to be in no hurry.

"I see you got a TV set up in there," he said. "You get any reception?"

"I'm just driving," she said. "Not going anywhere. It makes the driving go faster."

"You watch while you drive?"

"Cruise control," she said. "Sometimes I read, too, so it's like doing three things at once. Or more, depending what I'm thinking about."

Her voice was high-pitched, wavering, and he realized that her silence before was only the gradual surfacing from driving alone. She didn't mind talking. She had time.

"All the engines now are just aluminum," he said. "They sound different; you can't feel them rumble in your spine, like this one here."

"I watch videos," she said.

Shifting, he looked over the front seat and saw the VCR nestled in the passenger's foot space, half buried under videotapes. He kept scrubbing at the sticky rear window.

"*Rockford Files*, mostly," she was saying. "Old episodes. Whole seasons' worth."

"This is the same car Jim Rockford drove," he said. "I guess you know that."

"I always did kind of want a Trans Am," she said. "Instead, I mean."

"I once owned this same car," he said. "Same color, even."

"And what happened?"

"It just got taken away."

"Bank?"

"I don't know," he said. "No, not the bank. My wife. Haven't seen either one of them for twenty-five years."

The young woman did not express sympathy, or say anything at all. She stood there in that thin yellow dress, the sunglasses, the cowboy boots. Her hair still looked blown sideways, and there was no wind. She tore the beef jerky in half, one end in her teeth, her hand pulling down, her neck straining. She watched him watch her do this.

"I left a dollar on the counter," she said, chewing and swallowing. "It was the last one."

He pictured the jar of jerky, full this morning.

"Last dollar, I meant," she said, watching him think.

"The gas," he said.

"Exactly. I'll have to pay you some other way—like washing dishes at a restaurant, that old thing."

He looked past her, to the garage's open bay, the Cutlass up on the lift. She turned, following his gaze.

"Know anything about replacing struts?" he said.

"A little," she said. "Probably not as much as you do."

"So what are you suggesting?" he said.

"Don't you have any ideas?" She did not smile when she said this, only seemed disappointed at his lack of imagination.

Turning back to the Firebird, he saw for the first time that the left rear panel was bent, Bondo-ed. He scrubbed again at the sticky window; the heat of the car was suddenly getting to him.

"Stubborn," he said. "What could this be?"

"Piss," she said.

"What?" Startled, he stepped back.

"Don't be such a prude," she said, closer now, laughing low. "I hate to stop, you know, unless I'm out of gas. So I have a cup I use, a jar with a lid. And when it's full I just empty it out the window, start filling it again." She shrugged, her thin, bare arms sliding up her sides. "No big deal."

"I'm not a prude," he said. "No one ever called me that."

"How about a massage, then?" she said.

"Pardon me?"

"For the gas."

He dropped the squeegee back in its bucket of dirty water. "Fourteen bucks," he said, coughing, pointing at the numbers on the pump. "I've been taken for more. Maybe you'll pass through again."

"Never," she said.

He felt the pressure of all the deserted miles around them as he watched her say this. Behind her was the station—his station, and his home, his room upstairs. A pyramid of Pennzoil cans, dents turned back, stood against the wall. Their yellow matched her dress.

"When you say 'massage,'" he said. "What do you mean?"

She smiled, at last. "Aha," she said. "No, it's not that, whatever you're thinking, the old Nevada massage. When I say 'massage,' I mean you not moving at all, not trying to touch me with your hands or anything else."

"I wasn't thinking anything," he said.

"I'm licensed," she said. Holding up her hands, she flexed her thin fingers. The short nails were painted black.

She followed him to the station, and stepped through the office door when he held it open. The Judds were on the radio, singing "Mama, He's Crazy."

"This song works since they're mother and daughter," Kent explained. "Naomi's the mother, the hot-looker, but Wynonna's got the voice. Listen to that growl, there."

"I prefer to work in silence." The young woman stepped to the radio and switched it off.

"People tell me I ramble more, lately," he said. "I can talk and talk, like I didn't used to—sometimes I'll start and people will wander away from me. I can't help it. Maybe it makes me more honest, though?"

She just looked around the small, cluttered room—at the half-finished crossword puzzles, the grease-smeared telephone, the schematic diagrams of engines, hydraulics, electrical systems.

"I prefer jazz," he said. "It works better in the desert than you'd think."

"I'll need you laid out flat," she said.

He leaned against the dusty blinds so they clattered. He pointed to a door in the corner.

"I got a bed," he said. "In my room, upstairs."

"You live here?"

"I own it."

"Bed's too soft," she said. "Gives way too much. I use more of a table. Let's clear this desk off, here."

They did so, piling receipts and papers on the chair, along the counters. When he began to lie down, though, she stopped him.

"I can't work through your clothes."

"What? You want me to strip down?"

"No," she said, her hands up to slow him. "No, no. Just up top; I need your back bare."

He unzipped his coveralls to his waist, shucked out of the arms, pulled his T-shirt over his head. He lay himself down on his stomach, the dusty desktop against his skin.

"You're in pretty good shape," she said, "for someone your age."

"You don't know how old I am."

"How long you been out here?" she said.

"Since seventy-six."

"Bicentennial."

"Exactly."

"So," she said. "Twenty-five years."

She jerked off his work boots, one at a time, so his kneecaps jumped on the desktop.

"I'm not sixty," he said. "If that's what you were thinking."

Her cool palms came down first, smooth, circling from his waist, up to his shoulders, startling and then slowly familiar. He opened his eyes and saw only the dirty vinyl floor. He closed them again.

"Shh," she said. "Don't talk. Relax."

She continued, taking handfuls of his flesh, fingers spiderwalking down from his shoulders to his waist. Then she pounded with her fingertips, then used them as pincers, and then came karate chops, then the warm smooth palms again. She leaned gently against him, only that thin fabric between the warmth of their bodies. Her fingers clattered across the back of his ribcage, solid, and pressed into muscles, finding electricity, unsnarling knots. How long since a woman had touched him like his, how long since he'd allowed it? Alice, it had to be Alice. His wife. All those years and everything gone wrong, the photographs and then the disagreement that led to the leaving.

Alice—he remembered one time on the shoulder of a night highway, her spread out on the hood of that very car, the Firebird, a night when they could not wait the half hour it would take to get home. Now the fingers worked down the tendons of his right arm, across his wrist, spreading his palm, pulling on each of his fingers, stretching his thumb, then returning—wrist, elbow, shoulder, clavicle, and down the other side. The air conditioner chuffed and shivered, then cycled trembling to a stop. There was no sound except his breathing, and hers. No wind outside, nothing for miles as he recalled another time, off a hiking trail, the voices of other people suddenly so close as Alice rose, astride him, jolting him into the sharp twigs beneath his bare back, the sharp stones he could hardly feel.

"Roll onto your side," she said.

He did so, turning toward her, resting on his hip and shoulder. She stepped back. He looked up at her face and she looked back at him; she didn't pretend not to notice his erection. Despite his bunched up coveralls, it was apparent, tenting out the fabric, pointing right at her.

"Maybe we should take a little break," she said.

"How's that?" he said, startled, not sure how he wanted to understand her.

"Why don't you go into the other room and take care of that situation," she said. "Then come back in and I'll be able to finish the massage."

Her tone was so matter-of-fact that he could not deny its logic. He swung his legs around over the edge of the desk and sat there, thinking how to get down, to walk without hurting himself or looking ridiculous. Clasping the gathered material of his coveralls at his waist, he shuffled, hunching toward the door to the stairs—no, it would be too hot up there—and, still keeping his back to her, through the door with the EMPLOYEES ONLY sign, into the garage. He took only one step and stood there, the door closing behind him, between them.

He let go of his coveralls; they fell down to his knees. He pushed down his underwear and took hold of his cock, trying to remember the feel of her skin, but his fingers were far too rough and it was difficult to make himself believe. Standing there, eyes closed tightly, he tried to imagine her grasping the hem of that yellow dress and pulling it over her head like liquid slipping away from her skin so she stood there bowlegged in her cowboy boots, squinting in the sun, standing next to the Gold Firebird, the same car that Alice had taken, and now he thought of Alice, spread-eagled across the hood, and he remembered how she loved to gun that big engine, the tires she went through, the whooshing sound of the gas sucked down as the carburetor's second set of throats opened. *Machine eats landscape,* she would say, her thin arms out straight, fingers tight around the steering wheel.

That's how she'd driven away from him, after the argument about the photographs. He'd always had control of his body, he told her, always kept it under control; his mind wandered, but whose didn't? He played in bands, back then, different outfits in San Francisco, and in that world there were always women getting in your mind. He liked, he likes the shapes of different bodies, the mysteries, the places hair grows or doesn't, the wrinkles and scars. That's natural. And now all those events were twenty-five years back, the Bicentennial, the last time he can remember so many American flags everywhere. Why wouldn't she believe him? Why did her mistrust seem to have some basis to him? He hardly knew a thing anymore—these days, people flew airplanes into buildings—except for how he felt back then, watching her drive away.

He opened his eyes. His memory had taken him; he had forgotten what he was doing; his coveralls were at his ankles, his underwear at his knees. His hands held each other, rather than getting to business, and down below he was flaccid, loose, all forgotten. Bending, zipping, he fumbled to the window, checked and saw the gold Firebird, still there, dull in shadow, tumbleweeds collecting in the barbed wire across the highway. One blew free, in that moment, and skittered along the hot pavement, through the open garage door, and bounced off the back wall, under the Cutlass, which was still suspended.

Kent looked over the dirty rags, the wrenches hanging on their pegboard, the crooked black pillars of worn tires. Shuffling in his stocking feet, he opened the door and stepped back into the office. She was not there. He checked another window—the Firebird sat motionless, empty. Would he have heard her footsteps on the stairs, if she'd gone up to his room, if she'd stretched out on his bed? His bed gave way too much, she needed a table, but how would it be to simply lie down beside her, the length of her inadvertently touching his side in the heat? He kicked his feet into his boots, didn't bother lacing them.

The stairs creaked. The air thickened as he climbed through it. She was not there, the room empty—the sagging mattress, the jazz magazines and warped records, the broken television with its bent antenna and half-assed tinfoil, the dull-bladed fan in the window, the heat. Through the sand-scratched glass he saw the white desert stretching away. Nothing but hot clumps of sage, pathetic Joshua trees.

And yet something was different; something was wrong. Out behind the station, a hundred feet away, a black square marked the desert floor. Not just a square, not a lost sign or piece of metal or scrap of black plastic bag—it was, he knew, a hole. The trapdoor of the dugout was slapped open. That's where she'd gotten to. He wheeled from the room, kicked down the stairs.

The dugout was nothing more than an underground space, a kind of room with dirt walls and floor, the earth held overhead by stout wooden pillars, the sunken roof covered by dirt. Back when the station was a house, the dugout had been for storage, a cool place against the desert; in fact, jars of preserves and pickles remained from that time, stacked dusty next to his cleanser, toilet paper, and other supplies.

He hurried across the heat, stopping at the open trap door. Looking down, he couldn't see a thing; perhaps a hint of light, a glow on the ladder's lower rungs? He imagined her hiding back in the station, just waiting for him to descend so she could run out and lock him under. He looked all around, turning a slow circle, then laughed at himself. What good would that do her?

"Hello?" he called down, crouching, hands around his mouth. The dark hole swallowed his voice, answered with silence.

His back to the hole, he stepped onto the ladder. He descended slowly, unable to see behind him, his eyes focused on his hands, which grasped the splintery rungs and became harder to see.

She was here. He turned to face her, in the light of one candle. Her shadow slipped out behind her, legs bent where the floor met the wall. The pockets of her dress were jammed full, weighted down with cans and jars. In her hand she held his trumpet.

"How long have you been driving?" he said. He'd meant to ask why she'd come down here, how she'd found it, but this other question came out. She just smiled, not answering, not at all nervous.

"Take whatever you want," he said. "Anything."

They stood ten feet apart, on opposite edges of the candlelight. Had there been candles down here? Had she brought it along? Now she glanced away, confident for a young woman alone with a strange man, underground, perhaps a hundred miles from the nearest person and no promise, then, that that person would care. He had not even told her his name, had he? And yet he did not know hers, either. Suddenly he realized he should not have followed her down here, that nothing good could come of it. He bent his neck and looked up, at the blinding square of blue, above and behind him; a black crow slid across it, then angled back, slashing across the line of its first pass to make an X, returning as if it wanted a second look.

"You play?" she said, slightly lifting the trumpet; the candle's flame doubled in the brass.

"Well, yes." He looked back at her, his eyes still blind from the sky, the crow.

"Down here in the dark?"

"Yes," he said. "I like the silence between the notes. The lack of echo, you know? And in the dark I can imagine, pretend I'm anywhere, like I don't know where I am."

"I see what you mean," she said, now setting the trumpet down on a shelf. "Sometimes closing your eyes is close, but never quite. You really want to turn yourself inward. Inside out, almost."

"Listen," he said. "Really—take whatever you want. I'm sympathetic with your situation, whatever it is."

"No," she said. "We're not even, yet. Not square. Not even close."

"Pardon me?"

"How about—" The pale skin of her face flickered with the candle's flame. "—instead of the rest of the massage, I tell you a story? It's a good one."

"We could go back to the station," he said. "No reason to stay down here. I'll buy you a Coke. Anything."

"I haven't always been driving around like this," she said, as if not hearing his offer.

"I didn't expect you had been."

"I was married," she said. "Well, technically I guess I still am married. A married woman. A wife."

This last word was cut short, as if she were smiling an ironic smile he could not quite see.

"We bought a chest of drawers," she said. "A dresser. An antique. My husband and I bought it, secondhand. At a garage sale. An estate sale, actually, a dead person's empty house in a little town. Six drawers, heavy, dark and varnished. It rattled when we carried it, and I remember thinking that there must be something inside, the clatter when we wedged it into the car, driving with the trunk tied down and yawning."

He watched her as she spoke, as well as he could, her hand at her mouth, perhaps her fingers wetted as she reached out to touch him or to put out the candle's flame, to pinch it out. He could almost hear the sizzle, the hiss, but that wasn't it, either. She bent her elbow and it was as if a wire or transparent line stretched to the trap door, which slapped shut without warning, with a hollow sound, raining loose dirt over his head. The candle blew out.

"The wind up there," she said.

In this new darkness it was as if the space had bent inward, the black air itself twisted and tightened and still. This, he realized, was how it always was, when no one was here, all day and night, no difference between the two; he imagined snakes, tortoises burrowing beneath the desert floor, the space suddenly opening up on them as they tumbled into this darkness. He shivered. Any rattler here would be slow and cool. Torpid.

"For months and months," she said, "I forgot that sound, that rattle. Half a year, maybe, of taking out my bras and underwear, wearing and washing and folding and replacing them, before I felt the small thing that had been left behind, rolling there in the back of the drawer. Do you know what it was?"

"The candle," he said. "The door—"

"A roll of film," she said.

"Wait—"

"Thirty-five millimeter," she said. "Undeveloped, all wound and hidden inside itself, waiting all that time."

The black air smelled of damp dirt. He heard the squeak, the slide of her fingers on the brass of the trumpet again. Was she closer to him? Was that her breath, the warm shiver of air on his face? She was whispering; they both had been, for quite some time; there was no reason to whisper.

"It wasn't waiting," he said, trying to raise his voice. "Film doesn't wait."

"That's exactly what *he* said—that was the seed of the disagreement, its beginning. He said to throw it out, the film, and I wanted to see what pictures might be in there. What would you say?"

"Well," he said. "They were somebody else's, and probably there was nothing. Costs money, too."

"What?" she said. "Six, seven dollars? That's nothing to pay, to turn a mystery; besides, we bought them all with the chest of drawers. We owned them."

"So they were a dead person's pictures?"

"Maybe," she said, "maybe not. Don't you want to know what they were of?"

As she paused, in the lost underground silence he thought he heard the sound of an engine, four hundred cubic inches growling to life and slowly fading, sliding away. His mind flashed on the gold Firebird, and in that flash he saw Jim Rockford pull one of his patented J-turns—reversing at high speed, jamming on the emergency brake, skidding 180 degrees, speeding off in the other direction—and also saw that that was the same way that women left. And yet he was mistaken, this was some sort of mirage, for he was still here, underground, and she was right here, silent, awaiting his answer.

"There's no reason to pry like that," he said. "You should have thrown it away."

"I've heard this before," she said.

"Maybe you were mistaken," he said. "Maybe the roll of film got put in the drawer, slipped in after you bought the thing."

"I took them to the drugstore," she said. "And the next week when I picked them up I could not wait. I sat there in my car in that parking lot and went through them, one at a time, all twenty-four photographs. They were pictures of my husband, every one of them—"

"Like I said," he said. "Could have slipped in—"

"Only they were not times," she said, "not places I remembered; they were shots of him standing in bedrooms with beaches visible through open windows behind him, in a field of wheat, in a waterfall with a wild smile on his face, his bathing suit balled up in one hand. And it was really his expression in these photos—that dreamy smile I'd never seen before, never saw him so happy. What's the word? Blissful."

"Hold on," he said.

"No," she said, "you wait. Because an even stranger thing was that in every picture there was the hint of an arm circling his waist, or a pale, blurry figure behind him, or a slender leg half in the frame. Women? At first I wondered about other women—he was not younger in the pictures, and he wore clothes I knew well, and there was even that period of the mustache experiment. The photos were from times I was around. Our times. And he didn't seem to be smiling at anyone, or even aware that his picture was being taken."

"Ghosts," he said.

"Exactly," she said.

"On the film, I mean," he said. "That's all. A problem with the processing—"

"He tried to say that," she said. "He tried to explain. He couldn't explain. He seemed as perplexed as I was, and I did believe him—at first I thought I could even forgive him, that we could keep on."

"A developing mistake," he said. "A mistake turned everything inside out between the two of us. I can't believe that, still, won't accept it."

"Ghosts," she said.

"They were not ghosts," he said. "And they weren't women, either. Or maybe they were ghosts, if that's what ghosts are. I recognized the times and places, I did, but that did not mean they were actually times and places where I had been. They were pictures of daydreams, I guess, times when I was not where I was, exactly, moments where I was thinking of other women. Imagining them. That's all."

"It made me so uneasy," she said.

"Who could do that?" he said.

"I realized," she said, "that the film made visible what was always there, that those ghosts were always around him, part of him, between us."

He imagined himself turning and climbing, felt the splintery rungs of the ladder in his hands, the press of hot, sage-fresh air slicing down as he lifted the trap door, the intense sharp brightness and the disequilibrium it could bring—the stumbling, the surfacing bends. Yet the darkness did not thin. They could have been anywhere, in a city, at the bottom of an ocean, any year or month or time of day, their faces, ages, and names unsteady as they talked, lashing the moments.

"He wanted to know," she said, "just what I was blaming him for, but it wasn't like that—there was no judgment, it was just facts, ghosts, the photographs still stacked in my glove compartment—"

"That gold Firebird," he said, "she didn't care about sense, anymore, the way she saw me, it was only me talking my way in deeper, trying to explain myself when being myself started it all. Who else could I be? It's our bodies that can be blamed, not thinking, not thoughts. I don't even know where that comes from."

"Once you know something about a person," she said, "you can't not know it."

"It's not a thing you can run from."

"You have to run," she said.

"A person," he said, "a person can come to see that what you do is circle, that you're circling back to where you started, where you left, however it is now."

"In a way," she said, "I felt those cold arms around me. I still do. Driving can't shake them, but maybe the motion keeps them from settling, taking me down."

"Wait," he said. "Wait, wait, wait. That's all. I don't know how, or who could take a picture like that. They were places I hadn't been, times that never exactly were."

"It was those ghosts around him that held me away," she said. "They eased the temperature and shivered my skin and would not let me rest. They wouldn't let the doors lock, and they made the highways shine. They packed the car and turned the key."

IMAGINING BISBEE

Alicita Rodríguez

FEW PEOPLE LIVE IN BISBEE; the town's history makes it so. When miners decided to strike in 1917, the sheriff's deputies, with their big guns and small teeth, rounded them up like cattle, packed them into train cars, and shipped them to New Mexico—dumped the strikers, with their soot-covered faces, smack in the middle of desert. A few of the miners walked back to Bisbee, each step, each raising and dropping of the foot, taken amidst the jumble of hallucinations. These are the forefathers.

And so, their progeny.

Bisbee Bob, drug dealer, father of two suspected arsonists.

Walking Bob, Francophile, tours the Côte d'Azur every summer, raves about the country's footpaths.

Bible Bob, eighty years old, thin as a pencil, eats only carrots, skin hangs in folds, scribbles in notebooks, recognizable by red rubber raincoat.

Crazy Nancy, bright lipstick, black hair, junkie. Reportedly a brutal suicide.

Library Girl, reads, looks for forest fires with *perro callejero*.

Built into the mountains, Bisbee is a town of steps. Natives decorate their steps in many ways. Some string colored electric lights along the treads. The more creative choose novelty bulbs in the shape

From *Ecotone*.

of bumblebees or cactus trees or cowboy boots. Others paint the risers with bright colors; some imitate the designs of the surrounding Indian tribes. Still others paste tiny pieces of broken glass onto the stairs. The paths to their homes glisten and blind in the Arizona sun.

Bisbee's inhabitants want to disappear. They use PO boxes and first names. They hide under straw hats and melt into the horizon. They don't see movies and they only sleep with foreigners. They never get biblical with one another.

It is a town that exists only in relation to other realities: south of Tombstone; east of Nogales; north of Mexico; west of the Arizona/New Mexico border. Bisbee often does not appear on maps. It is not there.

　　　　　　　　ALICITA RODRÍGUEZ

REASONS FOR CONCERN REGARDING MY GIRLFRIEND OF FIVE DAYS, MONICA GARZA

John Tait

THAT SHE CURSED TWICE in the first full sentence she spoke to me, even though she was trying to pacify me after my accident with her uninsured younger brother. That she also drives uninsured and seems to view this as a lifestyle choice. That she is twenty-four and I am thirty-nine. That she has tattoos: two visible, one partly visible, unknown invisible. That in that first meeting, after her uninsured brother's truck crushed my Corolla's right front bumper in the Sack 'n Save parking lot, and after he next tried to drive off before I blocked him in, and after he then swore and threatened for fifteen minutes before getting on his cell phone, Monica appeared and actually tried to convince me not to call the police. That she succeeded. That after she and I talked for another half hour, I decided to forget the matter entirely, even though between my divorce settlement and credit card debt I'll have trouble paying the repair myself.

That she asked me out first, to my surprise, pleasure, and suspicion, said she'd enjoyed our conversation and I seemed nice, then asked if I wanted to see a movie. That she made the first move four hours later, at a picnic table up on the levee along the artificial lake, or at least nuzzled me in the evening chill when the conversation fell off and gave a series of soft, impatient sighs until I kissed her.

From *Crazy Horse*.

That she seems more impressed than she should that I am an adjunct professor of English at the local college. That she probably thinks I'm wealthier than I am. That she refers to her job in the Wal-Mart auto center as a career. That her determination to work slavishly to support her doltish brother's education seems more misguided to me than admirable. That she wears shorter skirts and larger earrings and is better looking than any woman I've dated since high school. That she's less educated than any woman I've dated since high school.

That for two hours from the time I dropped her off that night to the time I climbed into my bed, nearly forgetting to take off my shoes, I couldn't form a single coherent thought.

Notable Insecurities at the Two-Week Mark with New Girlfriend, Monica Garza

Because I am so white and so lame at times when I'm with her that I feel like Lawrence freaking Welk. Because I know she humors my attempts to be cool, like when I asked yesterday about a song on her radio, "Is that banda or grupera?" and she said wryly that it was neither, then changed channels. Because my best friend is named Doug, who is an actuary who is married to another actuary, and they live with two golden labs in a gated community called Idle Pines, and Monica's best friend is named Analeticia, who is a manicurist who dates a guy I think is named Puppet who drives a chopped Civic with "¡Chingalo!" in gothic script on the back windshield, and both Analeticia and Puppet stared at me with stony incomprehension the only time we met. Because whenever I talk politics, art, literature, or the intricacies of human behavior with Monica, while she appears to fully understand, she seems utterly uninterested and just watches me with an amused, indulgent look like I'm a precocious child. Because when I finally convinced her to read chapters from my latest unpublished novel, she at first declined to comment then said mildly that my characters seemed to have much free time, and they spent a lot of it staring into the rain and agonizing over decisions they would never make or staring into the rain and contemplating actions they would never take. Because, though I thanked her for her feedback, kissed her forehead, and made a show of noting her comments on my draft, I actually felt hurt and misunderstood.

Because when I force myself to be as brutally honest, I can't for the life of me see why someone like Monica Garza would want to go out with someone like me.

Because I question my own motives. Because I worried for an hour the other night, while preparing for my postcolonial lit seminar, that I view Monica, with her mestizo cheekbones and glossy black hair, as some objectified, exotic "other" to colonize with my white maleness. Because I have imagined, more than once, running into my ex and have pictured in exquisite slo-mo her every grimace and twitch at seeing me with a pretty girl fifteen years younger, before remembering that she would probably laugh. Because I have both fretted about running into neighbors, colleagues, or students while with Monica and secretly hoped that we are observed, discussed.

Because for the first time I can remember, the physical relationship has advanced faster than I feel comfortable. Because after our first time making love Monica interrogated me about what I liked and didn't like, then gave her own preferences, after which I said I usually liked to discover such things naturally, to which she said that it was just as natural to talk about them, to which I said that her way took away from the spontaneity, to which she said that my way guaranteed that one or both of us would never enjoy activities that the other was perfectly willing to join in just because we'd never bothered to ask, to which I had no real response.

Because she likes to go out dancing and I like to stay in reading. Because I speak softly and hear poorly, and she talks so loudly it makes my ears ring but can hear my neighbor's cat jump on the sill outside the bedroom window to watch us. Because she walks faster than me, drags me by my shirtfront into mall stores with gaudy signs and loud music where she buys her short skirts and large earrings. Because most of what sustains our relationship so far is what we find amusing or incomprehensible about each other, her snickering at my alphabetized New American Film collection and morning Tai Chi, me marveling at her girlish little charm bracelets and industrial-sized overnight makeup bag.

Because she grew up speaking a language I can barely form a sentence in. Because she can have a phone conversation with her cousin, and I can hear my name spoken twice but have no idea what she is saying about me.

Because I never care about any of these things while I'm with her, but only afterward, alone, late, pouring a glass of milk at my open fridge.

Troubling Revelations Regarding Monica Garza, My Girlfriend of a Month and a Half

The fact that, an hour before what I will refer to as our "big talk," at my place following our weekend away in Austin, she admitted that she flirted with me that first day mainly in hopes I wouldn't call the police on her uninsured brother, and I laughed a lot because I'd suspected as much, then laughed less because I hadn't really wanted to believe it. The fact that, immediately before the "big talk," while continuing a debate on whether I am either a cautious or a crappy driver, a clip of a girl crying beside a burnt house came on the TV news, and Monica's demeanor changed and she sat up straight in bed then told me, with grave expression and moist eyes, that she had some "important things" to tell me.

The fact that the first thing she told me was how she ran away at sixteen and became an exotic dancer in San Antonio, a story I tried to receive with the unflappable understanding of a man of the world. The fact that she went on to describe how, during the stripping years, she dated a dealer and became "half addicted" to methamphetamine and contracted one of the "not-so-bad" hepatitises, which I also tried to hear with cool equanimity. The fact that she next went on to tell me how at eighteen she was incarcerated in Wilson County Jail for fifteen months for kiting checks while involved with another man who is now dead, details which I tried, less successfully, to shrug off, distracted by the quiet, persistent voice that repeated, in case I'd forgotten, that SHE WAS IN JAIL.

The fact that, after our big talk, as I watched her sob and tell me that I wouldn't think the same of her anymore, she looked so miserable and I was still so dazed that I told her that everyone does things they regret, that I certainly had, even stealing a Christmas tree from a department store once while on acid back in college, and that we could only hope to learn from our mistakes. The fact that, as I said these words, I hated how much I sounded like some ineffectual youth counselor. The fact that, after she kissed me and went home, I absently took my wallet from the dresser and counted the cash, a moot action since I couldn't remember how much I'd had, and was so filled with self-reproach after that I threw said wallet hard against said dresser.

Reasons I Shouldn't Call My Quasi-Girlfriend of Nearly Two Months, Monica Garza

Because I haven't called for over a week following our "big talk," with a resulting buildup of anticipatory dread for the moment when I do. Because there was honestly some ambiguity about who would call whom. Because even in the message she left today, asking if I wanted to come out clubbing with her and Analeticia this Friday, though she tried to seem casual, the way her voice hitched at the end sounded so tentative and anxious that it made me feel the same.

Because my parents are visiting from Kansas City this weekend, and though our relationship has of late matured into a fellowship of adult equals who respect each other's life decisions, and though Mom and Dad have managed to adapt admirably to America's changing culture, I can't be sure what effect the combination of Monica's youth, ethnicity, social class, wardrobe, legal history, bodily decoration, and vocabulary might have on them. Because I get so mad that I would even care, at almost forty, about the above that I feel like inviting Monica over anyways, which another part of me recognizes is an immature and dangerous rebellious impulse, much like the one that led me fifteen months ago to go out for drinks with a woman I knew had a crush on me just because my wife had made some belittling remarks, though the marriage-ending tryst that followed was pretty much my own dumb fault. Because I just got a new cell phone and haven't transferred all my old numbers yet. Because I would actually think of the previous issue as an excuse not to call someone.

Probable Reasons Why Monica Garza, the Girl I Was until Recently Involved with, Hasn't Called Me

Because when she last appeared, at two-thirty on Friday night/ Saturday morning, dropped off by best friend Analeticia after their night of clubbing, and she hammered on my door, waking my parents on the foldout in the front room, I didn't answer until she'd wailed my name and shouted in a voice both playful and severe that I was a dick and better take what was coming to me. Because when I did answer, I told Monica that we should talk some other time. Because when she then laughed and started to walk away, swaying on her high heels, then wheeled back to call me a coward and hypocrite, I acted like I didn't understand. Because when she suddenly darted inside my apartment, then lost her balance on the slippery hardwood and fell and only then looked up to see my parents in their plaid pajamas and smiled at them with heartbreakingly hopeful timidity, Monica received back a look I could call arctic. Because, in my parents' defense, one of the reasons for their reaction might have been that, as Monica fell, her skirt rose the small distance necessary to show she wasn't wearing underwear. Because, instead of helping, I stood over her and felt an irrational fear that she might grab or grope me in view of my parents. Because, when she rose and I introduced her, we all noticed that the hand she waved in greeting before stuffing it hastily into her purse held the same panties she should have been wearing. Because I then called a cab for her. Because when I led her outside and she stood, facing away, shivering and sniffling, I didn't touch her or speak until her cab arrived, just paid the driver then went back inside where my parents waited, their faces stricken and very pale.

Feelings I Must Fight in the Wake of My Split(?) from Monica Garza

A malaise that makes it hard to focus on what I should—my teaching, my writing, my income tax preparation—a tiresome funk I can only alleviate by writing long, self-involved lists. A compulsion to go to Wal-Mart and walk the aisles, approaching the auto center with dread and hope until I glimpse her, maybe over by the spark plugs, and flee. A painful awareness that never before in my life has

JOHN TAIT

a pretty girl banged on my door and wailed my name in the middle of the night, and it's unlikely this will ever happen again.

A dread that, by losing Monica, I've lost my one late opportunity to become a person who continues to grow and change along with a growing and changing world rather than shutting myself fearfully away with the rest of the people like me. A naïve optimism, fueled by well-intentioned movies and TV shows, that we Americans can overcome all barriers between us and embrace each other based on our shared humanity. A recognition that even though the above is a crock, it shouldn't be. The worry that I am more concerned with what others think of me than with my own happiness, a fact that makes me wish I was miles from every other human being— maybe on some unpopulated island or at least archipelago, though when I imagine myself in that desolate place it seems only natural to add a companion, leading to fantasies (about M. G.) that are both pleasant and troubling.

Consolations to Remain Mindful Of Post-Monica G.

That a year from now I will be dating a woman more age-, ethnicity-, and background-appropriate, a librarian, journalist, or real estate agent who wears long skirts and small earrings, a relationship I will find pleasant, comfortable, comprehensible. That a year from now, if I do see Monica Garza, maybe at the mall, clinging to the arm of her young, tattooed novio, I won't be as torn up by that image as I am now. That I shouldn't be expected, at nearly forty, to undergo changes I am unequipped to make. That, though our brief time together is over, at least the pleasures I remember are mine to store fondly in my memories. That even though the preceding is a crock, it really shouldn't be.

Questions I Wish I Had Been Able to Ask Monica Garza, the Woman I Can No Longer Quite Believe I Dated for a While Last Year

What did she come to talk about that night, drunk and banging on my door?

Why did she say I was a coward and hypocrite, or at least did she think I was those things in ways I don't already know I am?

What was it like to run away at sixteen and be alone in the city?

What was it like to be in jail at eighteen?

What dreams does one give up to work at the Wal-Mart auto center to support an uninsured, doltish younger brother?

Did she hope that, if we continued dating, I would help her financially?

If not, did she hope I would help her in some other way?

If not, why did she want to be with me?

Could she understand that, the more I think on it, those revelations about her past didn't bother me so much for what they said about her as much as for how they contributed to my larger worry that she lived in a different world than mine—not just a different culture or different neighborhood, but a place I could never inhabit, a place from which somebody, looking over, might find someone like me quaint, dull, complacent, undeservedly protected?

What is she doing right now, while I write this?

Where is she now?

If, just suppose, Monica, I was passing by the Wal-Mart auto center with my cart of groceries and was to run into you, maybe over by the spark plugs, and was to overcome my impulse to flee, and we were to talk, maybe laugh at what happened between us last year, how would you look at me now and what would you see and what might we talk about with the honesty possible in the brief moments allowed for such things?

And would I be able to handle it as I waved then walked away, feeling you watching me, steering my grocery cart through the aspirin and diaper displays back toward the checkout?

PASSAGE

Patrick Tobin

TODAY THEY BROUGHT IN a lot of new prisoners. For the next week we'll have to listen to these guys go on and on about how someone's going to straighten everything out. That this has all been a terrible mistake.

Those of us who've been here a while will listen, but we won't say anything to contradict them. That would be unnecessarily cruel.

After the first week or so the new prisoners will realize they aren't going anywhere. Their eyes will glaze over with despair as it dawns on them—*this* is it.

Their lawyers aren't going to get them out. Their families aren't going to get them out. Their friends aren't going to get them out.

Today is the beginning of the end of all hope and they don't even know it.

I think our rations have been permanently reduced, although nothing official was said—not that you get any explanations here. Now our meals are:

Breakfast: Something that resembles oatmeal, and water
Lunch: A sandwich with ham/bologna (not sure which—
        too bad if you're vegetarian), and water

From *Literary Review.*

Dinner: A tiny piece of some kind of meat in a very
sweet barbeque-type sauce (again, tough if
you're vegetarian), frozen peas and carrots, and
watered-down fruit punch

We used to get a small bag of chips with the ham/bologna sandwich. Not any more.

I've lost about forty pounds. If I were home I could easily fit into my linen pants with the thirty-two-inch waist.

The guys who were already skinny to begin with resort to eating bugs and weeds. I suppose crickets and grasshoppers aren't bad for you, but I worry about what some of the weeds are doing to them.

It seems like a waste of time to worry, though.

Almost all of the prisoners work in the gypsum plant. The prisoners who aren't strong enough to lift fifty-pound sacks, like the guys with AIDS, have to work in the garden. Only the soldiers and commanders get to eat the produce from the garden, but every once in a while one of the prisoners will smuggle out strawberries or tomatoes. It's like Christmas around here when that happens.

The gypsum plant is next to the camp, so we just march there in the morning after breakfast. There are some Mexican civilians who work at the plant too. I've never talked to any of them. It used to annoy me that the Mexican civilians looked at us with pity, but now I don't mind. It's a harmless bit of human kindness and I'll take any I can get these days.

There are about eighty soldiers total. It's hard to tell because they're never all in the same place at the same time. They live at the camp too, but they stay in air-conditioned dormitories and they get to shower every day.

The prisoners sleep in permanent tents that are always filled with dust. The prisoners only get to bathe once a week, less frequent in the summer when water's scarce. They line us up naked in front of one of the water towers and we each get one minute under the makeshift shower. They don't give us soap, so basically you're just rinsing off the dust. The water is always cold, even in the summer.

It will only get colder now that winter's coming.

I tell the new guys they have to be careful not to provoke the soldiers. You can tell who the short fuses are. Their dead, bloodshot eyes and the way they chomp on their gum like they're trying to kill it—these are the things that give them away. The analogy I use is this: it's like when we were in junior high and high school and the bullies teased us about being fags. I try to get the new guys to remember walking through the hallways, the way you had to avoid any eye contact, because if you returned a bully's stare it only provoked violence.

I tell the new guys that the bullies are running the show now. Not only that, the bullies have machine guns and hunting knives and they don't mind using them.

There's a really nice kid in my tent named Jason. He's been at the camp about six months. He was sent here at the same time as his boyfriend Kyle, although the two of them were careful not to say anything about their relationship. That was smart. If the soldiers find out you've had a relationship with one of the other prisoners they go out of their way to make your life miserable.

Kyle was assigned to one of the other tents. Every day when we marched to the gypsum plant, Jason would wave at Kyle when the soldiers weren't looking.

About two weeks ago we woke up in the middle of the night because there was yelling. You could hear feet running on the gravel outside our tent and then the dogs started barking. We heard the dogs running, faster and faster, chasing something. Someone said "please"—just that one word. After that all you could hear were the dogs tearing something apart.

Next day it turned out the something had been Kyle.

It used to be when someone tried to escape you would hear his screams when the dogs attacked him. Someone said they've trained the dogs to tear out a guy's throat first, so the soldiers don't have to listen to a bunch of screaming.

That wouldn't surprise me at all.

We have to force Jason to get out of his cot in the morning. He just shuffles along with a dead look on his face, like he's sleepwalking. I've been covering for him at the gypsum plant. I don't want the soldiers to notice he's falling behind, otherwise they'll do something awful to him, like make him crawl on his bare belly through the desert, or force him to eat their used toilet paper.

I worry about Jason even though I know I should only worry about myself.

It rained all day—at one point the dirt floor of our tent was an inch deep with mud. The only good thing about the rain is you can get a little cleaned up, especially from a downpour like we had today. If it's just a light shower you end up smelling like a wet dog and there's nothing you can do about it.

Jason's getting worse. He has nightmares and sometimes he wakes up screaming. Those of us who sleep nearby quiet him the second he starts screaming—the last thing we need is the soldiers paying a visit after dark.

One time when I quieted Jason down, I asked him if there was anything I could do to help. He said there was nothing, so I just held him. After a couple of minutes he told me a cold beer would really help.

For some reason we all found this funny, until even Jason was laughing. One of the soldiers yelled at us from outside, saying if we didn't stop laughing he'd give us plenty of reasons to stop laughing.

Then we heard him cock his rifle, so we knew he meant business.

There is a way I could get Jason a beer.

I'm not sure when Passage started, it already existed when I got here. Passage is when some of the soldiers let a prisoner leave camp for Vegas. The reason they do this is because the soldiers can't ever leave this place until they get dispatched somewhere else. The usual tour of duty seems to last about two months, so there are more than a few of them who start missing their cigarettes and pot and booze. With Passage, a prisoner procures these things in Vegas without the soldiers getting in trouble.

It's dangerous. If you're caught on the outside and the police find the ID tattoo on your neck they'll shoot you on the spot. The other thing is, if you don't come back to camp the soldiers start killing your friends, torturing them one by one. The last time some guy didn't come back they nailed his friends to the base of the water tower. We had to listen to them scream while we took our showers.

The soldiers who do Passage are smart—they only pick the kind of guys who wouldn't be able to do that to their friends. Guys like me.

I approached the only decent soldier at the plant, a blond kid named Gary. I had a feeling he might be in on Passage from the way he marches—his face always says he's not too impressed with the military.

I walked next to Gary when we were coming back to camp for lunch. I asked him in a low voice if he had any interest in setting up Passage.

"You know where to get pot?" he whispered.

I nodded and we didn't say anything more.

During lunch I noticed Gary talking to one of the other soldiers and the two of them kept looking at me. I tried to act like nothing was going on, but inside I was terrified. For all I knew they might be setting me up—then God only knows what they'd do to me after dark.

But it turned out I'd been right about Gary. When we were going back to work, he slipped me a note that I read during a bathroom break. The note had a list of what the soldiers wanted me to get. It said I'd be given a backpack and my civilian clothes, but I was supposed to wait to put on my civilian clothes until I got to Vegas. At the bottom it read:

Be ready tonight.

Gary opened the front of the tent just a crack so the others wouldn't wake up. When I went outside I noticed they'd turned off the flood-light next to our tent. I also didn't see the dogs anywhere.

Gary was silent as we walked to the gypsum plant, where one of the Mexican civilians was standing by a beat-up truck with Baja plates. Gary said something in Spanish to the guy before he told me I had to be back by nightfall. I said that wasn't very much time, but Gary said I wasn't in much of a position to negotiate. He told me I was to meet Emilio, the Mexican civilian who was driving me to Vegas, by four in the afternoon in the back parking lot of the Excalibur. He asked me if I knew where that was—I told him I did because I lived in Vegas my whole life.

Emilio had a picture of his wife on the dashboard and pictures of his three girls on the inside of the sun visor. They all looked very happy. I assumed Emilio was trying to earn enough money to buy his way back to Mexico.

There wasn't much traffic on I-15, which was strange. Usually there are lots of people heading to or from Vegas, even at the crack of dawn. Every once in a while we came upon military cargo trucks loaded down with equipment.

In a way I was glad Emilio didn't speak much English. I'm not sure I would have remembered how to have a conversation.

We stopped to get gas at the Terrible's off Blue Diamond. I used the outside restroom to clean up. After I was done I put on my civilian clothes, the ones I was wearing when I first came to camp. I had to laugh because my jeans hung past my butt. Emilio lent me his belt because I didn't have one and then he made sure my collar was hiding the ID tattoo.

The soldiers who went in on my Passage put together about $500. Not that much money. Still, I thought it was only fair to get Emilio a cup of coffee and a doughnut. The clerk inside the convenience store was a greaser/loser type who must have been too stupid even for the draft. He stared at Emilio and me the whole time, like he was going to pull out a baseball bat and bash our heads in.

No one trusts anyone anymore. Not that I'm saying people should.

Emilio dropped me off in Henderson. My mom was up fixing coffee. After she hugged me she said I stunk to high heaven. I told her I hadn't had time for a decent shower.

She made a big deal out of getting me a towel and a washcloth. I stood under the hot water so long my mom knocked on the bathroom door and asked if I was okay.

Afterwards she fixed me breakfast. At first I wolfed everything down like a starving man. But then I paced myself, because I wanted to savor every bite. Raspberry jam and toast. Scrambled eggs with a little bit of salt and pepper. Fresh coffee.

The whole time my mom didn't mention the camps, so I figured she didn't know anything. Not that I expected her to. At one point she asked me how I liked living in France, and I asked what made her think I was living there. My mom acted like I'd lost my mind. She brought out some postcards, all from me. Mailed from France.

I held them in my hands and it was like I was reading my own obituary.

I wanted to tell her she was being deceived, that those cards weren't from me, that if she looked carefully she'd see that the person writing for me wasn't even doing that good a forgery.

But that would accomplish nothing. There would be nothing she could do to help me and that would cause her incredible pain.

Instead, I told I was glad she liked the postcards. She said she shows them to all her friends. She asked if I wouldn't mind sending her some French lace—ever since she was a girl she always wanted some fancy French lace. I said I'd try.

I asked her if she had any liquor in the house—one of the soldiers wanted bourbon and my mom used to drink a lot of bourbon. She said it was impossible to get rations for alcohol anymore and she certainly didn't have money for the black market. She said it seemed a little early to be drinking anyway. She asked me if that was a bad habit I'd picked up on the Continent—drinking before noon.

She laughed. She laughed like she was proud I had a glamorous life, like she couldn't wait to brag to her friends about her son who was going to send her French lace.

That was the hardest part.

My mom said she knew I'd probably be busy catching up with all my friends, but she asked if she could fix me a nice dinner. I told her it wouldn't work out, but I'd try another time. When I kissed her good-bye she said I smelled a whole lot better.

Then she told me to lay off the diet already, I was getting too skinny.

Gordon was my boyfriend for five years, right up until everything went to hell, when he moved out of our apartment and wouldn't return my calls. I figured if anyone knew how to get pot it would be him.

I hired a cab after I found Gordon's address in my mom's white pages. We pulled up to an old tract house with a dead patch of lawn in the front. The color of the house was like one big water stain. Uncollected garbage was piled up by the curb.

The place reeked of despair.

Call me an asshole, but I was thrilled to death Gordon was living in this dump.

When I knocked on the door a woman answered. She was in her early thirties, fat, wearing an MGM Grand uniform and nurses' shoes. I told her I was a friend of Gordon's.

A little boy, just barely walking, stumbled out and gawked at me from behind the woman's legs. He had Gordon's eyes.

Gordon came out and I almost didn't recognize him, he'd aged that much. He was polite enough at first. He shook my hand and said it had been a long time, while the woman stared at me with a suspicious look on her face.

She finally interrupted us, saying she had to get Bobby (the boy) to daycare and she was late for work. It was definitely an awkward moment, because I think she expected him to leave with her. Gordon kissed her on the lips (not much enthusiasm). She left in a huff with the baby, driving off in their minivan.

I stood there waiting to be invited inside. The smell of Gordon's house reminded me of my mom's. I don't know why but that made me sad.

Gordon's mood changed the minute the woman left. He said he couldn't let me inside, that he didn't want the neighbors thinking he let homosexuals visit him. "It would be a disaster" were the exact words he used.

I told him it looked like his life was pretty much a disaster already. He asked me what I wanted anyway and I said I wouldn't waste any more of his precious time if he would just put me in touch with a dealer. He got a condescending look on his face and said that obviously nothing had changed—I was still just a party boy. I told him the pot wasn't for me, it was for the soldiers back at the prison camp.

Gordon said I had to go, but not before he told me how glad he was that he now had a normal life.

I pushed my way into the house and slammed the door behind us. These are the exact words I screamed at him: "Do you have any idea what's going on or are you the dumbest fucking faggot who ever lived?" Then I tried to calm down. I asked him if he didn't know what had been happening to all of our friends, including me.

Gordon just stared at me the whole time. When I finished talking he got this weird smile on his face and said he knew what was going on. Not only did he know, he approved.

I started punching him and there was no way he could stop me, not after two years of lifting fifty-pound sacks of gypsum. He yelled and cried and I just kept punching him. When he fell on his knees and begged me to stop, something broke inside of me. There we were on the floor, both of us crying and hugging, when all of a sudden Gordon grabbed a lamp and bashed me over the head.

I fell flat on my face but I didn't pass out. Gordon ran to the phone. I got up and told him to put the phone down. He said he was calling the police, that it was going to be a pleasure to watch them kill me.

If I didn't show up back at the camp, Gary and his buddies would start torturing Jason in ways I couldn't even begin to imagine. And it would be my fault.

I'm sorry his wife will have to find his body. I really am. I left a note taped to the front door:

If you have the boy with you leave him outside before you go in the house.

I stole someone's bike and raced to the Mirage. It was after noon and I only had one other option: Vic, my very first boyfriend. He was a partner in the Mirage, a real bigwig in town. Tons of money and a chauffeur. Always taking trips.

To be honest, when I was with him I never loved Vic. He was my sugar daddy. I used to laugh with my friends because he was older than my mom. Vic loved me though. I was everything to him but I just took his heart and cut it up, because I was young and stupid.

I never talked to Vic after I broke up with him. When I saw him out on the town I could tell it hurt him to see me. I could tell he hated me for the way I'd treated him.

I can't say I blame him either.

Vic looked like a million bucks in his Italian suit. What was left of his gray hair was perfectly styled. His eyes lit up when he saw me and I was relieved. While we were hugging he whispered that we had to go to his house because it wasn't safe to talk at the hotel.

We didn't say much during the drive. Vic finally closed the window between us and the driver. I told him I'd just killed Gordon. He fixed me a stiff drink.

When we got to Vic's house he gave the housekeeper the rest of the day off. After she left I told Vic everything. The camp. The fake postcards to my mom.

Passage.

Vic listened without saying anything. When I was done he called a friend of his and told her he needed to get some pot. Then he called a guy at the Mirage who worked in one of the bars and told him to bring a few bottles of liquor to the house.

He brought out a couple of cartons of Marlboro Lights from his office. He opened a pack and we both had a cigarette. It was my first one in two years and I nearly passed out.

I told Vic I was deeply sorry about the way I'd treated him. He tried to stop me, but I made him listen. I told him I'd been heartless. I said I wouldn't blame him if he hated me, but I still had to ask him to forgive me.

Vic told me his one hope these past two years had been that I'd managed to escape to Canada or Mexico. He knew about the

PATRICK TOBIN

camps—he'd been using his money to keep himself out of them. He knew it was only a matter of time before the money didn't work anymore.

I asked him why he didn't take off to Canada or Europe. He said the government canceled everyone's passport because of the war. International travel was impossible.

I felt bad for Vic. I could see the fear in his eyes even though he was trying to act like he wasn't scared.

Later we lay down on his bed, with the windows open and the curtains blowing in the breeze. Vic stroked my hair. He told me he'd heard rumors about what was coming down the pike. He said things were going to get even more ugly at the camps.

I just stared at the curtains—the way they seemed to be waving good-bye. Vic got up and opened his safe. He pulled out a small box filled with gold coins.

He said I could use the gold to hire a runner to take me to Mexico. I told him he should use the money for himself, but he said he didn't have it in him. He said he'd had a long life with no regrets, but I was still relatively young. He told me he could make the arrangements in one phone call.

"I want to do this because I still love you," he said.

"I love you too." I kissed him on the forehead. "But I can't."

I waited in the parking lot of the Excalibur until the sun started to dip behind the mountains—that's when I started to freak out. I decided to take a sip from the vodka.

When I pulled the bottle out of my backpack I discovered why it had seemed so heavy. Vic had hidden a baggie full of gold coins inside.

I watched some military vehicles go up I-15. All the windows were black with heavy tinting, so you couldn't see any of the soldiers inside. It made it seem like the vehicles were driving themselves.

Emilio showed up and we started driving back to the camp. Because we were both pretty stressed, I opened one of the beers to share with him. I'd decided when we got closer to the camp I would try my best to make Emilio understand why I was giving him the coins and the Passage money, that he's to use them to buy his way back to Mexico. Maybe he'll have enough to save someone else too. That would be nice.

I hoped Jason would like his beer. Maybe it would cheer him up, even if it was just for a few moments.

A military jet flew overhead and the inside of the truck rumbled. I looked up in the sky, but in the fading twilight I couldn't make out which way it was going.

BAT

Valery Varble

THE RENDING SOUND when I unzip his pants makes us both flinch. Hey, your zipper's just about rusted shut, I say, but not meanly. A joke, just to ease things a little. Good thing you came in, I say. If you'd waited any longer, it might've been too late. You might've required surgery, advanced pants removal. I'm tempted to keep going, to mention a zipperectomy, but I don't. I'm not funny, I know that; my New Year's resolution is to stop trying.

It's late afternoon and we're in the Gemstone Motel in the desert outside Quartzsite where I've set up shop this year. It's a small place on an unpaved road gradually fading like a scar. As I slip my hand inside his pants (boxers, surprising) to move things along, I can't help thinking that at least this man is nice looking. The last one was a salesman who made unrelenting eye contact, his grunting breath spearminty, hands barnacled with warts. This one has wavy hair and a dimple in his chin. I'll bet his mother never stopped telling him, with a little pinch to the chin and a pleased sigh, that her boy was the handsomest around. I imagine her cloud of tea rose perfume. Even so, I'd bet that at school he was teased without mercy about the dimple. Now his face is slightly deflated around it, his hair tarnishing at the temples but he's good looking all the same. He's older than I am, but not old enough to be my father.

From *Mid-American Review.*

He's crushably soft in my hand and suddenly I'm reminded of the bat that got trapped in my bedroom a couple of nights ago. For a moment, I'm dizzy; my heart speeds up. But I don't want to think about that now. I'm just about to decide whether to talk dirty or murmur encouragement when suddenly he makes a little gasp. Okay, we're getting somewhere. When I glance up at him, his eyes are squeezed shut.

Then he blurts out, "My wife has cancer."

I stop what I'm doing. One of his legs is trembling, just one.

"Look," I say, "it's extra if you talk about your wife."

I'm only kidding (see? I remind myself, not funny) but he gropes around in his drooping pants pocket and takes out his wallet. He caught me off guard, that's all. He sits carefully on the bed and I fold back a corner of the bedspread to sit beside him.

I take the bills the man offers.

"I'm sorry to hear that," I say about his wife's cancer. "Is it serious?" I reach over to flip his fly closed so he won't seem so vulnerable, and after a dazed moment he says, "I don't know. Yes. But we hardly talk about it. She sits there in that hospital bed and pretends she's fine. We talk about the TV news and weather. But if you could see how she . . . sinks when she thinks no one's watching." He swallows. "She's scheduled for surgery in a few days. They're removing," he hesitates, "some of her female parts."

"Oh, those," I say. "Sugar and spice and everything nice." That's what little girls are made of. He looks so stricken, gripping the motel bedspread, that I remember why I hate sarcasm, its edge of spoilage. I take a breath. "Breast? Uterus? Ovaries? Is it a hysterectomy?" Of course I think of Janey.

"It could be," he says, nodding. "I kept going blank when the doctor was talking. I don't remember a thing he said. When he asked if I had any questions, I asked him for the time." He lets go of the motel bedspread, its old green fringe stiff as a comb against my bare leg.

"Well, maybe she has ovarian cancer, then," I say. "Or uterine. A friend of mine had that. Uterine. Or endometrial, it's called." Whenever I think of Janey, I try to imagine her as she looked at the potluck she'd organized a few years ago back home in Nevada, trying to start up a union. United Brothel Workers Local 121. "God, I should've known better," she told me. "It's like trying to herd cats." We were sitting on the tailgate of her pickup and I was scooping ice cream. She'd brought a whole truckload of the famous "Hearts o' Gold" cantaloupes from Fallon for the picnic. "Even the bowling team was a flop," she laughed, as we served cantaloupe halves with a scoop of ice cream in the middle. "You'd think us whores would want hobbies." Her laugh was so raucous you expected it to go flapping up into the trees; you couldn't help laughing, too.

"What happened to her?" this man says.

I hesitate. "She had a more rare kind of endometrial cancer," I say, finally. "Hers was clear-cell carcinoma."

A long silence. He waits. It's one of my favorite things, a photo from that afternoon: Janey grinning with the sun in her eyes, holding a cantaloupe in her arms. On the back she'd written, "Here I am!!! Hooker with a Heart o' Gold."

This man's still waiting, I guess for me to say something hopeful.

"Your time's up," I say.

It isn't until after the man is gone that I realize he's left his wallet behind. Oh, well. He'll be back for it. I put it in my purse, lock the door, wave at the motel manager (who takes a cut of my earnings each week but still treats me like a guest), and head home to my trailer. It's in the Oasis Kampground and RV Park, my home for these couple of months. Janey was the one who started us coming here to Quartzsite for the winters. "Why shouldn't we be snowbirds, too?" she pointed out. She'd been working practically nonstop, her sights set on retirement. "It's got to be soon," she told me. "There's no way I'm gonna end up as the world's oldest pro in the world's oldest profession, you know?" And besides, she said, she was really tired. We needed a vacation, and if it turned out to be a working vacation, that was okay, too. "Hey, we can put up a sign that says, *Get Your Rocks Off Here*," I told her, and she laughed, although it wasn't very funny. It was just that Quartzsite had originally been known for its Rock and Mineral Show and swap meet.

Bat

I wasn't sure I could sleep. A few nights ago I'd been awakened by a scrabbling sound in my window. The sound of a zipper. No, I realized, it was something rasping across the metal screen. Then a fluttering. I lay there in the dark, my heart thumping, before I realized it must be a bird that was caught. Damn, I'd been meaning to fix that window screen. The bottom was loose and one corner flapped up where it was torn. But when I turned on the light, I saw it wasn't a bird at all but a small bat, crumpled like a dark leather glove between the screen and window.

I eased the window up so I could reach in and push the bottom of the screen out. The bat pulsed there weakly, caught fast. "Hold on just a minute," I said, trying not to hurt the thing, "and you'll be free." It never even occurred to me that the bat might come inside instead but all of a sudden it was swooping wildly around the trailer. And I was screaming.

I stopped abruptly and turned off the light; I didn't want the neighbors to hear. My heart was pounding and I felt as if I had shards of glass in my throat. It was shocking, this panic. And now that the fear was receding, I was aware of an odd sense of shame and grief, too. I shook my head to clear it. Growing up on the ranch, I used to see bats all the time, their odd, jerky flights in the dusk as if they were yanked by strings but with a peculiar grace, too, that left me feeling wistful. They were harmless, beneficial creatures who ate insects, I knew that. But all of a sudden here I was remembering every story I'd ever heard about bats. That they tangle in your hair and you have to cut them out. That a bat in the house means someone will die. My father told me these things at the dinner table with the same flat voice he ordered me to get him more bread or mend fence or wash myself. One time as a boy he'd had to beat them off the meat in the smokehouse with a shovel. There were gnaw-marks all over the bacon. They crawl into your mouth at night. You can't keep them out.

When my eyes adjusted to the darkness, I could see the shape of the bat atop a pile of folded towels and laundry. Okay. No big deal. I put a sock on my hand as a glove. "Look," I said. "We've got to do this." I grabbed the bat, then relaxed my grip when I felt how

VALERY VARBLE

soft it was, how crushable. I pushed open the trailer door and set the bat down next to the steps. It fumbled along the ground for a moment and then lifted itself into the dark with astonishing ease.

Anyway, since that night, I haven't been able to sleep much. It isn't bats that I'm afraid of, I know that much. I don't know what it is, exactly, except maybe the old dread that used to swoop and flutter and dive in the plunging darkness of my childhood room when at last I had to turn out the light. And wait.

Now I sit outside, just to breathe. I love the desert, its scouring beauty. This particular landscape seems more complicated than the high desert of Nevada, although it may not be in reality. I doubt I could live in another kind of place, in a different kind of terrain. The desert always helps to remind me that I don't matter, at least not much, and that's a relief.

Sunrise is pinking the horizon when I finally go inside for a glass of milk. I see the man's wallet on my table and I open it. I can't help but laugh: his name's John. I flip past a photo of him and his wife posed in matching jeans and chambray shirts against a studio back-drop, and then a picture of his wife by herself. I go back. She's wear-ing a black dress with a low, sweetheart neckline. How funny. I study her streaked blonde hair, plump mouth, her long collie's nose. I shake my head: too much of a coincidence, I tell myself. But the more I look at the picture, the more sure I am. Lori Singleton, my old "best friend" all through school. Something cramps in my stom-ach. Now that I think about it, I remember hearing she'd ended up in Blythe, which isn't too far from here, just across the state line.

Lori. I toss the wallet away from me, gulping the cold milk so fast I have an instant headache. Not funny at all.

John calls to make a date for late that afternoon. When I let him in, he's carrying an ice bucket and a paper sack. "Here," he says. "Are there any glasses?" When I bring some tumblers from the bathroom, he sighs and rubs his face, then shucks the bag away from a bottle of scotch. "Do you mind?"

"No," I say, so he splashes some scotch into a couple of glasses and adds ice. I hand him his wallet and wait. "It's the same price today, depending on what you want to do." He pays me and then we're silent for a moment. An ice cube in his drink gives a startling crack.

We sit on the bed again and I wait for him to say what he wants, the glass turning cold and slick in my hands. Finally he says, "You can't believe how thin she's getting."

Oh, I can believe it. I can easily picture her getting pared down to the truth of herself that I probably know better than he does: cruel, petty. Afraid. "She's never been what you might call big," he goes on, "but now she's almost like a child, so small I'm afraid to touch her."

His leg vibrates again, a plucked string, and I imagine an afternoon after school in the sixth grade when Lori's idea of a good time was to sit around topless, smoking cigarettes. It struck me as an especially stupid thing to do but Lori was my best friend, so I didn't say anything. We were down by the creek on my father's ranch, hidden by willows. I wanted to collect some squaw tea from the bushes nearby—the *Girl Scout Handbook* called it Mormon tea, my father called it "whorehouse tea"—for the plant collection we were supposed to be making. Instead we sat there, our feet gone numb in the creek. Lori had small, pointy breasts and even sharper shoulders. Her pale skin was goosebumped, washed with pink. I thought she looked plucked, somehow, and defenseless. "Yours don't match," she announced about my breasts, exhaling smoke. "One's bigger." I looked down at the right one, the runt, the underachiever, but mostly I was planning how, as soon as she went home, I'd roll around in the creek so my father wouldn't smell the smoke on my skin. I'd rub mud into my skin and hair and let the cold creek rinse it away. Lori was humming, a high falsetto like the droning of an insect. Then she said casually, "We're going on a family trip to Disneyland," stabbing out her cigarette, watching me from the corner of her eye. "My parents said I could invite a friend." Oh, God. The rush of hope so strong it felt like pain. "When?" I asked her, "When?"

"Thursday," her husband says. "To tell you the truth, it's not much of a medical facility. I told her, 'We're already down here. Let's go to Mayo's for the best.'" He makes it sound like a restau-

VALERY VARBLE

rant, an Italian eatery with great spaghetti puttanesca or something, and for a moment I'm confused. Oh, the Mayo Clinic.

"But she won't do it," John says. He takes a gulp, looks at his glass. "Why wouldn't someone want the best treatment available? For the life of me, I don't get it."

"Maybe she doesn't deserve the best treatment," I say and there's a pause. "I mean, maybe she doesn't think she does."

"Maybe not," he says and sighs. "I guess she didn't exactly have the easiest life growing up. She was an only child, she didn't have many friends. There were a lot of problems between her parents. Just a lot of stuff, apparently. And now this."

Problems? I take a sip of scotch, slip an ice cube onto my tongue. That's interesting to hear. Lori's dad managed Kaye's, the department store in our small town. All I really remember about him is that he had the resigned, bloodshot eyes of a basset hound, he loved to shoot skeet, and he'd once bought a side of beef from my father to put in a new deep freeze he'd installed in the garage. Mrs. Singleton was as narrow and elegant as her family line, which she traced back to the *Mayflower* and England. She hosted an annual spring party featuring dishes like tomato aspic and jellied beef consommé which made the guests unsure of themselves, hungry and irritable, and finally, because they ate so little, very drunk.

But strangely enough, I'd liked Lori's mother. Once, when I was helping to clean up after one of these parties, she looked around at all the wobbling, quivering food left untouched on the trays, the frilly and complicated hors d'oeuvres, and started laughing. "Oh, what a fool I am," she said to me, laughing until she sagged next to the kitchen sink, gasping, sobbing merrily. "What a complete twit!" I was frightened for a few moments, but when I helped her up, she clasped me close for a few steps of breathless, mocking waltz. Then she curtseyed and we both laughed. And then suddenly she was herself again, smooth and composed. "Thank you," she told me, smiling sadly, and shook her head.

When I went to find Lori she asked me, her voice hot and flat, "Aren't you glad your mother's dead?" I knew then she'd seen us, and was jealous. I felt bad for her, that I'd been given something she wanted, but the realization still gave me a small, fleeting warmth. But of course now there'd be a price I'd have to pay.

I'm thinking about this later, when the day's over. What I gave Lori was this, the one complete memory I had of my own mother: I was very young. My mother toweled my wet hair after a bath, and then combed out the tangles. I could remember the steamed-over bathroom mirror striping with condensation, the frayed corner of the towel, the scent of golden shampoo, my mother's breath against my face. She told me a funny story, pretending to read it in my hair; she kept parting my hair in different places with the comb, like turning a page in a book. She'd read for a while and then part my hair again. It was so silly we couldn't stop laughing. "And they lived happily ever after," she said finally, "The End," and kissed my ear.

Lori looked at me doubtfully when I finished. "You mean that's it?" I barely kept from flinching, but I wasn't exactly surprised. She had to punish me a little; it was just part of this strange, intricate dance girls seemed to do. I knew all the steps although I wasn't sure when I'd learned them or how I knew. But I was upset at myself, too. The memory was diminished somehow. It was what I'd hugged to myself at night and now the whole thing seemed puny. This was what I'd always known in some secret part of myself—in the end it was better not to tell.

But now it was Lori's turn to reward me, and that's what happened. She started talking brightly about our trip to Disneyland. The restaurants where we'd stop and eat on the way, the banana splits we'd order. The motel in Anaheim where we were staying, with its own private pool. And Disneyland: the Matterhorn and Monorail. Fantasyland. Sleeping Beauty's castle. Her father was going to pay for everything. It was going to be so much fun. My heart quickened painfully in my chest.

At our Girl Scouts meeting we carved bars of Ivory soap into turtles. It was a craft project, a gift for our parents, although in my case, there was only my father. Cutting into the soap made my eyes burn. I worked as slowly as I could, trying to put off the moment we had to gather our things and go home. We painted the turtles with watercolors, which only just weakly tinged the soap. Mine looked less like a turtle than a beetle—a *dung* beetle, Lori announced but then added that I'd done a good job on the tail. It didn't matter what my turtle looked like; I'd already planned to lose it in the wastebasket where it would sink beneath the crumpled brown paper towels, or to accidentally leave it in Mrs. Singleton's car. My father used soap with grit in it; his hands were callused hard as horn.

It was dusk when Mrs. Singleton drove me home to the ranch, my legs locking stiff as soon as I got out of the station wagon. My father emerged from the dark hole of the barn door and gave a terse nod. I pretended not to see him but I could feel him watching me. Mrs. Singleton noticed, too; she told me brightly, "Good-bye now. You have a good night," looking away as I shut the car door. Lori gave a limp wave.

They were halfway down our lane before I took off after them. "Wait!" I called out, running as fast as I could, choking on the dust billowing up behind the car. "Wait, wait!"

The car's brake lights lit up and it skidded to a stop in the dirt. I was panting, breathless when Mrs. Singleton rolled down the window. "I left my turtle," I told her.

"Oh," she said and the relief in her face scared and saddened me. What had she thought I wanted?

A few days later after school I walked downtown to ask Mrs. Etchemendi at the Kaye's perfumes and toiletries counter if she'd like to buy some soap turtles. It was my new idea to earn some money. I'd whittled ten bars of Ivory soap into turtles until the dark of my room had smelled almost pure and clean. I told Mrs. Etchemendi they were a Girl Scout project and she could display them on the counter in a big shell, if she had one. She studied my sample turtle a little doubtfully but then said, all right, it was pretty cute. She'd buy all ten for the store, assuming Mr. Singleton wouldn't mind, but she hoped I wouldn't hit her up to buy cookies this year, too. She couldn't resist those Scot Teas and heaven knows, she was getting broad enough in the beam as it was.

I went directly to the lingerie department, just to look. I wanted a pair of baby doll pajamas more than anything. Miss Wilson, the saleslady, looked at me and said, "We certainly carry those in your size. But you're a little old for baby dolls, dear. Wouldn't you rather have a nice nightgown? We do carry Lanz." When I didn't say anything, she mentioned that I'd just missed Lori Singleton and her friend Elise Tapper shopping in the Young Miss department for new outfits. Some really darling things. Maybe they'd wear them to school tomorrow to show me.

Tomorrow was Friday. Lori had already told me she and her mom would come by to pick me up after dinner on Friday at seven o'clock. I'd spend the night at her house and we'd leave early in the morning for Disneyland. We'd probably sleep in the car for the first few hours, and she was bringing big pillows for us, just in case. Her father had said it was a long drive. "I'm not even ready yet, are you?" she asked and I said no, although under my bed, my suitcase was already packed.

"You're so easy to talk to," John says. "Guess you're not from the Midwest." He huffs a brief laugh. He looks crumpled, head down, shoulders sagging, like he's folding in on himself.

It's late and I'm tired.

"I wish I could talk to her like this," he says. "But I don't even know how to start. What would I say?" He clears his throat. "Jesus, will you listen to me. It's pathetic. She's my wife and I don't know how to talk to her, not about anything important."

"Maybe you could pay her," I say.

We look at each other and I see something, an ugly flash of contempt in his eyes. But I'm not sure it's for me. Mostly what I see in his face is desperation and pain; he's no longer handsome.

He puts my hand on his lap. "Will you?" he says.

It's funny what I feel inside. I can't even explain it. "That's what I'm here for," I say, almost surprised that words can literally taste bitter. I unzip his pants as he tells me how when he asked Lori to marry him, she cried so hard another woman's husband in the restaurant stepped up to make sure she was okay, that John wasn't threatening her in some way. "Thought I was going to have to fight the guy," John says. His chin is like a rasp, and I imagine my father's whiskers in the sink like iron filings. The knotty pine paneling of my room, all snouts and eyes and mouths. My little blue suitcase, packed with everything I owned.

He stays soft, so soft, too soft. There's not much a man can do by now that will shock or even surprise me but when John starts crying, it's like he's choking.

Sometimes even now I have the strangest sensation that I'm still out there waiting in the twilight. I waited for an hour, then almost two, afraid to go back to the house, afraid to miss my chance. I stood with my suitcase at the end of our dirt lane where it met the highway, where the mailbox was, watching the road. Behind me, there were nighthawks plunging through the darkness over the corral. And bats. And my father, a shape in the yellow light of the door, watching as no one came to take me away.

"Do you think she knows what I feel about her? God, I'm scared," John cries. "I'm so afraid."

"Imagine what she must be feeling," I hear myself whisper, and I don't mean his wife.

I'm not sure why it is that when I go home, I take out my friend Janey's picture. I remember how that night after the picnic as we'd driven away, the truck's tailgate dropped open and the rest of the Hearts o' Gold cantaloupes had gone rolling out of the back of the truck. Some of them broke apart; others bounced and rolled down the highway in every direction, careening off the road into the desert. "Hey, just like our bowling team," Janey said, laughing, when we'd pulled the truck over and walked back.

I remember looking at the wreckage spilled across the road, the pulpy mess. "That's what happens to good hearts," I said.

Janey turned to me in surprise. "You don't really believe that, do you?" she said.

I try to go to bed early but it's the same old thing; I lie there with my heart pounding. There's no way I'll sleep. I get up and turn the lights on. I look at the torn window screen, check the place where I've taped it shut. When I close my eyes, I can still see the bat's wild, jagged flight in the room, and how it finally came to a rest.

I take a deep breath and dial the hospital's number. I ask the operator for Lori's room.

As they connect me, I turn out the lights. When she answers I hesitate, my eyes adjusting. Then I say, "I want to tell you something about your husband." It's like darkness, her silence. My heart flutters against my chest, and I wait.

APPENDIX

Publications Consulted

The following print and e-journals were consulted for this volume:

A Public Space
African American Review
Agni Review
Alaska Quarterly Review
Alligator Juniper
American Literary Review
American Short Fiction
Antigonish Review
Antioch Review
Apalachee Review
Ascent
Atlantic
Baltimore Review
Bat City Review
Bellevue Literary Review
Bitter Oleander
Black Warrior Review
Blue Earth Review
Blue Mesa Review
Bomb Magazine
Bordersenses
Boulevard
Callaloo
Calyx
Carve
Chattahoochee Review

Chicago Review
Cimarron Review
Cincinnati Review
Colorado Review
Confrontation
Conjunctions
Cottonwood
Crazyhorse
Cream City Review
Crowd
CT Review
Cue
Cut Throat
Dalhousie Review
Dancing with the Wind
Denver Quarterly
Descant (Fort Worth)
Descant (Toronto)
Diagram
Dirty Goat
Dispatch
Downtown Story
Ecotone
Edgar
Elixir
Ellipsis

Epoch
Event
Exile
Fence Magazine
Fiction
First Line
Five Points
Florida Review
Fourteen Hills
Georgia Review
Gettysburg Review
Glimmer Train
Granta
Great River Review
Green Mountain Review
Greensboro Review
Gulf Coast
Hanging Loose
Harper's
Harrington Gay Men's Literary
    Quarterly
Harrington Lesbian Literary
    Quarterly
Harvard Review
Hayden's Ferry
Hudson Review
Image
Indiana Review
Iowa Review
Isotope
The Journal
Kalliope
Kenyon Review
Ledge
Lit

Literary Review
Long Story
Louisville Review
Madison Review
Main Street Rag
Malahat Review
Mandorla
Massachusetts Review
McSweeney's
Michigan Quarterly Review
Mid-American Review
Minnesota Review
Mississippi Review
Missouri Review
Natural Bridge
New England Review
New Letters
New Orleans Review
New Yorker
Nimrod
Ninth Letter
North American Review
North Dakota Quarterly
Northwest Review
Notre Dame Review
One Story
Ontario Review
Other Voices (Chicago)
Other Voices (Edmonton)
Paris Review
Passager
Passages North
Paterson Literary Review
Pearl
Pikeville Review

Pinch
Pindeldyboz
Pleiades
Ploughshares
PMS
Porcupine Literary Arts
  Magazine
Portland Review
Post Road
Potomac Review
Practice
Prairie Fire
Prairie Schooner
Prism International
Provincetown Arts
Puerto del Sol
Quadrant
Quarterly West
Queen's Quarterly
RE:AL
Red Rock Review
Red Wheelbarrow
Redivider
River Styx
Rock & Sling
Salamander
Salmagundi
Salt Flats Annual
SandScript
Santa Monica Review
Seattle Review
Sewanee Review
Shenandoah
So to Speak

Sonora Review
South Carolina Review
South Dakota Review
Southern Indiana Review
Southern Review
Southwest Review
Southwestern American Literature
Spinning Jenny
Spork Magazine
Subtropics
Sun
Tampa Review
Terra Incognita
Terrain.org
Tex[t]
Texas Review
Thema
Third Coast
Threepenny Review
Tin House
TriQuarterly
Virginia Quarterly Review
Walking Rain Review
Weber Studies
West Branch
Western Humanities Review
Willow Springs
Xavier Review
Xconnect
Yale Literary Magazine
Yale Review
Zoetrope
Zone 3
Zyzzyva

CONTRIBUTORS

ALAN CHEUSE is a fiction writer, journalist, and the book commentator for National Public Radio's *All Things Considered*. He is the author of, among other books, the novels *The Grandmothers' Club* and *The Light Possessed*, the short-story collections *Lost and Old Rivers* and *The Tennessee Waltz*, and a memoir, *Fall Out of Heaven*. His latest book is an essay collection titled *Listening to the Page*. He has new short fiction coming out this year in *Ploughshares, New Letters*, the *Antioch Review, Prairie Schooner*, and the *Southern Review*.

The story has it that after spending the night on a sofa at his friend Leigh Hunt's cottage next to the wall where hung a painting of Apollo, the god of poetry, riding his fiery chariot across the sky, John Keats sat up and wrote "Sleep and Poetry," one of his loveliest early poems—in which Apollo makes a grand appearance, giving life to the world by the powers of poetry. I'm not comparing my story to a poem by Keats, but I realize that I've had an experience similar to his. About five years ago, my wife gave me as a birthday gift one of my favorite photographs, Ansel Adams's beautiful and mysterious "Moonrise, Hernandez, New Mexico, 1941," and had it framed and mounted on the wall next to our bed. Every morning, all these past years, I've awakened to the sight of that gorgeous piece of light and shadow, image and counterimage. One of the differences between me and Keats—one of many, of course—is that it took him one sleep for his poetry mind to focus on the subject of the nearby painting. It took me five years before my fiction mind got me to see that I wanted to write a story about the origins of that photograph.

*I'd written fiction about the Southwest before, particularly
a novel about an artist similar in many ways to the real-life
Georgia O'Keeffe. I was happy to return to that brilliant,
light-struck landscape, however briefly, in this short story.*

MATT CLARK's novel *Hook Man Speaks* (Putnam/Berkeley, 2001) was chosen for the Texas Monthly Author Series. When he died in 1998, at age thirty-one, Matt was coordinator of the Louisiana State University creative writing program. While a graduate student at LSU, he was fiction editor of *New Delta Review*, which now sponsors the Matt Clark Prize. His work has recently appeared in *American Short Fiction, One Story*, the *Southwest Review*, and the *Yalobusha Review*.

LORIEN CROW is a freelance writer/reporter and student of English literature in rural western Connecticut. She is an avid humanitarian and world traveler, and will begin pursuing her doctorate in literature in the fall of 2007.

*This story was written on a plane while I was returning home
to Connecticut from my grandmother's funeral in northern
New Mexico. She lived a hard life, but one filled with
unwavering love and devotion to her family. I wanted to
memorialize her, but also myself at that difficult moment in
time. I also attempted to point out the stark contrast between
my grandmother's life and mine while highlighting the tension
that still exists within families and between genders and
cultures respectively. It is with great humility and pride
that I dedicate this story to the loving memory of my
grandmother, Ellen.*

KATHLEEN DE AZEVEDO was born in Rio de Janeiro, Brazil, but came to the United States as a young child. She grew up in a blue-collar community in northern California. The nearest large town was Reno, Nevada, where "Together We Are Lost" takes place. At that time she was not interested in her Brazilian heritage; her dream was to run off to Hollywood to be in the movies. She moved to San

Francisco, where she eventually gave up theater to focus on writing, which at the beginning explored non-Latin themes. Years later, she realized that Brazilian and Latin themes were what she had wanted to write about all along. She taught herself Portuguese, and during the process wrote *Samba Dreamers*, a novel published by the University of Arizona Press. Her work reflects both her Latino and "Americana" roots and has appeared in many publications, including *Américas, Michigan Quarterly Review, Boston Review, Green Mountains Review, Hayden's Ferry Review, TriQuarterly* and *Gettysburg Review*. She currently lives in San Francisco and teaches English at Skyline College.

> *When I write of the U.S., I love to write about Nevada and its metaphors and oppositions. Nevada's desert still has abandoned opera houses in ghost towns from the silver mining boom. The long lonely roads of earth and sky lead to cacophonous unreal cities like Las Vegas where casinos contain unreal miniworlds. The mystical stark Pyramid Lake, which belongs to the Paiute Indians, draws dirt bikers and old hippie stoners. Nevada reminds me of people who have grandiose dreams that never materialize, but who struggle to create beauty all the same. The characters in "Together We Are Lost" create beauty in their desolate lives. They are the true heroes of the Southwest.*

ALAN ELYSHEVITZ is a poet and short-story writer from Norristown, Pennsylvania. His fiction has received awards from *Antietam Review*, the *Cream City Review, Pebble Lake Review*, and *Briar Cliff Review* and has been nominated twice for a Pushcart Prize. He has also published two poetry chapbooks: *The Splinter in Passion's Paw* (New Spirit) and *Theory of Everything* (Pudding House). In 2001 and 2003 he received fellowships from the Pennsylvania Council on the Arts. Currently he teaches writing at the Community College of Philadelphia.

> *The idea for the story "Hermano" first occurred to me years ago, after I had spent several months in New Mexico. For me,*

a nearly lifelong Easterner and city dweller, the Southwest was
an acquired taste. However, once I began to understand and
appreciate the subtleties of its social and physical environment,
the region proved to be a source of inspiration for my writing.
The landscape of the American Southwest, with its ambiguous
beauty, as well as its cultural and political complexity, strikes
me as an appropriate setting for the emotional drama of
Maury Sandoval, the main character of "Hermano."

MARCELA FUENTES is a native of the Texas-Mexico border. She is a graduate of the University of Texas at Austin and Central Michigan University. She has worked as a librarian, a translator, a grant writer, and, most often, an English teacher. Recently, she was the fiction editor for *BordeRevolución* and an English instructor at Southwest Texas Junior College. She is currently an MFA candidate in fiction at the Iowa Writers' Workshop.

In 2000, I worked at the library at the University of the
Incarnate Word in San Antonio, where my younger brother,
Robert, was going to school. Although we lived in the same
city, and even once lived in the same apartment complex,
our lives were completely separate. We weren't estranged—
my brothers and I have always been close—but we were
very much involved in our own agendas. I saw him only
occasionally, and his visits were sudden, unexpected, and
completely nonchalant. He might show up at my office door
wanting a dollar, a couple of paperclips, or to take me to
lunch. Then I wouldn't see him for weeks. This story began
in that office doorway—the surprised-but-unsurprised feeling
I got when he literally appeared out of nowhere. At that time,
he was also heavily into bull riding, and while I loved the
sport as a child, seeing my little brother ride was an entirely
different experience.

DENNIS FULGONI is the winner of an AWP Intro Journals Award and a James Kirkwood Award for Fiction through UCLA. His stories have appeared in *Parting Gifts, Quarterly West,* and the *Colorado Review.* He teaches high school English at John Marshall, in Silver Lake, California. He, his wife, and his son live in Highland Park.

The impetus for this story came from something my wife related to me: the son of a friend of hers lost his nail in an accident, and because the nail didn't grow back properly, the doctor recommended a nail plate transplant from a cadaver. The idea of this kid walking around with a dead man's nail (I assumed for some reason that the donor was male) struck my imagination. Right then, I knew I'd write a story in which the protagonist had this quirky thing happen to him. A few months later, I sat down to write a story about an event from my childhood in which I watched some teenage boys jump off a two-story roof into a shallow pool. The danger of that moment—they were drunk and high and seemed barely capable of walking, much less jumping off a roof—always stayed with me. I wrote the scene on the roof in first person and then worked backwards from there. But something didn't seem right about the voice. So I tried to rewrite it, from beginning to end, in second person. Once I'd made that choice, the story took off, and I was able to have just the right distance from the narrator while still having enough access to his consciousness. In reflection, I think the second person adds another layer to the story in that this boy lacks a sense of self, and the narration with the "you" narrator instead of the "I" narrator suggests his sense of being invisible to those around him.

RAY GONZALEZ is the author of *Memory Fever,* a memoir about growing up in the Southwest; *Turtle Pictures,* which received the 2001 Minnesota Book Award for Poetry; and *The Ghost of John Wayne and Other Stories.* A collection of essays, *The Underground Heart: A Return to a Hidden Landscape,* received the 2003 Carr P. Collins/Texas Institute of Letters Award for Best Book of Nonfiction, was named one of the Ten Best Southwest Books of the Year by the Arizona Humanities Commission, was named one of the Best Nonfiction Books of the Year by the *Rocky Mountain News,* was named a Minnesota Book Award Finalist in Memoir, and was selected as a Book of the Month by the El Paso Public Library. He is the author of six other books of poetry, including three from BOA Editions: *The Heat of Arrivals, Cabato Sentora,* and *The Hawk Temple at Tierra Grande.* His awards include a 2003 Lifetime Achievement Award in Literature from The Border Regional Library Association, a 2002 Loft McKnight Fellowship in Poetry, a 1993 Before Columbus Foundation American Book Award for Excellence in Editing, and a 1988 Colorado Governor's Award for Excellence in the Arts.

ANNA GREEN considers herself fortunate to have moved from Alabama to Arizona at the impressionable age of thirteen. That drastic change of landscape and culture has been the inspiration for much of her writing. She has published short stories in *Clackamas Literary Review, Palo Alto Review, Alligator Juniper,* and the anthology *Open Windows.* Her honors include the Santa Fe Writers' Project Literary Arts Series Grand Prize, the Ghost Road Press first-place prize for fiction, and the summer residency at the University of Arizona Poetry Center. Anna has an MFA from Texas State University and teaches in South Texas.

I wrote "Food Stamp" while in a graduate workshop, far away from my homeland—the Gila Valley of Arizona. I was nostalgic for my hometown friends, who have constantly inspired me with their remarkable stories. And I was missing the local hangouts, like Thriftee's Food and Drug. A grocery store contains so many microcosms that it seemed a natural setting for this story. A day at Thriftee's Food and Drug is a day in southeastern Arizona; where else could you find metatés and vigil candles alongside Cocoa Puffs and every flavor of toothpaste under the sun? Since I moved to Arizona as a kid, I have been fascinated by the intersection of cultures and personalities in the Southwest. "Food Stamp" was born of this fascination and is a tribute to the rich and volatile friendships I've made there.

DONALD LUCIO HURD grew up in Southwest, Texas, a community that took its name from a prominent filling station. Outside of the local school library, the most common printed materials were seed catalogues and *The Farmer's Almanac*. He attended one of the worst school districts in Texas, where his dual ethnicity (his mother is Mexican American, his father Anglo) allowed him to experience the true meaning of alienation at a young age. Following an altercation with the school counselor, who attempted to "knock some sense" into him, Donald dropped out of school at the age of twelve. After obtaining his General Education Diploma, he attended San Antonio College. Over the next ten years, he became an active organizer and participant in the San Antonio literary scene. He was soon offered an assistant editorship with *ViAztlan, the International Journal of Chicano Arts and Letters,* and eventually took over as editor. He was the founder of NO CONCEPT ART, an extremely successful series of poetry/music performance extravaganzas that often lasted from eight to ten hours. He was also organizer of the Paperbacks . . . y Más reading series, founded by the poet Ricardo Sanchez. His work has appeared in *Talebones, BIGnews,* the *Trinity Review,* and *Southwestern American Literature,* among others. He teaches English to economically disadvantaged students in San Antonio. He is married and has two children.

Guadalupe Lopez was named after my grandmother, but she owes her cantankerous nature to my grandfather, Lucio Lopez. The citizens of Espantosa are loosely based on the people I encountered in and around La Coste and Macdona, Texas, two small towns that have become even smaller over the years. This environment was rich in folklore and mythology. Growing up, I heard tales of the Chupacabra and la Llorona, of la Lechuza and the Donkey Lady. These tales were more vivid in my mind than those of the Brothers

*Grimm or the Arabian Nights. I am now at work on a novel
in progress titled Espantosa, set near the mythic lake of the
same name.*

TONI JENSEN is métis and is from the Midwest. She teaches creative
writing at Texas Tech University. She has published fiction in *Fiction International, Passages North, Tusculum Review,* and the *Dos
Passos Review,* among others. Her short story "At the Powwow
Hotel" won the 2006 Katherine Anne Porter Prize for fiction from
Nimrod International Literary Journal. She earned a PhD in creative
writing from Texas Tech University in 2006.

*"At the Powwow Hotel" came about when I had what I
thought were two ideas, which turned out to be stronger,
better, if linked and made into one story. The first idea
involved a moving cornfield. I grew up in Iowa and spent
summers detasseling corn—the only job I've ever liked much,
other than writing and teaching. I liked the rhythm of pulling
the tassels from the corn, the quiet of the cornfield. There
were not many other Indians in our part of Iowa, but there
were some, and though my story is not based on any old,
traditional corn story, it's an effort on my part to bring
Indians into this place where they hadn't been acknowledged—
an effort to say, "We're here, too."*

*At the time I wrote the story, I was living at the edge of
Blanco Canyon in West Texas, and like Lester and Jack in
the story, probably, I felt a little isolated from other Indians,
from any larger sense of community, so the second idea for
my story grew out of those feelings. There's a historical
marker on the one road to the canyon and the house where
I lived that tells about the Texas Rangers "eradicating the
Indian menace" in the region. Every time I'd drive by it, I'd
think, "not quite." The story, then, comes from the impulse
to bring Indians onto landscapes deemed "non-Indian," to
create a present where healing comes from community,
where there is hope at the end, not tragedy or eradication.*

CHARLES KEMNITZ's father prospected for oil, gas, and uranium on the Colorado Plateau, then worked for the Atomic Energy Commission as the drilling supervisor on Amchitka Island. He grew up during the Cold War at the edge of cultures in transition—Navajo, Ute, Alaskan Athabascan. After high school he dug archaeology sites along the Alyeska Pipeline and served as the captain of the fire department and physician's assistant for a tiny Alaskan bush village. While working toward his PhD at Tulsa University, he began publishing poetry, short stories, critical essays, and creative nonfiction, and now has approximately 150 publications. His first book, *CopperHawk*, won the Eikenberry Poetry Award; he has also won the New Millennium Writing Award and a National Endowment for the Arts Literature Fellowship in creative nonfiction.

For the past decade he's been slowly going blind. His wife of thirty years is his best editor and reader—rigorous, unsparing, and appreciative. They live in Williamsport, Pennsylvania, where he teaches literature and the history of science at Pennsylvania College of Technology, a member of the Penn State system. His favorite pastime is to sit on the deck and listen to bats hunting moths beneath a nearby streetlamp.

"The Fifth Daughter" began many years ago as a lengthy essay about the personal and cultural effects of uranium mining in the Southwest. I based the essay on research and interviews with Anglo, Navajo, and Ute uranium workers and their families. After submitting the essay, then titled "Seep With Yellow Frogs," as creative nonfiction, to a dozen literary journals, I put it aside for a couple of years and continued research to expand the essay to book length.

A couple of years later, I dug out "Seep" and realized that the framing nonfiction narrative about Doll was, itself, a story. So I spent several months struggling to revise her history into what, when I finished, could only properly be called "fiction." But, as Mark Twain said, "The best story tells the truth in such a way that everyone thinks it's a lie." Characters who are drifting between cultures face either

assimilation or annihilation—it is the writer's job to
explore the impossibilities of life.

ELMO LUM currently lives and works in San Francisco. He is currently
trying to locate an agent for his first novel, much of which takes
place in the Southwest. His past work has been published in *Sto-
ryQuarterly, Bitter Oleander, Effing Magazine*, and the *New England
Review*. He is also finishing the preliminary research for a new novel.

*"What I Never Said" got its start, like many of my stories, with
a phrase—in this case, the first line of the story. Originally,
this sentence began "This was we." I was later convinced to
change this to the more conventional "This was us" since
this was the only place this strange grammar seemed to
manifest itself in this story. By then, of course, the story had
gotten well past its beginnings, and I agreed. Its setting in
the Southwest was the result of a road trip I had taken two
years before to visit a friend who lived in Austin. Initially
my setting the story there was mostly a convenience of
memory, although the desert setting (the heat, the space)
contributed to how the plot unwound. A number of my
stories unwind of their own accord this way, although this
one perhaps a bit more than others, seeing how it finished
in a manner I still don't fully understand.*

TOM MCWHORTER was born in Abilene, Texas, in 1961. Although
he was raised in the military and moved frequently as a child—living in Okinawa, Japan, and all over California—Tom's family eventually returned to Texas, where he attended high school in the towns
of Sweetwater and Haskell. Following high school, he moved to
Salt Lake City, where he earned several degrees and engaged in various occupations. Most recently, after a brief career as an attorney,
Tom received an MFA in creative writing from the University of
Utah in 2006. He is currently living in Pittsburgh, Pennsylvania,
with his partner, Todd, and his cat, Simon, where he writes and
does freelance editing.

Many of my stories end up being about me, but not in any autobiographical way. This story seems related to the fact that I spent much of my childhood separated from my father and from Texas by my parents' divorce. During much of this period, my father farmed—mostly cotton and wheat, but occasionally and intermittently, of course, pigs. By the time I returned to Texas, my father had leased his land and had entirely given up farming for a post office job in the city. Once or twice, however, I saw the hogs my uncle was raising with my cousins' help, and they were similar to the hogs my father had farmed and the pigs in this story. Viewing these hogs with me, my father told the first of many pig-farming tales. I think the compelling image of these animals and the vividness of my father's stories somehow became implicated in my unconscious with a particular brand of emasculation, linked to the absence of sons and to the inability to continue farming.

More specifically, this story began in my mind with the image of the fire that Fred had inadvertently started with Maybelle's discarded coupons on their wedding night. The parallel created in this scene between their faces and "the pigs' at sunrise" evoked for me these characters' hopes for fertility and prosperity which I play against in the rest of the story.

S. G. MILLER's stories have appeared in a variety of literary magazines. She is a native of the Pacific Northwest, has lived an important number of years in the Southwest, and is doing the best one may in New York City, until further notice.

"Old Border Road" was conceived with an image and born with a first good sentence.

PETER ROCK was born and raised in Salt Lake City. He is the author of the novels *The Bewildered, The Ambidextrist, This is the Place,* and *Carnival Wolves,* and a story collection, *The Unsettling,* published in 2006. Rock attended Deep Springs College, received a BA in English from Yale University, and held a Wallace Stegner Fellowship at Stanford University. He has taught fiction at the University of Pennsylvania, Yale University, and Deep Springs College, and in the MFA program at San Francisco State University. His stories and freelance writing have both appeared widely. The recipient of a National Endowment for the Arts Fellowship and other awards, he currently lives in Portland, Oregon, where he is an associate professor in the English Department of Reed College.

I spent my first two years of college at a place called Deep Springs, on a cattle ranch just north of Death Valley. We had a strange dugout storage area in the desert, and one of my troubled peers used to go down there and play the trumpet in the dark. Twenty or so years later my wife and I bought a piece of used furniture with a roll of film in it. The Bicentennial is rich to me, and that edition of the Guinness Book *remains burned into my memory, a seminal text. The desert of Nevada is my favorite landscape. I've spent a lot of time driving back and forth across it, the whole experience a kind of hazy dream. It's a place of rare encounters, people stuck and others in flight, where past and present and dead and living seem like fairly arbitrary distinctions.*

ALICITA RODRÍGUEZ lives in a Colorado ghost town with her fiancé, the writer Joseph Starr; their two girls, the doggies Jessa and Mina; and the specter of their beloved male wolf, Wiley. She teaches at Western State College in Gunnison. Recently, her work has appeared in *Denver Quarterly, Mississippi Review, Ecotone, Divide, New Letters,* and *TriQuarterly.*

I wrote "Imagining Bisbee" after hearing someone who lived there describe the town. Between those few personal details and some historical research, I figured I might invent a place that already existed. If, as neuroscientist Steven Rose states, "the world we observe is constrained—some would say

constructed—by the architecture of our brains/minds,"
then my fictional perception of Bisbee must represent some
truth; and if fiction is an architecture, then the story is an
architecture of an architecture—what could be better than
that construction of the double?

JOHN TAIT is a native of Ontario, Canada, whose stories have ap-
peared or will soon appear in *Prairie Schooner, Crazyhorse, Tri-
Quarterly, Michigan Quarterly,* the *Sun, Meridian* and elsewhere.
He is an Assistant Professor of Fiction Writing at the University of
North Texas and editor of the *American Literary Review.*

"Reasons for Concern . . ." is the latest in an alarming number
of stories I've written while avoiding people. This particular
story was written in the Sunnidale Arboretum in beautiful
Barrie, Ontario, Canada, during a summer visit to my parents'
new home there. My parents were having dinner guests, one
of them a notorious gossip. I was in the middle of a divorce
and not looking forward to being grilled about it, so I drove
around for hours, ate at a diner, and finally landed at the
Arboretum around dusk. I saw some lovely things there—a
blind woman touching ferns and fronds, children playing in
a gazebo—none of which (unfortunately) made it into the
story that I hacked out. It was one of those rare cases where
the story seemed to land, ready-made and whole, on the
page. The structure arose quite naturally from the voice,
which arose quite naturally from the title and first lines. I
wasn't even sure if I was writing a story when I began (and
equally unsure when I finished), but it emerged the way it
wanted to. Ironically, considering the northern latitude
where the story was composed, it's definitely my most
Texan story to date. It was fun to try and capture a
quality, a mingling of exciting possibilities and frustrating
impossibilities, that I associate with Texas's changing
culture. And a love story—albeit a strange one—felt like
the best way to do it.

PATRICK TOBIN's stories have appeared in many journals, including *Agni*, the *Literary Review*, and the *Kenyon Review*. His nonfiction, published in *Grain*, the *Florida Review*, and *New Delta Review*, has been nominated for a Canadian National Magazine Award, and his essay "Reunion" won the 2006 literary nonfiction contest sponsored by *Prism International*. He also wrote the award-winning film *No Easy Way*. He currently works as a graphics designer and photographer and lives in Long Beach, California.

For years I've wondered what was on Zzyzx Road, an exit north of Baker, California, on I-15. To be honest, I've been too lazy to take a five-minute detour and find out, but I've always thought there was something vaguely sinister about the way the road goes up a small hill and then disappears. Cut to November 2, 2004. Bush was reelected and everyone was crediting (blaming) the gay marriage issue. My partner and I spent Thanksgiving with my very Republican family in Las Vegas—I could barely breathe the entire time—and on the drive back to Long Beach I continued to read Viktor Klemperer's I Will Bear Witness: A Diary of the Nazi Years, 1933–1941. *As we came upon the sign for Zzyzx Road I began to imagine what was on the other side of the hill.*

VALERY VARBLE grew up in Reno, Nevada, and although over the years she's lived in at least eleven different states, it's the desert regions of the Southwest that continually call her home. She's a graduate of the Iowa Writers' Workshop, received her PhD from the University of Nebraska–Lincoln, and was the first Axton Fellow in Fiction Writing at the University of Louisville in Kentucky. She's currently home again in Nevada, teaching at the University of Nevada, Reno.

"Bat" was one of those rare stories that seemed to write itself. The bat incident is one I actually experienced. I've never been afraid of bats—if anyone asked, I would've sworn that I actually like them—so I was shocked to find

how powerful and primal my fear was when, in trying to free a bat from the window screen, I accidentally let it into my bedroom instead. Surprised, too, at the tenderness I felt toward the bat once I'd caught it, how soft and vulnerable it seemed to be in my hand. That experience was the story's genesis, and in fact, trying to catch a wildly winging bat in the dark is probably a great metaphor for the writing process as well.

CREDITS